Saint Teresa

A Novel

BY
HENRY SYDNOR HARRISON

AUTHOR OF "QUEED," "V. V.'S EYES"
"ANGELA'S BUSINESS," ETC.

BOSTON AND NEW YORK
HOUGHTON MIFFLIN COMPANY
The Riverside Press Cambridge
1922

To

STEWART AND ANNE

" Nectaire, you fought beside me before the birth of the world. We were conquered because we failed to understand that Victory is a spirit. . . ." ANATOLE FRANCE, *The Revolt of the Angels*.

Saint Teresa

Saint Teresa

.·.

CHAPTER I

THOUGH the setting was as secular as need be, the suggestions of the scene itself were not a little devotional. It was Sunday, it was Easter Day, very early in the morning; the wonder of dawn was hardly gone from the skies, and nothing stirred the unearthly hush but the cheeping of birds in the ivy, and the liquid chimes from the great Cathedral, ceaselessly intoning. The bells called the faithful to worship and sinners to repentance, and the pose of the woman at the window, where the room's dimness lightened to the new day, seemed wonderfully attuned to the solemn cadences. She was kneeling; her figure, maidenly and slim, was clothed in a straight white robe; and her pure gaze, turned upward, celestially lost itself in the auroral dome. The whole look of the colorless young face was rapt and ascetical. The hands met in the changeless attitude of the devout; the slender fingers moved, and it was as if she told her beads; the lips moved and surely she spoke her heavenly passion. In the instant, to the airs of that holy music, this woman might have been the virgin of tradition, Saint Teresa at her orisons. She looked the true figure of the Nun of the ages, classical and pale.

Her gaze descended, she moved a little for convenience: and all was changed. Something unsullied, something cloistral, did indeed cling to her expression, for it belonged there; but the medieval illusion was shattered at a stroke. It was seen that the long robe was no uniform of a celibate order, but just a night-

3

gown, by no means of hair, but agreeably silken and soft. The genuflexion was disclosed as the posture of comfort only, by a woman's mysterious and supple-jointed standard, and the thin haze of smoke which rose above the bowed figure came from no Catholic candle or swinging censer, but from a cigarette of excellent Russian tobacco which she now lifted to its uses.

As if to make the ruin of the tableau complete, the murmur of the virginal lips became audible:

"Hell's bells! . . . I'll die before I give it up."

In almost the same breath she added, in a different tone: "You cute little monkey." And unconsciously her left arm, crooked like a cradle, pressed more closely, but still gently, to her side.

One does n't tell beads in that fashion, obviously, and from this neck, white as a swan's, there hung no crucifix. Inside the diaphanous gown, under the hard round breast, there lay at his ease a snuggling small puppy, very drowsy and warm. He was a wire-haired terrier, of a famous strain which the damsel herself had imported many years earlier; this puppy's grandfather was none other than Highland Brushwood Boy, who took the blue as the best dog at Madison Square Garden, in 1910. But the promising descendant was as yet only a bit of fluff and soft flesh, with lively legs and helpless endearing ways, and at the moment, heedless that he was loved, he was fast asleep.

Nor were the surroundings, once one had looked at them, at all suggestive of a nunnery. There was beauty, costly beauty, all about. The room itself — on the third floor of an enormous mansion — was seen to be a sitting-room of the more personal sort, a warm and luxurious boudoir which both conveyed a definite point of view, and had the air of having been lived in, intimately, a long time. It was charmingly done; the liberal use of purple in especial gave it, in the curtained dusk, a striking richness, sensuous and lovely. A deep-cushioned window-seat

4

offered the semblance of a prie-dieu; and the window gave upon no flagged area or whitewashed wall, but upon palaces flanking the most magnificent avenue in the world.

To-day, by chance, the view from these windows was exceptionally brilliant. The maiden was gazing at the glittering spectacle, the marvellous spectacle, of a white Easter.

It was the fourth of April, which should have meant spring, and the soft breeze blowing through the half-opened casement was vernal altogether. The street lay silent, none the less, under a thick carpet of snow. Yesterday, all day, untimely and incredible, a blizzard raged, and hearts that were full of the pride of raiment had been sad indeed. There was snow on stately roofs and cornices and towers; light snow covered the carved stone balconies and wrapped the boughs of trees already swelling into bud. The scene, just touched with early gleams, had a shining splendor, pure and cold: but already it was breaking up. Between evening and morning twilight, the abrupt change had come again; the thermometer bounded upward, and there came from eaves and copings the little noises of snow resolving into its element. Faint wet splotches began to darken the sidewalks; tiny rivulets, forming under the softening crust, turned their faces toward the sea. The day's promenade, it seemed, might yet be saved.

"It's the biggest thing I've tried, far and away.... And the best," mused Teresa at the window; and the exalted look shone strong in her eyes.

Without doubt, there were many in the city who, overhearing that remark, would have observed in satire, "Well, that's something to say, certainly!" For the simple fact was that this slim was the true heir of "publicity," the predestined child of the spotlight. Born to great advantages, of position, of power, of encouragements to freedom, she had also drawn from able and wilful forbears the dynamic personal quality which does not leave talents wrapped in napkins, or lights under bushels. These things make for a vivid biography.

The woman was no child now; she was twenty-seven years old, and she had been famous — or, as an increasing number of people preferred to say, notorious — for a decade at least. That is passing over the juvenile episodes, naturally. The memorable time when she ran away to be a gypsy, and the later day when, walking a rusted gutter-pipe on a dare, she had fallen from a third story and been picked up for dead, were of course duly recorded — the gypsy adventure, mistaken for a kidnapping, had indeed filled the newspapers for days — but these were the mere typical feats of high-spirited youth, empty of morals and meanings. As early as her second year at college, however, the young woman's exploits had taken on a more substantial character; and with her too noisy expulsion from the halls of learning, at that time, she might be said to have passed definitely from the news columns, where even people who become engaged and die and violate the ash-can ordinance have a place, to the editorial page, reserved for those whose conduct offers food for thought. Teresa's conduct at that time offered food for thought; and it had continued to offer it to the judicious, with few intermissions, through the ten years succeeding.

By the multifariousness of her life and deeds, this kneeling virgin resembled, not a saint in a cell, but Theodore Roosevelt. Locally, at least, she was as well known as a great actress or a great murd but they were details. Issues, public issues of the livelier sorts, were the field of the young woman's real activity, fierce issues were the breath of her nostrils. To an odd and peculiar degree she had moved, in late years especially, in the atmosphere of violence. Slender as she was, cloistered as she looked, this girl knew what it was to be hit with a brick, not accidentally; that knowledge had come to her on the State-House steps at Albany. She had been struck with a fist in a hotel lobby. Proud men, going unwillingly to what she considered justice, had sworn upon her a terrible vengeance....

"My poor grandfather!" said her voice, just audibly.

Down the street the ploughs were out; from afar, above the bells, there came the gritty sounds of scraping shovels. Over the rim of the world, the face of the sun came peeping; and a bright beam shot into the bower. Somewhere in the dimness a small clock struck in a fairy tone: it was half-past six. The young woman started from her reverie, abruptly, and rose.

She removed the youngest Highland — Hotspur II in the stud-book — from his snuggery; she, who had bred him, softly kissed his small moist nose, and laid him down in a padded wicker basket in the window-seat. He had opened his eyes, jolly and wide-awake at once, but perceiving that the moment for play had not arrived, he resigned himself, with a dog's fine philosophy, and was instantly asleep again. From the chaise longue she took a robe, brought with her from the bedroom just now, and put it on. It was of satin brocade, the color of a plum, and was cut straight and short like a man's overcoat; it was the upper half of a Chinese house-suit. Her dead cigarette she dropped into the fireplace; from a capacious crystal box she took another and fitted it abstractedly into the holder, which was of ebony, very long, convoluted and curious. Then for a space she strolled about in her small pattering mules, and scarcely thought of the task to which she had so willingly awakened.

Books lay in wait on the reading-stand, books lined the three walls of the spacious chamber. Antique cases, dark and handsome, held the variegated rows, heavy leaded-glass doors guarded them from dust and weather. Yet the books themselves, by the look of them, were far from being a priceless collection. Assembled by a personal taste clearly, gathered to read and not for the bindings, many bore the marks of hard usage; some were ragged in paper covers; a few were backless. Now and then as she walked about, the owner of the library loitered, staring through the glass, perhaps, at some title which had transiently caught her eye. But her heart was not here, it was plain, and she did not cease humming softly to herself the victorious airs of the Easter chimes.

Soon she stretched herself on the stuffed chaise, drew toward her an ash-tray on a pedestal, and from the stand at her elbow took up the two volumes that attended her. Having placed upon her classic nose a pair of large spectacles, which sometimes she wore at such moments, the girl settled herself to read. One of these tomes, held propped up on rounded knees, was Taylor's "Modern System of Office Management"; the other, to which she soon passed, was lettered in gold upon its blue covers: "High Speed Steel."

For a long time then, while the sun climbed steadily and the stirs and sounds of the wakening city grew louder, Teresa in the cushioned chair hardly stirred. Something ascetical, something passionately pure, clung to the girl's face while she read, and the look of exaltation did not depart from her eyes.

CHAPTER II

WHEN George Davis at last emerged into view, it was seen that the prolonged splashings from the bathroom, the incessant goings back and forth in the bedroom, had by no means been for nothing. George was warm from his preparations, his noble nose shone overmuch, but he was magnificent. Mrs. Roorback, the entirely uncomic woman of the house who furnished breakfasts by contract, could scarcely take her sad eyes from him as she laid his tray. He accepted as meet that sincere and silent tribute; the more vocal gratification of his rooms-mate he as simply ignored. George's intentions this morning, like everything else about him, were serious; levity, frankly, did not appeal. He knew that he was garbed with absolute correctness, indeed with distinction, for the occasion: let that suffice.

The occasion was a real one, and no mistake, for George Davis was a pillar in a dissenting church. In the Sunday School, he taught a Men's Bible Class; after the class, he was head-usher in the church — no small responsibility to-day certainly, as any one would admit; after the crowded church he was an Elder, or whatever they called it in his sect, and would help to count the takings of the plates, on the size of which depended many a diocesan plan through the coming months. On the religious side, it was unquestionably the big moment of George's year, and he was visibly conscious of his interesting situation. He invested the small business of breakfast with an indescribable augustness: while his mind, at intervals, ran over once more the remarks he intended to address to his class at the opening. George's central idea was to use the season (Spring) to exemplify the ordered recrudescence of life.

9

However, he ate rapidly too, and his oxlike eye turned often toward the clock.

At the last moment his rooms-mate rose suddenly from a hail of newspapers, saying: "Half a minute, old fellow — I believe I'll go along."

The Elder, if such he was, in the act of tugging on an excessively new glove, lemon in color, stared at him with some displeasure.

"Why! You just said you were going to spend the morning here working!"

"Yes, but a breath of air first might do me good. Look at that sunshine!"

George Davis grumbled: "Well, get a hump on then, for pity's *sake!* Don't know your mind from one minute to the next, looks like. I'm late now, if I'm going to walk."

The rooms-mate, whose name was Masury, laughed and vanished through the portières, to reappear promptly enough. Within two minutes, the pair were emerging from the new English-basement front of the old brownstone house, and George, taking a lungful of the soft air, was saying interestedly:

"By gad, these sidewalks are *dry!* You wouldn't have believed it possible, this time yesterday."

They skirted the private park, where a single shrub, venturesome beyond its fellows, showed tiny feathers of green, now wet under melting snow, traversed a block of Twenty-Third Street, crossed the Square by the meandering footway, and so came into the Avenue. The secular bells in the tall tower hard by, which perpetually remind the just and the unjust of the passing of all mundane things, began to strike. It was quarter to ten, and already the great thoroughfare, deserted by commerce, was astir with the special preoccupations of the day. Numbers of the faithful moved to or from masses and services, or upon didactic missions similar to George Davis's; others, if appearances did not belie them, were for taking the day outdoors in the pure holiday vein, neither caring nor having heard that the groves were God's first temples. The new modes were out in the unexpected sunshine, hats, gewgaws and frippery; and now and then, through the mere feminine display, there obtruded a sterner note, indicative of the troubled times. Spurs and sabres gleamed among the costumes. At the Holland House corner, Masury gave greeting to a British officer who came swinging by, a handsome bronzed man, very smart and bright-harnessed.

George Davis said: "Who's that bird? Howdedo, Mrs. Penfield? Happy Easter."

His friend answered absently; "Fellow named Hedley-Black. Attached to the British Purchasing Mission. I'll set Forty-Second Street as my limit. Suppose I must get on with those confounded articles."

"When have you got to have 'em in?"

"A week ago Tuesday. Like Peter Dunne in the story."

The sun shone on George's tall hat, on the starched white edgings of his vest, on his brilliant and enormous shoes. Masury, in workaday clothes, overcoat-tails flapping in the light breeze, made him the perfect foil. But the mutual adjustment of these two was in all ways harmonious and complete. Temperamental poles, wholesomely disagreeing on every subject under the sun, they got along wonderfully, like an old-established married couple of the best tradition. Seven summers and winters they had lived together now, a model to the neighbors, and neither saw the shadow of any parting, this side the demise of one of them.

Now and then the two men spoke to acquaintances along the way; by a coincidence each of them was that rare creature in New York, a born New-Yorker. For blocks, their conversation was desultory. George's silences had a pontifical quality; he was possessed by the beauty of holiness. But something else, definite

The younger man, unobserved, smiled faintly. The smile was far from derisive; rather it recognized and appreciated the authentic flavor of these remarks. While he never argued with George, Masury often listened to him with attention, frankly considering him rather wonderful. His faculty for the general amounted to genius. Through George, mysteriously and unmistakably, pulsed the tide of the common; touch him at any point, day or night, and he would give you instantly the colossal reaction of the mass. He was miraculously national. The gift indeed was well known in George's circle; and Heming, the newspaper columnist, a friend of both men's, had more than once printed paragraphs beginning: "As George Davis, the American People, would put it" — etc. While George affected to be annoyed by this publicity, he was in truth much gratified, and never failed to buy an armful of the paper mentioning him, which he dispatched to relatives and admirers, far and near. Thus, gradually he himself had become aware that he possessed an institutional significance.

"Because an Austrian fellow was blown up by a Servian fellow — a *Slav!* — at *Serajevo!* — you're talking about going and driving an ambulance at Nooyey! I can't see — Hi! Whatchu doin' out so early, Ed, you sinner? Happy Easter!"

Masury again made no reply: this time he really did not hear. His eye, happening to go down the side-street, had just then fallen upon the figure of a friend: one whom, as it chanced, he had not seen for months, one whose conversation, as it further chanced, he preferred even to George's. He started a little at the unexpected sight, and stopped short. At the same moment the friend — a young woman it was, who had just tripped out from a tall white apartment-house down the block — saw him; a radiant look broke over her comely face, and she waved a white-gloved hand.

"Hello! There's Mrs. Flanner back."

"Where? ... Oh!" said George, having followed his gaze; and he swept off his tile with the distant gallantry of a man constitutionally afraid of women.

"I leave you here," resumed Masury.

"H'm, lot of work you're doin' this mornin'. Well! — won't see you till night —"

"Happy Easter, George!"

The pillar, quickening his long stride, was gone into the crowd. Masury, having joined his home-come friend halfway, gladly caught step with her.

The two met in a fire of greetings and questions. Mrs. Flanner had been wintering in Florida, recuperating from influenza and doubtless thoroughly enjoying her new wealth, yet spending each morning at a desk nevertheless, it seemed. She was thirty-one or two, perhaps, but looked six years younger at least, and was then in the first agreeable flush of the discovery of a talent. A beginning scenario-writer, though by no means an amateur, she had lately won an abrupt and dazzling success, the dimensions and future possibilities of which still literally startled her. Her sudden triumph, following much adversity, had been to Masury the pleasantest happening of a year not memorable for pleasantness.

Mrs. Flanner was not the oldest friend he had, by many. He, for his part, was hardly a dependent or confiding person: he positively looked to no one to "inspire" him. But good minds and hearts were dear to him, if not necessary, and it seemed to him now that he must have missed this young woman considerably in these three months.

"But what luck meeting you this way! When did you get in?"

"As stated in my postcard — Thursday! I actually thought you would call me up instanter!"

"Yes — yes. I was going to. But — well, I was n't exactly certain where you'd be, you see —"

She told him with rapture of her new apartment — where she possessed among other agreeable things, it appeared, a maid-servant all her own.

"Lucy! This becomes positively nouveau!"

"Is n't it the most ridiculous —"

"Do you mean to say Palm Beach did n't break you flat?"

"I spent something beside the winter, I own! But I can make more! I —"

"What about the new pictures? — how are they coming? You 've hardly written me a thing!"

"Oh, Dean, really well! One 's practically done and the other well along. I have n't hurried as you see, but I honestly do believe they 're both good — really good. And I picked up a lot of loose material down there, characters and situations — I 've three more sketched out in my mind, did you ever?"

However, being an agreeable creature, she soon turned the talk.

"I 'm inspecting you as I walk, my friend," said she, "and I don't consider that you 're looking just right. You look bored — and indolent, and — Dean, is it true that you 've thrown your job at 'Parson's'?"

"Yes — yesterday! But how on earth did you —"

"Bad news travels fast, shall we say? But what made you do it?"

"Bad news! — how you talk! Why, my dear girl, I 'd been there nearly a year!"

"And you were doing such splendid work too. Everybody said —"

"No, I was n't. That 's the point — just doing the same thing over and over, that 's all."

He spoke with unconscious assurance, like one disposing of ignorant objections, and she, glancing somewhat quizzically at his habitually grave face, understood him readily enough. She was by now quite familiar with this man's original platform as to work, faithfully exemplified by his life, namely, that when you had been in a given position long enough to know and understand it thoroughly, that was the moment to move on to something else. True, he was fundamentally a journalist, a publicist, and practically all of his activities had been threaded on that central interest; but he had persisted in being as scattering as he liked. Thus it happened that while he had done a great many things, some of them decidedly interesting in themselves, and even distinguished, perhaps, he still did not stand for anything in particular, and her private feeling was that he had failed to take the place to which his abilities entitled him. . . .

She said, a little less merrily: "What are you going to do now, Dean?"

Having no idea of being drawn into a further discussion of the secret chancelleries of Europe (though she, as a fact, was passionately for all the chancelleries, outside the Central Empires) he said that he had no plans; and thereon drew her attention to the municipal snow-ploughs, which were driving wide swaths through the soft waste, already melting away under the traffic, and to her overshoes, which he cited as superfluously prudent. Stepping briskly, for she was an admirable walker, and he had clearly abandoned his plan of turning back at Forty-Second Street, they were coming now into the more fashionable regions. On every hand appeared the lilies of the field and the hothouse; the lines of shining motor-cars thickened; everywhere was the gala air, a little hushed, the hum of voices and the tolling of bells.

"But explain yourself, Lucy," said Masury, returning to the muttons. "I'm idling, I confess it without shame. But you look as purposeful as George Davis himself — only maybe not quite so religious. Where are we going from here?"

Mrs. Flanner said that she had business to attend to. "In

fact, I expect I've got a whole day of business, as it happens. Not that I mind —"

"Spending Passover with picture-kings! How delightfully decadent!"

"No — I'm not."

She seemed to hesitate, and then — for argument could scarcely be escaped in these days, and as he was walking with her he would soon know anyway — she plumped it out:

"I'm spending it with Teresa DeSilver."

Her companion was silent for at least five seconds, and when he spoke it was in a changed key: "Easter with Saint Teresa! By George! — that's the sweetest fancy I've heard in weeks. But — why exactly!"

"Why — *work!* Very simple! She asked me if I could put in my Sunday, helping her out — so many people were away over the holidays, and it was urgent. Of course I was —"

"You can't mean — *Whitestone?*"

"My dear Dean, what do I know about steel?"

"If it comes to that, what does Teresa?"

"Well, a great deal more than you or I, depend upon it. But no — I didn't even know she had bought the company till I got back. This is the Eight-Hour League — she's resigning there of course. They closed the office yesterday, and I'm useful for packing up and things. Of course that's all I've ever been good for, unless you'd count making eyes at a Congressman or two!"

"I never," said Masury slowly, "heard of anything so absolutely public-spirited in my life."

Mrs. Flanner, holding down the brim of her large hat against a gentle gust, said: "On the contrary! — selfish altogether! Haven't I told you it's been one of the most valuable experiences I ever had?"

"Working for the Eight-Hour League?"

"Association with Teresa."

"Well!... What's your trip south done for you, then? Hasn't broadened you a bit. Still sticking to it that you admire —"

"Isn't it ghastly? What's more, I stick to it that you'd do the same, if only you had a chance! The trouble is she'll never give you one!" She spoke in a lively and merry manner, plainly provocative. For her part, she would have preferred to avoid this topic altogether to-day, convinced as she was that, under the circumstances, it was capable of lasting them the walk. Nevertheless, she had of course no idea of yielding anything; and if she irritated him, it couldn't be helped. But now, all at once, her graceful head turned sharply, as if jerked round by a hand, and she fixed the man beside her with a curious stare, and became silent. It was as if, with the sound of her own light words, a positive thought had thrust into her mind, momentarily arresting her processes.

He, unconscious of her scrutiny, was replying, a little patiently:

"A chance to 'know' her, I suppose you mean? My point is exactly that I do know her, you see. It doesn't matter that I've never seen her; for as I've mentioned before, she's merely the worst living example of a perfectly familiar type. Take this last performance, this Whitestone business. Can't you see how offensive that is? What could — "

Mrs. Flanner, rousing, exclaimed: "For a woman to assume control of the business she owns? I must confess —"

"Grabs, let's say —"

"Why, it was her father's business, Dean. You know he left her —"

"A little stock — exactly — exactly! — and she ferrets around and secretly gets hold of enough more to bag it — and throw on the sidewalk the experienced men who were successfully building it up. Why? Nothing could be simpler. Steel's in the lime-light, as never before in history — all right, let's jump into steel. Why —"

She interrupted spiritedly: "Honestly, that's the most prejudiced thing I ever heard you —"

"I am prejudiced where that woman is concerned, and I'm glad of it. But enlighten me. What is her idea really, shoving herself forward in such a grotesque way?"

"I pass over your terms, since you admit, at last, that you're unreasonable. As to this steel company, I fancy Teresa had special reasons for wanting to take it —absolutely cogent reasons. as she saw it — "

"Such as what? Specify!"

"Well," said Mrs. Flanner, and paused a moment. "I'll tell you what I really think. She's always wanted and expected to go into business on a large scale — I know that — as a logical part of — well, a sort of demonstration that she's giving her life to making."

He shot her a glance, then, full of speculation.

Some days earlier an item in the newspapers had briefly announced that the Whitestone Steel Company, an inconspicuous concern of which he knew next to nothing, had passed into the control of this restless daughter of an arrogant house, the enormously wealthy, the altogether too celebrated, Miss Teresa DeSilver. At the time, among more important news, he had paid small attention to the incident, merely noting it as a characteristic bit of self-assertiveness. Now all at once, under the impetus of argument and of his friend's somewhat evasive manner, it had occurred to him that the performance might have deeper significances. It was certainly no moment for a born fool to be monkeying with one of the world's vital industries. Steel, some were saying, would "win the war" — was it possible that there was something ulterior here?

Biding his time, he said mechanically: "Oh! — a demonstration. How do you mean?"

"Well! — I think I'd put it this way: demonstrating that a

woman can live a life of large public usefulness without being conditioned in any way by her sex, just as a man does. In fact, completely unconditioned by sex, which a man seldom is."

"Really! That's cute. So you do admit she's a typical man-hater?"

Mrs. Flanner laughed, and then sighed.

"Did you happen to see an article about her two or three months ago — one of those awful Sunday specials? An unknown hand sent the paper to me in Florida — I suspect Mr. Steinfeldt. It was called 'The Woman Who Hates Love.' I thought of you as I read it!... But no, Dean dear, I should n't call Teresa typical at all. She's merely decided that marriage is not for her —and she has to protect herself, that's all."

"I see," he said, in the same preoccupied manner. "She's convinced the horrid brutes are just set on springing out and conditioning her. Those perfectly rabid man-haters usually think —"

"Think! — she could have married fifty times if she'd wanted to! That is, but for the laws.... How do you do!... Yes, just back!... Thank you. Yes, lovely time!"

"It's hard to believe there are that many really desperate fortune-hunters about."

"To be young, beautiful and charming is also something of a lure, don't you think?"

"*Charming!*"

"I speak of her offers — let's put it another way. I have n't the slightest doubt Teresa DeSilver could marry anybody on earth she wanted to!"

"She's crazed you!"

"You, for instance, Dean! — with your admiration for strength and beauty and — competence and — what is the other quality? — well, say, invincibility — say victoriousness. Why,

I don't doubt she'd gather in your scalp in no time if she happened to think it worth the trouble!"

Beside her the man walked in a silence, in which an inimical interest was fed by a certain human exasperation.

To him, this noisy Miss DeSilver, with her conspicuous position and her extravagant activities, had long stood as an example and a warning. In his thought, and he did some thinking, she had come to personify the inevitable seamy side of all "reform"; she was the living embodiment of all that was undesirable and untrustworthy in causes not in themselves unpromising, perhaps: of everything in a woman, everything in a human being, that was self-assertive, harsh, unlovely and untrue. She was all advertising and pose. That Lucy, just back after months, just off the train as it were, should be making herself the creature's ardent champion —

"Now!" said she, abruptly, after a pace or two. "How about testing that — would n't you like to?"

"Testing what?"

"Oh, Dean! I dare you!"

"Dare me what?"

"What I just said to you — you heard me!" said she and gave her sudden, pretty laugh. "I just thought — a new and rather exciting idea! I was up here, at the League offices, for a little while yesterday morning — such a time! — the place jammed all day and I hardly saw Teresa. But I did hear her say this to somebody — listen, for it's curious. She's looking right now, or was yesterday, for a man — of the clerk type, she said! — an expert, to take charge of reorganizing the city office of the steel company — it's a fact! You know — put in modern systems and equipment, coach the personnel and all that. Well! Did n't you tell me you'd make a study of office efficiency at one time in your career?"

"At all times in my career."

"Well!— you're idle and free! Why not apply — embracing the remarkable opportunity of seeing her for yourself."

"Why, indeed?"

"Seriously! I said you'd never have a chance to know her, since she goes nowhere and meets no one, eligible men especially! Well, here *is* a chance, such as many would jump at! Be game!"

She spoke banteringly; he answered with perceptible irritation: "Associate myself with that freak — great Lord! And even you'll have to admit that a person's an unutterable freak who spends a lifetime 'demonstrating' something or other that isn't worth knowing."

"Not worth knowing! Really, Dean!"

Lucy, having given him a stare, went on spiritedly: "Do you honestly forget the perpetual argument against us — that we're hopelessly creatures of our sex — that our interest in business or politics or things of the mind is only incidental and pretended; that we're actually stalking men all the time, dreaming always of sinking into a pair of stout arms at the first opportunity — murmuring, 'Dear, I'm only a woman after all'?"

"But, you see, you are women after all, just as I'm a man after all. Why do you suppose we were made beings of sex? Hardly that we might pass our lives trying to prove there's no such thing as sex, do you think? Suppose this woman makes her demonstration, as you call it, what would she have proved? Merely that an abnormal person can lead an abnormal life, which everybody knows already. How many normal women would imitate her — or should, in your opinion? Most of the women who are leading lives of public usefulness to-day are personally normal. They are mothers. They are grandmothers."

To that she replied briefly, with some thoughtfulness it seemed: "Maybe so. But — well, she's different." The retort seemed so ineffective to him that he willingly let it stand in silence. In fact, his thoughts ran in a different direction.

"But let's see — about this steel company," he resumed, with admirable casualness. "What did she buy it for anyway? You mentioned that she had some — compelling special reasons?"

"I suppose you're familiar with her views? — You know so much about her!"

"Her views about steel?" he said, with a faint inner stir. "Why, no, I did n't know she had any."

"Well I won't attempt to conjecture for you....I simply imagine," said she, staring straight ahead, "that as the largest stockholder in the company, she was dissatisfied with the way things were being run. Therefore she decided to run them herself. As I say, she never talks, never explains."

Dean Masury was certain then that Lucy was consciously evading him. He was certain that the wild-woman was up to something with the captured steel company, deeply certain that, whatever it was, it was wrong....

Mrs. Flanner, who could hardly have found the topic of Miss DeSilver and steel indefinitely engrossing, but was unquestionably interested by the evidences of his interest, went on with sudden animation:

"Her complete independence, her strength and courage, pass anything I've ever known, I think. For the life of me, I can't see how even you, with all your male prejudice, could help admiring her for that. Just her courage alone — the kind that makes a person stick to the death to what she thinks is right, no matter how unpopular it is, or how cruel the opposition."

"Don't you think that's a sort of courage that comes naturally to — certain types?"

"Every sort of courage comes naturally to the type that has it.... But yes, I do think it seems perfectly natural to Teresa to decide for herself what is right, and then go ahead and do it, if the skies fall. If you knew," said Lucy, and the addendum seemed to him remarkably like an afterthought, "how the Manufacturers' Association has hounded her."

Her companion looked at her sideways, looked away up the Easterly street, looked back again. His expression, in a hardly definable way, had undergone a certain stiffening.

Suddenly but still casually, he spoke:

"So you really want me to meet her, Lucy?"

With a glance, she threw out: "If wishes were all!"

"Well, I'll tell you," he said, with a handsome air. "We've argued about her enough — it's absurd. You think I'm just a mass of ignorant prejudice, that if I knew her at all, I'd feel differently. All right! — I accept the test. I'll go in with you now — and have a look at her."

The young woman gazed at him; on seeing, with surprise, that he was entirely sincere, and most masculinely confident, she gave an odd laugh. "She isn't under wire in the Zoo, Dean. Having a look at Teresa — well, that's not so simple."

"Doubtless. But — we can arrange a pretext or so if necessary. Come! — I mean it. Perhaps I *have* been extreme in my criticisms — perhaps I'll recant, who knows? I really want to meet her."

"My dear Dean, there are fifty thousand men in New York who want to meet Teresa DeSilver. Don't be absurd. Her appointments are made weeks in advance."

"Rubbish! Do you mean to say you're afraid to walk in and say, 'Teresa, I want you to know my old friend' —"

"She hasn't a minute for her own old friends — why drag in mine? She isn't a bit like you, you see. She works sixteen hours a day, the year round."

Having reduced him temporarily to silence, she added gaily: "But it's rather a pity, for now that I've thought of it, I should like immensely to have you know her, even a little bit. I think it might do you lots of good! Well, here I am."

She paused on the corner to which they had now come, and the two stood looking together at the mighty pile of gray stone, the building of which had been a nine days' wonder in the nineties.

"There's where I'm going — in the wing."

On the whole, the famous mansion had been well done. Huge as it was, magnificently pretentious as it undoubtedly was, it yet achieved a certain massive beauty. The imposing entrance was on the Avenue, but the length of the palace ran down the side-street, the widest of the Fifties. Here, through a paved court, which held an enormous black-marble fountain dense with statuary, a short gallery led to the so-called "wing" which was in fact a three-story house, the mansion done again in miniature. The wing, as was well known, had been first projected to house a collection of pictures which Josiah DeSilver had intended to gather, presumably by way of giving a concluding artistic touch to a long life singularly unrelated to the arts; but a stroke of paralysis had robbed the old gentleman of his aspiration, and the building had been converted to other uses.

"Who owns the place?"

"Teresa."

Mrs. Flanner added, ruminating: "Old Mr. DeSilver deeded it to her on her twenty-first birthday. I've heard that he lost it to her on a bet. I suppose he regrets that now."

"Why?"

"That's a long story to go into offhand. But I imagine Teresa's unwillingness to marry has been a disappointment to him."

"Possibly her desire to go into big business has displeased him also?"

She glanced at him, caught by his tone, and was struck anew by the pointedness of his gaze. She considered that, for a kind man, Dean's eyes could look rather hard at times.

"Possibly."

"By the way, what *are* her views about steel? I'm afraid you forgot to mention."

"But then you'd hardly expect me to discuss Teresa's private affairs?"

Dean Masury echoed the words gustily. "My dear girl, the control of an important corporation isn't anybody's private affairs! Stockholders, investors, bankers, dealers, railroads — all the world's got a legitimate interest in it. Good heavens, don't you ever look at the financial pages in your newspaper?"

"Perhaps you'll read about Whitestone there some day, then! Let's wait and see.... Really, Dean, I know next to nothing about it, and what I do know came confidentially, I must feel. Good-bye! This talk leaves something to be desired, from my point of view. When will you —"

"No, no! Wait a minute! — please! —"

The man's glance slanted off toward the sunny Plaza and the Park, and he stood motionless, for the instant altogether lost to his surroundings. In fact, the conversation had increasingly interested him, in the most hostile fashion conceivable.... Might not this, at the least, be worth looking into? Might it not indeed be somebody's duty to look into it?...

"I was due at ten o'clock, Dean. It's quarter past now."

"All right, I won't keep you."

Turning his gaze down upon her, he announced in his bluntest manner:

"I've made up my mind. You're to take me in and introduce me now."

She was literally taken aback by his insistence, and by the look, keen as a hawk's, which suddenly peeped out of his nondescript light eyes. Her own expression changed perceptibly.

"But I've told you, Dean, that's impossible! You know the President, don't you? Suppose I casually demanded —"

"I'd do it! — and make it easy and natural too. And since you're so awfully timorous, I was just thinking I'd have to show you — I'll fix you up with the patter —"

"Splendid! I'll merely assume an air of girlish brightness and say, 'Oh, Teresa what fun! — here's an editor with nothing to do who's dropped in to pump you about Whitestone!'"

He retorted in a flashing way: "No! Say, 'Here's a qualified efficiency expert whom you'd be very lucky to get for your little job.'"

"Dean!"

On the spacious and breezy corner, where many persons passed, the two friends stared at each other. Lucy's look, all at once, was strange, and a little fixed.

"Do you really mean that?"

"For purposes of the introduction? Certainly."

Her face relaxed instantly, and she shook her head with a flatness in which impatience was not wanting.

"You don't seem to understand me at all! I respect and admire Teresa more than any woman I've ever known — yes, and love her too. I'd not dream of subjecting her to an impertinent prank."

But the man's thought, it was clear, had decisively quickened toward action.

"No, no! — You misunderstand — I'm not pranking at all! No, what you've said makes me think that I might find this, honestly, an interesting commission — interesting both from the business and human standpoints, and — in short, for various reasons of my own. It would only be a temporary thing — of course she would n't want an expert long — just to put her shop in shape for her. A few weeks at most — what's that? Now — here's absolutely my only reservation. If, after talking with her, I don't seem to grasp the possibilities of interest that you, in your enthusiasm — and so on — somehow suggest — why, then — "

28

She prompted, as he obviously reflected: "Then?"

"I'll so conduct myself that I'll *just miss landing it!* — don't you see? Your celebrated friend will be left thinking — in no sense that she's been trifled with, but actually that I was exactly the man for her — but for one little thing! On the other hand, if it seems as promising as I — as it now looks," he paused, seemed again to deliberate, and then said positively: "I agree to take the job.... Now! How's that?"

In the woman's intelligent and beautiful eyes he perceived the light of a mounting interest: an interest, perhaps, far different from his own, but it seemed hardly less strong. Still, seconds passed, chimes tolled, pedestrians brushed by; and she did not speak.

"Fair enough, is n't it?... Oh, come, Lucy! Modesty aside and all that, you know she'd be jolly lucky to get me. Have n't I organized half a dozen offices at least? Have n't I been made office-manager practically everywhere I've worked? Did n't I write almost the first efficiency articles ever —"

"All right!" said Mrs. Flanner abruptly, expelling a breath, and glancing away. "I'll do it — if I can."

"Good! Come along!"

At that folly, she merely shook her head. After a moment, she began to speak in a low rapid voice: "It's Sunday — it's moving day — and she's as busy as the mischief. Getting an appointment's going to be.... And to-morrow may be too late. And I'll have to explain you completely — prepare her mind for the idea of —"

"Oh, come, people's minds don't have to be prepared for me as if I were a death."

If he thought to lighten her absolute momentousness, his failure was complete. He thought she took the sudden project — which might prove nothing but a journalist's interview, artful but routine — with a somewhat absurd seriousness. And still, there might be matters here for her to ponder over of which he knew nothing, and still again, inevitably, her frame of mind in some degree reacted upon his own. He was aware of an expanding anticipation.

After a space, the engrossed young woman turned down her glove, glanced at her watch, gazed off for at least a minute at Miss DeSilver's official entrance, and then said decisively:

"I'll do the best I can. Come there at twelve o'clock. Ask for me."

Impelled by her conspiratorial gravity, Masury dropped his voice to a hoarse stage-whisper, openly mocking:

"*I'll be there — as the clocks strike twelve!*"

On that, without another word, the friends parted instantly and completely, like clandestine lovers who, the next tryst made, dissolve all traces of their fleeting union outside a subway entrance.

CHAPTER III

BY noon, the churches were beginning to empty. From houses and side-streets, from buses and car lines, appeared those also who but came for the walk, rejoicing in the sudden glory of the morning.

It was a festival atmosphere, doubtless; yet there was an undertone by no means merry. Before a stately church with a mighty steeple there stood a group of extremely dignified-looking personages, one of whom was said to be the Secretary of War; many passers noted the marked earnestness with which these gentlemen talked together. From ordinary citizens, from Jersey taxpayers and good plain burghers of Brooklyn and the Bronx, there fell, too, words that had nothing to do with the normal decorum of the day. Blocks below the stately church, eastward at Twenty-Eighth Street, a cluster of youths in felt hats and caps, for the most part visibly of foreign extraction, discussed some theory of national behavior in voices loud enough for all to hear. Here a fight broke out, sudden and fierce; in a wink a crowd gathered and three patrolmen came running. Still farther down, in Madison Square, another crowd was forming around a violent orator on a cracker-box.

It was, in fact, a time of controversy, of sharpening differences and deepening concerns. As the passions released in the previous summer had had as yet small practical outlet, it was also, preëminently, a time of talk. Everybody talked in these days, and talked again; millions of words to-day poured audibly upon the soft April breeze.

Dean Masury had withdrawn himself from the currents of discussion. In a corner of the dim, empty library of his club, surrounded by manuals, corporation directories and files of

31

newspapers, he had become very busy — expertly seeking to improve his knowledge of the Whitestone Steel Company, and its new president and treasurer, Miss Teresa DeSilver.

His time was short; and the results of his researches were proving unexpectedly meagre.

Regarding the woman herself, indeed, he scarcely needed references. Old Josiah DeSilver's granddaughter had been "written up" sufficiently, in all conscience; and his peculiar distaste for her had long served as a magnet for evidences and instances.

On the bus just now, his memory, which was a good one, had turned backward. Very distinctly he recalled the stir created, ten years earlier, by the girl's expulsion from college: the occasion, no doubt, when he had first definitely taken note of her. Her exploit then was a mere speech at a sophomore banquet, her subject being, as he recalled it, the ascetic life as seen in contrast with bourgeois marriage; however, the vigor of the young student's attack on some pretty well-established institutions had shocked the possibly Victorian dean, who somehow got wind of the affair. The Associated Press, which is never shocked, also got wind of it, and the piquant story had spread far and wide. So had originated what might be called the tradition or legend: for the wittiest editor in New York, making the girl's disaster the subject of an amusing article which became widely quoted, had then coined and fastened upon her the satirical nickname which seemed destined to be permanent. The wag averred that "Saint Teresa," like the pious Carmelite, wore a hair-shirt; that she scourged herself, slept on straw and bathed with hyssop. Thus at seventeen, she had advertised in the most public possible manner the beginnings of that misogamist pose which especially roused Masury's distrust, and which she had notoriously kept up ever since. . . . The thing was n't, to be sure, a crude or typical "man-hating," born of mere want of opportunity, and completely reciprocal in nature; no matter how he talked to Lucy, for argument's sake, applicants for the hand that held this tremendous dowry had, of course, been many, by common knowledge. This much-advertised celibacy seemed born, rather, of a general flair for picturesque sensationalism, no doubt pointed up and reënforced by an absurd sentimental egoism, an amusing arrogance of expectation, like the difficult princess in a fairy-tale. At any rate, the pretences to a noble sexlessness, classic superiority to nature and the ways of men, seemed to him particularly objectionable and false. . . . However, the young Teresa, as if only blooming under that unripe disclosure of her "complex," had gone on blithely gathering "publicity," now here, now there. She bought a speedy motor-boat as big as a yacht, and used to run around the Harbor at night, dressed in masculine oilskins and accompanied only by a prize terrier; a police-boat arrested her for running without lights, and so she was in the headlines again. She went hunting in the Canadian Rockies, and got lost; she went fishing at Catalina Island and caught a sea-serpent; she bought an early airship from Wilbur Wright and fell with it into the waters of Chesapeake Bay. While still in her teens, the maiden was known to have shot one man, a burglar, at the family place near Rhinebeck; a few years later, it was rumored about that she had shot another, a Frenchman, and her suitor. Amid such and many diversions, the daughter of the glare came loudly to her womanhood. Having completed her education with a year of post-graduate work at Radcliffe and a year of European travel under the chaperonage of a French maid, she had thrown herself abruptly into "public life," as she no doubt considered it.

The suffrage issue was her first obvious prey. She had, of course, joined the extreme Left of the cause, becoming a picketer, etc. One of the early advocates of the Federal Amendment plan and programme, she was generally credited with having originated the punitive card-index system, by which the "personal

17462

record" of every Solon was investigated and tabulated, and his life, if need was, turned into a hell. Here she had clearly displayed the overbearing qualities, indeed the ruthlessness, for which the men of her family were celebrated. Then, having risen high in the councils of the women, she had suddenly withdrawn from the work altogether, taking the position that the issue was settled. He recalled a typical smart-Aleck saying of hers that somebody had quoted to him: "Are n't people funny, going on arguing about suffrage? The question's as obsolete as slavery." But of course she had not remained idle. For a while she had busied herself with something public-spirited — a plan of coöperative apartment-houses for working-women, as he remembered the thing; but there was small publicity in coöperation in those days, and the grand notions had lapsed. Next, in 1911 or 1912, she had joined, taken over and swallowed up, the Women's Federal Eight-Hour League, an organization which in times past Masury had more than once assisted with his typewriter. A quietly effective body, marking steady progress on intelligent lines, the so-called "Saint" Teresa promptly made the League the noisiest thing in the State. In suffrage she had met resolute adversaries indeed; but such matters are milk-and-water to the bitterness of vested interests when attacked. In the Manufacturers' Mutual Protective Association, the implacable young woman had found a foe fully worthy of her steel. Her name in those days was gratifyingly often in the headlines; counter-charge followed charge, "fight" stepped on the heels of fight; the State was filled with uproars.

And then the war had come along and she had abruptly dropped out of sight. The great cataclysm had simply obliterated that trivial sound and fury. For months Masury had scarcely heard the name of Miss DeSilver mentioned. Now, as if unable longer to bear her obscurity, she had emerged with this curious yet characteristic feat.

Yes, but for what? Why this little steel business? On that cardinal point, the facilities of the library seemed to offer no light whatever.

As a professional commentator on affairs, Dean Masury's stock-in-trade was to know something of everything; in the case of the Whitestone Steel Company there seemed nothing to know. The available facts of record were these: In 1901 or 1902, Frederick B. DeSilver, having gathered in an old mine and smelter, apparently on a debt, had decided with characteristic impulsiveness to enter the steel industry; forthwith he had formed a corporation, christened it, floated it, built furnaces and mills, and opened for business. If the original lists of directors and officers meant anything, the corporation was of the "pocket" sort, virtually a proprietary concern: they were all "DeSilver people." As to how the stock was distributed, then or now, there was no means of knowing: that would have to be otherwise ascertained. The company history had been obscure. Though Frederick DeSilver had cut a more vivid figure in finance than his high-handed father, he lacked the old man's administrative grasp; some of his irons regularly cooled from neglect, and the small enterprise at Cohaxie had never paid a dividend. Following DeSilver's death, in 1911, however, there had evidently been some sort of reorganization; new officers and directors appeared, a man named Walter E. Ball was called to the presidency, and in the two years succeeding, as the manual showed, the company's gross earnings had more than doubled. There unluckily the official history ended: the latest reference book in the club did not go beyond January 1, 1914. The next notice of Whitestone to be found was in the newspaper accounts of the incident ten days ago.

Here again results were disappointing. All the papers had printed substantially the same paragraph, a bare statement obviously given out by the company. This statement merely ·

reported that the stockholders, at the annual meeting, had
elected a new board of directors (names given, Miss DeSilver
among them); and the new directorate, at its meeting next day
— of course under her domination — had duly elected the new
set of officers. One paper only, in its "Talk-of-the-Street"
column, offered a little mild comment on the emergence of a
woman steelmaster; this was "The Republic," which Masury
read regularly, and it was here that he had learned that the
young woman's inheritance from her father was a one-fourth
interest in the company and no more. But even "The Republic" exhibited no concern with Miss DeSilver's "views" and
intentions. On the whole, it seemed to him strange, even amid
the exciting general news of the day, that her raid and capture
had not attracted more attention.

Yet what perfect poetic justice this indifference of the public
was! For surely limelight was the true object of the thing,
exactly as he had said to Lucy.

Yes, again — but how? — what? Granted that the restless
young woman was moved in her various activities, not by genuine
interests and convictions, but only by an insatiable desire for
"self-expression," profoundly egoistic and essentially vulgar —
still, what did she see in the Whitestone Steel Company? Those
small paragraphs the other day could not be described as
"emerging" exactly.

Letting the file drop to the floor, Masury lighted a cigarette
and stared out into the sunny Sabbath. Had he been over-
suspicious, through his mere antipathy? Did Lucy's feminine
talk about courage and opposition refer to something else,
personal and unimportant?

That Miss DeSilver's choice of steel as her new "vehicle"
connected itself somehow with the explosion in Europe, he did
not doubt: but that of itself led nowhere. The steel industry, lan-
guishing domestically, was being kept alive largely through its

foreign orders: orders for rails over which the staffs could move men and supplies, orders for shell and shrapnel, of which England especially stood in dire need. Orders for shells. . . .

All at once he seemed to remember having read something about the Whitestone Company, back in the first period of the war: some stray item in the news — a long time ago. What might that have been about? His mind focussed intently on the elusive point. And then, just as he seemed to be vaguely groping toward a fact of interest, the silence and the solitude of his dim retreat were suddenly shattered together.

"Well, I'll be damned!" said a loud, bluff voice, nearing. "There's old Dean, getting up stuff for an article, I'll be bound!"

At the same time, another and more amiable voice said: "Hello, Dean! Not worshipping to-day either — how-come?"

The tide of talk, briefly escaped, came flowing back resistlessly. However, glancing at the wall-clock as his two fellow-members strolled up, Masury perceived that the time for his appointment was almost at hand.

For five minutes the three men stood talking together. One of the newcomers, Wilfrid Winslow, a drudge in a bank whose gentle bearing concealed a passionate addiction to sport and a rare adventurousness, wished to discuss a matter that really was interesting: the project of forming and financing a volunteer all-American flying squadron to serve with the French. The other, Horace Checkerman, wished to discuss things in general, and as Horace was the more determined man, and possessed by far the more powerful vocal chords, he had his way. A man with a considerable, though eventless, National Guard experience, who liked to be introduced as Major, Checkerman had early assumed the rôle of the club military authority, and more latterly that of its leading expert on the international situation as a whole, including diplomacy. The Major had long been recognized, by Masury at least, as one of those thrice-blessed beings who are constitutionally impervious to argument, or fact: whatever did not coincide with his own particular set of preferences, he invariably brushed aside as "pro-German."

So several of the leading questions of the day had to be thrashed out over again.

In the upshot, Checkerman, still talking, accompanied Masury uptown; for when the latter decisively mentioned an engagement, the bull-necked Major cried: "Righto! Give you a lift! — got to go up myself. I just want to tell you..." It seemed that his new racing-car, canary in color, with a Daimler engine, was waiting at the door. There being no convincing way of declining the offer, Masury accepted it; however, he salvaged something by listening not at all.

The probings into memory were not quite fruitless, for now, as he passed up the Avenue for the second time that morning, Masury suddenly recalled that his Uncle James Parmenter was counsel for the Blagden Estate, which in turn was involved through family connections with most of the DeSilver enterprises. That at least offered something definite to go on. Should the approaching interview develop anything of interest, Parmenter could certainly supply further details — how the Whitestone stock was distributed, for instance, who else besides the woman was interested, and in general what it was all about....

"Soft easy living, and all this cheap foreign spawn that don't think of anything but living safe and making profits. Profits — my God!" rumbled Checkerman's voice beside him. "Old England that our ancestors came from fighting for the freedom of a helpless little country — France that gave us Lafayette and Rochambeau fighting to the death for liberty and civilization — and we lolling over here thinking how we can make money out of their sufferings! Yes, and when those dash-dashed swine snort up and smack our faces for us, we have n't got the guts to stand up and resent it. No, we just write 'em a little note, like a tea-party, may-I-not this, and may-I-not that. It turns my stomach when I think about it ..."

Dean Masury neither answered nor heard. The rakish car slid to a standstill before the great gray pile beside which he and Lucy Flanner had darkly parted, two hours earlier, and he sprang out with an instantaneousness which left one of Checkerman's clauses forever hanging. His mind went forward.

"You seem to be in an awful rush," said Horace petulantly, bereaved of his audience.

"Awful!" said his friend cheerfully. "Stirring times, and this appointment's important — it's an interview. By the way, don't give up all hope of us yet, Major. There's a little life left in the old country still."

He saluted, thinking of something else, and turned away smiling.

He was in his mid-thirties, well known in his profession and well regarded there; he had reported wars and many occasions, been about a great deal, met nearly everybody, and read and studied considerably; he was himself the author of half a dozen scattered volumes, principally of a journalistic and "timely" character. In capitalizing his equipment he was characteristically careless; "Parson's" — "the international weekly" — had paid him a higher salary than they had ever meant to pay an editor, but now he had resigned from "Parson's"; in fact he was bored by routine, and genuinely indifferent to "getting on." His desire of life, whatever it may have been, clearly ran otherwise. He had no domestic complications, and no special softness where women were concerned; by preference he was footloose, and by temperament he was free.

There were no bells to be rung at the DeSilver "wing," no guardian of the gate to ask the countersign. This strange resi-

dence seemed as free as a city hall. You pushed open the vestibule door and went in.

Having pushed open the door, the caller found himself in a
wide, chill hallway, floored in black-and-white marble, and disappearing into shadows at the back; it was entirely bare save for
two oak benches, which had rather a second-hand look. On the
right, as one entered, was a large arched double-door of heavy
walnut; it bore, actually, a neat black-and-gold sign, lettered,
"Women's Federal Eight-Hour League." This door stood partly
open, and Masury opening it farther, stepped briskly over the
threshold.

He came at once into the full swing of the DeSilver activities.
The scene was as un-Easterly as could have been imagined. The
room, which was by no means a small one, was divided trans-
versely near the lower end by a stout oak railing; it was the
typical outer room of a well-ordered office. On the farther side of
the rail a Sabbath-breaking stenographer was busily clicking
away; a well-dressed woman in a hat was talking loudly at a
telephone, while another, even better dressed, seated at a table
heaped with odds and ends, was apparently taking an inventory of stationery and the like. The general sense of activity
was further heightened by an automatic typewriter in a corner
which, seemingly unnoticed, was running off form letters with
startling precision and speed.

On the visitors' side of the rail, upon a narrow bench which
might have been designed to discourage waiting, sat an elderly
rabbi, an exceptionally shiny negro, and a lady in a fur hat like a
helmet.

The thick door at the farther end of the room opened and
shut, and a woman in a severe black dress, a secretary evidently,
came into view. With a manner of noiseless efficiency and assurance, she gave a direction to the stenographer, received a message
from the lady at the telephone, and jotted a note on a small pad

hanging from her waist. Then, perceiving the caller standing at the rail, she came forward.

She was a smooth-looking creature, with sleek black hair and dark eyes set in a little slantwise; her "tactful" manner made it clear that your wishes were her own. However, at the caller's mention of Mrs. Flanner's name, she shook her head, regretfully.

"Ah, Mrs. Flanner. I'm afraid Mrs. Flanner is n't here just now."

"Not here? Why, that's singular. I had an appointment with her at this time — twelve o'clock."

"Yes — yes, certainly. But I'm afraid she was obliged to go out on a business matter for Miss DeSilver, and has n't returned as yet."

" Do you happen to know when she'll be back?"

"Ah, that I'm afraid I could n't say. I'm sorry. . . . If you would care to wait — ? Or, perhaps there's something I could do for you?"

Not a little disconcerted by the turn of affairs and having no idea how the land might lie, the caller said reflectively: "Thank you. Well, possiby you can. Mrs. Flanner, whom I saw this morning, was to make an appointment for me with Miss De-Silver."

"Ah, yes — with Miss DeSilver. And you are Mr. —— ?"

"Masury. Dean Masury."

"May I know what was the nature of your business with Miss DeSilver, Mr. Masury?"

Mr. Masury felt upon him the eyes of the waiting visitors, the pink-haired stenographer and the well-dressed Leaguer who was taking the inventory. He did not like this publicity; on several grounds his swift thought censured Lucy for having tamely let herself get sent out at just this juncture. However, he said without hesitation:

"I'm calling about a position in the office of the Whitestone Steel Company. I'm an office expert."

"Ah! — yes, certainly. . . . You are an applicant for the position, Mr. Masury?"

"Well, yes," said Mr. Masury. "Yes, I am."

A kind of interest came into the secretary's bland olive face; her look seemed to explore him. He returned her gaze in the firmest manner, defying her, as it were, to find anything the least odd in his being an applicant for the position.

"Will you wait just a minute, Mr. Masury? I'll speak to Miss DeSilver for you."

"Thank you."

She vanished through the patent-shutting portal that guarded the way to the sacred regions beyond. The caller was prepared for patience now; possibly for insistence. But Lucy Flanner, it seemed, had not made a total botch of it, after all. In less than a minute, to his distinct surprise, the secretary was back again, with her slight smile and nod, mysterious and understanding. It was as if she shared with him a pleasant secret.

"Miss DeSilver is expecting you, Mr. Masury — she'll see you in a few minutes. Won't you sit down?"

At these words, discreet though the voice that spoke them was, a little stir went through the waiting-room, as of endurance taxed just too far. The shiny negro sighed deeply, the stout old rabbi muttered something that might have been rabbinical, and together, as if moved by a common string, they rose and stalked out of the room. The lady in the fur helmet, on the contrary, crackled her newspaper defiantly, glowered about for a moment and went on reading the "Help Wanted" columns in an indignant manner.

Dean Masury sat down on the mourners' bench by the lady, and gazed unseeingly after the receding backs.

To say that he was devoid of anticipations at this juncture

would have been to underestimate his seriousness. Here he sat in the famous old mansion, where he had never set foot before, and had never expected to, awaiting an audience, and a battle of wits, with its not less famous young owner whom from a distance he had long so cordially disliked. At the moment, it was true, the exact scope of his intentions, the precise degree of his sincerity, were not altogether clear to him. Yet his distinct sense was of something impending, perhaps something important; and yet again, beyond mere curiosity and obstinacy, he undoubtedly had a purpose, and a definite one, which he fully expected to carry through. Motionless beside the helmet, he was now running over the plan of approach he had sketched in his mind in the beginning; the astute plan by which, while the woman supposed that she was pumping him as an applicant for a job, he would be cunningly pumping her as to what she was up to with steel. . . .

His eyes, becoming conscious of movement, focussed, and he found himself staring, through the open League door, at a strange old gentleman in a wheeled-chair. By chance they had come to a halt in the sunless hallway, directly before him.

Both the vehicle and the gentleman, in fact, repaid a stare. It was a very large chair, equipped with pneumatic-tired wheels, cantilever springs, a curved glass windshield, and a one-man top. It seemed even to possess a storage battery and apparatus, which made it, doubtless, more or less self-propelling. The occupant of this accomplished seat sat silent, looking straight ahead of him. From the bundle of furs in which he was enveloped his head, in profile, emerged with a singular salience. He himself was certainly no giant, but the head was a large one, high in the forehead and big in the back, and set at an aggressive angle on the shoulders; it was closely covered by a brilliant plaid gold cap. The gentleman had also a high thin beak and a beard which resembled a stiff white whisk-broom. From the whisk-broom

43

protruded an unlighted cigar, a very long one; sticking from the hard jaw at a rowdy tilt, it seemed as fixed a part of the countenance as the nose. You could see but a few square inches of the old fellow all told, but still he was an arresting presence.

Masury had scarcely gathered in the picture, in an all but instantaneous eye-sweep, when the gentleman spoke, in a throaty, rasped voice:

"Have n't I told you to see that this is closed?... These gapin' unsexed asses. Close it. God blast ye, close it!"

The face of a harassed-looking attendant appeared in the opening. At the same moment, unexpectedly, the face and figure of the sleek secretary came into view from the other direction — not harassed-looking at all, but cool and solicitous and suave. She bent above the great chair, saying something in a soothing tone. Then the League door banged shut, blotting out the scene. The lady in the helmet looked shocked and angry.

"The grandfather!" thought Masury. "And he did n't want her to buy Whitestone. . . . He has my sympathy."

The two typewriters clacked steadily; somebody talked tirelessly on the telephone; the well-dressed woman at the table counted blotters to herself; buzzers sounded, people came and went. After a time, which might have been long or short, there came through the noises a spoken name:

"Mr. Masury."

The universally helpful secretary, having returned to her official duties through some inner door, stood at the oak rail, mysteriously smiling.

"Will you come this way, please? Miss DeSilver will see you now."

She held the gate open for him; he passed within. Hat in hand, light overcoat on his arm, the seasoned interviewer threaded his way past typewriters and tables, to the thick door which commanded the presence. This door the secretary pushed

open for him; she preceded him through it, she smiled him over
the threshold; and then, turning toward the open spaces ahead,
she said in her confidential voice, hardly raised at all:

"Mr. Dean Masury."

She faded from view; the door clicked shut.

Masury found himself in the outlying parts, as it were, of a
large room, an enormous room full of light and noise and movement. By the accident of position, however, the very first thing
that his eyes fell upon, as he stepped over the sill, was the figure
of a woman. After that, for a space, he saw nothing else.

The woman was standing near a large desk at the extreme
farther end of the room — a long way off. She was, in fact, one
of a little group of women gathered about the desk; so far as he
was concerned, she stood alone. She was young, slender and
clear-skinned, and her effect was literally devastating. She wore
a long black dress like a cowl, girt about the waist with a cord; on
her head was a black cap that might have been a cross between
an old gentleman's skull-protector and a Turkish mourning-fez;
beneath this her hair, drawn back straight from her forehead,
bulged out in two large puffs over her ears. Her nose supported
a pince-nez, the most curious thing in the way of an eyeglass
that Masury, for one, had ever seen. Framed upon a straight
black bar which ran across the forehead like part of a mask,
the glasses themselves were as large as butter-saucers, and
divided horizontally into halves; from them depended a black
ribbon, almost broad enough for a sash. The creature was smoking a cigarette, set in a spiralled holder nearly a foot long, and
unnaturally looped in the middle.

Masury thought he had never seen such a looking object in
his life. He stared with fixed eyes, affronted and incredulous.

To the announcement of his name by the secretary no one had
paid any attention; announcements were constant in this centre
of unrest. The woman in the black cap and pince-nez went on

smoking and talking with those about her, her hands went on turning over the batch of papers she held. However, when Masury had slowly traversed about half the length of the room, the cluster around the desk dispersed; three women drifted away, the fourth, the appalling woman in the cap, moved toward the chair behind the great desk. In this movement her head turned a little, and the eyes behind the grotesque glasses met briefly and casually those of the advancing caller.

The woman's expression, thus fully seen, was curiously blank; had her face indeed been made of white wood it could hardly have been more signally devoid of expression. Her glance was in character, as empty as a doll's. And still, in an inexplicable way, that glance came upon Dean Masury with an impact; it struck him like a blow, and he was aware of a start and recoil which seemed to have literally a physical basis. The sensation was really extraordinary, and altogether without precedent in his experience.

No guide was needed to tell him that this was the insatiable "Saint Teresa." He advanced upon her with a thrill of profound antagonism.

CHAPTER IV

THE high ceiling emphasized the really noble proportions of the old picture-gallery, the floor was of fascinating stone in the Italian style, and immense curtained windows on two sides — doubtless cut when the artistic impulse had been abandoned — bathed the fine spaces with subdued, cheerful light. It might have been a splendid salon, or a medieval hall on a ducal scale; it was actually, by the look of it, a humdrum combination of working office and auditorium. The piles of camp-chairs ranged along the walls were the homely equipment of a meeting-place, and all the stock furnishings, mostly tables and filing-cases, were as clearly utilitarian. Prints in sober uniform frames sparsely relieved the walls, while the spacious floor was dotted with cheap Western rugs, imparting an unhappy gay note to the whole. The prints, it was seen, were all of women, modern celebrities ranging from Mary Shelley to Jane Addams; and in the farther corner, beyond the commanding desk, a large bust of Susan B. Anthony stood and gathered dust upon a pedestal.

For its present uses, the vast chamber seemed to be divided, like the ancient territory, into parts. The bustling and various activity which struck the visitor upon entering centred in its lower parts, the parts about the door. Halfway up the room, the noise and motion seemed to peter out, as if at an invisible barrier; and on the other side of the barrier there were space and bare stretches and quiet.

In the quiet, at a point about three feet distant from the great desk, stood Dean Masury, waiting to be "recognized."

The young woman who owned it all, having seated herself, had become, as he viewed it, unnecessarily busy. Several newspaper cuttings lay on the glass top of her desk (characteristic that

47

surely!) — these she fastened with a clip and pushed aside. She pushed aside also a considerable litter of papers, and having opened a large loose-leaf memorandum-book, plucked out a fountain pen from a pocket of her cowl and began to scribble down some notes. The caller was left free to eye her at his leisure.

He gazed at Miss Teresa DeSilver with that strange sense of predestined hostility, at once absurd and most genuine, and at the same time with a frank and simple amazement. He tried to imagine this face bare of its wilful disfigurements; he honestly tried, as a cold hypothesis, to conceive of the beauty mentioned by Lucy and others; but the effort was hopeless, like an impossible "catch." Some regularity of feature she might — and did — possess; the mouth and chin were not bad, the colorless clear skin was good enough; but — beauty! He thought of Lucy's strange adjectives, of her saying, "she's got to protect herself," and the words came back to him like a jest from the mad tea-party. The woman, surely, was at the last extremity from beauty or charm: she was ridiculous.

Without preamble or greeting, she suddenly spoke:

"Why do you want this job?"

If the caller was hardly prepared for so pointed a query, still less was he prepared for the voice which posed it. From this lady, by all the legend, one would have counted upon a voice like a steam-hammer or a klaxon. This voice on the contrary was of a piece with her general expressionlessness; it was deliberately small and flat, unnaturally inanimate, devoid of all character. But its artificiality gave it, to his ear, a wilfully offensive quality.

The whole matter, in a strange way, became more personal still. Masury answered instantly, in a manner odd for either interviewer or applicant:

"I'm not at all sure that I do want it, you see."

It could not be said that she paid him the compliment of surprise. But her blank eyes (which she did not trouble to keep more than half open, it seemed), lifting and dropping, just touched him. Again he had the stirring sense of having received a box on the ears.

"Why have you asked to see me, then?"

"Naturally, to discuss that very point."

"But the point, don't you know," she retorted flatly, "is one I have no disposition to discuss with you."

"Then I have called under a misapprehension, indeed. My understanding was that you were seriously looking for a qualified man to do a special work for you."

"You have no misapprehension there certainly —"

"In that case, the question whether or not you can make the commission attractive to me is decidedly material, I should say. I am, of course, an exceptionally qualified man."

"Ah? Well, that, naturally, is the point I prefer to discuss."

She tossed her pen down on the glass.

"An exceptional man, are you? Well, Masury, I find an unsteadiness in your record, and now a sort of senseless truculence in your tone, that make me, frankly, doubt your statement, and incline me to question the recommendations I have had this morning, from two sources, in your behalf."

Dropping the memorandum-book into a drawer, gathering papers from the desk-top, shuffling them rapidly, she threw out:

"Are you a drinking man?"

"I beg your pardon?"

"I say, are you a drinking man? Do you drink? Do you use intoxicating liquors?"

"May I ask what suggests such an extraordinary question?"

"Extraordinary hell!" said Saint Teresa, without the smallest change of tone. "You're thirty-six years old, a chronic drifter, and out of a job to-day. You've moved from one place to another, never satisfied, never sticking at anything. So far as I

can learn, you've never succeeded at anything in your life. Why?
You appear to object to my suggestion of drink? All right, all
right! — what *is* the matter with you, then? What's your
trouble?"

The interviewer, standing motionless before her, seemed to
feel himself turning a little white.

Forgotten now was his whim of drawing out this woman's
"views"; rather it seemed, indeed, that the woman, for reasons
impossible to fathom, had a fancy to draw out her applicant.
In that moment he felt that nothing on earth could induce him
ever to come within a mile of her again. And still something
deep in him was perfectly aware that merely to insult her, and
shake off the dust of his feet, would by no means suffice this
need new-born within him. No, his longing now was for a more
substantial declaration, beyond anger, some permanent souvenir
of his immeasurable distaste.

He said, with marked quiet: "Why assume that I have a
trouble, that there's anything —"

"No assumption about it. I've given you the evidence,"
interrupted the young woman. And stuffing the papers she had
been sorting into a long envelope, she licked the flap thoroughly
and pressed the buzzer.

"No, you've merely supported one assumption with a series
of others. For example, that I've never succeeded at anything.
Everything depends, should n't you say on reflection, on what is
understood by 'succeeding'? If one's idea of success is to dry
out of one's life everything that gives it flavor and value, to pursue some sterile desire like money — or fame — or shall we say
frankly, for illustration, a loud, empty notoriety — then I am
gladly counted a failure."

The woman's head lifted a little, and she looked at him; or
rather she peered or squinted at him, through her abominable
glasses. It might have been expected that she would close the in-

terview then, perhaps with violence; so far from that, after the briefest pause, the calm, flat voice said only:

"Well, I'll be darned!"

And then, in precisely the same tone:

"Call a messenger, Janney, and send these off. Let him bring back a receipt. Now what about Keeley and Ellison?"

The secretary, gliding on rubber heels into the range of vision, smiled her slight but understanding smile.

"The operator at Cohaxie's on Mr. Keeley's track, Miss DeSilver — we'll locate him very soon. Mr. Ellison's expected in from church at half-past twelve —"

"Bravo!"

"Colonel Hedley-Black is calling, Miss DeSilver. He wants to know if you can possibly give him a few minutes some time to-day?"

"Whew! — he's dogged. Tell him Tuesday at the company office. No — that would hardly do. Tell him this afternoon here — five o'clock. That'll spoil his tea."

"Undoubtedly, Miss DeSilver."

The secretary vanished, and the president of Whitestone Steel Company, returning to her tasks, pulled open another drawer rather thoughtfully. To him, her acceptance of his "senseless truculence" had come as a definite surprise. Had Lucy's advocacy interested Miss Teresa in his "qualifications" to this extent?... Or was it just possible that in the unmistakable challenge of his bearing, in this rude and instant male antagonism, there was something perversely gratifying to the creature's strut — "The Woman Who Hates Love?"

Behind him was the unceasing bustle of the departing League, of the coming activities of the steel company; for all he heard of it he and this woman might have been confronted in a void. Garb, look, word, gesture, everything about her perfectly supported his conception of a nature essentially theatrical; beyond and over all that was this curious cultivated colorlessness, unexpected and puzzling. The odd thing was that she did seem actually colorless — or almost. . . . Difficult indeed it was to associate this preposterous person with the Teresa DeSilver of legend, the heroine of a score of adventurous exploits.

She was saying, with a little air which in another might have been supposed to have a humorous intention:

"I had n't understood from Mrs. Flanner that you were a sensitive plant exactly! If my rough business ways wound your sensibilities, I am sorry. The work I want done is in itself very simple — the modernization of an antiquated run-down office — but it might easily develop into a permanent position, perhaps one of considerable importance. From that standpoint the question of stability is pertinent, and your record that way, if I have it right, is hardly promising. However, I need an efficiency man for a short time in any case. Passing over the purely temperamental questions for the moment, suppose you give me some idea of your equipment and experience."

Dean Masury stood, divided between two motives. The request, undoubtedly, was a victory for him; it was precisely the sort of opening he had framed in fancy fifteen minutes earlier as giving him his opportunity. Unluckily matters had changed since then; he could not bend himself to diplomacy now. On the other hand, in a distant way, he did desire her to offer him the job, that he might at least shake her by the manner of his rejection of it.

He said with sarcastic urbanity:

"For theory, I might cite you to my book, 'Profits by Efficiency,' a compilation of my articles in 'The World's Work' — almost the first articles ever written on the new ideas in business administration. For practice, I might refer you to various concerns, like the United States Zinc Company, who, following the publication of my studies, called me in as adviser. But —"

"You can offer the United States Zinc Company as a reference?"

"I can. But why should I?"

"Let's put it this way: why should n't you?"

"Because, as I said in the beginning the only real question involved is whether or not I would care to do the work for you."

"Ah, there we are again!"

The young woman blew smoke. Her hands were constantly busy with papers and more papers. She was packing a cardboard box. She said rapidly, yet in almost a mollifying way:

"All right — I don't seriously question your technical qualifications. The work is commonplace for any trained man — and I have an unusual confidence in Mrs. Flanner's good opinion. Besides, I've talked this morning with Mr. James Parmenter, who also speaks highly of you. What I do question is what might be called the seriousness of your intentions — originating so casually in a chance conversation on the street. Let's return to the beginning, then — the point of your interest. What did put it into your head that you would like to drop in, and at least discuss the position?"

The question brought the interview to the turning-point. Unconsciously the caller girded himself.

"I can answer you very simply. As no one doubtless knows better than you, the steel industry offers decided points of interest just now, and I, as I have ventured to point out, am an amateur by choice. I work for the love of the work, I work for the interest. It occurred to me that association with the Whitestone Steel Company at this juncture might offer special possibilities of interest. Therefore I dropped in hopefully, to look them over."

"And now that you have dropped in?"

"I confess that my hopes are practically extinguished."

Miss DeSilver's eyes glanced round the room: quite as if

she expected to find something somewhere that might have
extinguished her applicant's hopes.

"I don't follow your processes in the least," she said, but
hardly as if his processes interested her particularly. "However,
I can promise you at least that association with the company
is n't likely to be dull, if that's your point. Affairs that I'm
connected with are usually lively enough — sometimes quite
painfully so. ... Is n't that a fair statement, Mary?"

A middle-aged Leaguer, approaching from the rear, was in
the act of silently depositing on the desk-top two or three open
telegrams, with answers attached. At the sudden question she
said in a gentle, gracious way:

"I'm afraid I did n't hear, Teresa. Forgive me."

"Should you say that life with the Whitestone Steel Company
for the next few weeks is likely to be just a dull horrid bore?"

"I say foolish things sometimes, Teresa, I'm well aware, but
no, I should not say that."

"Thank you for the support — I need it! But probably,"
said the swift monotone, with the first faint hint of impatience,
"you are not of those who enjoy that sort of interest? Come —
tell me plainly what extinguished the nascent hopes with which
you dropped in."

Into the eyes of the visitor came a sudden gleam, faint and
cold. After all, what better prospect did the *manqué* interview
offer him now than this: to stamp himself upon her spoiled
complacency with an unforgettable candor?

"Willingly. But perhaps you, on your part, are not of those
who enjoy truth for truth's sake?"

"On the contrary — on the contrary!" said Teresa. "I especially invite it."

"Then I'll confess," said he, with an inner leap, "that in
dropping in here I was probably animated, more than I was
aware, by what I fear can only be described as vulgar curiosity.

I imagined that to see so — well-known a person as yourself, with whose celebrated points of view I myself had often differed so strongly, might be interesting to me — as a student, if I may so describe myself. I suspect I even thought — in addition to the other side of it, the interest in steel — that the association itself, for a short while, might prove more or less instructive. You perhaps perceive my predicament."

The young woman regarded him briefly through her glasses; it was rather as if she were peeping at him through a stereopticon.

"I may understand you to be speaking — somewhat personally? You're saying, are n't you — and mind you, there's nothing I like so much as good plain speech — that now that you've satisfied your curiosity, you don't find any promise of interest in the prospective association with me?"

"I can't deny that you've gathered my meaning adroitly."

The small busy hands had become quiet. The dreadful Miss DeSilver was gazing at a point on her desk-top.

"I believe I've been doing you an injustice, Masury. I think I've underrated your power of sincerity — your seriousness, in short. Now see if you can't make that a little more explicit — and convincing."

At another time and under other circumstances, Dean Masury would have found this incredible assurance purely diverting. It was otherwise now; and the distant hint of amusement in her flat voice was additionally exasperating.

He smiled darkly. "You find that difficult to believe? But my point's really very simple. I don't find anything to detain the student — beyond this single conversation. I don't — since you like plain speech and insist on the personal — I don't see any interest in you at all. You appear to have some gift for pointed speech — doubtless there is more that escapes me: I can only say that, speaking for myself alone, I don't, quite bluntly, seem to find anything — literally nothing at all. I don't find significance or force or character, I don't find reality. That's it above all — I see no reality in you. You seem to —"

He ended. The woman had interrupted him, she had silenced him, with a little gale of all but girlish laughter.

"By George!" quoth she. "Who would have thought it!"

The swivel-chair rolled and she was standing; her back turned as she rose.

Dean Masury said nothing. Oddly enough, while he doubted the woman's genuineness at every point, it did not occur to him to question the authenticity of this merriment. A difficult color mounted on his lean grave face.

It was no scene in a stage farce, however, no case of a little misunderstanding now about to resolve in badinage or jollity. She, whatever her small failings and foibles, was doubtless a busy person; even he would not have taxed her with a merely frivolous spirit. In five seconds, no more, she turned again; and her tricky countenance looked as blank as before: or nearly so — for perhaps there did survive somehow the slight reminiscence of enjoyment: as one may see in the west, after twilight has fallen, vague hues hanging.

Saint Teresa stood looking at him, just touching her lips with a handkerchief. She was of fair height, no more; slimly built, in bearing not ungraceful. Her eyes behind the slightly tinted butter-saucers were darkish, gray or blue; oddly enough, they were fringed with lashes which might have done duty for a village belle. However, part of her pose, it seemed, was never to look at anybody longer than for a second or two. Now the lashes fell; and putting out a hand, she slowly crushed the fire from her cigarette in a cheap glass ash-tray.

"Tell me," said the flat voice, "how can I induce you to come and work for me?"

When the applicant seemed disinclined to indicate how that could be done, she suddenly took another key, rather brisk:

56

"Oh, come, Mr. Masury! You came in here, it's perfectly clear, in the spirit of adventure, not to say of — boyish prankishness. Well, I'm meeting your prank, should n't you think? I offer you your adventure. And I'll tell you why frankly. I like to have about me men that are, not fat as the poet says, but — straightforward, truthful, impolite when need is — it's a whim, let's say. I want you in Whitestone, and I guarantee that you won't find even this casual connection with the company altogether tame or uninstructive. As to the other part, the personal part, I assure you that won't be nearly so dreadful as it now seems to you. In fact, I positively guarantee that you won't have to see your unhappy employer more than two or three times at most. Brief necessary conferences — and for the rest I keep studiously out of your way.... How's that?" said the voice, unmistakably mocking now. "Two or three times — an hour all told! Surely you are n't such a tender adventurer that you would wilt at that?"

Clearer and clearer it grew to the silent man that that sensation which had startled him at the first sight of this woman had not been for nothing; he, and no other, was her destined adversary. His lidless gaze upon her had become full of hostility: not sentimental hostility, nothing rhetorical, but enmity positive and ultimate....

"Stay! — a thought," said she, unmoved. "Possibly the question of salary interests you? I can offer a hundred a week for this work, you to decide how long —"

Out of the near spaces, in fact at the caller's back, the bland secretary said: "Mr. Ellison is on the wire, Miss DeSilver."

"Oh, good! — good!... Do you know something, Janney?"

"What, Miss DeSilver?"

"You'll certainly get your reward in heaven for putting in your Easter at hard labor for me."

Still standing, the appalling woman let her eyes touch the

motionless applicant, confronting her; and as she gathered up the instrument, she threw out smartly, with her flat effrontery that passed belief:

"Life is short, young sir. I think you'd better make up your mind, yes or no, while I'm having this talk."

She proceeded with her conversation, which began: "Ellison, Keeley'll be up Tuesday morning for a conference... plans, specifications and costs..." and seemed to go forward chiefly, on her part, by such phrases as, "By no means," and "Under no circumstances whatever." However, the young sir who was to make up his mind did not hear her talk. He had removed his eyes from that detestable cowled figure, and by a natural accident they came to rest upon the desk-top.

They came to rest upon the desk-top, and at once something happened. At the parting of the ways, chance jogged at his elbow. In this instant he was checkmated and knew it; nothing remained to him but an angry withdrawal. Within three minutes, which was as long as the telephone conversation lasted, the whole face of his outlook was changed.

His eye had fallen upon a newspaper clipping — the topmost one of the little sheaf, lying there almost under her hand. He was not consciously looking at it: the paper was indeed upside down to him, as well as some distance away. None the less, his eye, as if intuitively discharging its function, had suddenly picked up a word in that small and remote caption; and that word, as it happened, instantly fascinated him.

He was exceedingly familiar with newspapers, and by type, headline, and column-width had identified the clipping at sight: it was from the morning "Republic." There had, then, been news of vital interest to him in his paper to-day — probably to-day — and he had not seen it. Now in Miss DeSilver's presence, to the sound of her maddening voice, he set himself, with intense absorption, to catching up with current events.

"The Republic" uses an admirable type. The deciphering went forward rapidly. Masury's heart gave a bound like a ball as he read:

WHITESTONE CO. SHELL-PLANT
CLOSES; 2,000 LAID OFF

An hour's exposition would not have told him more of Miss Teresa DeSilver's "views about steel." He understood instantly what she was up to now. All was clear....

It was the direction his distrust had vaguely taken from the start. It was precisely that "something" which in his researches at the club had persistently eluded him. He had not remembered that this obscure company had already embarked in the munitions business; therefore even conjectures had been impossible. Now it came back to him dimly out of the past that the Whitestone outfit had been very early in the field; one of the first concerns in America to rush up a shell-making plant, disproportionately large, after the outbreak of war. Unquestionably that had been the item in the newspapers — a long time ago. Around this trade, the neutral arms trade, there had since arisen, as even the children in the street were aware, a bitter controversy. And it was to assert her perverse position in this controversy that the woman had raided and captured Whitestone.

Perhaps she was a "pacifist." Perhaps she was a Quaker. Perhaps the love of notoriety accounted for everything. Perhaps she loved the Kaiser. Whatever she might call herself or be, her wilful intention was, to the extent of her power, to deprive the European Allies of the supplies upon which their lives might hang.

Every atom in the visitor resisted this intention. The void of his irresolution was suddenly filled with purpose. He stood like a man transfixed....

The telephone receiver clicked up.

Miss Teresa DeSilver was gathering up the telegrams the gentle-voiced woman had laid before her a few minutes earlier. Standing and glancing through the proffered replies, she O.K.ed them with a flowing scribble. Having pitched the batch into a wire receptacle, she said suddenly, as if just remembering him:

"Well, Mr. Masury, which is it to be? Yes, or no, take it or leave it?"

The applicant said in even tones: "I take it, Miss DeSilver."

She was hardly a woman to betray surprise, if indeed she were capable of any feeling so human: yet it was certain that she was not prepared for his reply, or the manner of it. Her eyes, dropping, moved about a little: was it by accident or design, that they came to rest in their turn upon that significant sheaf of clippings? At any rate, lifting at once again, they seemed for the first time to rest upon him fully.

For the fraction of a second the two stood, almost as if they were frankly measuring each other. Then something flickered over her face which might have been mere amusement, and her inflectionless voice spoke with sudden business-like rapidity:

"Spoken like a man. Glad the student can be detained after all. City offices are at 500 William Street. Report there — to-morrow morning — to Mr. Kappus. No, I'll spare you Kappus. Ask for Harger — head clerk. He'll be expecting you — he'll show you everything. No need to tell you what to do, is there?"

"I think it will be found that I understand my business, Miss DeSilver."

"Good. Begin with a memorandum, outlining in a general way what you'd recommend to put the place in first-class modern shape, space, equipment, system, personnel, organization, everything. At minimum expense — *must* keep a close eye on costs. It's not a big place — if possible have your outline ready to-morrow night. Quick action's important. That's all. Thank you!"

"Just one question, Miss DeSilver, please."

"Make it brief," said she; and pressed the buzzer.

"In view of my casual — and temporary — relation to the company," said Dean Masury smoothly, "I assume that my — my views would not be regarded as of any importance in the matter? My personal views, that is, as to the general policies of the company?"

The expressionless eyes, again, briefly touched him: briefly met the scarcely mistakable challenge of his gaze.... Had she gathered his meaning, was it conceivable that she had followed his intricate "motivation"? That indeed scarcely seemed possible; and her voice, as she answered, conveyed again only the distant suggestions of condescension and assurance.

"I assume you're not a spy, Masury. I assume you would feel the rudimentary loyalty that the taking of a salary implies. I assume you would do the work you are paid to do in every way to the best of your ability."

"Naturally, those things are understood."

"Then what you think about it, or what you do outside of business hours, need not concern us. As a temporary clerk in the local office you will obviously have nothing to do with my management of the company."

"Thank you. Thank you, Miss DeSilver," said Dean Masury respectfully.

He turned away with a thrill of exultation, while behind him the toneless voice flowed on: "Get off these telegrams, please — collect. And Janney — did grandfather happen to mention to you whether he'd be in to lunch?"

"Let me see, Miss DeSilver. Oh! He didn't say definitely, but I somehow gathered that he expected to lunch with Mr. Lovering."

"Ah! — Well, show in Mrs. Carson — there's no help for it. Gosh, half-past twelve and nothing done yet ... "

Five blocks down the Avenue, striding swiftly toward his Uncle
James Parmenter's, Masury came face to face with Lucy Flanner.

His mind had become extremely busy. It was not a position
in an office he had picked up this morning, but a rousing gage to
battle. The thought of any conflict with this woman now would,
of necessity, have powerfully allured him. In the flesh, she
incredibly surpassed the worst that he had imagined of her:
she was a personified insolence, made strong only by the power
of an immense fortune; she was a soaring, perverse, and insufferable poseur, in desperate need of a thrashing. But what perfectly
substantiated this particular challenge, lying under the intense
personal antipathy and as it were validating it, was that the
basis of the encounter would be supremely worth while. For
weeks, restless under continued inaction, he had been planning
and speculating as to what he would do; now marvellously, in an
instant on a Sunday morning, he had found his "bit," in a task
as important as it was difficult and delicate. To circumvent this
entrenched adversary, somehow to preserve those vital trainloads of shells, would be a service indeed worth a regiment of
infantry. His anticipations waxed. . . .

Yet, perhaps the thought of his fellow-conspirator was not so
far from his consciousness, even then. At the first glimpse of Lucy
without any emerging process at all, he stopped short. She had
already stopped; her greeting was exclamatory, and, confirming
as it were the instant inquiry of her expression, she threw out the
one word: "Well?"

Masury said succinctly: "Very well. I have met the enemy."

"So I see. And you are hers, I suppose?"

"On the contrary, I took the job."

"Dean!"

Her eyes seemed to explore his face. She gave a sudden little
laugh which somehow puzzled him.

"I knew you would. What did you think of her?"

"She's young," said Masury — "you were right about that."

He added easily: "I think she's as beautiful and charming as a sick hedgehog. I can't imagine there's any doubt that she's the most obnoxious human being now alive."

"Not what I should call a bad beginning, not at all," said Lucy rather briskly. "Why did you take the job, then?"

"Why, of course to continue my study of the demonstration."

"Oh! — then it's nothing to do with her views about steel?"

"Yes, those views too. But it's a long story, not yet worked out. I'll tell it all to you when I can."

Her gaze, leaving him, lost itself down the crowded street.

"Well!...I must run. When can we meet, Dean? I have lots and lots to tell you."

They agreed to lunch on Tuesday; she said she would come downtown for the purpose.

At the last moment, when they had already said good-bye, Mrs. Flanner, pausing, spoke with a certain effect of abruptness:

"Oh, Dean! I — on second thoughts I think I'll tell you one of the things right now. You're not the man to believe me, I know, but — just remember afterwards that I told you, in a friendly manner. Will you?"

"You know I treasure your lightest word, Lucy."

She hesitated briefly, and said: "Well, then! — I don't know what you think you're starting with Teresa, but — whatever it is, she'll get the best of you. Don't forget. She always gets the best of everybody."

Her shining blonde face, as she turned away from him, wore a look that he was far from understanding.

CHAPTER V

HOW much stock did the woman own, how much was against her — or might be turned against her? That was the first, obvious and vital question. The hope had sprung up instantly within him that Miss Teresa DeSilver's control of the Whitestone Steel Company might still be wrested from her.

To his surprise, Mr. James Parmenter, to whom he immediately repaired, proved altogether uncoöperative. It was soon evident that Uncle James was perfectly familiar with the situation, and could have told him everything. All that Uncle James actually produced, however, were laughing evasions and odd, quizzical looks, and an invitation to lunch. The frustration, being quite unlooked for, was proportionately annoying.

He had found a number of people gathered and gathering for Easter luncheon in the hospitable old house; they were mostly relatives, mostly dull, and the three Parmenter girls, his cousins, whom he did not like, were excessively in evidence. However, Mr. Parmenter, greeting him with twinkling eyes, almost with a wink, had drawn him aside at once, into the little retreat off the library. It somewhat surprised Uncle James, evidently, and it somewhat intrigued him, that his nephew should have sought out this particular odd job, but then his nephew's activities had always somewhat surprised Uncle James; he clearly viewed the thing as a characteristic impulse, dictated perhaps by the queer newspaper inquisitiveness, more probably by some rash interest in the celebrated heiress; and his conception of the present talk was that Dean should thank him for his efforts in his, Dean's, behalf, while he twitted Dean a bit, in dignified yet roguish fashion. It seemed that the woman, whom Uncle James had known more or less from infancy, had telephoned him as he was in the act of

64

leaving the house for church, asking no end of questions; also that his, Dean's, ears would have burned, by Jove, if he had heard the flattering nature of Uncle James's replies, etc. When his nephew, however, succeeded in pointing out that he, in his personal or extra-office capacity, was firmly opposed to Miss DeSilver's policy as implied in the newspaper story, Mr. Parmenter had become at once, in what seemed to the nephew an odd manner, genially "diplomatic" and markedly less expansive. Masury had previously explained the strict honorableness of his position, his employer herself having assured him that his views were of no importance, and as he felt entirely sure of his ground — Uncle James being almost as staunch a German-hater as Major Checkerman — he presently said in real astonishment:

"But great heavens! You can't possibly think the woman is doing *right!*"

Uncle James, who was refreshing himself after worship with a cocktail and a plump Turkish cigarette, smiled amiably. He was a handsome man and not unaware of it, and possessed the most courtly and charming manner.

"My dear boy! How shall I put it to you? There's no question of 'right,' should you say? All of us, I take it, are opposed to war, you and I and everybody — except, if you like, a few West Point jackasses. Miss DeSilver is opposed to war. She happens to be, in addition, a non-combatant by conviction. She's a fighting pacifist, a militant for peace. As such, she would inevitably consider it wrong in principle to assist war in any way. And wrong in practice, too, since she would doubtless argue that to assist war is practically to encourage it, both now and for the future —"

"I understand, uncle, but —"

"Now," continued Uncle James pleasantly, "do you ask me, my boy, if I, personally, agree with her views? As you should know very well, I do not. In fact, as I have been advising her in respect to certain matters, as her attorney, I have strongly urged her not to take this step. My little block of stock — for you may remember that I formed the corporation and drew all the papers creating the company for DeSilver — back in 1901 — my little block, I don't mind adding to you confidentially, was voted against her at the stockholders' meeting the other day. All this, however, must not blind us to the fact that she, like every one else, is fully entitled to her own views, and that after all she is making, on conviction, on principle, an interesting experiment in a fairly debatable field. In this time of passions," said Uncle James, turning the shaker bottom upward, "I think we would all do well to try to keep a certain open-mindedness, to cultivate a certain tolerance. . . ."

To the conventional but unexpected defence of "pacifism," there were, naturally, a dozen pointed retorts. However, the opportunity for pumping Uncle James would not be indefinitely prolonged, and Masury resisted the rather strong desire to argue back.

With only the sketchiest transition, he had soon plumped out his inquiry:

"By the bye, if you don't mind my asking — how is the stock distributed at present? Just how much of it does she own?"

But to that, Uncle James, laughing, held up his hands in mock dismay.

"My dear fellow! Really! — had n't you better ask her that? That's it! — ha, ha! — you just ask her! — "

"I'm quite capable of it, if it comes to that. But I thought you'd prefer to give me the information yourself."

"My dear fellow!" remonstrated Mr. Parmenter. And then his lingering gaze upon his nephew grew arch. "By the bye, I wonder if you know the soubriquet that was given her by one of your bright newspaper men? 'The Woman Who —'"

"Yes, yes," interrupted Masury hastily. "I know that — I've heard it."

"Ah, you know it! A most interesting and original young woman! Well, my boy, you won't find it easy to come round her, that I must warn you. A word to the wise! Now —"

"But you see, uncle, I have n't the faintest ambition to come round her. My position is merely that, since munitions are vitally —"

"Have your fun, have your fun!" laughed Uncle James. "You adventurous free lances must get your experiences — I know! Well, you'll get experience out of the affair at any rate, I promise you! Ha, ha! Now come on in and make your peace with the girls. They were complaining the other day that they had n't seen you for months. . . ."

So the conference on which he had confidently counted for help oddly expired in talk of a " jollying" nature with the Parmenter girls, and talk of a depressing nature with Mrs. Parmenter, who was a long-time sufferer from a liver complaint, dark in her outlook and wanting in reticence. Moreover, he found himself dragooned, literally dragooned over three firm refusals, into staying to lunch. (Delia Parmenter was the sort of person who, when one says, "I'm sorry, I have an engagement," brightly retorts, "Can't you telephone and break it?" — assuming in a simple, odd manner that one will then say, "Why, the very thing!") The whole episode was exasperating to Masury; and the loss of valuable time was especially unwelcome.

However, he more than made up for it. His next inquiry, as it proved — and he had had several lines to windward — yielded surpassing results. Before the busy Easter Day had ended, he had his novel case almost in hand.

He found the facts wonderfully satisfying. In truth, he had uncovered a situation more encouraging than he had had the smallest right to expect.

At half-past ten o'clock that night — which was five minutes before George Davis's key clicked in the lock — Masury sat down at his work-table in the cheerful bachelor diggings on Irving Place. Here he had meant to spend the peaceful Sabbath at literary composition; in fact, he had that moment returned to his work-place, after more than twelve hours' absence. Seated under the green-shaded desk-lamp, he was looking at a sheet of paper, scribbled over with his handwriting. The paper contained, not notes for a war-article for "Parson's Weekly," but the pregnant secrets of the ownership of a steel company. He stared at it, engrossed.

He had got these facts, not half an hour before, from the late president of Whitestone Steel Company, Mr. Walter E. Ball. There remained a slight gap in the record before him. He confidently expected that gap to be filled by Mr. Ball....

Seeking an informant who would feel neither confidential restraints nor a funny "tolerance," Masury's thoughts had naturally turned at once toward the man whom Miss DeSilver had so recently set upon the sidewalk. The preliminaries of approach had not been easy: it had taken him hours to equip himself with suitable introductions, and another hour at least, with the aid of the switchboard boy at the club, to locate Walter E. Ball. In the upshot, at quarter to nine o'clock, he had presented himself by appointment at the residence of the deposed president, a rococo apartment-house in the West Nineties.

The interview had proved in some respects a difficult one. It took place in the "den" of Walter E. Ball's apartment, a strange room furnished with gold divans, a roller-top desk, a daybed and bachelor pictures on the walls. Masury had explained himself, with great firmness, as speaking for an "outside interest" which was on several grounds opposed to Whitestone's reversal of policy and was prepared to spend time and money in resisting it, provided there was any possible way of resistance. That was convincing enough; it could even be defended as true. However, his host proved wary; had it not been for the state of his feelings, it seemed probable that he would have remained completely uncommunicative.

Masury had counted upon some resentment from Walter E. Ball; he was hardly prepared for the extreme vindictiveness which the gentleman, in fact, exhibited. He himself was a good hater, not easily forgiving or forgetting, but Mr. Ball's verbal malignance passed beyond his repertory. Of Jewish extraction, a practical steel man as he said, the late president of Whitestone had a domineering voice, a gimlet eye, and large hard hands, which he used in gesturing. Masury frankly did not find himself drawn to him. In particular, he did not like the practical man's persistent interest in the fact that he, Masury, had taken a temporary position in the Whitestone office. He had thought it best not to conceal that, and Mr. Ball — not unnaturally, perhaps — at once understood a great deal that was not so. "You'll be in position to get us information of a valuable sort, possibly of great value," he insinuated, with dark eagerness. When Masury explained that he could not use his position in that way — that in fact he had taken the commission on more, well, psychological grounds — Mr. Ball, though puzzled, had clearly not believed him. "You're a pretty slick young fellow, I can see that," he said presently. "I guess you'll find you can work all right with me." And in fact it was then, as if heartened by the thought of the young fellow's slickness, that he began at last to show his hand.

Thus Masury had learned, with some surprise, that the intention of combating Miss Teresa DeSilver's designs with the Whitestone Steel Company was by no means original with himself. On the contrary, it appeared that he was precipitating himself into a struggle which had been maturing for months, the lines of which had long since been sharply laid. The discovery gave, at a stroke, unlooked-for dimensions to his private project. Far more important, he learned by degrees, that there was, in fact, a substantial basis for conflict, difficult certainly, but possible and positive.

In short, the hope which had struck and dazzled him while he still stood by the woman's desk, began to take on the quality of an intuition. She had not succeeded in getting a final grip upon the company; her raid and capture the other day had been effected only with a majority of the voting stock *represented at the meeting*. The somewhat stirring truth was that there existed a block of neutral stock, "dead" stock, which, if it could be bagged, would turn the scales decisively against her.

That bagging this stock was no simple matter went without saying; otherwise, obviously, the woman would have bagged it herself. Still, there it was, indisputably holding open the door to a brilliant opportunity....

The going campaign for the recapture of the company, as Mr. Ball had gradually confided it, seemed to be following three principal lines; first, an action for an injunction restraining Miss De-Silver from closing the highly profitable shell-plant; second, a stockholders' suit, pleading that the solvency of the company was threatened by the arbitrary policy of the new management; third, a special called meeting of the stockholders — provided for by the by-laws, on petition of one-third of the stock — "to consider, review and pass upon the acts" of the president. Such a meeting, it appeared, would have full powers for whoever could control it. In all these plans, now well advanced, the aged Mr. Henry Lovering — fellow-trustee with Mr. Parmenter of the Blagden Estate, and lifelong friend of Mr. Josiah DeSilver! — figured as the public protagonist against Miss Teresa; who else was included in Mr. Ball's guarded first person plural did not appear. That still other plans were afoot, for vengeance at least seemed extremely probable. When Walter E. Ball spoke of the enormous war-business which he had developed, and the lady thrown away, his swarthy face purpled. "She's a dash-dashed trickster; she's a dash-dashed pro-German!" he kept saying, using the two terms interchangeably. And now and then in his bitterness, he dropped mysterious hints: "There'll be disclosures — soon too! Big developments. You'll see. I'm not the man to take a stab in the back laying down. . . . "

Yet it remained perfectly clear that the true crux of the conflict was in that pivotal block of "missing" stock. That Ball himself so considered it was evident from the fact that it was at this point precisely that his confidences thinned out and expired. Still, in the end his reserve had come only to this: he would confer with his associates and communicate with his visitor again, within a day or two.

Meanwhile, the new employee of Whitestone, the office expert, was assimilating the following interesting facts:

Distribution of Stock

Miss DeSilver — inherited		2,000 shares	
purchased		2,700	4,700
Blagden Estate	1,500		
Mr. Josiah DeSilver	700		
Mrs. Wilmot	500		
Mr. Lovering	500		
James Parmenter	400		
Mr. Ball	400		
John DeSilver Wilmot	300		
Unknown			1,000
			10,000

That was to say, out of a total of 10,000 shares of common stock, Miss Teresa DeSilver owned but 4,700; beyond what she owned she did not control a share. The 4,300 shares were firmly and finally, and for the most part fiercely, against her. "Don't you fret there!" Ball had snarled. "Not all the money the dash-

dashed trickster's *got* would buy her a share off that list." What Ball had withheld was the identity of Unknown, with his controlling block of 1,000 shares. All that Masury now knew was that the unwitting master of the situation was an eccentric connection of the DeSilver family who, though known to be alive, was said to have "practically disappeared"; he had last been heard of in French Indo-China, and his stock had not voted since 1907. However, if Mr. Ball, on reflection, should decide against further confidences — which now seemed unlikely — Masury was certain that he could unravel the secret of that name and individuality for himself.

And then! . . .

That vigorous efforts had already been made on both sides to gather in the lost stock, there could be no reasonable doubt. That all the chief possibilities of advantage in the "fight" had long since been combed over and preëmpted was equally unquestionable. Yet Masury, convinced as he was that nobody "disappeared" nowadays, until dead, by no means felt himself a mere belated supernumerary here. . . . Were not the lengths to which a person was willing to go to attain an object determined by the depth and intensity of that person's desire for the object? No one's desire for this all-powerful block — not Ball's or Lovering's or Miss Teresa DeSilver's — was quite like his own. He thought of that untamed wilfulness and overweening conceit, absurd yet dangerous; he thought of that speech about the "temporary clerk," that unforgettable taunt — "you've never succeeded at anything"; and, alone in the cheerful sitting-room, with the sound of old George's step on the stair, he felt the blood rise within him.

There was dynamite enough in this situation, he was now convinced, for a fight that would wake up the country. Nevertheless, by his more urgent need and his more unappeasable hostility, the eminence would be his.

George Davis had had a happy Easter. Church over, his complex duties most honorably discharged, he had laid aside pure religion for the time, and gone to lunch with his friends of many years, the Williamses, who lived in Brooklyn. After lunch, Alice Williams, who was fourteen years George's junior and therefore only thirty-four, and for whom he was believed to entertain sedate sentimental feelings, had given him a pink for his buttonhole, and they had walked for an hour in Prospect Park. Then, having journeyed to the neighborhood of Columbia University to pay an Easter call on his next best friends, the Tweedales, he had returned to West Ninth street, as usual, to have supper with his revered aunt, Miss Sophy Winterbotham. Easter or not, rain or shine, summer or winter, it was George's inflexible habit to take Sunday supper with his aunt. Miss Winterbotham was more devout than she was deaf, and she and George had earnest evenings together, usually discussing the subject of Foreign Missions.

"'Lo," said he, entering, setting his tall hat on the centre-table and beginning without more ado to unlace his patent leather shoes. "Workin' away on those articles, hey?"

"No," said Masury, looking round. "That reminds me — I must telephone Hendricks not to expect that stuff yet awhile." He made a note on a slip of paper, adding as he did so: "This is a new job I've taken on — temporary thing. How'd you find Miss Sophy?"

"Fine," said George, kicking off a shoe. "She's got a new aurophone that's a wonder. 'The Little Marvel' they call it. Miss Sampson was there too. We had some singin'. There's a lot of music left in that old organette, lemme tell you...."

After a moment he continued, as he was certain to: "Say you've got a new job, hey? Have n't gone and signed up with that ambulance-driving outfit, have you?"

If there had been a time, perhaps, when the rooms-mate had

rather deplored having to tell George everything, that time was now long past. He answered readily enough:

"No — this is a little job with Teresa DeSilver."

And then, after only the briefest hesitation, he turned in his chair and rehearsed in bare summary, for his good friend's benefit, the unexpected story of his day.

On the whole, George received the curious news rather better than might have been expected. He was astonished, he was puzzled, he was by no means sympathetic — he frankly lauded Miss Teresa's neutral principles, her Americanism and her unmercenary courage — yet he was immediately and deeply interested.

At first, indeed, mere bewilderment and disapprobation must have their way with him.

"Craziest thing I ever heard of," said he, beginning to pace about. "Shuh! I declare! Start off in the mornin', and you're goin' to write some war articles, or else you're goin' to go with some ambulance-drivers at Nooyey. Come in at night and you're goin' to chase up a fellow in Indo-China to get a block of steel stock. Tck! Looks like you don't know your own mind from now till breakfast."

Masury laughed.

"I contend that consistency is my middle name, and those are all parts of an 'identic' thing. . . . There, there, never mind. I was just having you a bit on."

"But what'd you need to take the position in the office for at *all?*" George went on presently, frowning. "You can't use that *against* her! Why, great Scott! — how can you be workin' for *her* and for this fellow *Ball* at the same time!"

To explain to George the peculiarly personal aspects of his enterprise, which had seemed to make face-to-face contact a fundamental necessity, was naturally out of the question. For the third time that day, Dean Masury set forth his strict though somewhat complicated honorableness.

"Call it an impulse," he finished firmly. "Call it a rational attachment of one's self to the centre of interest — anything you like. But mark this well, old fellow, I'm not working for Ball. On the contrary, I'm working for myself, and Ball, as I look at it, is working for me."

George observed that he would need more than Ball working for him before he was through. His interest mounted. At least this new project, though downright crazy, was better than going and mixing up in the foreigners' mess; and as the various possibilities sank into him, George's heart, which was that of a good lawyer and a sound male, stirred toward the conflict. Walking up and down in his stocking-feet, standing and rubbing his bald spot with his thumb-knuckle, he pointed out attorney-wise the improbabilities of success in the injunction proceeding; ditto in regard to the suit; the months and months that would pass before a suit would come to trial, and the like — all at considerable length. As to getting that dead stock upon which everything turned, as to finding either the missing fellow himself, or some one who might possibly hold his power of attorney — the latter was Masury's plan — George described that chance as "fat." Whatever there was to do there, he said with great conviction, Miss DeSilver would already have done it.

He did not, indeed, exactly say, as Mrs. Flanner and Mr. Parmenter had said in their several ways: She'll get the best of you. Yet, curiously enough, his romantic or Sunday-paper belief in the woman's power seemed hardly less strong than Lucy's.

"She's a good-lookin' girl," he ruminated intently. "Yes, sir, a handsome girl. And you'll notice she's got a jaw on her too. Mighty fond of havin' her own way — just like her father and her grandfather before her. I know what I'm talkin' about," he added, rather unexpectedly. "I've watched her a couple of times — in the movies."

"Oh!"

The Elder leaned against the table, absorbed; and while Masury lighted a pipe and on the whole wished for solitude, he talked on:

"I've watched her — twice. One time she was just christenin' a battleship with a bottle of wine, and wavin' an American flag. The other time — well, she was in action sure enough! No, sir. I don't guess I'll ever forget that picture. She was comin' out of a courthouse with a young girl who was cryin' — had her handkerchief to her eyes, the young girl did. Well, you could see right away, by her look and the signs she made, that she was tellin' the movie man he mustn't take them. You could see her pointin' at him, and callin' out at him and then startin' runnin' toward him — but the picture kept right on comin'. His mistake.... Well, then there was kind of a shift in the film and you could see her again from a different side — you know, where another machine took it up — and there she was just knockin' the daylights out of that fellow. Yes, sir. I declare, it was a treat to see her sail in, just like a man and a blamed good one too! First thing, she knocked his camera over with her fists and jumped right on it with both feet — she wrecked it, I tell you. And then she lit right into the fellow, big fellow he was too, and gave him a smack on the jaw that nearly floored him. Well, hanged if he didn't grab up what was left of the machine and make off round the corner as hard as he could go, and that girl right after him. Fact. It was all in the picture," said George. "She was goin' right after him, far as you could see."

Masury, having listened to this edifying anecdote with some attention, laughed amiably.

"Characteristic, I don't question. Still, I can't say she looked exactly dangerous to me."

"Wait till you see her mad," said George.

He began at last to gather up his things, for the hour had grown late with much conversing, and the long Easter Day had tired him. Turning in the doorway, tall hat askew on his sparse hair, enormous shoes dangling brilliantly from his hand, he gave his rash rooms-mate a sudden parting stare; and he then shook his great head with something like concern.

"Yes, sir," said George soberly. "You've certainly bit yourself off a mouthful this time."

CHAPTER VI

DEAN MASURY'S first day with the Whitestone Steel Company proved to be an excessively busy one. The job itself, as distinct and separate from all private designs, was as concrete as carpentry. It had exactly that visible interest always yielded by making something with the hands; and the object to be wrought here was of itself entirely worth while: more and better work, with less trouble and at less cost. For several reasons Masury was determined to attain this object perfectly; he intended to make his reorganization of the Whitestone office as good a piece of work as he had ever done in his life. Nor was he troubled with any thought that this outward purpose was at variance with his deeper one. In his secret mind, of course, he was not working for his present employer at all; no, his resolve was precisely that the ultimate beneficiary of his services should be not Miss Teresa DeSilver, but Miss Teresa DeSilver's successor.

The captured steel company occupied offices on the eighth floor of an antiquated twelve-story building, set up on a narrow lot, in a typical downtown canyon. The accommodations were poor. The rooms, and there were plenty of rooms, did not even have the advantage of being a "suite," since they were on two sides of the public corridor; they were unattractive to begin with, they were dark, and their arrangement in relation to use seemed oddly haphazard. In fact, that note, the note of casual indifference to the executive end, appeared to be generally characteristic of the company. Masury had not been in the place an hour, before it was clear to him that Mr. Ball, though he might be a genius at making and selling steel (and several people during the day made a point of assuring him of that) was not an administrator; and that Mr. Kappus, the titular office executive, was not a competent person. By mid-afternoon, when the sheaf of notes in his hand had grown thick and his mind turned to the preparation of his preliminary report, he had to concede that the new president had known exactly what she was doing in setting up the reorganization of the office as one of her first official acts.

In each of the three fundamentals of efficiency, in equipment, system, and personnel, this "shop" was manifestly weak. A curious slackness pervaded everything, not at all concealed from the eye of the expert by an atmospheric excitement just as obvious.

Having reached his place of employment at eight-thirty o'clock, the "new man" omitted lunch without even noticing it. The hours sped, in a succession of "conferences." He met and talked with all the "heads" and subheads: the vice-president, the assistant secretary, the sales-manager and the purchasing agent, the freight and export clerk, the clerk in charge of accounting, statistics and reports, the chief file-clerk, the correspondence-clerk, and the cashier. He inspected the equipment, which was old-fashioned and often defective; he inquired into the organization, and found it uncertain, with much overlapping; he called for the payroll and made the first glance toward his general study of costs. He examined the systems of printed "forms" in use in the office, and those through which the mill reported and cleared to the office, and found them just so-so; he examined the files and found them deplorable. He made notes upon the distribution of floor-space, the allocation of offices and the placing of desks. He investigated the lighting arrangements, the ventilation, the drinking-water, and the rest-room. He interviewed the doorman upon the method of handling visitors and "checking" employees (it seemed that they were n't checked), and he talked with the correspondence-clerk about outgoing letters and the mail-clerk about incoming letters.

"Correspondence" was in a sad state. No less than seven people in the office signed company letters in their own names, it appeared, the letters themselves exhibiting every variety of tone and "style.". . . And all day, wherever he was and whatever else he was doing, consciously and unconsciously, he was "inspecting the personnel."

He was early convinced that discipline in the Whitestone office was lax and " morale " low. It was not merely that idleness was over-prevalent, and visiting about too general: that, in fact, was natural enough under the circumstances. The violent lopping off of a large part of the company business had unquestionably left the establishment overmanned, and cutting the payroll was indicated as one of the first "things to do." However, there were other and more significant signs that the machine had wanted for a long time the persistent attention of some one bent upon "measuring results against standards, quantitatively and qualitatively, and in relation to the ideals or purpose."

The unexpectedly close connection of the city office with the plant also opened possibilities and problems. The office remained, perhaps, but an incident of the mighty manual labor, the mighty making of steel, that went on in the furnaces at Cohaxie; still, it was an integral incident. Much of the buying for the mills was done here, all the product was sold from here, all the costs were checked over here, and in addition, practically all the mill records of whatever sort, eventually found their way to this file-room. The systematization and coördination of this business, the scientific handling of these masses of records, offered opportunities for technical planning on a scale beyond expectation.

Decidedly his work here would prove no matter of buying spring-back chairs for anæmic stenographers or selecting inkwells guaranteed against evaporation. There would be plenty to do.

Of the principal people in the office, none made any impression on him, expertly speaking, except the purchasing agent and the sales-manager. The vice-president, Mr. Tillinghast — the only one of the old officers who had survived the recent débâcle — was a dignified figurehead. Mr Kappus, who was not a member of the firm and whose title of assistant secretary was honorary, was — simply Mr. Kappus. The various clerks, with one or two exceptions seemed rather below than above a general average; and the two who were perhaps most important from the organizer's point of view, the chief file-clerk and the statistician, were clearly not equal to their duties. On the other hand, Mr. Van Hoefen, the purchasing agent, seemed to know his business thoroughly, and the sales-manager, Ellison, gave an even better effect of wide-awake responsibility and competence.

Everywhere, as he progressed from room to room, Masury saw symptoms of disturbance, due to the sudden change of ownership, everywhere the liveliest signs of interest in the woman president and "what she was like." At the same time a certain reserve, not to say mistrust, toward him was also perfectly evident.

He had, of course, been prepared for some guardedness, even for some hostility: the natural and human attitude of the worker toward the stranger who comes to inspect and "improve" him. The unassuming and friendly air he adopted — an air which said, like a cheery doctor, "Now what can we do to make you a little more comfortable?" — was designed to disarm such small resentments, and it did in fact have that effect, appreciably thawing the air about him as the day went on. However, the atmosphere had seemed thicker than the normal, and soon it had dawned on him that the people of the office, high and low, saw in him not merely the critic from without, but the special representative of the new dispensation. On this day, the active control of the company passed into the hands that had lately seized it; the only new faces that had appeared in the establishment, marking the violent transition, were those of Miss DeSilver, Miss DeSilver's secretary, and himself. All the rest of the company were "old people"—Ball's people, no doubt. So—not unnaturally but humorously enough—he found himself looked upon as the terrible young woman's confidential henchman and right-hand man. By lunch-time, a dozen little signs had made this unmistakably clear.

He not only could not contradict the quaint misconception; on the contrary, his bearing inevitably tended to confirm it. Instinctively resolved to lean backward, if necessary, in the matter of technical or "rudimentary loyalty," he steadily ignored the openings offered him to make some comment upon President DeSilver. That in itself resembled a denial of his true feelings; a brief exchange he had with Mr. Kappus about noon, carried the matter, oddly, farther.

The assistant secretary was reported to be a cousin of Mr. Ball's, though manifestly he had not followed Mr. Ball into adversity. He was a bald young man in a plaid waistcoat; and his interests, if one could infer anything from his use of his newspaper, ran toward sports and the drama. Mr. Kappus's general fretfulness under what he called "this new regimen" had been accentuated by an order found on his desk at the opening of business: an order signed in autograph "T. DeSilver, President," and directing Mr. Kappus to have all mail, incoming and outgoing, routed hereafter to the desk of Miss Janney. "This is one of your whims, I suppose," he said to the visiting expert, in a sneering way. When Masury answered briefly that he hadn't heard of the matter until that moment, the assistant secretary's feeble resentment turned. "Well, it's a fool thing, breaking up my system like this, and I'm going to tell her so—to her face," quoth he. "Can't you see yourself, that it's a—a most unwise thing to do?" Masury replied that, on the contrary, he thought it quite natural under the circumstances. In fact, the reasons for the order seemed glaringly obvious. It was n't merely that the dominant young woman wished on general principles to keep an eye on everything; beyond doubt she had extraordinary grounds for vigilance. In this aggregation that she had inherited from her predecessor, now her bitter enemy, who, in short, was for her and who against? Masury had no sooner seen the mail-routing direction than he thought: "Just what I should have done in her place."

"What sort is she, personally?" Kappus continued point-blank. "Is she easy to get along with?"

"Oh, I don't imagine," said Masury, with a pointed gaze, "that anybody who attends to his business and does it competently has anything special to fear from her."

Turning away on that, he became a little struck with the tenor of his words. Certainly they had been prompted less by any sense of official propriety than by an active distaste for Mr. Kappus. Yet a bystander might have said that he had actually "taken up" for the woman, whom he was here solely to overthrow. In that moment he became aware, as it were from afar, of impending awkwardnesses in his position. . . .

Was Mr. Ball's cousin scheming to overthrow Miss DeSilver too? Was Ellison, was Van Hoefen, were the clerks in the file-room? He had a sense of pervasive undercurrents, of masked hostility all about, and in an odd way he did not like it. It was not only that he disliked intrigue and concealed things generally; beyond all that, the more people there were who felt hostile to the woman who had bagged the company, the less easy it might be to distinguish his unique hostility.

About four o'clock he said to Harger, who had been his helpful escort through the day:

"Well! that's about as far as we can go this afternoon — and

I think it's pretty far for one day too! Now if you'll let me have a stenographer — a good one for choice — I think I'll get after my report."

The old head-clerk said that he would send in the best girl in the place — Miss O'Neill, Mr. Kappus's stenographer. That seemed the more fitting in that the hospitality of Mr. Kappus's office was already being enjoyed. The assistant secretary had gone, half an hour earlier; it seemed that he had an important business engagement uptown.

"Anything else I can do?" said Harger, rising. "Of course I have n't forgotten about the forms and sheets — I'll have a set made up for you right away."

Masury, thanking him, said there was nothing else for the moment. "Of course," he added amiably, "you must expect me to be trotting to you with questions right along for the next few days. I've a lot to learn."

"Happy to serve you in any way in my power, Mr. Masury. Very happy."

Aged before his time, gray-bearded and nervous, Harger carried on his breath the whiff of the solaces in those days so temptingly obtainable. A predestined clerk, he was yet an excellent clerk. He had been "with" Whitestone since its birth, and to the expert's fire of inquiries through the day, he had returned unfailing replies, detailed and accurate.

At the door, pausing, the old man cleared his throat and said, with a slight flush:

"And — I — er — if it should come in the way to say a good word for me to — to the president sometime, why, I'd appreciate it — greatly. Of course — I don't want to start looking for a new place at my time of life, if I can help it."

Masury smiled kindly.

"I don't know that a recommendation from me would help particularly. But I'll remember, Harger — certainly."

Left alone in the little office, he began to pace about slowly, sorting his dozens of disjointed points into ever clearer order and sequence. It was in his mind, that, in demanding a sketch report practically on the spot, the woman had desired to put him, the clerk who had so casually "dropped in," to an immediate test. He found the thought stimulating. . . .

The ground-glass door opened and a girl came in; or rather a girl flounced just over the threshold and halted there, rather defiantly. Masury, pausing in the floor, regarded her.

"Oh! Miss O'Neill?"

She just nodded.

"Good. I understand you're the best stenographer in the shop."

The girl said, in a loud twanging voice and with an indescribable enunciation: "I don't guess I'm any better than anybody else. They only try to work me harder, that's all."

"Well, that's the way to keep happy, they say — hard work and plenty of it. Can you take some stuff for me?"

"Don't guess I got no choice long's I got to work for my living."

He looked at her, reflecting once more that Mr. Kappus was an unsuccessful disciplinarian. Miss O'Neill was a carrot-haired, buxom girl, decidedly handsome in a bold way, and superfluously dressed for the steel business. She wore a "Georgette" blouse which could only be described as exceedingly communicative, her person supported a quantity of jewelry, both fixed and pendant, and she released into the close air of the little office an all but overpowering fragrance. A certain "niceness" in her large blue eyes was effectually offset by touched-up cheeks and a coarse, sensuous chin.

"No, I really suppose you have n't. But as for your going on working here, that's — "

"I don't care much whether I go on working for this outfit or not."

"It's a point we'll settle between now and Saturday night. Sit down. No," he added hastily, as she sulkily swished toward the seat by the desk, "take that chair there. That'll be better. I walk up and down when I dictate."

He flung open a window.

"Just for a minute, don't you think? These rooms get so stuffy. And, by the way, put up that book, and hereafter when you're sent for to work, don't bring any reading matter along."

The stenographer, in fact, having entered with a paperback copy of "Confessions of a Nun" in her hand, her finger marking the place, had on seating herself at once resumed her reading, or pretended to. She answered:

"What'd you say?"

"You heard me. *Come!* — get rid of that."

With a sudden movement the girl threw the book across the room; it struck the partition smartly and tumbled, pages awry, to the floor. Masury laughed. Her childish violence seemed funny. He rather liked the girl.

Though obviously out of humor, she did not seem exactly an ill-humored person, and as he proceeded to business, saying, "That settles that; now — " she interrupted, with complete moral inconsistency:

"You're English, are n't you?"

"I? Not a bit of it. Why?"

"Why, the funny way you talk, I guess."

He pulled out the leaf of Kappus's locked desk, opened his portfolio of notes and papers and looked at his watch.

"It is n't funny. It's only that you're used to the pigeon-English and bad voices of these foreigners that are all over the place. Now — "

"Pigeon-English is what I talk, I guess. I can't talk good. I quit school when I was twelve."

"You ought to try to make it up — it's not too late, and it

would be worth your while. Now we're in a rush. This is my first report — it's important, it's going to be pretty long, and I want to turn it in before closing-time — "

"Report? ... Who's it going to? To her?"

The girl, whose restless hands had been tearing a sheet of paper into strips, raised her head suddenly.

"To the president of the company. Let's see, just as a stunt, if you can't do the whole thing without a single mistake — "

"To *her?*"

"Look here, I think you ask a lot of questions for one so young. You know who's president of the company at present, don't you? To work! — to work!"

Miss O'Neill opened her note-book, and said in a quieter manner than one would have supposed her to possess:

"I'm ready. And I guess you'll find I won't make no mistakes."

The boast, thus put, seemed vaguely unconvincing. The best stenographer in Whitestone need not, after all, be very good. However, she was at least the best he had.

"All right. Main heading — full capitals. Begin. Preliminary Memorandum on Conditions in the Offices of the Whitestone Steel Company, with Recommendations Looking toward Increased Efficiency in Operation. Got that? Now, first subheading, capitals across the page — A. Offices. Paragraph — the numeral one — period dash. ... "

He was talking more or less steadily for forty minutes. Though he made his sentences as compact and pointed as he could (and he flattered himself that he could make sentences very compact and pointed), and though he explicitly reserved some subjects — such as Organization and Coördination, and Records and Files — the report, for a preliminary memorandum, ran rather long. The arrangement was correspondingly elaborate. Moreover, he talked, in spurts, very fast. Yet Miss O'Neill, not interrupting him once, kept pothooking along.

At the end, Masury said, with another glance at his watch: "Now I want that done as fast as you can, and at the same time I want it well done too. That's a hard order, I know. All I can ask is that you'll do the very best you can."

Rising at once, the girl tossed out: "You want her to have it before she leaves to-night. You won' be dis'pointed."

"That's the spirit.... Oh," the expert added in a changed key, "come in, Mr. Ellison."

A shadow moving upon the opaque glass of the partition materialized in flesh as the stenographer opened the door. The sales-manager, his plump figure rather suggesting a well-fed partridge, nodded pleasantly from the threshold.

"Don't want to interrupt. Just a little thing I've got in mind — in line with our talk this morning."

"I've finished," said Masury —"very glad if you've time to talk with me. Good advice is what I need...."

Ellison came in, stroking his neat mustache. Beyond any one else met in the establishment that day, the sales-manager gave the impression of being responsibly identified with all the interests of Whitestone. He had come to it in Frederick DeSilver's time, years before Ball; and his bearing was that of an officer, one who belonged to the company and it to him. Naturally, the general uneasiness which pervaded the office to-day had not passed him by. Under his air of confident alertness, of "red-blood" and "pep," Mr. Ellison, as Masury had seen in the first five minutes this morning, was deeply troubled.

The little thing that he wished to talk of now — or which at least he made the occasion for a talk — was an improved millsheet: giving in compact form, for the information of department heads, a daily digest of the various operations at the mills. The improved sheet, as he expounded it, seemed admirable. Ellison said he had more than once recommended it to Mr. Ball, but nothing had come of it. Talk slanted off to the general problem of the records. The expert's plan to set up a separate "dead" file, to help unclutter the present broken-down system, proved pleasing to the sales-manager, who confessed that, as the files were now, he was frequently guilty of "holding out" on them. 'T was n't right, but what was a man to do?

Masury laughed. "I made a test this morning — about the first thing I did. I had Harger specify three typical papers, none of them more than three months old — a letter, an assay sheet, and a bill of lading — and sent a slip to the file-clerk calling for them. I got the sheet in ten minutes, the letter in two hours, and they 're still looking for the bill of lading."

Ellison said: "There you are! — They 're rotten, are n't they?" Presently, with increased confidence, he asked naturally enough: "I suppose you know the new chief pretty well?"

"Never saw her till yesterday when I applied for this job."

"Oh. Well."

In Mr. Kappus's smart little cubicle there fell a brief silence, indefinably tinged with expectancy. Masury knocked the ashes from his cigarette. He was aware of Ellison's eye upon him, surprised and exploring.

He said casually: "Do you?"

"Well — yes and no," said Ellison. "I've known her for a long time — known her by sight, that is. She used to come in here often enough when Mr. DeSilver was alive — when they were going out to lunch together or to the country for the weekend — or maybe down to the mills. Funny, she was always interested in Whitestone — in steel. I've heard she used to pester the life out of her father to take her with him to Cohaxie — when she was just a kid, you might say, running round with her hair down her back. Never got tired of poking around the furnaces, they say. Funny.... But no, I can't remember that I ever really talked with her, more than to say howdedo — well, till last Monday. We had some conferences last week, of course. First time I'd seen her for about four years. She — she's changed a good deal."

"Yes?"

"Well," said Ellison, "I guess she knows what she's doing all right."

" You think so?"

The sales-manager had spoken with a faintly interrogative inflection; the expert spoke without any inflection at all. The effort required a certain control. In the same detached way, he went on:

"Market conditions are still pretty bad, I understand?"

"You said it. Just a few signs of beginning to pick up, but still pretty dead — and cut-throat competition for what there is. I haven't sold better than sixty per cent of capacity any month since the war broke out, and I've had to jump to do that. Of course," he said, in measured tones, "as long as we had the war-trade that did n't make so much difference. We could show a big gross profit, even with the plate and billet mills going half-time or less. Now — well, it's different."

"Of course."

"You don't know Mr. Ball, I suppose?"

"I've met him."

"Some hustler," said Ellison, and sighed.

Addicted to candor by taste and habit, Masury felt, despite himself, vaguely uncomfortable. He would have liked to say: "The fact is, I'm expecting to see Mr. Ball to-morrow." Moreover, if he did say that, there was no telling how far, and how valuably, the unsettled sales-manager might not "open up." However, confidences were of doubtful wisdom, and these secrets were not wholly his.

He pointed out that the change in operation raised problems, even from his own small end. In especial there was the indicated reduction of personnel, clearly desirable on the present basis of business. On the other hand, if the disused shell-plants started producing something else soon — if it were converted into some sort of specialty mill, for example — any cut at all might be premature. Ellison, palpably pricking up his ears, said with a keen look:

"That's it — yes! Er — s'pose she has n't told you what she means to do?"

When Masury said that he had no information at all, the sales-manager, glum beneath his "pep," looked disappointed.

"Well," he said slowly, "guess we'll all know more about it pretty soon. O' course that's the centre of the company's problem just now — what to do with that useless new mill and equipment. There's going to be a conference to-morrow — guess you know. She's got her plans, of course. Making parts on contract, I suppose. Oh, I guess we can make some money on that sort of stuff."

He was silent for ten seconds, and then suddenly exploded: "But my God! — *it is n't the steel business!* Our business is *making industrial steel* — not turning out needles for *sewing-machines!*"

The genuineness of the little outburst impressed Masury: he could sympathize with this bitterness. However, Ellison immediately " caught himself," with a laugh at once rueful and chagrined.

"But then, I suppose you might say making shell-cases was n't strictly the steel business either! And that's right too, I guess! — that's right. It's just that we already *were* in that, don't you know? — and cleaning up pretty big on it too. . . . Don't think for a minute that I'm criticizing, old man. That's not my angle at all. They don't hire me to dictate the policy of this company; my job's just to sell what the mills turn out, and I'm going on doing it, the very best I can — long as I stay. Still — well, I don't have to tell you that the change of policy hit me, that is, hit the selling end, a pretty stiff one."

"I can understand that, yes."

"Got to change all my selling plans from the bottom up," said Ellison abstractedly, and rose. "Well, come see me whenever you feel like it — glad to have you drop in any time."

He nodded, turned toward the door, hesitated, and wheeled again. Masury saw that his pleasant face had become suddenly solemn.

"You understand — it is n't my way to knock. But just to give you an idea of the change from my point of view, I cancelled a ten-million-dollar contract last week. Ten million dollars," repeated Ellison in a hushed voice, and shut the door gently behind him.

Masury, standing, gazed on at the spot where he had disappeared. For the moment he was thinking, not of efficiency from any aspect, but of the unbelievable perversity of a woman, and that woman his employer. The figure that the worried sales-manager had so quietly thrown at him was not only larger than anything he was prepared for; beyond that, in the nature of figures, it made the whole matter appallingly concrete. Dean Masury stood staggered by the dimensions of the wilful sacrifice. Ellison — doubtless — thought of the huge loss in terms of sales and percentages. But in Masury's thought, what the mad woman was juggling with was life and death on the Western Front....

He stirred, shook himself. Old Harger came in, bringing the specimen set of forms, bringing also an exhibit that Masury had suggested earlier in the day: twenty jackets plucked at random from the badly messed files. Time passed. The door opened again, and Miss O'Neill flounced in. Supposing that she had come to ask some help with her notes, he was taken aback when she held out the typewritten report: three copies, each neatly bound in a blue-paper cover.

"You *have* been quick!"

"I am quick — when I want to be," said Miss O'Neill, not without complacence.

"Sit down — sit down! Let's have a look at it."

Such speed indicated an extremely slap-dash style, and he scanned the first page prepared for the worst. On the contrary, he saw at once that the work was admirably done. The document, as he ran through it, proved practically errorless. Considering the girl's speech, her orthography seemed well-nigh incredible, like the mysterious feats of genius.

More important, the expert found himself well pleased with his own work. Bowed over the leaf of Kappus's desk, he read his paper through a second time, editorially. He saw small omissions; there was a sentence that he would have liked to change, a section that could have been recast to advantage; but by and large he was perfectly content. . . . Let her decide for herself now if he was "exceptionally qualified."

He leaned back in his chair, and looked at his vivid assistant.

"What was that you gave me about not being better than anybody else? You know as well as I do that you're a crack stenographer. If you're thinking of leaving at the end of the week, I intend to ask you to stay."

The girl neither bridled nor made other acknowledgment. Without taking her staring and rather pretty eyes from him, she surprised him by saying:

"Kin I take it in to her, then?"

"Take it in to her? Well, no. That would n't be regular This must go to her secretary."

Her look of disappointment was so childlike that he could not forbear adding:

"But why do you want to?"

She made a little movement that might have been the gutter equivalent of a shrug, and glanced away.

"I dunno. I just wanted to hear how she talks, I guess."

She added, after a pause, as if this would explain everything: "I seen her — goin' through the file-room this afternoon."

Still more surprised, Masury felt like saying: "Well, it's best that you should n't hear her talk. It only makes you want to hit her with something hard." But he made, instead, quite a different answer:

"You can see — that would hardly be the thing. But you can take it to her secretary if you like. How's that?"

Miss O'Neill took the blue-covered memorandum with something like eagerness and silently vanished through the door.

He lighted his pipe, and re-attacked the set of forms and sheets. After an interval rather longer than he had realized, he rose and moved toward the files. The clock in the long-deserted "general room" showed quarter past six — dinner-time for the lunchless, now that one stopped to think. From the other direction came the sound of footsteps, and Harger appeared in hat and overcoat. The old man had a letter in his hand; he was fussed and apologetic.

"This seems to be for you, Mr. Masury. I just found it — quite by accident, on Elmer's — the office-boy's — desk. I'm sure I can't imagine why he failed — ?"

"It's all right, Harger. Thank you."

He glanced at the superscription; the writing was unfamiliar and his name was misspelled. The moment the clerk had bowed himself away, he ripped open the envelope.

The letter, written from a lawyer's office hard by, was from Walter E. Ball. The late president of Whitestone stated, just legibly, that he would be glad if Mr. Masury would make it convenient to call on him at his apartment that evening, Monday, any time after eight-thirty.

Standing alone in the still room, Dean Masury gazed off into space.

On the whole, he had been successful, throughout the day, in keeping the two compartments of his undertaking honorably divided and dīstinct. Single-minded in devotion to his task, constantly preoccupied, he had scarcely admitted a thought of anything ulterior. Now, inevitably, there occurred a reconnection between his presence in this office and the plans and purposes which had brought him here. . . .

There had remained a possibility that he would never succeed in getting Mr. Ball's last secret — from Ball or elsewhere. The scrawl in his hand disposed of all such doubts. This prompt summons meant nothing at all if not that he was to be given a share in the practical struggle to eject Miss DeSilver from Whitestone; and that was all the favor he asked. Once he had a fair foothold, he would take care of the rest.

He stared intently at the dingy office-wall, and upon his inner ear, without effort or intention, sentences were forming and sounding. Quite clearly he heard again that insolent and affected voice: "What you think about it, and what you do outside of business hours, need not concern us. . . . "

A gleam came into the expert's eyes. In the same moment a bland voice spoke at his elbow:

"Pardon my interrupting you, Mr. Masury. Miss DeSilver would like to see you for a few minutes, if you please."

Dean Masury emerged from his absorption with a little jump. The noiseless secretary, appearing as if on wings, was standing not five feet from him. He saw that she smiled her slight mysterious smile, while her slanted glance just touched the open letter in his hand.

CHAPTER VII

NIGHT had fallen. A cluster of naked bulbs on the ceiling threw a bright light over the room, and the glass top of the desk reflected also the light of a bronze reading-lamp: the only thing in the president's office — not excepting the president — that looked new.

Whose taste the executive chamber represented at the moment, whether Frederick DeSilver's or Ball's or the present incumbent's, could only be surmised. Frugally and even cheaply furnished, without a touch of ornamentation, it suggested rather the first quarters of a young professional man than the place of business of a going "magnate." The bare and tidy room was cold; the three windows were open wide, and from somewhere came wafting, oddly enough, the faint sweet odor of cut flowers.

Behind the new lamp sat Miss Teresa DeSilver, in her full "protective" accoutrement; and open on the desk before her, as Masury saw in stepping over the threshold, lay the blue-bound copy of his memorandum.

She nodded up at him absently as he came to a halt on the worn rug, and said in an extremely "business-like" manner, flat and brisk:

"This seems to be satisfactory. In fact, I think it's good — very good."

The "chief" exhaled smoke through her nostrils, she thumbed the pages of the Preliminary Outline, she skimmed paragraphs here and there. Meanwhile, in brief snatches, she shot off opinions.

"It's interesting in itself. It's discriminating.... Not extravagant.... We'll save some salaries at once — that's to the point!... H'm.... D' you know, I'm rather struck with how closely most of what you say here follows the line of my own observations? . . . Made last week."

Dean Masury, standing hands in pockets, regarding her, laughed monosyllabically.

"That's hardly an accident, perhaps? To those familiar with office method, the standards are, of course, quite definite."

"No doubt — no doubt. Prompt application of standards to unfamiliar conditions isn't so easy, all the same. I'm trying it myself! . . . It's comprehensive too. You've covered the field here pretty thoroughly. . . . Good — better than one could have expected, on one day's work —"

"Allow me again," said he, pointedly. "The memorandum, being intended only as a first tentative sketch, makes no pretence at being 'comprehensive.' It is concerned with general conditions only. It hardly touches the special conditions, those peculiar to this company at this peculiar point in its history — which may well prove even more important."

The young woman squinted up at him. The broad ribbon from her pince-nez dropped over her clear-white cheek; she shook it back with a practised toss.

"What conditions are you speaking of?" she demanded bluntly. "Those involved in the change of business and policy, d'you mean?"

"Quite so. . . . Such changes necessarily — have reactions. They affect the questions of personnel and payroll and space. They involve the organization of the office, the coördination of —"

"Yes, yes — to be sure," she interrupted busily, returning to the outline. "A certain amount of time will be needed to adjust some of these matters, naturally."

How was it possible to listen unmoved to such a creature? To cover the sensations she aroused in him, the man, her sworn adversary, laughed again, gently. The fingers of his hand rested on her desk.

"More than time is needed, should n't you say? There must be fixity; there must be continuity and definiteness. This office is in a state of transition, not to say of fluidity, which makes intelligent planning, in some fundamental matters, all but—"

"Patience, patience, Masury! You're at a momentary disadvantage in some respects, I'm aware, but I daresay you'll find that these little difficulties will work themselves out very quickly. Meanwhile — as this thing of yours well indicates — there's plenty to do. Plenty."

She paused to scrunch the coal from her cigarette, and the stillness of the bright bare room, of the nearly deserted building, became noticeable.

"Now, then, I'll run through this with you," said the chief, "and indicate a little programme for immediate action. Never mind for the moment the hazy topics and those you've reserved for further study. We'll proceed now for quick results.

"Results," she repeated lingeringly, as if she liked the flavor of the word. And then suiting the action to the promise, she began to dash through his outline, item by item, throwing out rapid comments in her curious manner, as juiceless as a bone; but still displaying, it had to be confessed, a good deal of grasp of the technique of office mechanics.

"She's picked up the patter somewhere," thought the expert, and was annoyed by the strength of his inner resistances. Why? Why did the very sight of this woman fill him with a longing to hurt and punish her?...

It was strange; it was like nothing whatever in his experience — except, perhaps, one remembered episode. It had made him think, in a sort of way, of Willie Connaught, a boy at school, long ago; Willie, his enemy, who had thrashed him well, who, in fact, though no bigger than he, had thrashed him well seven times in a period of three years; at the end of which time he had been finally convinced that Willie was his master, that never so long as the world lasted would he be able to thrash the red-headed and hard-handed young devil. That knowledge had gone curiously deep with him; in the classroom or in the playground, he could never look at Willie Connaught or hear his gritty young voice, without feeling the blood flow away from his inside, and the pulses throbbing in his temples. And even now, after twenty years, when he and Willie met, there was an odd, funny sense of strain: some weakening consciousness of a high hope left forever unfulfilled. . . .

"There!" said the small voice — so totally different from Willie's! — almost animatedly. "That makes a fair schedule for a starter, I think. Yes, very fair. It's detail largely — necessarily so, to begin with — but it's confoundedly important detail. And it enables one to get things *going!* — results from the first day!"

She glanced upward with her little business nod, her manner indefinably suggesting that he would probably desire to take up the conversation at that point — perhaps to commend her "programme." As her expert, however, merely continued to regard her with his steady gaze, she went on with no loss of time:

"You've kept a copy of this?"

He bowed.

"It's understood, then, first, that you're to follow it up, as quickly as possible, with separate memoranda covering the larger subjects in detail — Organization and Coördination — Personnel — Utilization of Space — Forms — Files and Records. That's your plan here — right. Well, then! Regard this memorandum as approved as it stands — and go ahead!"

He drily broke silence: "Exactly how am I to go ahead, if you please?"

"How? Why, along the line I just indicated to you!"

"Doubtless. But 'going ahead' requires form, and procedure;

it necessitates instructions. The procedure here," he stated in the manner of a mature and experienced person explaining something elementary to a child, "would be in three steps; the plan, by me; the approval — by somebody; the execution, which involves authority — by somebody. You have failed —"

"No! — there's authority. For the time being, we'll do our going ahead this way: the plan, by you; the approval, by me; and the execution, on my order, by Kappus."

"No, I can't accept that."

"You can't accept it!"

Masury shook his head.

"It is n't worth while submitting plans at all, unless there's a chance that they'll be competently executed."

To his surprise the woman gave a little laugh, extremely brief but almost merry.

"By George! — I don't blame you for that! Well, I eat my words gladly. By no means let's interfere with Kappus's other engagements. Execution by you — through Harger, for the time being. That all right?"

"An improvement. However —"

"Yes. Harger's authority is ample for points such as these — We'll have it that way."

But the man's profound disagreements with her were not appeased so easily as that.

"However," he continued, where she had interrupted him, "should n't you say that this confirms, in rather an extraordinary way, a point I faintly indicated there — for the subject hardly comes within my province at all — as to your curious weakness here?"

"In the organization of the office, you mean?"

"In the disorganization of the office. I've never seen anything like it in my experience. The double function of operation is clearly recognized on one side. There's a general manager at the mill. Why the assumption that the office does n't need the same constant direction? A head-clerk, however good — and Harger is —"

"I confess I can't explain the omission, Masury," said the bagger of the company briskly, and pushed back her chair. "Remember, won't you, that I just took hold this morning?"

"I too," said Masury evenly. "Still, I'm in position to point out to you, this evening, that the work here will be badly handicapped, so long as —"

"But, you see, I don't need to have that pointed out to me. I thought I'd just made it clear that I realize it perfectly. I thought that was precisely why we were taking up, to begin with, a programme that does n't raise any troublesome questions. A little time, Masury, a little patience! For the moment — well, I'm afraid you'll have to consider Me as the general manager here."

She nodded as she spoke, as if that disposed of everything, and rose; her hand, definitely laying aside his memorandum, moved toward the buzzer; or perhaps it was toward one of the three telephone instruments which stuck out, on brackets, from the side of her bare ugly desk?

"Thank you — thank you," said Miss Teresa.

Her expert answered with a deeper dryness: "I must detain you further, I fear, since you seem to miss the fact that all these things — down to the very placing of lights and desks — are bound together. To put off even considering the fundamental matter of organization seems well enough in theory, perhaps; unfortunately, in practice, all the coördination of the functions hangs upon the organization. So do personnel and payroll, and systems and —"

"Oh, no, no!" she broke in smartly. "My dear man, you're gloomy! Take personnel, for example — take personnel in particular — and *go ahead* with it, that's all! In fact, the sooner you —"

"'Go ahead!' — on what basis? — toward what objective?"— the man bore her down in his turn. "For how much business? Don't you grasp the point that the place is overmanned only if the company's business is to stand where it is to-day? — while if, on the contrary, the business is to go back to the volume —"

"Never mind the company's business. Don't concern your-self in the least with the past or the future. I have n't employed you as either an antiquary or a prophet."

The notorious woman flicked him with a direct gaze, transient but hard in its way.

"Go ahead strictly on the basis of what you find to-day," she commanded. "On that basis cut the force to the bone. Don't hesitate. If the cutting is done judiciously, resulting in the hardpan of a firm, competent organization, you'll find that in the process you'll have picked up all the flexibility you'll need."

"Are n't you just a little optimistic," said the efficiency man quietly, yet quick as a pounce — "under the somewhat peculiar circumstances? You seem to be assuming, in what appears a hasty way, that having developed the basis of a sound organi-zation on paper, you can hold it; that, in short, this situation here is completely in your hand. You —"

"I assume nothing. The situation here is in my hand."

Miss DeSilver glanced at him again, through the hideous pince-nez, through the dusky eyes that, by her curious affecta-tion, practically never opened. Dean Masury's hand, in his coat pocket, touched by chance his letter from Walter E. Ball. He smiled abruptly.

"Really? I had n't been in your establishment here an hour before I saw that the whole place was eaten through with dis-affection — fully accounting for the lax discipline, the bad tone, the poor morale. And those things, as I say, go deep. Why, have you seriously supposed that this sudden and highly controversial change in policy, such as the stenographers neglect their lunch to discuss, can be carried out —"

She stopped him by suddenly striking her hands together: an odd gesture and, from her, rather an effective one

"Listen, Masury. If your interest in pressing these points is the impatience of the technician to show results, well and good. If it's a continuance of the talking-to you gave me in our other conversation, then neither well nor good. I'll put the matter for you plainly, once and for all."

She paused again, as if marshalling her words, and went on with marked deliberateness:

"I am new here. The organization is neither new nor mine. There will be people here who would like to put me out. I don't intend that they shall do so. There will be people here that I shall want to put out. I intend to put them out. D' you think for a moment I'm going to muddle along and waste my time and energies with a lot of slack-twisted incompetents — some I don't doubt disloyal to boot? Hell's bells!" said Saint Teresa. "I'll sack the whole outfit if necessary, from Tillinghast to the messenger, between breakfast and lunch on a fine morning — and never think of the matter again. And then I'll start fresh all by myself, and build up, person by person, the sound and dependable organization I spoke of and which I'm determined to have."

She stood slender in her long black robe, not very tall even with the fez, and gave him back a look as steady as his own, and just as hard. The contrast between those forceful words, and the controlled flat monotone which voiced them, produced its positive effect. In that moment some corner of Masury's consciousness received the impression that the creature, over all her ridiculous artificiality, did somehow yield the effect of a real executive, a person of consequence, able and resolute. There *was* some force in her, there was power.

That thought, to a hard adversary, was anything but unwelcome. On the other hand, the woman's unexpectedly firm grasp upon her situation, and her quite astonishing frankness, proved faintly disconcerting.

He bowed, slightly and easily.

"If you are really prepared for all that, you're of course fully acknowledging the weight —"

"I'm prepared for anything, my dear sir, literally anything — make no mistake about that. I'm going to get this office *right*, no matter who's hurt. Don't suppose for a moment that, because my predecessor slighted administration for sales, I shall make the same error. The mills are no more necessary to the office than the office is to the mills. Second only to producing the best possible commercial steel at the lowest reasonable costs, the problems of this office are the centre of my enterprise. On the skill and thoroughness with which we do our work here hangs the success or failure of my whole undertaking. Thank you."

But that was the word too much.

"Why do you say this to me?" said Masury instantly. "You're perfectly aware that I have no part with your undertaking."

Teresa DeSilver's hand, again reaching toward the buzzer, returned slowly to her side. A look of astonishment, faint but genuine, came into her face. After an instant, she gave an annoyed laugh.

"No part with it! — bless my soul! Then I am indeed laboring under the oddest of misapprehensions —"

"There should be no misapprehension about the matter. None whatever," said he. "If any exists in your mind, allow me to clear it up now. I am temporarily employed by you to do a special technical work, separate and distinct, inside the office. This work I shall do to —"

"But merciful powers!" said Miss DeSilver, almost with a groan. "Must I explain for the fifth time that I consider this special technical, et cetera, work you're doing as of the utmost importance to the company —"

"No, don't trouble — I'm afraid that would be a little belated now. You remember, I have prior authority for stating that my position here is merely that of a clerk, and that my attitude toward your enterprise as a whole is of no interest to you."

"Ah," said Miss Teresa slowly.

The clustered lamps above, frank for beauty, shone down upon the man and woman confronting each other: turned the president's ugly glasses into a shining smudge, glinted back from the eyes of the totally insubordinate subordinate. For the first time in their two conversations, he could believe that he had somehow struck her. The stupendous egoist, gazing at him, looked not only puzzled; in that instant it seemed to him that she looked actually offended.

So that was that.

Dean Masury smiled civilly. He bowed, released her gaze, and turned away.

She was — in a sense — a woman, and therefore doubtless entitled to the traditional privilege. However, no effort at a successful last word went after her expert, withdrawing. The stillness followed him down the room, and he shut the door upon a silence.

CHAPTER VIII

IF he had struck the woman with his hostility, however, it was at best but superficially; quite probably she, in her incredible assurance, viewed it as only more "senseless truculence" — surprising, perhaps, but devoid of significance for her. So Masury thought next morning, looking at an item on his daily memorandum which read, "Lunch L. F. 1 P.M.": thought it directly apropos of Lucy Flanner, whose parting taunt, or warning, on the Sabbath had not been forgotten, and was n't likely to be. True, even Lucy could not have said that Miss Teresa had "got the best of" him last night; but then, on reflection, neither could it be said that he had bested her exactly. It had to be conceded, on the evidence of the woman's manner, that she viewed him strictly as a cog in her office machine — doubtless a pretty good cog, now that she had got a line on his work! — and that she meant to utilize him thoroughly as such, with complete indifference to any sentiments of his own. However, there would be plenty of time, and plenty of opportunity to set her straight on those points: that, in a word, being what he was here for. Meantime, the thought of talking with Lucy to-day had a positive allurement for him, despite the pressure of work. Water had flowed under the bridge since they had last conversed together; and whatever might have been thought of his little passage with the woman, no one could have denied that his later and more important conference the same evening had put him a long step forward. With that knowledge came a secret strength. . . .

He had secured his foothold now; Walter E. Ball had yielded up the clue. Going about his tasks this morning, Masury knew everything that was essential about the mysterious absentee who held the future of Miss Teresa's "enterprise" in the hollow of his hand. The man's name was Josiah DeSilver Coit; he was a grandson of the grandfather's sister. In the West Side "den" last night, at a late hour, the excitable Ball had finally pronounced the strange cognomen in a whisper, with dramatic portentousness — quite as if he had expected Masury to bound from his chair, smiting his forehead and crying: "Josiah De-Silver Coit! No! No! You can't mean that!"... Still, there the man was, living, and owning one thousand shares of stock in the Whitestone Steel Company. And so one could now fairly think of a day when Dean Masury's present employer (and Lucy Flanner with her) would discover that the machine he had been a cog in here was not Teresa DeSilver's at all, but that of "my predecessor," Walter E. Ball. . . .

Though the late president of Whitestone must by now have satisfied himself as to his new acquaintance's reliability, his was a nature not marked by a sunny trustfulness. "Suppose I let you in on this," he had demanded, the first thing, "and you find that stock, what do you want to do with it?" When Masury stated that he wanted the stock in his own name, at least for the coming "protest" meeting — for his thought had soon come to that — Ball had literally sprung from his gold divan, his swart face darkling: "Then it's off! — nothing doing! — I don't split this with Godalmighty!" To that the visitor had replied, with a brisker confidence than he felt, perhaps: "All right! Of course you understand, then, that I'm going to get the information somewhere else within twenty-four hours. Naturally that releases me from any possible obligation to you." The counter, luckily enough, had unsettled the predecessor, and possible successor, at once. Had he been in this young fellow's place, undoubtedly he would have pumped one of the old clerks, or made an opportunity to peep in the stock-book; he of course presumed that the young fellow would do the same. The beady eye had bored into Masury like a drill: "I don't get you at all,

Mr. —'' he said at last. "Why're you so hell-bent on getting into this?" Masury had then said firmly: "Part of it is due, as I told you on Sunday, to the way I feel about the war. My belief comes just to this: unless the Allies get more ammunition, there's going to be a bad smash. I don't want that to happen. The rest of it," he said deliberately, "is altogether personal. I can't go into that." Clearly relieved, Mr. Ball had soon fallen back on jocosity — lady in the case, *shershay la fam*, etc. The ex-president sparred about for a time, showing an annoying inquisitiveness touching present conditions in the Whitestone office. "She won't be able to hold my organization together another week — you'll see," he declared, with a look of malevolent significance; and spoke again feverishly of coming "disclosures." In the end there had been a "little agreement" composed by Mr. Ball with a dexterity suggesting a past largely founded on the sworn word, duly typed and signed, and witnessed by a Korean butler and a singular-looking niece. The agreement had it that the party of the second part, in consideration of and in the event, etc., should sell the said stock to the party of the first part, at the price the former had paid for it, and not later than sixty (60) days after the special called meeting, thereinbefore designated, etc.

Thus emerged Josiah DeSilver Coit, "Unknown" — an original by all odds. The runaway, by Ball's account, was a valetudinarian, an ethnologist, a spendthrift, and a crank. Besides that, he was a "mean little cuss" and, in a tame way, the black sheep of his famous flock. At the age of forty, having succeeded by that time in estranging all his family and friends, DeSilver Coit had migrated, accompanied by a still faithful Swede named Christophersen, who doubled as valet and comrade, and had then drifted into the curious nomadic habits which had gradually become fixed. Nowadays, it appeared, he seldom even communicated with Paris, which was his nominal home; he gave himself up to "poking about in outlandish countries," studying races doubtless, and at any rate losing himself and Christophersen under an impenetrable silence for months or years together. However, it gradually transpired that it was neither health nor folklore, in their purity, that had inspired so excessive an absentation on the part of the interesting Mr. Coit. The lamentable truth was that he had got himself into a difficulty in the year 1907, involving among other little lapses the forgery of the name of Mr. Josiah DeSilver; and for that his hard great-uncle had never forgiven him. Josiah DeSilver Coit was "wanted."

All this, needless to say, was told to Masury "absolutely Masonic" — "your honor as a gentleman," etc.

"I suppose, of course," he had prompted casually, "you've started somebody out after him?"

Mr. Ball preferred mysteriousness there; however, it was conceded bit by bit that he and his associates might have done something of the sort. By good fortune it happened that a certain party — personal matter, nothing to do with Whitestone — had received one of DeSilver Coit's infrequent communications early in March. That letter was postmarked Saigon, and thus the wanderer was definitely located. The last address previously known — obtained from his Paris bankers, who represented him but had never heard of Whitestone — was Shanghai, in December. The letter, in a word, fairly opened the trail toward the owner of the stock; and this was the secret advantage possessed by the ousted minority. When Masury suggested that perhaps Miss DeSilver had started out a courier or two of her own, Ball had shouted with an oath that that was impossible; she had no possible means of having the information, he declared positively, with a few hard names for the lady to whom he referred only by synonym and paraphrase. Nevertheless, the thought somehow emerged that the predecessor was less certain on this crucial point than he would have liked to be. In the air of the den there seemed to hang the voiceless fear that the woman might, in fact, have started out a search-party — that in fact it might be her search-party, not Mr. Ball's, which would find the shy Coit and rush at him with an offer for his steel stock. There the grave matter had narrowly skirted the humorous. In his mind's eye Masury saw the competing expeditions bounding wildly through the tropics; he saw the lush jungle peopled with searchers for Josiah DeSilver Coit, hot men in pith helmets, dozens and dozens of them, all with great whiskers like moving-picture detectives, leaping out at each other with cries of triumph from every bush.

Well, that was Ball's affair. Ball and his backers were going to find DeSilver Coit if they could. He, Masury, was going to find DeSilver Coit's local representative or agent, if such there was. That was the sum of the "gentleman's agreement" arrived at, in supplement to the legal contract. That Ball on the whole doubted the existence of an American agent was probable enough; to find the hypothetical being might in any case prove impossible, with literally nothing to start on; hence the practical man's readiness to let some one else spend time and money on the off chance. "No harm letting the fool scratch" — you could easily follow the thought behind the hard jaw and through the black eye — "and who knows but it *may* get me something?" But Masury, for his part, was exceedingly content. The thought of the agent had, in fact, drawn and convinced him from the start. A man of means, with many holdings and sharp about money, DeSilver Coit had kept his Whitestone stock through all these years; that he had retained other American interests seemed almost certain; that he employed no one to keep an eye on them in his exile seemed all but inconceivable. What had lacked, obviously, was a person of sufficient determination to seek and find, through whatever difficulties, the unknown delegate. Ball had made a few inquiries of local banks and stopped there; as for Miss DeSilver, she undoubtedly felt herself secure in her practical ownership.

All the later part of the evening, in the libraries of his two clubs, Dean Masury had been busily poring over college and fraternity rosters, club directories, scientific society membership lists and the like, pursuing the broken threads of the life of the distant stranger whose backgrounds had suddenly become of so powerful an interest to him. His private thought was that a third search-party was now in the field, competing with both the others. Ball was not racing against Miss DeSilver more definitely than he, Masury, was racing against Ball.

Lucy Flanner's fine eyes, which never squinted or hid behind butter-saucers, regarded him fixedly over the table at Donovan's, which some call the best eating-place between Park Row and the Battery. In the firmest and easiest manner, he had resisted her pardonable curiosity, heavily colored with the personal as it was.

"You are *working* against her?"

"But also for her — as it seems. She herself told me only last night that my work was discriminating and of the utmost importance to the company. Please take that!"

"But *against* her?"

"Is n't it exciting? A new sort of double life."

"But what are you *doing?*"

"All, all, I'll tell you everything a month from to-day."

Mrs. Flanner, gazing at him, was silent for at least thirty seconds, a long time out of certain moments. Undoubtedly his air of confidence and his calm reserve had impressed her, as they were meant to do.

"Does she know that you're against her, as you put it?"

"Have n't I told you three times that I'm the soul of honor? Of course I told her where I stood when I took the position. I told her again last night. My plan is to tell her every time I see her."

"She knows you're opposed to her," said Lucy slowly, "and she takes you into her office. She knows it again, and she praises your work. That's fine — and it's exactly like her."

Masury smiled faintly.

"That's one way of looking at it, of course. Another is, if you've got a good man, keep him — especially if people who are not opposed to you don't happen to be plentiful. . . . After all, what do a clerk's views matter?"

"You do think, then, that there are many — opposed to her?"

"When the facts become public — and they're sure to, I think — I imagine that pretty nearly everybody'll be opposed to her, except the Germans. Why, are n't you?"

Lucy's thoughtfulness markedly increased.

A waiter came and took their plates. A "captain" stood and told him how to do it. While Donovan's was a costly place, many people seemed to think it was worth it; the place was crowded. Standing on top of a mighty building, two of its sides all glass, the long room commanded a magnificent view — city, rivers, and harbor. It was a mild, hazy day; zephyrs blew through the opened windows.

"Do you know old Mr. DeSilver?" said Lucy; and captured his attention at a bound.

"No — but I'd like to! I believe he and I'd be awfully congenial."

"Then — whatever you may be doing, you are n't — working with him?"

"I'm working with nobody. It's my private feud, did n't I mention?"

He looked at her with a twinkling eye, completely confirmed in his surmise that the renowned financier was one of those "associates" to whom Mr. Ball so darkly referred. In the last analysis, was that comic contest in the Oriental jungle actually between grandfather and granddaughter?

"I'm glad of that at least," said she. "I don't think I could quite bear your conspiring with that dreadful old beast — eaten up with self-will and malice and hatred — Ugh!"

Masury felt that the time had come to put a few questions of his own. Indeed his hostile curiosity about the woman, his adversary, had grown apace.

"Good gracious! — what's he taking on so about? Can't tolerate the notion of a lady steelmaster, I suppose?"

Lucy said briefly that all that was a detail: at most it had brought matters to a head. She was silent for a moment, looking out the window.

"No," she said soberly, "he's never been big enough to forgive her, you see, for not giving him what he wanted more than anything else."

"What's that? — a little quiet at home, perhaps?"

"Great-grandchildren," answered Lucy.

She continued to gaze out into the spaces and her face took on the sweetly pensive look natural to the best women, no matter how modern, when they speak of children that were never born, even to the second and third generation.

"Ah!" said he, with a scrupulous absence of controversial accent. "But I suppose you can't sympathize with him at all?"

"In that? Oh, I do. I think he's a monster without a scruple and without a single virtue — except courage, maybe — but oh, yes, I can sympathize with him there — in a way.... Life's hard, say what you like. All very well for people to be crossed — especially those who need chastening as much as he — but how ingenious to cross them at just the point it hurts the most!"

"Yes, indeed.... Only this is rather the eccentricity of an individual, shouldn't you say, than the inscrutable workings of Providence?"

"Perhaps the eccentricity of individuals *is* the inscrutable workings of Providence."

Having again appeared to reflect, Mrs. Flanner resumed deliberately, as if consciously meeting the reality of his interest:

"Old Mr. DeSilver's a natural patriarch, you see. His ambition was to form a dynasty. His dream was of DeSilvers and De-Silvers — all over the place. Well, you speak of the dark ways of Providence. Look what's happened to him. He had five children. All of them died unmarried or childless but Frederick De-Silver. Frederick had four children. All died young but Teresa. ... No multiplying or replenishing the earth at all — no hope left but in her. How nice for him if she could have turned out another old woman who lived in a shoe!'... But have n't you noticed, Dean, how nature marks some stocks for extinction, and it does n't make a particle of difference what you do? You can struggle, hope, yearn, pray, and fast — and marry! — but that fatal Will has got you beaten before you begin. 'No,' it says, 'I've gone as far as I can with these combinations. This is n't what I'm looking for — thumbs down!' Oh, yes, life is hard. There are those two admiring each other extravagantly — he's the one person in the world that Teresa really fears a little, I do believe — and yet for the last few years they've done hardly anything but quarrel, over this ... this fixed and inevitable and incurable difference — quite hopeless. It's sad, I think. ... And he'd stick at nothing to punish her."

"Well!" said he, with perfect politeness — "but seriously — could n't she oblige? I mean, just a few years — *part* of a few years — withdrawn from the demonstration?"

Mrs. Flanner smiled seriously.

"It's considered helpful, don't they say, to begin by falling in love? I'm afraid she's never managed to get as far as that. Suppose she's a born bachelor? You," said she, "would n't critize her too severely for that...?"

And then, as if she were pledged by something deep in her to try to make him see as she saw, the young woman went on, rather abruptly:

"Why, look at her face sometimes, Dean, when she's natural, if she ever lets you see her that way! — when she's forgotten her mannerisms. There's something in Teresa's expression — something ascetical — withdrawn — that I've hardly ever seen in the face of a young person before. Don't laugh.... I don't pretend to know, for of course she never explains herself — never seems to think there could be anything to explain — but I have thought about it a good deal — before Sunday and since. I do think Teresa has a natural taste for celibacy, a sort of inviolability — a simple aversion, perhaps — born in her to begin with, and gradually strengthened by the circumstances of her life. Take for one thing the intense concentration on sex that has always flowed over her, by precept and example, from that old man: who knows but what the recoil from that was the true cause of her famous speech at college, years ago! ... And then there's the practical side that I spoke of the other day; her instinctive feeling that marriage and motherhood would go deep with her — change her — soften her — put out her fires.... Guesses, of course. Still, I remember the only talk I ever had with her even skirting the subject. I said, 'Don't you think you would be happier with children?' — for the fact is, you see, she adores them. She looked at me as if I were about ten years old, and said, 'Do you think what you call my happiness has much to do with it, my dear?'... Her values are different, that's clear — and that brings me to my end! I think I've said enough to show why Teresa can't possibly be like her extremely different grandfather — but I personally don't stop there. I do believe that, as time goes on, all these motives have become somehow merged and transformed into — something less tangible, but unifying — into — well, a personal ideal. You'll understand that.... That half-mystical longing for purity, which is nearly as old as history, and which in the Middle Ages scattered the Christian world with convents and monasteries."

It seemed to her listener an elaborate and superfluous defence, indeed, of a strut which in its essence any schoolgirl could have hit off in a simple sentence, namely: "The right man has n't come along yet." ... However, influenced somewhat by his good friend's seriousness, Masury had sat gazing at his plate, effectually concealing his cynicism, and looking indeed quite respectful. Now he began amiably:

"You're a good champion, Lucy, and what's even better, an interesting one. The touch about the cloister is good. A real Saint Teresa — admirable! But I must —"

"Well, is n't it possibly a link, then, Dean — really?" she interrupted suddenly. "You don't forget that the convents were also — havens of peace?"

"I recall that."

"I 've wondered if it was n't the same qualities of temperament that gave Teresa her aversion for men — and her deep aversion for men's worst and most characteristic activity — war."

He stared at her, a little struck by her ingenuity, more than a little irritated by the feminine logic and the strong sentimental partisanship against him. Mrs. Flanner was returning his gaze; and as he opened his mouth to speak, she stopped and surprised him with her sudden pretty laugh.

"Never mind — I 've finished! ... And at least, Dean, it occurs to me, you should n't resent Teresa's little peculiarities *too* much — since I imagine they had a great deal to do with her accepting you as a fellow-worker!"

That deflected him at once; a changed look came into his eyes.

"Really? By the way — I meant to ask," said he. "Just what did you tell her about me on Sunday — by way of preparing her mind?"

"Oh, that!" smiled Lucy. "Why, naturally everything I could think of to convince her that she'd be lucky to get you."

"Thanks. More personally?"

"Again, whatever I thought would do the most good."

"For example?"

She laughed, looked at him, looked away.

"Well, I believe I did mention that you were superbly monastic."

He was conscious of a reminiscent note in that brief speech. He and this woman had had their moment, their unforgotten passage. It had come abruptly, within a month of their first meeting; and had not been repeated. His eyes fell from her face.

"Ah, yes. . . . Thank you!"

"I imagine," said Mrs. Flanner serenely, "that Teresa, with her prominence and her position, was troubled over this plunge into a purely masculine world. I suppose exactly what she wants most is to surround herself with capable men who are 'settled,' don't you know. Don't imagine that we were two débutantes swapping gossip, Dean dear. It was very apropos."

"To return," said Dean rather abruptly, annoyed at the thought of having been talked over with that woman. . . . I resist an overwhelming desire to controvert your diagnostics, your psychology, your history and your bad Freud. Time's short, and I've an earnest question or two — and then I won't have to catechise you again. First: Admitting the reasonableness of every word you've said — need she, in your opinion, be so tremendously disagreeable about it?"

"Why," said Lucy, with evident surprise. "That's the point of all I've been saying — she need. She must. She was a nun, but she could n't go into a convent. She was a nun, but she had no veil to advertise her — dedication. No, to the eye of others she remained an excessively eligible and attractive girl — and they behaved accordingly!"

"I sit at the feet of Gamaliel," said Masury crisply. "We come fairly to point number two. As you hope for salvation, do you consider that woman *charming?*"

"That depends," she answered at once, rather unexpectedly. "To me, of course. To most intuitive persons, yes — for the facts prove it. To you, as you see her now — hardly. In fact, that's her triumph. It's precisely what she's been working toward all these years — latterly with a doctor to help her."

He threw out, all but aghast: "*A doctor!*"

Mrs. Flanner went on spooning the particular confection in a slim glass which was dear to her heart. She spoke firmly:

"You understand, I'm trying to be judicial for your sake. When I first saw Teresa DeSilver, three years ago, I thought, at sight, that she was absolutely the most fascinating person I'd ever met. I may add that I still hold that opinion, only more so. It was just by the merest good luck that I'd been introduced to her — at Carnegie Hall, it was, one Sunday afternoon — and I went back to my room and lay awake most of the night, plotting how I could make her my friend. . . . As I say, she's changed since then — and especially in these last few months. Naturally I don't mean her appearance, the way she disfigures herself. That's a detail. No, it's something subtle and mysterious that she's learned to *do*. . . . It's as if personality were a light, don't you know, and she had caught the trick of *turning it off.*"

That again seemed to him rather clever, and even, in a humorous way, illuminating. He thought sarcastically of those half-shut eyes, that toneless voice, that countenance more expressionless than a pan of milk. . . .

"But," he prompted mildly, — "what about the process you hinted at? That's interesting, for it's my observation that, in the essential sense, people rarely change much."

"She has — and she has n't. It is extraordinary, I think."

Mrs. Flanner hesitated, gazing out toward the Statue of Liberty.

"Well!" she began with a kind of resoluteness. . . . "Right or wrong, she had this conception of herself and her life, and from the time she was grown, she was a sort of social recluse, practically going nowhere. But of course she was n't the sacred cow, she was interested in life — more interested in life than any one I ever knew — she had to meet people, including men who were anything but 'settled,' and at first she did the inevitable thing. She gradually became, for public purposes, just what you mean by the man-hating type — rude, boisterous manners, loud, slangy speech, masculine dress — oh, quite a shrew, no doubt. The strange thing is that it did n't work at all; the intuitive males saw through her right away. . . . Do what she would, they took up a lot of time and thought that she preferred to spend in other ways. By the way, I need n't put this altogether in the past tense either — more of that another time. . . . Well, then, about a year ago, she went to Dr. Oscar Kessler — professionally. Did you ever hear of Kessler?"

Masury, avoiding her glance, said in a slightly muffled voice: "Yes. Oh, yes."

"I believe he 's considered one of the greatest psychologists — psychiatrists? — what do you call them? — in the country. Well, Teresa consulted him, asking him to consider the whole matter in a scientific way. There was the problem, you see: What is the cause and source of individual attraction — especially between the sexes? What 's the basis of the mysterious thing called charm from a woman to a man? Everybody 's wondered about that," said Lucy, more and more interested in her thesis, "and incidentally I 've my own pet theory, which I may or may not expound to you some day. At any rate, I don't believe anybody 's ever gone into the thing scientifically before, as to an individual case, and Dr. Kessler, I 've heard, was extremely interested. The question was to analyze this elusive thing, and then proceed to break it up scientifically — to dispel it. He started a series of experiments —"

Her host's unnatural silence exploded in a bark of laughter.

"Whe-e-e! I don't mind coals to Newcastle or painting lilies — but old Kessler working nights in his laboratory to dispel Saint Teresa's charm! It's a knockout! Why, can't you see yourself that it's pure low comedy —"

"No, I can't," said Lucy quietly, too quietly in fact. "But I'm glad I succeed in amusing you, at any rate."

He saw that she was really offended, and checking his biting mirth at once, became genuinely contrite.

"I beg your pardon, Lucy. I'm really sorry. I — it was only that it — it seemed a little unusual —"

"I thought I was telling you what you wished to hear. Never mind — let's talk of something else."

On the whole, after more apologies, it seemed best to comply with that suggestion. Though he chafed under it, Masury was yet capable of admiring the staunchness of Lucy's loyalty; it was one of the manifestations that had persuaded him long ago that she was as true-blue a person as ever lived. Still, there was no hope of any harmony here: and he told himself firmly that he would avoid this subject for the future.

He got her to talking of her two new "pictures"; the topic was of real interest to him, but he hardly heard a word. Looking over the table at Lucy while she obligingly conversed, he found himself thinking how much more worth the attention of men was this fine, free, generous fellow-being than the loud poseur of whom they spoke, to whom she so curiously looked up. Was Lucy married as they sat here? He had no idea. This girl was not of those he had rolled hoops with in Washington Square in the later eighties, and had lived to dance at their diverse weddings. About her past, which had certainly been shadowed, she preserved a reticence he had never pressed upon. She came from the Southwest, and at nineteen, had met and married one Edward Flanner, a man twice her age, of whom Masury knew literally nothing except that he had no settled business and roved persistently from city to city. He did know this, however, that as the pair drove away from the church on their wedding day, the bridegroom had let drop a few words which convinced Lucy, at a stroke, that she had made a terrible mistake. What was the nature of those few words, and why, if they were that sort of words, the groom should have let them drop, Masury had no notion. Why Lucy had stuck to him for nine years remained also a mystery. This she had done, by the calendar: though he had gathered from a single remark, made early in their acquaintance, that the essential marriage had ended at the honeymoon. Toward the end of 1910, whatever had bound her to her husband ceased to operate and she had left him. Had there been a divorce, then or subsequently? She had never mentioned and Masury had never inquired.

He looked over the table at the maidenly ex-wife, who had preserved through deep waters an oddly girlish beauty, with quantities of honey-colored hair crowning a delicate and piquant face; and he was thinking that you could say of Lucy what was perhaps the best thing you could say of any human being: she was hard and soft in the right places. Was there any one really whose good opinion he valued above hers? . . .

Nevertheless, their talk in the end returned to its centre, to its controversy, after all. When the time had come, and more than come, for him to go back to his efficiency, and the waiter had satisfied his lower nature and withdrawn, Lucy herself made the reversion unexpectedly. She alluded with regret to that "opposition" he had hinted at, in and out of the office; and thence crossed directly to their topic.

"I'm sorry if I seemed over-touchy just now, Dean. That

would be silly of me.... It's true I can't understand your attitude — about this — and of course as you know how I feel about
Teresa, you'll know how I'd hate to see her — get hurt. Well!
Perhaps it's one of the things that can't be argued about — an
instinctive antagonism, shall we say, and let it go at that? But
as to whatever you may be doing with the company — trying
to obstruct her somehow, I suppose — I really don't feel quite
happy.... Not, of course, that I feel any responsibility, because
I introduced you, or anything like that. You and she are both
fully responsible people, more than able to take care of yourselves.
But — I don't know — it's as if I felt somehow that — morally
speaking — you were on the wrong side."

The speech conveyed so unmistakably a real regard that he
received it with no signs of irritation at all. Still, its controversial aspects seemed impossible to pass over — the more so as
her positions seemed to have an unquenchable interest for him.

Smiling at her in the friendliest way, he said: "So then you
really are with the enemy?"

"You forget, I hardly know what the war's about yet."

"At least you're familiar with her 'views about steel,' which
really do seem to be the heart of the matter. I take it I'm to
understand now that you sympathize with all that?"

Lucy, drawing on her gloves, was silent.

"Do I sympathize with what, Dean?" she said at last. "If I
had a steel mill, would I make shells for the side I want to win?
Of course you know I'd sit up nights and make them with my
hands if I could. Do I sympathize with people's doing what they
think is right, whether their views of what's right agree with
mine or not? Yes, I do absolutely. Do I sympathize with attacking and hating everybody who doesn't agree with my views?
No, Dean, I don't sympathize with that a bit."

"But why should you mind my attacking and hating her,
really?" said he smoothly, rather nettled after all. "What

difference does it make? You know you think that, whatever I do, she's sure to get the best of me."

Lucy gave him a straight look.

"That's it too. That's it especially, perhaps. I don't want you to get hurt either. I don't."

She saw that his grave face, as they rose, had fallen subtly into the "hard" lines which she liked least. But he said, easily enough:

"Well, make no mistake about that, my dear. One of us is pretty sure to be hurt. I can't answer for her, of course, but I'm not in this just for fun."

CHAPTER IX

THE expert's hour-to-hour activity in the Whitestone office
had now taken shape along two principal lines. First he
was carrying out the specific changes already approved — the
"little programme for immediate action"; second, he had to
study piecemeal all the fundamentals of operation involved in a
complete reorganization and prepare his findings, step by step,
for official approval. However, in practice no rigid procedure
was possible; his line was broken by many things, some as large
as Organization, some as small as pen-nibs and Mr. Kappus.
In fact, in this helter-skelter office, he could not remain the pure
adviser, technical and aloof; perforce he found himself also a
sort of floating office-manager, and already there were signs that
the employees distinctly viewed him as such. To-day, the
correspondence-clerk sought him out to press an ancient claim
for a window-desk; three stenographers waited on him asking
for a large mirror in the cloak-room; Gertrude, the conversational
telephone girl, whose switchboard stood in the anteroom — a
misarrangement that he meant to change — complained to him
about the draft. The difficulty was as yet that, though he had
to do an office-manager's detail, he did not have an office-
manager's authority. That, however, was a matter he intended
to press more pointedly with his employer, at his convenience.
Meantime he was going ahead under the wing of the head-clerk
or outside of it, just as seemed best.

He had taken for his own an unoccupied desk in a corner of
the "general" room: that room which in its random conglomera-
tion of stray clerks and stenographers from sundry departments
was an offence to an orderly mind, yet which, unquestionably,
afforded an excellent position for the observation of Personnel,

Coördination, etc. Here as he sat toward four o'clock, with the gifted O'Neill beside him — for at last he had been able to get at some minor dictation — Ellison, the sales-manager, passed by on some errand, and passing, greeted him with a brilliant smile and a buoyant wave of the hand. In the middle of a sentence as he was, Masury's thought was diverted by that exuberance; and he thought again of Lucy....

He had hinted to Lucy at "opposition" here: what would she have said of this quick conversion of opposition? "I told you so," without a doubt. But for him that odd result of the momentous conference this morning had the subtle interest of surprise. His eyes, unconsciously following the "red-blood" salesman, showed a sudden flicker of amusement. He thought of Ellison yesterday, groaning: "My God, Masury, making sewing-machines is n't the steel business!" He thought of Ellison to-day beaming: "I guess this old company's going to get on *all right* — say, the new chief's a wonder!" ... Oh, yes, undoubtedly she had got the best of *him!*

Ellison had reported his own phenomenon fully, in the vein of manly apology. Feeling guilty of "croaking" the day before, he had made a point of hunting up the new man directly the conference was over, which was just before lunch. For his gloom yesterday the good fellow could only say that the sudden closing of the new mill had been "a bolt from the blue"; he was "frank to say" now that, speaking as a salesman, he had n't been able to "see his way clear" at all. It appeared that one day last week, the new owner had just lined the heads up in front of her and announced: "Whitestone's going out of the munitions business at noon Saturday. Any of you gentlemen who don't like that can take a month's pay now and resign." ... "First hint we'd had of what was coming," explained Ellison, with eagerness. "You can imagine what a bombshell.... It's true, nobody resigned right there, but — well, I guess it's an open secret that some of us have been carrying our resignations round in our pockets, as you might put it. Just did n't seem possible to swallow that terrific loss and keep going — know you can see my angle. And then, by gad! — we come to the conference, and blamed if she has n't got a big, convincing plan all worked out to a decimal! — facts, figures, specifications, blue-prints — everything — you would n't believe it. Made old Keeley eat his words on a technical question — question of assays. And *markets* — and *customers!* I guess I can claim to know something about markets — been studying 'em for twenty years, that's all — but I'm hanged if she did n't have an edge on me — some respects. Made us a speech, too, that was a whanger! By gad, you ought to have seen them flopping...."

That tale of an incipient walkout quelled with blue-prints, and profit-loving men converted more easily than the shell-plant, had seemed to Masury, by a little, to pass belief. He had easily discounted the mercurial Ellison's optimism in his rebound from hopelessness; and in fact the whole matter, while psychologically interesting, had little importance for him. He had learned from Ellison that the proposed conversion of the closed plant would not be carried out till after the stockholders had passed upon it, which put it at once beyond the range of his interest. By that time, his affair here would be settled — one way or the other....

He resumed his dictation. The task was one of the lesser items on the immediate programme: a style-sheet and set of rules for stenographers, with a "model letter" accompanying. The smallness of the job was typical of the scattering and fussy day.

"That's all of that," he said presently. "The routing-slip's for the printer, the two sheets are for the mimeograph. Single space the rules and style — they must go on one page. Sign it ... sign it, By Order of T. DeSilver, President. Who's supposed to do the mimeographing?"

Miss O'Neill said that one Mamie Lestovsky, an indexer in the files, usually did it; however, in this case she herself would accommodate, if desired. She could do it better than Mamie, she averred with frankness.

"All right," said he, pushing back his chair. "Show me your copy before you start on the stencils."

"Sure thing.... By order of T. DeSilver, President," said Miss O'Neill. And then she added suddenly, in a lowered voice: "Say — you seen that piece in the paper about her, didnyer?"

"About whom, Miss O'Neill?"

"About *her*," said the girl, with a significant gesture of her head. "In the Sunday paper it was, the piece that called her 'The Woman That Hates Love'?"

She pronounced the lurid words of the "special" with an indescribable unction. Mr. Masury, concealing both surprise and displeasure, said:

"Never mind what I've seen. This —"

"I know where the paper is! Want me to get —"

"Certainly not. What's more, this reading of papers in the office, this talking and gossiping about, has got to stop. I'm not going to have it. Now get."

"I'm gettin' — I hear you," said Miss O'Neill, reluctantly preparing to depart; and unrepressed, she repeated in a slow, rapt voice: "The Woman That Hates Love.... Gee — I don't know. Don't you think there's something thrillin' about —"

At that instant, a different voice said close beside them: "May I interrupt just a moment, Mr. Masury?" And turning his head, Masury saw the rubber-heeled secretary, Miss Janney, standing before his desk.

The woman's identification with her principal was in his mind complete. He supposed at once that he was wanted for another interview, and the swift thought drew him; unconsciously he

half rose to his feet. However, the secretary was continuing in
her characteristic manner, which rather made one think of cold
refined oil:

"I don't see Mr. Harger, and Mr. Kappus does n't seem to
be in his office. I wondered if you could supply relief for me a
little later — about half-past four?"

Mr. Masury, sinking back in his chair, echoed with a certain
absentness: "Relief?"

"I've an appointment with the dentist uptown at five o'clock.
Miss DeSilver very kindly is letting me go. Could you send a
stenographer to sit in my office, in case —"

The husky voice of Miss O'Neill spoke up abruptly: "*Lemme!*"

Masury said: "All right, Miss Janney, I'll see that you have
somebody. Four-thirty."

Miss Janney glanced from him to Miss O'Neill and back again,
with her tactful, faint smile. No one could have been pleasanter
than the president's secretary; yet Masury's sense was that in
some way she was not pleasant at all. He never looked at those
curious eyes without seeming to be aware of something still and
cold, perpetually looking out from behind them; as one might
see a toad, say, gazing out motionless through the murky glass
of an aquarium.

"I'm sure," she said blandly, "from what we saw yesterday
of Miss O'Neill's work, that she would be satisfactory —"

"I'll see that you have somebody who is satisfactory."

"Thank you so much, Mr. Masury."

She glided away, and Miss O'Neill said at once, firmly but
now somewhat pleadingly too:

"Lemme — Mr. Masury."

He glanced at her. She was eighteen years old, a guttersnipe
vivid with rouge and life. She wore five rings, a necklace of
shiny pink, a rhinestone comb, a tinny wrist-watch, and at least
a pound of bracelets. Leaning forward in her eagerness, she

overpowered him with a heady sweetness.... More mystery! Was this, then, one of Lucy's "intuitives"?

"Why under the sun do you want to? She may keep you till seven o'clock."

"I wisht she would! Ooo!"

"She may give you a terrible blowing up — on several grounds. I myself think that you dress too — handsomely — for the office, and that your manner might easily be more quiet and — polite. Look at her own secretary!"

To his surprise, the girl flushed a little under her tinted talcum, and made no effort toward flippant repartee. In fact, she made no retort at all; her eyes, which were really pretty and oddly infantile in expression, fell, and she said only, still more to his surprise:

"Ugh! I don't like her."

Dean Masury, eyeing the point of his pencil, considered the application, managerially. The girl's skill spoke for her; so did her wish speak for her, for he liked her. Yet the thing, from several points of view, was odd, to say the least of it. In especial, the attraction of the full-blown child to the bodiless and affected "nun" was odd; the juxtaposition of those two would be odder than a meeting of poles....

"*Lemme*," implored Miss O'Neill. "I c'n please her. I know I can."

"All right," said Mr. Masury, after a brief silence and smiled faintly to himself. "I'll give you a chance."

The girl sprang up instantly, her eyes shining, and said in a subdued voice: "Gee!...Thank yer."

"Knock off that copy first. I'll put somebody else at the mimeo. And, Miss O'Neill," he added, "if you ever want to substitute for Miss Janney again — a word of advice. Keep your distance and don't speak till you're spoken to."

"I hear you. *I'm goin' a please her!*"

She flew to her typewriter — at the farther end of the large, ugly and crowded room, already dotted with random lights. Masury, consulting his notes, made a choice among his many "next things" and rose.

He sought Mr. Keeley, the general manager of the mills, who, having come up for the conference, was spending the day in the office; there were a number of points he wished to discuss with Keeley, bearing on the handling of mill-records and the like. Gertrude, the chatty switchboard girl, who wore an ostentatious shawl about her thin shoulders, opined that the general manager was with Mr. Ellison: she had put through a call for him a few minutes earlier. However, when he looked in at Ellison's office — or offices rather, for "Sales" had two — it was to learn that Mr. Keeley was closeted again with Miss DeSilver.

He got this information from Ellison's personal stenographer, a pleasant-faced girl named Alice Leeds, and noted with a mixture of amusement and disapproval that Miss Alice, who was returning to her sanctum just ahead of him, was so engrossed in a newspaper that she seemed to have some difficulty in collecting her thoughts. As he turned away, Ellison's vigorous voice came floating out from the inner room:

"Hello, there, old man! Anything I can do for you?"

"No, thanks — stalking Mr. Keeley. I want ten minutes with him before he runs back to Cohaxie."

"Well, we'll take care of you on that, all right. Make a note, Alice — conference between Mr. Masury, Mr. Keeley, and me. Say, that reminds me."

The sales-manager's plump figure appeared in his doorway, his smile not devoid of complacency.

"I explained that idea of mine about the mill-sheet to the chief and Keeley — they both thought it was fine! Chief told me to take it up through you. Well, I guess we'll agree all right.... Oh, say," he went on, with a glance at the stenographer and a backward nod of his head, "come in just a minute, can you? Want to tell you..."

Miss Alice Leeds looked up from her newspaper, and rose suddenly in her place. However, she hesitated; and the two men passed into the inner office and the door shut behind them.

Masury had scarcely desired another chat with Ellison to-day. It had become clear to him that the sales-manager liked to talk things over; also that there was nobody about the place, in particular, for him to talk them over with. He was not sorry that Ellison was learning to unburden himself to him. Yet this ingenuous assumption that he went about thirsting to hear praises of "the chief" began to grow irritating.

Sure enough, what Ellison wished to report this time was the saying of one of the old directors, after the morning's meeting, namely, that Miss DeSilver would probably make a better all-round operating head than Walter E. Ball! It was a fact. The director told him so himself.

"Oh, did he?" said Masury.

Ellison laughed expansively. "Yes, sirree! — I feel a whole lot better about things than I did this time yesterday, you bet! And after all — why, hang it, Masury, we've got to remember this war is n't going to last *forever!* We'd have to get out of the shell business *some day!*"

"True. Yes. On the other hand, we don't have to get out of it to-day."

Eyeing the sales-manager steadily, Masury felt himself stirred with a faint contempt for this so easy somersaulting.

"Look here, Ellison, it's nobody's business but my own, but as we're on the subject I'd prefer to have you know that I, speaking personally, am against the plans and policy of the present administration."

"You're *against* them?"

"Totally. And the war *is* lasting now."

The door opened with a sort of pop, and the sales-manager's stenographer came hastily into the room.

Ellison, who looked a little bewildered, glanced round frowning; he extended the flat of his hand in a quick, banishing manner.

"Not just yet, Alice, please. I'm in conference with Mr. —"

"I know — excuse me, but I thought you'd wish to see this at once, Mr. Ellison —"

"Well? — see what?" he barked, vaguely caught by her manner. "What is it?"

Miss Alice was holding out a newspaper; the forefinger of her free hand, in a large gesture, indicated the "what."

Thus Masury, who was opposed to talking and paper-reading in business hours, found himself become a party to both. This, it was true, was plainly not a dog-eared section of an old Sunday paper, such as might contain a special write-up on a highly colored theme of interest to this office: Miss Alice's offering was an evening newspaper, "The Blade"; it was just off the presses by the look of it. That Ellison, at least, found it interesting was also clear at once. The good fellow had received the sheet with more than a touch of impatience, doubtless anticipating a paragraph on Improving Conditions in Steel Industry, or the like. The abstracted frame of mind vanished instantaneously. The moment Ellison's glance, following the girl's forefinger, rested upon the place, it was caught; it was riveted. A second more and it was as if Ellison himself, the entire of Ellison, had become riveted. He stood by his swivel-chair quite rigid, his strong teeth just nibbling his little mustache, his dark eyes fixed. A minute passed in unbroken silence, while Masury and Miss Alice stood, perfectly still, regarding him: and then there broke from him, just below his breath:

"*God!*"

Through Masury's mind, also, shot a single word, but a different one: "*Disclosures!*"

The sales-manager looked up and around with a sort of jerk. His honest face, under the lights, seemed to have lost all its ruddiness. His voice came, at once repressed and hard:

" Seen this ? "

" I think not."

"It's Ball. He's spilled the beans. On purpose. Here."

With a turning movement of arm and body he summoned the other to look over his shoulder and behold; his own eyes darted back to the absorbing page. Masury advanced. His gaze preceded him, and — much as on that other day, in the woman's office — a printed word sprang out at him from a distance. It was the same word: WHITESTONE. Another second and he had the context:

INJUNCTION DENIED
IN WHITESTONE CASE

In one sweep he took in:

Sitting in Special Sessions this afternoon, Justice O'Laughlin denied the plea of Henry Lovering et al. for an injunction restraining the Whitestone Steel Co. and Miss Teresa DeSilver, President, from closing the company's extensive munitions plant at Cohaxie, Pa., and discontinuing the manufacture of munitions for the British and French governments. . . .

He was aware of an immediate reaction. Feeling but small interest in that part of the "fight" in which he had no share, he was conscious of no disappointment; in fact, he felt no emotion at all beyond a certain surprise at Ellison's perturbation. Then, exactly as he was thinking, "Well, what of it? Where's the bean-spilling there?" — his journalistic eye, running rapidly down the column, struck a new line, struck a paragraph beginning: "*The case is a chapter of an interesting story, not yet finished, which is told at length in another column.*" And that at once was something else. . . . His eye, shooting upward again, was smitten with a far bigger headline: a three-column headline streaming blackly across the "best" place in the paper. Once again, his heart seemed to leap within him as he read:

PACIFIST STEEL PRESIDENT ORDERS GREAT SHELL-PLANT CLOSED AND DISMANTLED; TERESA DESILVER WON'T SELL ALLIES AMMUNITION

Neutrality Reasons Assigned — Ousted Executive Hints Pro-Germanism

For a moment Dean Masury's eye travelled no farther. Motionless, he continued to stare over Ellison's shoulder; but he had the disclosure now, to the utmost reach; and his consciousness soared over the print.

The cat was out of the bag, indeed. The lady's fish were in the fire. That sense he had had on Sunday, that intuition of real conflict here, bitter and far-reaching, had by no means misled him. Those "views" about steel, but just now deemed too "confidential" to be spoken of, would to-morrow be argued by the boys in the street. . . . He stared at those damning words, "Ousted Executive Hints Pro-Germanism"; and his sense was like that of a warrior who, having set out secretly on a hazardous cause, wakes to see the world flocking to his banner. For that instant, perhaps, Dean Masury's feeling was as largely vindictive as that of Walter E. Ball himself. He felt a fierce thrill of triumph. . . .

"God!" said Ellison again, in a voice resembling a groan.

Vision returned to Masury's eye; he began to run down the page. The story, as he saw at once, was very much "at length." With the exception of the secret of DeSilver Coit and the block of "dead" stock, it told everything: the history of the White-stone Steel Company from its organization, the rapidly developing business — under Walter E. Ball — the building of the shell-plant — Walter E. Ball's idea — the enormous output of the same — developed by Walter E. Ball — and then the sudden disaster, the "fight," the protest meeting to be called: all that he, Masury, had dug up in seclusion, all the details of his entirely original and private undertaking were here flung large for the world to read.

For him the "interviews," gathered by the reporter to point up and give body to his narrative, were the real news. There was a statement from Mr. Henry Lovering, calling attention to the fact that the injunction proceedings were but the first step in the campaign to protect the rights of the minority stockholders — "the true owners of the company," said Mr. Lovering. The defeated plaintiff further declared that he, personally, considered the invasion of the "present president" a mere "act of piracy" which he would not cease to oppose while breath remained in his fleshly husk, or words to that effect. Even stronger, and far more damaging, were the remarks of the "Ousted Executive," round which, as Ellison had correctly perceived, the whole somewhat high-colored story had been built up.

"I don't know whether Miss DeSilver sympathizes with the rape of Belgium and the German Kaiser or not," said Walter E. Ball, adroitly enough. "It is not for me to judge the motives of others. All that I care to say at this time is that, as everybody knows, Germany is hiring criminal agents to blow up American munition-plants, in order to prevent us from sending the Allies the supplies they so sorely need, and which they are morally and legally entitled to have by every precedent of law and custom. This lady has saved the German spies the trouble by obligingly closing the Whitestone's splendid plant."

Toward the end, as if to show how just he was through it all, the reporter quoted Mr. Edgar Byers, whose true name was said to be Beierstein, of the so-called "American Rights Society," in warm support of "Miss DeSilver's courageous stand for strict neutrality." More interesting still was a brief statement from

Miss DeSilver herself — "popularly known under the soubriquet of 'Saint Teresa'" — whom the thoroughgoing investigator had reached, as he said, "with some difficulty." Over the
telephone, "the attacked president" — as distinguished from
Ousted Executive — had said (how clearly he could hear those
assured flat tones!):

"My action, I think, speaks for itself. I disbelieve altogether
in war as a means of settling national differences, and I think
that America can best serve the permanent hopes of the world by
preserving her position as a non-participating neutral — aloof
from the appeal to arms and steadfastly refusing to give it aid
or comfort. I believe that selling munitions to the warring
nations not only violates the essential spirit of neutrality, but
that it positively helps to promote, now and for the future, the
fatal principle of war. Therefore I do not propose that the
Whitestone Steel Company shall engage in this trade. The
minority stockholders will have no reason to complain that their
genuine interests are neglected."

But in his final lines, which included a hint of "interesting
developments to follow," the "Blade" reporter did not fail to
restore that "point of view" which only the pure in heart suppose to be absent from news-columns:

"Outside of the admittedly pro-German groups and a few
professional pacifists, it was impossible to find any one in the
city to-day who would defend Miss DeSilver's action. Those
who believe that the Allies are fighting the battle of civilization
were unanimous in condemning," etc., etc.

"*Well!*" said Ellison abruptly and expelled a breath of immense length. . . . "There's going to be hell to pay now!"

Having stared at Masury with a sort of startled air, all his
"peppy" buoyance shattered in an instant, the sales-manager
wheeled upon the stenographer.

"Mr. Van Hoefen see this?"

Miss Alice, who had remained standing by the door all this time, silent, attentive, an exemplary secretary, answered in her pleasant way: "Oh, I imagine so, Mr. Ellison. The newspapers are flying over the office — everybody's reading them —"

"*There you are!*"

"Mr. Dijon," added Miss Alice, rather sympathetically, "has resigned."

"Dijon!" echoed Ellison, and looked literally horrified: while even Masury felt a diversion of his thought, the able freight and export clerk — second only to Harger in length of service — being nothing less than one of the mainstays of the office.

"They say he did n't ask for his money, or anything," said Miss Alice. "He just read that and unlocked his desk and put on his hat — and went."

As the new man, Mr. Masury, continued to gaze at her, she explained, obligingly: "You know, he's a Frenchman."

"And I'm a Canadian, or just as good as one!" snapped Ellison, quite unexpectedly. "Thank you, Alice — that's all."

And in the same breath he said: "You'll excuse me, Masury. I — want to talk with Mr. Van Hoefen."

He started hurriedly toward the door, but stopped short midway, as if arrested by a force outside of himself, and exploded:

"I did n't think it of Ball! All very well to fight — yes! I expected that! Yes! — up to this morning, I *wanted* it, I'm frank to say! But dragging old Whitestone's name in the mud, so we'll never live it down! — so they can *ruin us!* — no, by God! I don't stand for that dirty fighting!"

Dean Masury nodded toward the crumpled newspaper on the floor.

"His argument seems to be that if Whitestone's name has been dragged in the mud, it was n't he that did it."

He spoke the simple words in his quietest voice. Yet perhaps his steady gaze upon the sales-manager, which certainly yielded little of sympathy, helped to interpret the unspoken meaning of his tongue: "*Have n't you considered that what Ball hints there is very likely true?*" Ellison, at least, seemed conscious of implications at once, without effort. Under the indignation and trouble on his candid countenance, there emerged a look of boyish ill-ease, of something like distress. It was his eye that wavered and averted itself.

"Well," he said, in a let-down way from the door, "there's no good crying over spilt milk. It's done. But — I'd give a thousand dollars out of my own pocket if Ball had n't given out that statement."

CHAPTER X

HE had asked himself what possibilities of advertisement Miss Teresa DeSilver had seen in the obscure little steel company; his answer had come with startling directness. The little steel company was obscure no more. It had become celebrated at a bound; and the already too celebrated young woman, its president, rode suddenly in the glare of a "publicity" unprecedented even for her. Every afternoon paper in New York, and every morning paper next day, printed Mr. Ball's story, strongly "played up," on its front page. Following the explosion of print, there was heard an extraordinary reverberation of talk, a clacking of tongues such as heralds and ushers in a genuine *cause célèbre*. On the streets and in the clubs, in drawing-rooms and behind counters, the new exploit of "Saint Teresa" was discussed with a zest sharpening often to heat. Within twenty-four hours, the affair had unmistakably taken shape as the loudest achievement, to date, of a signally noisy lifetime.

Dean Masury followed the detonations of his private story with more interest than surprise. For months, the issue of the arms trade had revealed a bitter liveliness; even small incidents had proved enough to set the worn controversy raging again, and yet again. But never from the beginning, perhaps, had these vital differences been so sharply raised, never had the "neutral" or "pacifist" principle been so dramatically asserted. Possibly there had been other manufacturers who had refused, on principle, to make ammunition; certainly there was no previous instance of a company which, having plunged deeply into the lucrative trade, had decided "conscientiously" to withdraw from it; effecting the recantation publicly in the teeth of intense opposition within its own ranks. That in itself, as had been obvious, had all the makings of a pretty tale. But here, as the last touch of picturesqueness, the will responsible for the strange proceeding was that of a young woman of wealth and position, already famous for many feats, and but this instant embarked as a captain of industry.

Not all the editorial comment, to be sure, was adverse to Miss DeSilver. More than one of the city newspapers was candidly or uncandidly sympathetic to the masters of the submarine (already viewed by many as fundamentally "an anti-munitions weapon"); one or another held strong pacifistic beliefs; these, naturally, like Mr. Edgar Byers, supported the "courageous stand," though with varying degrees of warmth. But the weight of the influential city press, as had gone without saying, was heavily against her. On Wednesday morning the dignified "Republic," the ablest opponent of ungenerous neutrality in the city and the least solicitous of the feelings of hyphenated advertisers, considered the whole issue in a two-column leading article, carefully written and restrained in argument. The dissertation, which followed a firm pragmatical line, was entitled "Enemies of Liberty," and the meat of it was carried in a single sentence at the end:

Whatever, therefore, may be the sentimental theorizing, whatever the claims of a foggy and emotional "non-combatism," it is impossible to escape the conclusion that this headstrong young woman has, in effect, and by the meanings and natural consequences of her own acts, aligned herself with the adversaries of liberty and the sworn enemies of the best enlightenment of her time.

That cold and formidable verdict — which the ex-editor of "Parson's" might himself have composed — sounded the general note of the city newspapers. And not of the city only, it seemed; for the telegraph brought in similar comments from editors in distant places, and a brief dispatch from "The Republic's" London correspondent, on the second morning following, showed that the singular "Whitestone case" had attracted instant attention there.

Among individuals, in Masury's personal circle, the preponderance of opposition seemed, if anything, still heavier. It appeared that that basic distrust of the woman, which he privately felt as so potent a motive, was unexpectedly widespread. Even "liberals and radicals," he found to his surprise, men and women whose convictions opposed the shipment of arms, seemed prone to find reasons for criticizing the president of Whitestone, or for damning her with the faintest praise. Even George Davis, stout champion of the maxims of Washington and of the principles and spunk of Miss Teresa, even the neutral American People, having read under the evening lamp columns and columns of unfavorable print, seemed to disclose a more guarded enthusiasm.

Dean Masury, in fact, was rather taken aback by the dimensions of the support so suddenly flowing to his lone difficult cause. To Lucy he had predicted a general opposition; the blare of this hue-and-cry passed somewhat beyond his expectations. That the vast white light entailed definite disadvantages for him was also soon apparent.

Dropping in on Thursday evening at the club which he frequented, he found that the apostasy of Whitestone was the principal topic among the loungers. Hailed upon his entrance, he was subjected to curious stares and a pepper-fire of questions, and Horace Checkerman, who did not count delicacy among the martial virtues, at once demanded point-blank: "Now tell us what the hell you mean by going to work for that pro-German she-ass? . . ."

For months it had seemed to Masury that his club was probably the talking centre of the universe, and the group he fraternized with the talking centre of the club. Interested in the shifting winds of opinion, he regularly looked in there "to tell or to hear some new thing." As his habit of mind was open, his friends had learned early of his new "temporary job"; it was known that he was arbitrary in his attitude toward his work, doing exactly as he pleased about it, and in the first day or two, he had met, at most, only a little good-natured chaffing. The public uproar had, of course, changed all that. Now he was not merely working for the notorious Teresa, he was working for a "pro-German outfit"; and his acquaintances were at a loss to understand his motives.

Around the table in the grill, facing a circle of inquisitive faces — Checkerman's the most inquisitive, as well as the reddest of all — Dean Masury explained the case of Whitestone as frankly as he could. That is to say, he told again everything that had already been told in the newspapers, and nothing more. To direct questions about his connection with the affair, he returned easy evasions of the just-you-wait-and-see sort. He mysteriously directed Checkerman's attention to the reporters' hint about interesting developments to follow. He said cryptically, "There are more ways of killing a snake than stamping its head off." To another he remarked, with an air of calm confidence: "Don't you know the Government agents have to adopt strange disguises at times?" Such glimpses at the truth could not be said to satisfy curiosity, but they did safely pique it; and, though he was less passionately militaristic than many of his friends and had lost prestige accordingly, no one seriously doubted that whatever his strange association might mean, he was himself "all right." In fact, the net effect of the quizzing that evening was perhaps more satisfactory to Major Checkerman and the rest than to him, Dean Masury.

The irritations he had felt at Lucy's praises of Miss DeSilver, his incredulity at Mr. Parmenter's tolerance and Ellison's swift admiration, seemed to be by now fully offset. Ball's disclosures were scarcely two days old, and already he was surfeited with abuse of the woman. To his particular taste, indeed, the pendulum seemed to be swinging rather too far. In the multiplicity of voices crying behind him, the force and distinction of his first solitary position seemed somehow blurred. In an odd way, too, the reaction promised to be actually weakening. The constant iteration of suspicions and conjectures as if they were proven facts — a method of polemics he had always particularly objected to — began to stir within him, despite himself, a certain dissent. On Sunday, even yesterday, he had thought it highly probable that the perverse woman, herself the disciple of violence, entertained personal sympathies for the lord of the shining armor. Now that a score of voices had shouted the fact in his ear, with much imaginative detail, he began to doubt that it was true.

He left the club restive and unsatisfied. He was annoyed by the cheery assumption that he had to explain himself; it was still more annoying that he could not explain himself adequately. "Working for her!" he would have liked to throw at those prying faces. "Why, you poor simpletons, I'm the man who's going to take Whitestone away from her. Give me a month — that's all." That perhaps would have made that easy-chair soldier Checkerman, who was perhaps as bigoted a fellow as ever lived, smile out of the other side of his face.

In his rooms, alone, he became very busy. From various sources and at infinite pains he was compiling a list of persons who had known, or might possibly have known, DeSilver Coit at some stage of his eccentric life. The list eventually ran to nearly two hundred names; to each of them would go a carefully prepared, confidential form-letter of inquiry, promising "something to the advantage" of Mr. Coit — personally or through any representative of his. In three of the city newspapers, he had yesterday placed a "personal" advertisement — "Information Wanted" — of similar purport. These chief lines of search he was supplementing by word-of-mouth inquiry, right and left, in person and by telephone. By the end of the week, barring accidents, he would have thrown out a dragnet such as, he was convinced, no one else — on either side — had even attempted; that it would yield results, he could scarcely doubt. It was a long time since the earth had swallowed Korah and his little group, and even Miss DeSilver's retiring cousin could not live in a city for thirty years without leaving behind abundant footprints. The crank himself, unconscious arbiter of the widening conflict, might be lost in the wilderness half the world away. But there was some one near at hand — a definite individual with an office not a block away, it might be — who was authorized to speak with the crank's voice and sign with the crank's hand: and he would not rest till he found that person.

They could start law-suits which would never be finished, and fantastic "expeditions" which were no more than extravagant gestures; they could write and jaw, and catechise and denounce, till they were tired: but all the time there were only two people who really counted in the nationally interesting "Whitestone case." Everything remained between him and the woman, just as he had planned it on Easter Day.

It was known that the company president had planned to spend Wednesday and Thursday at Cohaxie, where the production of "the best possible commercial steel at the lowest reasonable costs" was doubtless a more pressing need than ever, now that the "enterprise" was weighted with so heavy an odium. Instead, as Mr. Ball would certainly have been gratified to learn — and possibly he did learn it? — she remained chained to the presidential desk in the Edsall Building. Unenjoined, easily victorious in the first assault upon her ownership, she was yet caught in the backwash of those proceedings. All day, both days, as every one in the office knew, she was besieged with callers — a crowding miscellany —

reporters and more reporters, directors of the company, under-
writers of the company, her personal lawyers (with whom
she was closeted for the better part of an hour, it was said),
pacifist well-wishers and committees of protesting ladies, Hedley-Black, the British purchasing agent, Mr. Edgar Byers (or
Beierstein), Uncle James Parmenter — heaven knew whom!
What went on in these executive sessions none might say: but
the nature of the reactions in the office at large was common
property. Here the initial excitement was slow in dying down;
already it had boiled past the point of overflow.

Dijon the Frenchman, in fine, was not alone in his distaste for
"playing the Kaiser's game." Those resignations, mentioned by
the once optimistic Ellison as practically torn up, began to pop
out of the pockets that held them. Other departures, not contemplated by him, but not without importance to an office
organizer, proceeded coincidentally. At closing-time on Thursday, the score of casualties stood thus: Mr. Tillinghast, the vice-
president, had resigned; Mr. Kappus, the assistant secretary,
had resigned; Mr. Van Hoefen, the purchasing agent, was
reported as exceedingly shaky; and four employees had walked
out — demanding and not getting their money, which made
something of a scene — with rumors of others waiting only till
one o'clock Saturday. Thus — quite apart from mysterious
"pressure" from without, at which Ellison kept darkly hinting —
it was evident that disaffection from the DeSilver enterprise was
spreading from within, with a force and directness that seemed,
on the whole, a little puzzling.

Mr. Tillinghast's resignation, perfectly unimportant in itself,
was also perfectly understandable: undoubtedly he owed it to
his "position," whatever that was. Masury happened to see the
old gentleman in the hall, just emerging from his interview with
the "chief"; his senile face was quite caved in. On the other
hand, Kappus's exit, while an unmixed blessing, remained a puz-

zle: all the more so in that earlier in the day, Thursday, he had involved Masury in a strange, rambling conversation, the gist of which seemed to be that while many people "felt very strongly on the subject," and while this made the situation "very awkward" for the "responsible heads" of the company, he, Kappus, retained every confidence that the chief would fully "appreciate" those who stood by the old company in its dark hour. Masury naturally inferred that the titular office-manager — suffering as he was from some obscure complaint, resembling hookworm, which rendered all labor abhorrent to him — sought financial recompense against the hour's darkness. Sliding over him with his sly pop-eye, the assistant secretary had hurriedly declared that, so far from intending any criticism of the new chief, he, Kappus, invariably honored people who did things for principle's sake. "That's my nature," he insisted, with a furtive expectancy. "I honor principle. If that's a fault, if I'm too broad-minded, I'm sorry. I simply can't help it any more than I can help having brown hair." "Practically speaking, you have no hair," mused Masury; and walked away. What it all meant he had no idea; he was certain, though, that the loafer desired to stay, the thought of a raise being no more than a racial hope. Therefore the news of his abrupt resignation, which flew about in the late afternoon, came as a delightful surprise. The assistant secretary said no good-byes; and as he was constantly "out," it might not have been known that his departure this time was permanent had not Miss O'Neill confided the fact to a few of her closer personal friends. The girl's gossip had it that Mr. Kappus, on his own assertion, had given Miss DeSilver a talking to she would n't soon forget, mentioning to her among other things that he "would n't work for such a outfit if they was to give it to him." On the whole, this seemed unconvincing; Miss O'Neill's own verdict was: "He's a dirty liar — he'd never dast lip her."

She repeated her story to Masury in the tail of the hard day. Much preoccupied — for the chaotic conditions brought their own drawbacks — he listened without encouragement, merely nodded at the end, and went on with his work. The unlessoned girl did not take the hint, however; on the contrary, having hovered about for a space, she judged the moment favorable to proffer a small request, namely: whenever Miss Janney "had a bookfull," or was otherwise unavailable, might she, O'Neill, act as her stenographic substitute? Would Mr. Masury, in a word, make that as a promise?

The office organizer glanced up again from the paper he was looking at. The paper chanced to be his own — a memorandum of essential new equipment which he had finished and sent in to the secretary yesterday morning; at five-thirty to-day it came back, endorsed in a neat upright hand, "Approved — T. DeSilver." Thus the technical work went forward, under difficulties. ... "Approved!" Was n't she aware that desks and chairs cost money and that, with Kappus gone, there was no warrant for making expenditures in the office? ... Into this thought, into the whole current of his private thought, the stenographer's childish request fell as crosswise as possible. He eyed her abstractedly, with a touch of impatience at finding her still there.

"I don't know at all about that. ... How'd you get along the other day when I gave you the chance?"

The girl seemed to flinch a little. She hung her head, with visible loss of ease.

"I dunno. I ... But I'll get along good next time — I know I will! I'm goin' a please her —"

"You mean that she found fault with you? ... Come, speak plainly — you're wasting my time."

Miss O'Neill then blurted, shamefaced: "She near took the top my head offen me — just at first. Ooo! When I first went in — 't was on'y a naxident. It would n't never happen —"

"About your work? Out with it!"

Coloring, she shook her head; then, impelled by his gaze, she confessed in her lowest voice:

"She did n't like my puffume."

Nothing stirred on the expert's face.

"But," the girl hastened on, with an odd meeting of mortification and eagerness, "I don't use it no more. I — I'm off it. I'm goin' a be what she likes —"

"Ah, yes! — well, we'll see! I can't make any promises now. Changes are going on in the office — it may be necessary to assign you permanently to —"

"No! — no! Please, Mr. Masury. Leave me stay in this room and promise to lemme —"

But Mr. Masury, raising his hand, stopped her short.

"All I can say now is that your work is good, that I think it's going to be better still, and that I want to do what I can to keep you satisfied."

"Well — thank yer," said Miss O'Neill.

And then, as if only heartened for conversation, the child leaned forward hurriedly as he nodded dismissal, and said in a husky whisper:

"Mr. Masury, kin I speak to you confidential?"

"My good girl! — I've something to do besides that, if you have n't."

"Mr. Masury, it ain't true that she's workin' for the Choimans, is it?"

The query was scarcely more than a slight precipitation from the thick air of the office that day. Nevertheless, his orderly mind found it curiously provoking; and the girl's next words pushed the matter still farther.

"They say she's going to make submarines," whispered Miss O'Neill anxiously, "to drown innercent women and children. It ain't true, is it?"

That certainly had never been read in a newspaper.

"Who says so?"

"I dunno — everybody. It's what they say. It ain't —"

"Miss O'Neill," said Masury sternly, "I've told you once that I'm not going to have gossiping in business hours. Now, I'm not going to remind you of it again. The next time I hear —"

"Well, I did n't believe it! — I did n't!" she broke in hastily. "Why, Mr. Masury, she *would n't* I on'y —"

"Go back to your desk."

Miss O'Neill went quickly, looking for once almost squelched. Unquestionably she would have felt less flat had she known that Mr. Masury, on his part, was less single-minded than he seemed. In truth, her artless words had fairly confronted him with a somewhat vexing problem.

Twenty times in these days Masury had thought of the characteristic and hateful speech of the woman's when he had predicted just these possibilities: "I assume nothing. The situation is in my hand." Seeing how rapidly the situation was running out of hand, he had felt, at first, only a sense of inimical triumph. Inevitably the woman's discomfiture, on the direct point of her "principle," must in any case have given him a positive satisfaction; Dijon's fine, silent rebuke was wonderfully to his liking; and the whole matter came to this, that if she could not command loyal employees, she could not operate the company — which was the prime anticipation of all his labors. Moreover, his official position was clear, in that, warning her once about such contingencies, he had gotten only a cheeky reprimand for his pains. Very well, then — let her now find out for herself what a conceited young fool she was, and deal with her office "situation" as best she could.

That was on Tuesday afternoon; by now he was aware that his views, steadily pushed upon from two directions, were undergoing a certain curve. In the first place, he had pledged himself to do a certain work here; and to do it as thoroughly as he could. For the present, that was the sufficient vindication of his being here, in a position otherwise somewhat equivocal; for the future, as he trusted, it would be his satisfying gift to Miss DeSilver's successor. But how was it possible to organize the office, for the present or the future, in duty or in interest, if the fundamental basis of organization — personnel — was to be a constantly dissolving quantity? ... Beneath that now appeared this second consideration also weakening to the strict *laissez-faire* position: this sense of an inspired "agitation" within the office which he had scented from the beginning, and which Miss O'Neill's question seemed to make disagreeably concrete. Hostility to the woman might still be welcome, but the stealthy fomentation of hostility within the ranks was another matter, for which he, for one, had no stomach. ...

Next day, while reflections such as these pursued him on his busy way, the office-boy dropped into his basket an unexpected letter, or order, from "the chief," which he found inconceivably malapropos and proportionately exasperating. The woman's office was shaking to pieces about her, she herself was being denounced far and wide in staggering terms; yet it seemed that her cocksureness soared undiminished. He read with fixed eyes:

Loss of employees by withdrawal will be regarded merely as in lieu of an equivalent number of dismissals, already contemplated in general reduction of the force. It will not otherwise affect the procedure previously indicated to you. Go straight ahead with your plan to cut the working force down to the bone.

Rush along a plan for rearranging the offices, toward economy of movement and money. If this is well done I think we shall be able to dispense with two of the present rooms, possibly three — the sooner the better.

T. DeS.

She, it was clear, was one who learned nothing by experience. In substance and gratuitous tone, in its mixture of sheer ignorance and insolence, this "order" seemed to him to pass the limit. He thought of that pince-nez and that voice, and the blood warmed in his veins. Rearranging the offices! — when the only question of any moment here now was whether or not she had any offices. How in hell did the fool suppose . . . ?

A genial voice fell suddenly upon his ear: "Ah, here he is! — thank you, Miss Janney, thank you! Well, Dean, my boy! H'are you?"

The office organizer looked up to see Mr. James Parmenter, piloted by the model secretary through the rows of desks, coming to a halt beside him. The apparition brought him to earth with a jolt.

"But you've a very solemn expression this morning," said Uncle James, himself very bland and debonair — "staring at that paper! Nothing wrong, I hope?"

"Howdedo, uncle?" said Masury easily. "Oh, not solemn, I hope! — just serious and business-like. Sit down, sir — glad to see you."

"No, no, I must n't interrupt! It merely occurred to me to stop, as I was in the office on business, and see how things were going with you — in your — ah — new undertaking?"

"Splendidly, uncle — splendidly. I picked a lively one, as you may have gathered from the newspapers. Really, it's a gift I have, should n't you say?"

The two men, regarding each other, were both smiling. What Mr. Parmenter's thought was he did not state, but Masury was reflecting that Uncle James's business as attorney brought him here rather often.

" Good! And no doubt you've found out the answers to all those questions you were firing at me on Sunday?"

"Ah, that would be telling, uncle, and you recall that you would tell me nothing. Unluckily, that compelled me to turn my simple confidences elsewhere."

"Have your fun, ha, ha!" laughed Uncle James, glancing handsomely round. "It's something at least to work for the most remarkable woman in New York. These offices are n't very good, are they? I remember advising poor DeSilver to move into a better place long ago, but he'd never listen to me. A sound, thrifty fellow, DeSilver, and his daughter's in many ways like him. Now, good-bye! By the way, she tells me you're doing first-rate work for her — first-rate! Gratifying, eh?"

Masury walked with his uncle to the elevator. In the hall, he said casually:

"The news from Europe's rather discouraging, uncle, don't you think? I was very much struck with what Sir John French says about the urgent need for an absolutely unlimited supply of ammunition. . . . Were n't you?"

"Yes, yes, but a bit of a croaker, French," said Uncle James firmly, "and I've told him so to his face, years ago. And our own loyal newspapers are no better, not a bit — absurdly pessimistic in their outlook — shockingly suspicious and one-eyed, as they've just shown. There's no question who's going to win this war — that's written in the stars," said Uncle James. "The real problem to-day is to keep alive, in this hour of strong passions, the spirit of fair-play and of personal freedom. . . ."

The nephew, for his part, had never felt less attracted toward these noble attitudes. The moment the lift-door had clicked on Mr. Parmenter, he glanced at his watch; it was quarter past twelve, the slack hour. He became increasingly thoughtful. In the inner corridor, by chance, he met old Harger, seeking him apologetically to put a question of great pertinence. In short, who was in charge of personnel, since Mr. Kappus had "left us"? It appeared that the old clerk, whose nose looked purpler than ever since the "trouble," had just learned of two more resignations to come.

"That makes seven altogether, including Mr. Dijon," Harger

offered, nervously plucking at his goat-shaped beard. "I thought
— that is — it seems that something would have to be done —
at least — replacements —"

The organizer said in his business-like way: "You're right,
of course. However, we've got till Monday, and with the reas-
signment of work you've already attended to, we'll get along
till then. Now," he added, "pending the appointment of Mr.
Kappus's successor, my understanding is that the responsibility,
as far as there is any, belongs to you and me, and as between us
two, I assume it all. How's that with you?"

Harger returned to his book-keeper's cage relieved and satisfied. From his desk-drawer Masury drew out a long typewritten
sheet entitled, Officers and Employees of Whitestone Steel
Company. Paper in hand, he made the rounds of the offices,
briefly consulting with the "responsible heads." When he
returned to his desk, fifteen minutes later, there were four
further checks on his personnel sheet. That brought the gross
total to eleven. Eleven employees, some of them very well worth
keeping, were leaving the service of the Whitestone Steel
Company in the first week of Miss DeSilver's management.

He folded the sheet, put it in his pocket, and betook himself
to the neat little office adjoining the president's chamber. His
request was for an appointment with the president, at her first
convenience.

The refined secretary, looking up at him with her tactful smile
in which the slant eyes could never be induced to take part,
whose gaze in fact seemed to him now as searching as a probe,
said pleasantly:

"I think you come at a good time, Mr. Masury! — just a minute, and I'll see. Miss DeSilver's leaving for Cohaxie at 2.30,
but I believe she's at liberty now."

CHAPTER XI

THE "attacked president" glanced up, rather inquiringly, over an open Gladstone bag into which she was stuffing portfolios of papers.

"Ah, Masury? — come in. . . . A coincidence," said she. "I was on the point of sending for you."

If much had changed since Dean Masury last stood in this presence, here he could see no sign of change. The bare, quiet room, looking more than ever austere in the gray morning, seemed as removed from the noises of the world as a rural parsonage or an abbess's cell. Its occupant, who had just drawn upon herself the unfavorable attention of her country, looked equally untouched by recent developments. Manner and bearing, voice and face, the "headstrong young woman" seemed unnaturally the same.

Her expert's first words, uttered while he still advanced, were a contradiction of her.

"Not quite a coincidence," said he, dry and cool, "since I regarded your note as in itself a sort of summons. I think you can hardly understand the present situation in the office."

"Ah? . . . How so?"

"I should like to make that clear to you — in detail."

"Pray do," said Miss Teresa, and snapping her bag shut with a click, thumped it down on the floor. She seated herself, and reached for a pen, while he, standing tall and a little forbidding, began coldly to unfold his considerable story. However, he had proceeded scarcely five sentences on his way when the woman, who had already shown signs of restlessness, fidgeting about a little as he talked, bluntly interrupted him.

"Yes, yes — I know all that. Eleven, you say; my information was nine, but no doubt you're right — a detail. . . . Is that all you have on your mind?"

Through the stereopticon front, her eyes touched him again, and again he seemed to be aware of a fleeting inquiry.

The brief but entire silence that followed was punctured by the man's sarcastic laugh.

"If what I am saying is not enough to interest you —"

"Interest, yes," she broke in again flatly, "but I told you the other day that I was prepared for all this, and more. Eleven. . . . Looking at it practically, that's hardly more than it would have been necessary to dismiss — though, to be sure, I lose some that I might n't have dismissed. However, a little readjustment will easily take care of that; ditto with future quittings, and I expect a future there."

She paused to jot a note in her memorandum-book; resuming, she spoke with executive rapidity:

"As for the headless condition you complain of, that of course will be quickly remedied. By the way, you must n't count Kappus among the omens of destruction; that's an organizing step strictly. He did n't resign, as you put it. I sacked him for cause. As to the rest, this was not only to be expected, but up to a point it's entirely wholesome. I say up to a point. The sooner I shake out all the partisans and the weak sisters, the sooner I shall have a sound organization at my back. The fly in the ointment, of course, is that all this seems to lack the purely spontaneous touch. Had n't it occurred to you that the exodus seems — a little excessive?"

The woman was astonishing; hardly credible, in fact. Her air was of one who, of course, knows everything; a dreadful conceit. The trouble of it for him, and the surprise, was that she really did know something. In assuming to preëmpt everything that he had to say and then to go him several better, all in a few brusque sentences, she seemed to leave no content in him at all, but a knot of pure resistance. He had intended to give her fair notice of her "situation"—even to give her direct help, as she must see it, by the temporary but genuine identity of their interests; in a moment, she had completely dispersed that intention. Nothing would have induced him to admit now that he had, in fact, thought the exodus excessive.

"If you seriously ask my opinion," said he, with some signs of self-control, "I should remind you again that, in view of the widespread unpopularity of your policy—"

"No, no, that won't do," she interrupted once more. "That can account for a distinguished dotard like Mr. Tillinghast, with a British squire for a son-in-law, but for ignorant boys and girls, many of them not a generation out of South Europe—no. If you've nothing more to tell me than *that*," said Miss Teresa, rapidly, with a glance at her watch, "I'll tell *you* something!"

She tossed her book into a chair near by, and her colorless tone seemed to stiffen.

"There's an active disloyalty at work inside this office. I'd already discovered a leak—a bad one. Confidential matters, known only to one or two persons besides myself—decisions of importance—are being communicated to unfriendly persons outside. I've had proof of that this morning, for the second time—since I wrote to you. I don't doubt now that this excessive quitting is part of the same thing. Now, then! While I, of course, expected that Ball would plant somebody here to watch me and give me a few pin-pricks when he could—"

"Plant!" interrupted Masury forcibly, impelled to obstruct this flowing progress somehow. "Why not say simply that Mr. Ball, when thrown out after years of excellent service to the company, left behind some sympathizers and well-wishers who—"

"Doubtless. Strange to say, I'm one of them myself. However. we can't have anybody wishing him well so thoroughly that, while taking the company's money, they are working against the company's interest — possibly spreading disaffection through my office, certainly betraying information to my enemies . . . Well! — it was to bring this state of things to your attention that I was about to send for you. I'd even thought it possible," said the notorious woman, "that considering your opportunities for observing the personnel, you might already have become aware of the deplorable symptoms. . . ."

Once again he was aware of the bluish dusky eyes upon him, eyes which were rarely opened, and yet could look, as he had found before, with a penetrating regard; then the scrutiny was cut off by the curtain of lashes which the creature so incongruously possessed. In that instant, Masury was struck, to motionlessness, by a completely new thought. Was it conceivable that she entertained a suspicion of *him*?

The man's stillness took on a certain rigidity. The thumbscrew could not have extorted from him now what he had said yesterday to Miss O'Neill. . . .

"For of course," she was going on, in her sure way, "this disloyalty must be run down and stamped out immediately. Who is this person who is at the same time on my payroll and working for poor Mr. Ball? We must —"

"That," said he, rather stonily, "would seem to be precisely what you undertook to find out when you told me the other day that the situation was in your hand."

"Well, I'll try to find it out, I'll try to. To conceal nothing from you, I had rather suspected Kappus. However, I satisfied myself before I sacked him that Kappus knows nothing of Ball's activities. That leaves me, for the moment, I confess, considerably at a loss."

In the momentary silence which followed the dropping of these words the ticking of the small watch on the young woman's wrist became audible.

"I suppose you can shed no light on the mystery?"

"I?"

"Agitation in the office, leak outside the office — my question is, do you know anything about it?"

A spot of red suddenly darkened Dean Masury's forehead.

"Look here — may I ask you to say plainly what you are driving at?"

On that blunt demand, the eyes of the two met fully. Perhaps even she was conscious, this time, of a certain impact.

"Driving at! Good gracious! — could language be plainer? I ask you in one-syllabled —"

"No, I think you've been throwing out hints for some time. You seem to be trying to insinuate —"

"Oh, no, no, no!" said Miss DeSilver, and he fancied then a certain yielding in her tone, some faint essay toward the leavening of humor. "I never hint. I never insinuate —"

"Why don't you say plainly, then, that you rather think I may be this pleasant person who is spreading whispers about the office and listening at keyholes for information to hawk outside?"

"The very idea! Why, my dear sir, the very idea!"

The woman spoke with an indescribable air of drollery, in a changed and deeper voice, wholly unexpected, like an actor burlesquing a speech in a comedy. The odd thing about it was that under totally different circumstances it really might have been faintly amusing.

But she went on at once, hastily and gravely, with a sort of mollifying "graciousness":

"I'd merely forgotten, what you indicated clearly at the outset, that my forthright ways have a tendency to annoy you. To associate you with a crude betrayal of trust, after what my two good friends, and your own, have told me of you — that would be impossible! Oh, no! I question you, of course, only because your opportunities for observation in this office are necessarily better than anybody else's."

His instant sense was that she receded under attack, that she would not stand up to her own implications. The thought, if anything, increased his distaste for her. Only an act of the will enabled him to repress words that rose spontaneously to his lips: "You're a damned liar. You meant a great deal more than that, and you know it."

"In fact," she was finishing handsomely, "it's exactly because I consider that your work here entitles you — already — to a different status and authority that I wished to confer with you —"

The noises of the opening door sounded from the spaces, and the voice of the secretary, smooth and cool as an eel, dropped into the pause:

"Excuse me, Miss DeSilver. Mr. Byers is calling. I explained that you didn't receive at this hour, but when I told him you'd be away until Wednesday, he begged for just five minutes. And the young man from 'The Blade' is back again — he insists he has a story which it would be in your interest to —"

The woman, who was looking at her watch, shook her head slightly.

"Quarter to one now — h'm. I'll see Byers — yes — about one-fifteen. He can wait or come back as he prefers. Tell the reporter he's wasting his time. . . . And oh, Janney, my dear! — better send out for some lunch now, had n't you? The same as yesterday, shall we say?"

"With the caramel icing, Miss DeSilver?"

"Yum, yum," said Miss DeSilver, with a sketch of smacking her lips; and added directly, in another tone: "I'll be engaged now till I ring."

The door shut gently. Privacy enveloped the attacked president of the company and the temporary office-man who had sworn to capture the company from her. He sat on the arm of the oak chair reserved for visitors — bored with her assumption that he must stand indefinitely while she talked — and regarded her in silence, inaccessible to her graciousness. He had wished, and intended to demand, an enlarged authority; but the purpose, as now announced, merely stirred him to resist her will. Fair reason might rule in the outer office; here all was personal.

"And the first evidence of it," she sailed on, tossing back the ribbon from her pince-nez, "is right here: I want your help in stamping out this pernicious activity. You have the strategic position: I want you to use it to hunt the thing down — at once, even if other things must be sacrificed for the moment. Then either bring the case to me, or in my absence deal with it yourself on the spot, without mercy." Her tone was that of one who says, "There now, see how I trust you."

Masury answered quietly: "No, I won't do that. My engagement does n't contemplate anything of the sort."

Her capped head lifted a little, and she looked at him over the desk-top. She did not speak at once, and he became aware that her gaze upon him had a new quality, speculative and alert. Her voice came dryly:

"And just when I thought we had your position so nicely defined, too. . . . Did you, or not, show, in your first report, and again in coming to me to-day, that you consider morale an important element in efficiency — which is in fact your engagement? I take it you would n't argue that open disloyalty —"

"I argue nothing, Miss DeSilver. I merely tell you that spying is out of my line."

"Spying? But I should call this spy-catching, usually deemed an honorable —"

"Possibly — but outside of my technique, as I say. As you seem to be troubled with so many suspicions, why don't you call in the Pinkertons?"

"Oh, Lord," said Teresa DeSilver.

She drew her cigarette-box toward her, selected a cigarette, and fitted it, with some evidences of annoyance, into the absurd holder. The silence — which was of itself somewhat flattering, perhaps? — ran rather long.

"All right — all right!" she spoke up suddenly, brisk and ironic. "I simply must not, and will not, press upon your sacred instincts. I gathered, when I engaged you, that you had certain — inhibitions, as it were; doubtless it would n't become me to complain of them now. I 'll modify my first hasty request to this: If you, in your capacity as practical personnel officer, should inadvertently stumble upon treachery to the existing company interests, I shall count upon you to —"

"You 're counting upon me, are n't you," he interrupted suddenly, powerfully urged toward plain speech, "to help protect you from the natural consequences of your own acts? Well, I 've taken no retainer to do that, as I 've just said. On the contrary — my disposition, as you should be well aware, runs precisely in the other direction."

"Ah," said the woman, significantly, and nodded her "protected" head a little.

Withdrawn as she kept herself — personality turned off like a light, to dispel her charm! — it was sufficiently clear that a new thought had struck and possessed her. Without any haste at all she pulled open the top right-hand drawer of her desk, took out something — a slip of paper, a newspaper cutting again — and leaned forward with hand extended.

"Look at this, won't you?"

Dean Masury, reaching out his own hand, with reluctant compliance, received the offering from the commanding small fingers. He saw, in the act, that it was a cutting from the classified advertisement columns of "The Republic"; a strip of three or four classified advertisements, one of them marked off with heavy blue-pencil lines above and below it. His eyes then rested upon the following:

> INFORMATION WANTED. — COIT:
> Mr. DeSilver Coit, formerly residing at 2
> East 37th Street, this city, and at Tarrytown,
> New York (or his representative or agent in
> this country) will learn something highly to
> Mr. Coit's advantage by communicating im-
> mediately with WILLIAM BROCKENBROUGH,
> 900 Liberty Street, Telephone John 10,001.

He raised his head. The glassed bluish gaze of the young woman upon him was so level, so insistent and so hard, that sóme part of him, far down in the subconscious, wondered if he had been mistaken just now in thinking that she had evaded and yielded to him.

"Well?"

"Do you by any chance know who is responsible for that advertisement, and similar ones appearing in various city news-papers?"

"Yes. I am."

Miss Teresa said, in low tones: "Well, I'm damned."

Their looks clashed again. His bearing, which was quite imperturbable, was yet a manifest challenge: "*I dare you to show your white feather now....*" She, though she must have read that defiance easily, did not at once meet it; perhaps her mind needed some adjustment to assimilate his strange admission. However, had she not that moment declared that it was too late to complain of her bargain? — and beyond that was n't it suffi-ciently clear that on the whole she scarcely wanted to? Whatever the reason, this woman undoubtedly put a value on him, beyond his "inhibitions."...

"You are putting these advertisements in — for —?"

"I am putting them in for myself."

"Your object in wishing to reach my cousin DeSilver, or his agent, is, perhaps, to try to buy some Whitestone stock?"

"Naturally."

"For yourself?"

"As I said."

"And your object then would be to try to take the company away from me?"

"Not to try. To take the company away from you."

He would have sworn that, for the flying instant, the immobility of that countenance was touched by a flicker of amusement. It vanished, leaving no trace behind. She surprised him by giving a sudden whistle, low yet sharp. Thereafter she sat entirely silent, frowning faintly at her desk-top.

Dean Masury continued to regard her, still with a look that challenged her to dismiss him now, or otherwise to find fault with his position or conduct. Under his cool visage, lean and impenetrable, he was, to say truth, not a little unsettled by that phrase, "to try to take," by that just perceptible sign of amusement at his expense. What, after all, did he know of her hidden movements to protect and ensure her control? For all he could say of his own knowledge, or even Ball could say perhaps, the pivotal block of stock might be lying safe in her deposit-box at this moment. That, indeed, would give his advertisements for her the bouquet of an exquisite jest....

"Really, I had no idea," said Miss DeSilver suddenly, and as suddenly stopped.

She was looking at him again, with a frank curiosity, and her gaze this time said quite plainly: "But since you *are* too honorable to take any advantage of your position, why, in fact, did you wish to come here at all?" ... There was that outstanding declaration of his, that association with her offered no interest for him — was it likely that that rather obfuscating remark had

completely dropped from her mind? At least there were awkwardnesses here; perhaps it was to forestall possible questioning,
or any circumspection — that he spoke, abruptly:

"You're hardly expecting me to feel guilty, or anything of
that sort? I remind you once more that I made a point of indicating my views to you before I undertook the work here — giving you fair opportunity to object if you wished to. But possibly
you supposed that views are something people wrap in pink-
wool and lay away in a drawer?"

"I hardly think I can be taxed with holding that opinion of
views," said Saint Teresa, quietly, and on the whole had the best
of the exchange.

"Tell me," she went on presently, in a serious way which disclosed that the discovered extent of his lone hostility had impressed her — snowed under with hostility though she was —
"is this just a punitive — or personal — opposition, as we might
put it? Or is it possible that you really feel so strongly about one
small company's going on trading in the means of war?"

Dean Masury fell upon these last tempting words as swift as
lightning.

"*Feel strongly!* ... Great God! — how could any one help it!"

He rose suddenly from his perch, stalked a pace or two up and
down on his long legs, wheeled and flung at her:

"Do you read only those parts of the papers that concern
yourself? Don't you know that boys are being slaughtered by
the thousand every day simply because they have n't got the
ammunition to protect them? Don't you know the reason they
have n't got ammunition is that they're nationals of a country
that *did not mean war*, and refused to go armed to the teeth?
Don't you know the country that *did* mean war and *did* go armed
to the teeth has got the unfair advantage of its anti-social policy?
Don't you know that country's saying that if it can hold that
advantage, by however foul means, they have won the war?

Do you want to put the biggest premium you can on going armed to the teeth? Don't you know that neutral sale of arms has always been recognized —"

"Yes — *yes* — YES!" the young woman broke in, in emphatic crescendo. "I not only *know* all the arguments, but I don't doubt they're good enough — for *those who think in terms of war!* As for —"

"Why! — you don't deceive yourself into supposing that *you're* thinking in terms of *peace? Why* — the —"

"I confess to entertaining that small delusion, yes. However, this —"

"It's a stupendous delusion, if genuine," the man threw at her headlong — "can't you see that's precisely what I'm saying? Why, do you think I'm arguing with you about nationalities and cultures, Germany against the Allies? I'd not waste my time that way. I'm speaking exactly in terms of that peace which you profess to be a friend of. I am saying that there are no friends of peace to-day but those whose *acts* lead logically forward to peace. Your act here, as I should think you could hardly avoid knowing, logically leads to war and war again — and I can prove it. Your —"

"I assure you," the attacked president broke in, testily, flinging up the palm of her hand toward him, "I am altogether familiar with *all* the arguments. Some day we might debate them, perhaps — not now. Yes, we might," she added, with a rather unexpected humanness, "for I can respect a sincere opinion, so strongly felt, no matter how —"

"Good! Then allow me to point out to you," resumed Masury, mightily drawn by the argument, "that your *act* here — no matter what you may *mean*, in your mind — is actually this: arbitrarily and on your own opinion to change established law and custom, and to change it *against the more peaceful side*. To the extent of your power — and five thousand shells a day is a great deal of power — your act will help professed milita-rism to win this war. If militarism — anti-pacifism — with your help, wins this war, it will have been demonstrated once and for all, so that the dullest will never forget it, that professional swashbuckling and the mailed fist *pay*, and pay colossally. Every —"

"Thank you, thank you! I've heard it all before —"

"— Nation in the world will have learned that lesson, and that will be the end of peace on earth in your lifetime and mine. In law and in morals, every responsible person is supposed to intend the reasonable consequences of his acts, and the reason-able consequences of your act look toward turning the world into an armed camp and afflicting humanity with a century of war. You —"

"God save us!" cried Saint Teresa, in the liveliest voice he had ever heard from her. "Do my senses deceive me, or is the man really trying to convert me?"

The satirical note of that, mocking at his earnestness, into which a certain passion had crept, stopped him short; and his anger rose. However, to stop him was all that the woman wanted, it seemed; the moment she had her way, she herself took up the talk with a vigor betraying that he had now, through everything else that she had to contend with, somehow aroused her.

"By George! — if that's the range of your views, I can only congratulate you on your comfortable orthodoxy! It must be frightfully jolly to find one's convictions taking one along so snugly with the majority — instead of out into the wilderness, to lead a hangdog life with the miserable enemies of civilization!"

She picked up her holder with the cigarette in it, which she had forgotten to light just now, changed her mind again, and pitched the apparatus with a certain forcefulness into the tray again. In that instant, something in the woman's look, beyond her words, suggested to him that after all she had not been quite impervious to her abounding unpopularity.

"You *are* offering a nationalistic argument in my judgment — with the supporting hypotheses built up afterwards, as usual — and you base it on what? — your personal predictions of the course of history for the next hundred years! Why the deuce should I accept your prophecies as a basis of conviction? If it's a matter of prophesying, I prefer to do it for myself. I did n't assume the responsibilities of my position exactly on the spur of the moment, and my prophecy is that out of the universal exhaustion that will follow this war there will rise a universal demand that the lunatic self-destruction shall never be repeated. However, let that pass. . . . Your restricted view interests me. I gather it has n't occurred to you that there might be still bigger questions involved here — questions bigger than anything to do with any particular attitude in any particular war?"

The woman's unshakable assurance, her galling air of omniscience, and now this desire to evade the so welcome argument by lifting her performance to some foggy "higher plane," all worked together to infuriate him. He threw at her frostily:

"*No!*"

Miss Teresa, having tilted back a little in her chair, was looking at him fully. It proved to be the most personal look she had ever given him; and it noticeably prolonged itself.

"You rather surprise me," she said reflectively, and paused again. . . . "True, you 've been straightforward, and one need n't doubt that you have the normal prejudices of the Anglo-Saxon male. . . . Still, in the upshot — well, there's something about a good fight for a liberal idea that often appeals to young men of adventurous disposition and generous courage. My impression is that this controversy has already raised the issue of a basic human right — nothing less. To some minds, such an issue must always seem more important than —"

"If you're referring," he interrupted brusquely, "to your 'basic human right' to play with a notion of sentimental pacifism while the future of the world is being settled by force of arms, I can't say too quickly or plainly that I can think of nothing of less importance, literally nothing."

"Play with," she repeated quietly. "You'll find there's not much play about me before this is finished.... As for the rest I wonder.... While I think of it — do you happen to know a little book published three or four years ago, a little History of Freedom of Thought, by the Englishman, J. B. Bury?"

Nothing could have been more unexpected or seemed less to the point than such a question, like a random bit of "literary" chat at a dull party. Yet in a sense he was armed for anything here, and he answered shortly, with his rather threatening gaze:

"I know the book — certainly."

"In that book, you may remember, Professor Bury asserts that when the human family concluded that it was wiser to let opinions, however unpalatable or apparently pernicious, express themselves freely, without hindrance or penalty — it was probably the most important decision ever reached by man.... Do you happen to recall that very large statement?"

Her expert again gave his laconic and indignant assent.

"Well, you *are* the Mr. Dean Masury, are n't you, who wrote an article in a magazine about the trial of some so-called anarchists in 1912? — and who then quoted Bury's saying with approval — observing, in the first person, that no damage done by the folly or violence of anarchists could approach in harmful consequences even the smallest curtailment of the sacred principle of freedom?"

The forgotten utterance came back to him then; its tricky exhumation in this connection remained considerably puzzling, and correspondingly exasperating. The further revelation of her knowledge of him, suggesting reserves of information and power

— and of purpose too, perhaps? — much beyond what he had given her credit for, would, indeed, at another moment, have been decidedly disconcerting. But all such considerations were now quite thrust aside by her objectionable air of having trapped him to his overthrow.

"Certainly I wrote that. What of it?"

"That was three years ago, in time of peace. Possibly you, like many of my acquaintances, have modified your sentiments since then?"

"No! — what I thought then, I think now. Do enlighten me as to the object of this cross-examination?"

"I will!" said Teresa DeSilver in a changed tone, and struck one hand into the other. "You think that the fundamental issue here turns upon a few shells, furnished or not furnished to a particular side in this particular war. Well!...I concede that I thought of it that way too — once. I thought of it — yes, and meant it," she said, more slowly, "as just a simple assertion of a principle — just one unimportant fist shaken in the face of war — one insignificant step taken toward that voluntary boycott and outlawry of war, from which, as I believe, there will some day grow legal codes — and courts — and peace.... But that simple time's *past!* What's happened in these three days has made it only too clear that the real question I've raised is whether or not I can run my business as I think it ought to be run — so long as some people think I ought to run it differently. Like it or not, that's a question of basic human rights, and a big one, just as I said. The question that's going to be settled here is just this: Shall opinions be suppressed because they are unpopular? I say they shan't!"

The cheeky grandiloquence of these claims passed belief. Dean Masury gave a laugh, short and disagreeable as a hoot.

"You *are* interesting! Who, by the way, is suppressing your opinions? I was under the impression that the courts had just sustained, in the firmest way, your basic rights to shake your fist all you please."

"Fiddlededee! Don't pretend to think, just for the sake of a retort, that courts guarantee people in their human rights. You're an experienced journalist; you know as well as I do how power gets its way and unwelcome opinions are snuffed out by extra-legal processes. If you don't know, I'll tell you that the ordinary machinery and channels of business, which ought to be free like the high seas, are already being closed to this company — not because I've broken any *law*, or infringed on anybody's *right!* — but solely because my views don't suit certain persons in high places. If they're closed, I can't do business. . . . But no doubt all that impresses you as fair and desirable, and anything goes when you're stamping out heresy? Well, I prefer Bury — as you did when it was all on paper."

He fairly shot out, in a voice betraying at last a bitter edge: "Whoever's against *you* is against freedom? Come, that's the claim you're trying to set up, is n't it?"

"No," she answered flatly, and a certain repressed depth disclosed itself in her voice too. "But whoever is for me will be found in the end — whatever else may be said of him — to have supported free opinion. Think it over. Ask yourself plainly some time or other, whether the common good will be promoted by putting me out of business. I say, and I assure you I speak impersonally, that it will not, but the contrary. For what would have been proved is, not that I was wrong at all, but only that unpopular opinions can and will be snuffed out in America. But no matter," she said, pushing back her chair, "I see that all this is not for you — now."

Deeply stung, the man said furiously: "If you've supposed that I'm the sort of sloppy mutton-head who thinks he must dance when anybody chooses to pipe 'freedom,' I'm happy in the chance to set you straight. Crimes in the name of 'liberty' did n't stop with Madame Roland, and I for one have never held that freedom meant the unlimited privilege of every dilettante — like the right to sit on a park bench. Your persistent desire to claim all virtue to yourself, and wrap up plain and simple things in noble terminology, strikes me, in fact, as both curious and decidedly suggestive —"

The woman gave him a warning look; then, as he saw her hand moved deliberately toward the bell, he struck swiftly:

"You're hardly unaware that you talk very much in the strain of Mr. Beierstein — waiting to confer with you now, I believe — and his interesting group of demi-Americans. Therefore you won't take it amiss if people estimate your acts accordingly."

The speech was intended to arrest her attention; it had that instant effect. The attacked president's hand dropped to the desk-top; she eyed him with a new attentiveness.

"Pray what do you mean by that?"

"Is n't it plain? I'm saying that you have only yourself to blame if many people doubt whether sympathy with *peace* is actually your guiding motive, at all."

"Whether," she said, in a still voice. "Or ... ?"

"Naturally, sympathy with the cause of the Power you are so greatly assist — "

He jumped a little despite himself. The woman struck the top of her desk a blow with her clenched hand, and, with a movement extraordinarily quick, was on her feet.

He was quite taken aback, and, against his reason, faintly thrilled.

For the half of a second it looked as if Miss Teresa DeSilver, the celebrated heiress, the too celebrated president of Whitestone Steel Company, meant to come bounding over the desk and upon him. She, whose past had not been free of violence, looked suddenly and wonderfully capable of violence. She did not come bounding; she only stood, still as a statue, her hard gaze upon him, her breast rising and falling with marked rapidity, her face all at once unnaturally white. But for seconds longer the menacing intentions of that swift upstarting seemed to hang all about her.

Through those seconds, he was acutely aware, the woman looked marvellously changed. Her anger seemed to explode away all the affectations and pretences; real at last she looked in her long cassock, and her eyes, which had seemed out of place in a woman of action, had now the strange unconscious fixity, the single-minded hostility, of the fighting animal thoroughly aroused. For the first time in his knowledge of her, he could see, behind the ridiculous costume and under the superimposed mannerisms, the veritable Saint Teresa of legend: the girl who had boxed a Governor's ears and once at least had shot to kill.

Undoubtedly, the revelation was for him an interesting one; it pushed out permanently, perhaps, the frontiers of his thought. This woman not only had power; she had depth and dimensions; she had passion. There was blood and iron in her. Yes, she was dangerous. She was a fit antagonist for a man.

By some choice of her will, however, no outburst was to follow these threatening manifestations; her desire, it seemed, was to put down her anger, and this she did, though not on the instant. Slowly, her unnatural stillness, which resembled a physical seizure, relaxed; the naked ruthlessness of her gaze became obscured, and the undulation of her rounded bosom, which had been spasmodic, subsided and ceased.

When she spoke, at the end of a full minute of rather intense silence, her voice and manner were almost as usual.

"You understood that I just explained to you what my motive was, and is?"

"I understood you. Yes."

"You're apparently a reader of the newspapers. Possibly you

also saw a published statement from me, explaining why I have done what I have done?"

"Yes, I saw that."

"But you yourself think that I have lied about the matter, and my real motives are quite different?"

"I beg your pardon! — I have n't undertaken to say what I might think —"

"But that was what you meant to convey to me, was it not? ... That is what you do think?"

The man's eyes upon her did not waver. Still, he did not meet that peremptory challenge at once....

To recede before the attack of this woman, or even to seem to recede, was all but impossible for him; in some sense that resembled a physical fracture, it was like deliberately breaking his leg. Yet in this instant, as luck had it, he was perfectly aware that he did not think she had lied, or even evaded: that, in short, he believed her motives, however fatally perverse, were precisely as she had stated them. That awkward consciousness threw him straight upon the horns of a dilemma; perhaps he regretted that punishing thrust of his now. The struggle within him was stubborn.

After the unflattering delay, he spoke with the steeliest reluctance, as if the words were wrung out of him beyond his will:

"It's not my habit to form opinions without evidence. I cannot say I have any evidence that would justify me in — thinking that."

The dusky blue eyes, so unnecessarily large when opened, so absurdly and girlishly fringed, touched him with a look which, in its turn, scarcely complimented him upon his extremely guarded *amende*. She made a little gesture with her hand, a slight, conclusive gesture, and turning slightly, glanced toward the window.

He regarded her, unwinking. Oddly enough, in that moment,

hardly a triumphant one for him, his boundless distrust of her seemed somehow a little mitigated. Undoubtedly her resentment, in its pure humanness, was disturbing to his preconceptions; for that, something in his nature yielded her an unwilling dole of credit. And she had penetrated some part of him, too, with another thought, subtler, but in its way not less unsettling. Was it conceivable that the decidedly striking-looking woman who had just confronted him had, after all, some slight pretext for "protection"? ...

But the hand that had made the gesture of finality moved now toward the buzzer, and Miss Teresa spoke with her characteristic briskness, distinctly crisped.

"That's all, Masury. I don't believe in the coercion of opinion, especially on the part of employers, and I now withdraw the instructions I gave a few moments ago, which you find obnoxious to your principles and hopes. The fight's a public one; outside the office, I leave you free. ... As for your services within the office, though necessarily reduced in scope by your own desire, they will, I am sure, continue to be valuable and — rendered without prejudice from your opinions. Thank you."

The buzzer sounded.

He said, rather hurriedly: "This brings me back to the beginning again. The present disorganization of the office —"

"I will make my own arrangements. As for what you are concerned with, I will see that your authority is ample. Is Mr. Byers waiting, Janney? Good! — show him in."

The strange woman was as good as her word; indeed, he had to admit, a little better. Entering the office next morning, passing the new bulletin-board which he had set up at the general room door, Masury's eye was caught by a manifesto not placed there by his hands. This document, a copy of which he found a moment later on his desk, proved to be an official order; it was addressed To All Officers and Employees, and signed "T. DeSilver, President." The order gave notice to all concerned that pending the appointment of a successor to Mr. Kappus, Mr. D. Masury had this day been designated as acting manager of the company offices, with general charge of equipment, method and personnel.

CHAPTER XII

THE explosion in the newspapers had taken Lucy Flanner completely by surprise: those blasts of disapproval came upon her both as a shock and a continuing distress. But from the beginning Lucy found the unpublished evidences of hostile opinion still more upsetting. In her circle, too, the Whitestone story had fallen like a spark upon tinder, or a blow upon a wound. The animosity toward Teresa seemed to her extraordinary; she remembered the saying about Death and the shining mark. Not a few persons, to her astonishment, spoke of the matter with raised eyebrows and pleased, low voices, as old cats exchange the details of a friend's disgraceful lark, happily found out. More exuded a simple bitterness, unyielding and unmerciful. It was commonly said at first that the exploit had been prompted by an ancient grudge against the British Empire; soon the idea was put more briefly, as Major Checkerman put it at Masury's club. Presently the air was dense with whispers of all sorts.

Thus Lucy, being almost alone in defending her reckless friend, found herself suddenly plunged into an atmosphere of controversy, sometimes excited and tearful, sometimes merely sharp, but always unwelcome to her kindly soul. The matter, of course, quickly went further. She was to learn, not for the first time, that in differences involving the passions, few people pay scrupulous attention to the nature of an opponent's argument. That she herself possessed no "taint of neutrality," and in Miss DeSilver's place would not have done as Miss DeSilver had done, was easily brushed aside; that she argued at all in behalf of a person who was known to have received half a million dollars from Bernstorff (for the tale had come to that directly, oddly regardless of the fact that the person already had more millions than were necessary), this was for many enough, and more than enough. Before the Whitestone news was three days old, Lucy was aware that people looked at her a little askance. Good friends, and sometimes persons whom she did n't consider friends at all, drew her aside in public gatherings to advise her "for her own good" that her admiration for the notorious woman was causing talk. The experiences both startled and angered her.

The situation grew hard for Lucy. All at once she could n't work. The discovery was the more unlucky for her in that she confronted, at just this juncture, the opportunity of her lifetime. A long time she had slaved, through unhappiness and obscurity — an underpaid "rewrite" hack with a failing picture-company — before her chance had knocked at last, and found her ready. But the climb upward, necessarily, was by stages. It had happened that a script which some one had written, and she in her namelessness had rewritten, had caught the attention of Steinfeldt, the suddenest and most astounding of deities; and the great producer, having laconically inquired, "Who wrote them captions?" — had cautiously summoned her to his office. His offer then had been only the chance to "do the continuity" of a popular novel, and even this was given "on approval," though he liked her; for the nabob was not at that time one to mix business with pleasure, and no one had said of him as yet that there were talents he appreciated beyond the mimetic gift, and proportionately rewarded. However, the resulting picture, "Babs of the Boglands," played by a ringletted and adored young person, achieved a success so extraordinary that even the author of the novel confessed to being pleased with it. Within a few months, Lucy's first picture all her own, "Dark Happiness," had almost duplicated that triumph. Now she was executing an unconditional order from Steinfeldt, at a price which seemed romantically large; and, that test being successfully met, it was the director's desire to put her under a five-year contract at a salary which would have staggered most of the great ones of the earth.

But she could not work. Far along with the second of her two new scripts, all at once she could n't make it march. From the beginning, her magical luck had seemed shadowed by the trouble of the world; now this insidious personal thing, truly born on the Western Front, came reaching into her life like a miasma. Pictures had done everything for her; she was their creature hardly less than they were hers; and suddenly she cared nothing for pictures. Sitting down at her desk in the pleasant new apartment, which writing had won for her, she found herself thinking with bitterness, a dozen times a day: "Oh, if I could only really write! If I only could!" For now the successful scenario-writer desired nothing so much as to compose a tract, which should really be a sermon, upon a simple text: that intolerance is the sin against the Holy Ghost for which there is no forgiveness.

She wrote Teresa a note upon her typewriter, delicately conveying her sympathy and affection. She was to see her widely condemned friend — at least to see her — at the annual conclave of the League which was to gather within a few days now. Masury she had neither seen nor heard from since the day they had lunched at Donovan's, before the thing had happened; nor was there in his case any plan afoot looking toward a remeeting. In the matter of calls, "attentions" and the like, he was known to be quite undependable; if left wholly to himself, weeks, months even, might elapse before there would be an opportunity for the exchange of views. But Lucy herself, as the days passed, was increasingly conscious of a need to talk with him, her fellow-conspirator of Easter Day; hence in the end she decided to do precisely what any sensible woman, having her own kitchenette, would have done under similar circumstances. She called Dean on the telephone, and gathered him in for dinner.

The occasion was hardly a success. Since a woman must be

sure of herself, indeed, to summon single men to tête-à-têtes, Lucy had of course thrown the customary drapery over her fundamental design. She asked not only the Willy Masterses, but Helen Lupado and the gifted young cartoonist, George Henry James — six being the precise capacity (Hommes and Chevaux) of the combination sitting-and-dining room. Externally all went well, indeed charmingly. The subject of Whitestone, whether by a miracle, or by the tact of guests, was not touched upon except for a single rather nasty dig from Eva Masters; but Eva, though without doubt fantastically amusing, was intellectually and morally such a celebrated ninny that the scratch passed virtually unnoticed. The talk was good, it was constant and merry; the only criticisms from the hostess's standpoint being that George Henry James talked too much, and Dean Masury too little. She thought that Dean looked a little tired, and a faintly set look, with which she was quite familiar, seemed to hover continually over his long, keen face. This was unsatisfactory enough to Lucy, but worse, hardly had her little servant Hilda folded up the collapsible dining-table and the hired-in butler Alphonse taken away the coffee things, when Dean rose suddenly to go. He had mentioned over the telephone that he was fearfully busy; he repeated his amiable apologies now.

Lucy's heart sank a little. She had taken pains with the dinner and had put on her prettiest dress. However, she was no child, or even a helpless vine. Without troubling to make any excuse, she followed her friend out into the hall and shut the door behind her.

She had longed to hear Dean say something indicating, for her comfort, that he was at least "against" the hateful wagging of tongues. But now, as she tried to draw him out a little, he proved unexpectedly obdurate and uncommunicative. That reserve in him, which she had faintly noted the other day, seemed only to have stiffened with the passing days. However, he did say this, in quite a gentle way:

"How could I help being sorry for anything that distresses you, Lucy? Of course, you know I am. Still, you must n't let this little business grieve you too much — it seems ten times as terrible to you as it does to her, depend upon it. She's a seasoned campaigner, remember. Her name's been in the headlines, she's been under attack, many and many a time before to-day."

Lucy pointed out that Suffrage and the League had not been like this. She said that the sheer vindictiveness, flowing in from so many sides, made her literally afraid; she would never think the same of her kind again. But Masury, leaning idly against the wall, soon interrupted her, saying soothingly, yet with the greatest firmness:

"Everybody is n't against her, my dear. You must n't mistake the infinitesimal group of persons that you and I flock around with, at a single dot on the Atlantic seaboard, for the United States of America — that's a fatal error. The fact is, there are millions of people for her — throwing up their hats for her as we stand here. All the anti-Europeans and provincial Americans — all the peace societies and Quakers and turn-the-other-cheekers — all the England-haters, all the Germans and Irish, all the Vereins and Vierecks — they're all for her — millions of esteemed fellow-citizens, some of them exceedingly powerful and influential. You must n't vex your kind heart by thinking of her as a great lonely eagle."

When she resisted that as exaggerated, and cold comfort besides, he merely listened to her, unmoved; she even thought she detected a trace of impatience in his pleasant voice as he answered:

"Well, Lucy, no one can expect a martyr's crown, I'm afraid, without enduring something of a martyr's pain. You think of her as something of a hero, I believe? — but you see, it is n't by getting pats on the back and hearkening to honeyed words that a hero reveals the heroical quality. And by the bye, was n't it you who told me that she wants to make her life a demonstration of something — selfless and sexless service, something of that sort? Surely she is n't complaining at this late day that those large ambitions come high?"

Lucy shook her head. "The complaints are all my own," she said briefly, and felt herself set down at a great distance.

She was presently reduced to saying point-blank: "How are you and she getting along?"

"Splendidly," said Dean, picking up his stick. "We never meet. It could n't be better. — Well! You gave us a wonderful dinner, and your apartment's fine — about the cutest place I've seen yet. 'Night! See you soon!"

But he did not indicate when the soon would be, and Lucy, left standing alone in her tiny hall, felt — as how many women have felt, staring at a door that has just shut upon a back — that she had to bear her troubles alone.

And then on the heels of that, the next day but one, something happened which made the whole matter much worse at once. If the mists of rumor had seemed poisonous, at least they were mists; now they suddenly condensed, as it were, and precipitated a too definite "incident." In short, it befell Lucy to see her heroine publicly affronted, in a quarter from which affront might least have been expected.

The quarter was the Women's Federal Eight-Hour League, no less, which Miss DeSilver had herself helped to found in 1908, whose heart and soul she had been during the years of its rapid rise to national prominence. The scene was the convention of the active workers of the League, and the immediate occasion of the affront was, of all things, Miss DeSilver's voluntary abdication of her leadership.

The lamentable development came, to Lucy at least, as sudden as a thunder-clap.

The sessions were held — ineptly, as it seemed in retrospect — in the old office in the DeSilver wing; and at the opening session, on Thursday afternoon, Teresa DeSilver, as president, occupied the chair. A sensitive person, Lucy was not unaware of hidden currents; the vast chamber, which to-day had almost a crowded look, showed signs of a certain atmospheric coolness, different from other meetings; the competent feminine air seemed vaguely electric. Yet the idea of any outbreak, in this familiar and coöperative *milieu*, had remained quite unthinkable.

It was known throughout the League that its leader had determined to retire from active service, for reasons which were also well known; her intention had already been communicated to the executive committee, and there remained only the formal duty of accepting the *fait accompli*. For a time all followed the normal course. The distinguished Mrs. John B. Necker, of Albany, rising at the proper moment, offered a prepared resolution, rehearsing at length the services of Miss DeSilver to the League, warmly expressing the appreciation and gratitude of the membership, and deeply regretting her enforced retirement. Nothing could have been more strictly regular; and the chairman, whose brisk presiding manner betrayed no consciousness of anything whatever below the surface of Roberts's Rules of Order, put the question as dispassionately as she might have put a motion to adjourn. The meeting was thrown into a refined uproar when a chair-leg scraped abruptly and a member, rising with evidences of strong emotion not under perfect control, protested against the adoption of the resolution.

The member was Miss Shane, of Connecticut, long prominent in the work of the League and for the last year a member of its executive committee. A short, scrawny woman, with an odd cerise turban crowning a pale, pugnacious face, Miss Shane was clearly of those who never flinch from doing their duty as they see it. Her duty now was to take exception to what she called "the flowery and sentimental nature of this resolution." In a slightly shrilled voice, Miss Shane declared that the matter before the body was official business purely, and accordingly "these fulsome expressions" seemed to her, Miss Shane, entirely out of place.

Every occupant of every camp-chair gathered the woman's meanings instantly. Every eye in the old DeSilver picture-gallery was instantly riveted on the faintly fanatical face of the lady from Connecticut. There was, of course, an immediate stir; there were the beginnings of an uneasiness and excitement so general that only one woman in the room, by the look of things, remained entirely dissociated from them. That was the chairman, whose purely formal bearing disclosed no interest of her own in this unlooked-for response to her routine "Any discussion?"

Lucy, for her part, sitting on the last row of camp-chairs, listening with strained ears, felt the blood drawing from her cheek. She stared at the faces and heads about her, sick with incredulity.

By the secretary's count at the opening there were forty-seven women "present." While there was a scattering from distant States, and one energetic welfare-worker had journeyed all the way from Los Angeles, the majority of these active workers came, naturally, from the State, and nearly half from the city itself. These were the women who knew Miss DeSilver best, perhaps; an intelligent, serious-minded and resolute lot, some of them, certainly, were the closest friends she had. Popularity in the intimate sense, she might lack; popularity had hardly been her object in the world, perhaps; but at least she had always had, as Lucy well knew, the unbounded admiration of these, her co-workers. She was the unique centre of their common interest. Was it imaginable, was it endurable, that this utterly uncalled-for ...

She was quickly aware that she was not alone in her sensations. Others, many others, felt the unseemliness of the fierce spinster's foray. As she orated, the fluttering from the chairs grew louder. Voîces, interrupting, began to call: "Question! Question!" One gentle soprano said distinctly, "Shame!" And now two women were on their feet clamoring for recognition: "Madame Chairman!"... "A point of order!"

But the chair, quite unmoved, was saying in calm and measured tones: "Order. Miss Shane of Connecticut has the floor."

Miss Shane, her sallow face a shade paler, her small eye glaring round, went on a little jerkily:

"It was not my purpose, Madame Chairman, to raise questions of a foreign nature in this body — er — at this time. I regret that the issue has been forced upon me by others. It is not denied that the chairman has in the past done excellent work for the League — "

A voice, hoarse and rasped like a ballyhoo's, said: "She *is* the League. Really, this is — " The chairman's gavel rapped her silent.

"But circumstances have changed — since last August," cried Miss Shane, defiantly, her own voice keying up further. "There are some of us, and I say it reluctantly, driven only by a profound sense of my duty — in these terrible times — who no longer feel the confidence in Miss DeSilver's — ah — *judgment* — that we felt last year. I object particularly to the unnecessary expression, 'with the deepest sorrow and regret.' I feel, and I may say that I speak for others besides myself, that Miss DeSilver has — by her own acts — seriously injured her usefulness to the League, and that her resignation at this time is — is timely, and for the good of the —"

A sharp hiss brought the speaker to an uncertain pause. It came from the lips of Lucy Flanner. Not having planned anything of the sort, not having dreamed herself capable of it, Lucy was utterly nonplussed when the glances of her neighbors brought her offence home to her. She was colder than snow within; she felt ill. But the old gallery, all at once, was in a hubbub. There were gloved hands which clapped. However, the voices of protest drowned out that thin "demonstration." One after another was taking up the cry, "Shame! Shame!" A low, sweet voice — perhaps the soprano that had spoken earlier? — was saying, over and over, "Throw her out!" From all over the room came the insistent call, "Question! Question!" — and the woman with the ballyhoo voice, standing now, her heavy face purpling, was shouting: "Madame Chairman, I insist ... Madame Chairman, I demand ..."

But through the womanly uproar, to which the continual scraping of feet and chairs added itself, the gavel was sounding with increasing peremptoriness and the detached voice of the chair, only a little raised, made itself easily heard.

"Ladies!"

She had not lost her power over these women, it seemed. She could rule them still. In the sudden silence that followed, full of the tenseness of expectancy, the young chairman, her cool and somewhat ironic gaze moving over the gathering, sternly rebuked her colleagues. She said they seemed to mistake themselves for an assemblage of men. She said that they were accustomed to order and decorum in that body, that such discourtesy to a speaker was unprecedented and astonishing, that she must and did insist, etc.

Her eyes then turned toward the cerise bonnet, only to find that its owner, in the confusion, had sat down.

"Miss Shane has the floor."

Half-rising, the scrawny woman, excited almost to tears, said:

"I guess I've made myself pretty plain. I've put my objection in the record anyway — that's something."

Chairman DeSilver gently prodded her: "Do you not wish to make a motion, Miss Shane? For example, that the resolution be amended by striking out the words, 'with the deepest sorrow and regret'?"

"I — yes — Yes, I make that motion."

The chair called for a second to the motion thus made, and got one. The chair called for discussion, and the purple-faced woman, recognized at last, made a loud address, not very good, but containing several hard slaps at Miss Shane, indignantly protesting against "this unheard-of intrusion of partisan politics and personal predilections," etc. Miss Shane's motion to amend was put and lost. Mrs. Necker's resolution, as originally offered, was put and carried, with no spoken dissent. However, several voices had voted aye on the motion to amend, a decided "rebuke" under the circumstances — a somewhat bitter epitaph on three years' devoted work — and Lucy felt ready to cry.

The business of the meeting proceeded with perfect order. Mrs. Edgar Fairchild, of the well-known Philadelphia family, was duly elected president of the League and chairman of the executive committee, according to the plan of the nominating board. Miss DeSilver, turning over the chair to her successor with a few remarks of the "well-chosen" sort, took a seat in the first row of camp-chairs, a member only. In the discussions of general matters that followed, she took an occasional part. The session moved smoothly to adjournment.

However, there was a little aftermath of the deplorable incident, and Lucy, waiting to the last in the hope of a talk with her unpopular friend, was a witness of it.

The gathering, when the business was finished, dispersed quickly. Outside there was to be a great buzzing, no doubt; here the ladies seemed indisposed to linger. A few slipped away at once without ceremony; but most of the members politely paused to shake hands with the two presidents, the old one and the new. A changing group formed about Teresa DeSilver who, amiably calm, responded with ease to the flow of carefully pleasing speeches. But there was a want of complete relaxation and the drift toward the door was steady.

Mrs. Edgar Fairchild, the new leader, smiling and bowing about like a visiting prince, went out, taking a group of subjects in her train. Mrs. John B. Necker, of Albany, went out, and the up-State contingent with her. Then in the enormous room there remained, besides the woman who owned it, but five persons: Lucy Flanner, sitting motionless on her camp-chair in the empty row; a tall, pretty, middle-aged woman in deep mourning who hovered indeterminately near the door, gazing at the portraits of celebrated women; and Miss Shane, of Connecticut, with two loyal supporters.

Miss Shane, it was obvious, was by no means indeterminate. More unmistakably than Lucy she was waiting to speak to Teresa DeSilver; and now, seeing the meeting-place practically empty, she detached herself from her auxiliaries and sailed forward.

The president of Whitestone, the ex-president of the League, aware of the inimical descent, stood awaiting it. Eyes fixed upon her advancing opponent, she looked as hard and cool as a marble statue. Miss Shane looked hard too, and almost cool; she had recovered from the nervous excitement which had partially shaken her when she launched her declaration of war. As the two women faced each other, one young and of extraordinary appearance, the other fast drying into bony age, it seemed to Lucy that there was something implacable, something deadly, in the look of both of them.

She missed no word of the colloquy that followed.

"I assume that the newspapers have reported you correctly,

Teresa? I assume that I have not misunderstood your position and purposes?"

"You appear gifted in making assumptions, Amy. I can discuss your understanding better if you can manage to convey it."

The sallow cheek of Miss Shane showed a flag of red.

"I understand that, having seized this steel company, your first act was to close the munitions-plant, your motive being — for what reasons I do not undertake to say — that you do not wish to sell ammunition to the Allies?"

"Why not simply undertake to say that I do not wish to sell ammunition?"

"Because that exonerates you from your just responsibility. Because, as you know very well, it is not possible to sell shells to the Germans — no matter how much one might wish to do so."

"I am unhappily responsible for many things, Amy. I disclaim responsibility for the control of the seas, or the rules of the blockade."

"But hardly for the known consequences of your own acts?" said Miss Shane; and did not know that the ex-chairman had lately listened to just those words from another. "You are perfectly aware that, under the conditions as they actually exist, to set up this procedure now is simply to give aid and comfort to the German army — fresh from their unnamable atrocities. I have no love for any one who is helping the Kaiser to-day."

"It is possible that I shall help something bigger than Hohenzollern. But I must n't expect a mind never, if I may imitate your candor, either large or deep and now dark with passion, to follow me there. What is the purpose of this conversation?"

As Teresa grew harder and colder, the older woman's excitement more and more returned to her. Her voice squeaked up:

"The purpose? I 'll tell you very quickly. I preferred not to make a public demonstration against you, but to your face I'm glad to tell you that I've lost all belief in you, and all regard for you. I consider that, by your admitted acts alone, for I don't listen to the unsavory gossip, you have shown yourself hostile to what I hold dearest in the world. I don't like you, I don't trust you, and I am against you in everything you try to do henceforward."

"You're aboveboard, Amy; that's admirable of you. May I say that if I had nothing bigger than your enmity to concern me, just now, life would seem almost a song again?"

Miss Shane snapped a glove-button with livid fury.

"Take the high hand if you like. It was always your pose. But I warn you I'm not talking just for smart repartee. I'm going to spread my opinion of you as far as my voice can carry, and it carries pretty far. My enmity, as you correctly express it, will follow you wherever you go — it will stick to you like a shadow. Good-bye."

Teresa smiled wintrily. "Good luck, Amy, in all your undertakings. But indeed I'm not going anywhere — no, you'll find me right here when all this is over."

Miss Shane and her two satellites marched out in a hot silence, their righteous heads high. The lady in mourning, who also had listened to that sad parting of friends, moved aside from the angry exit. Seeing her then, Teresa spoke in a different voice.

"Oh, Mrs. Merrill! Were you waiting to speak to me?"

The tall woman, starting a little, turned, hesitated, glanced at Lucy and said in a gentle voice with an English intonation: "Well — not particularly — no, not now, I think. I merely waited —"

"If there is anything morally in my power to do —"

"No — thank you. Another time, perhaps. I merely — but I won't trouble you now. I — good-night."

She passed with a hurried, rather frightened air through the door. The late president of the League gazed after her, motionless. Then her eyes, moving a little, fell upon the figure of

Lucy Flanner, sitting quietly, hands folded in her lap, full fifty feet away. The fixity of her gaze hardly changed.

"Ah, Lucy. You still here?"

Lucy's heart ran out to her. She had recalled what she said to Masury, on the night of the dinner; surely now, she had been right: used as Teresa was to fights, she had never encountered anything that quite approached this. In this familiar room, associated in her mind with friendly quiet and useful work, Lucy felt herself to have been bathed in the ugly passions released by the sport of kings. She had scented the effluvia of war, and the odors had sickened her. Teresa, standing there alone, first gratuitously insulted, and now, as the fancy pictured it, deserted, her great eyes staring over empty spaces, seemed to Lucy, in that moment, a literally tragic figure. She yearned to comfort her.

Rising, smiling sweetly as she advanced, while all her being vibrated within her like a bowstring twanged too hard, she said, stammering a little:

"Yes — I have n't seen you for such a long time. I — I thought I 'd stop and say how-do-you-do at least, and —"

"Is there something I can do for you?"

"No — no, Teresa, thank you. I —"

Flustered by her friend's abstracted stare, Lucy was visited by a sudden inspiration.

"I hoped I could induce you to take a little walk with me — it 's so lovely out! And — perhaps it would blow the air of all *this* out of our lungs."

And then with a little burst, almost a cry, she said: "Oh, Teresa! — it was so dreadful! I can't tell you how sorry I am — and how ashamed for the League!"

The ex-chairman looked at her with some appearance of grave surprise.

"Oh!... The meeting? That 's nothing. Not worth — "

"It's everything! — it's the most shocking part of war!" said Lucy passionately. "Honest bloodshed seems clean and decent by the side of this hateful ill-feeling — this sickening injustice —"

Then Teresa, the unconquerable, having seemed to shake herself a little, laughed briefly.

"Those are hard words, Lucy! No — the meeting went off in most ways rather better than I had expected. As for Amy Shane and what she represents, I'd really think that was funny, if it were n't at the same time a little sad too."

"*Funny?*"

"Yes, but a little sad too."

She leaned back thoughtfully against the great desk, idly turning in her fingers the gavel which was no more hers to wield.

"Because, as I see it," said she, like one discussing an academic point of some interest, "they're all letting go something that *is* fundamentally important for something that, after all, is n't. And at just the wrong time too! Yet, Lucy, it's so darned human, it's so perfectly unconscious, it's so exquisitely pat, the way they flop, that you can't help being amused at it too. Amy Shane's a sworn pacifist. She fears and detests war just as much as I do — we've talked about it dozens of times in years gone by. But the last time she was down here, just after Christmas, it was very clear that the spring thaw had set in. Following the line of least resistance? — or shall we say, just the nice, human necessity to fit yourself in comfortably with the people you live with and love? 'I'm as much against war as I ever was,' she told me, 'but this war, don't you see, is different.' . . . It's the same with most of them, of course. I've had to smile as I watched them, one after another pouncing on something — just that one thing — which compels them to support this particular war. They've forgotten that every war has been 'different' since time began. . . . But they'll remember it again, no fear — and in 1920 or 1925, Amy Shane will think of this afternoon and be sorry."

Staring with wonder at the extraordinary girl, Lucy was struck, and moved, by the look of her face. . . . No, she had no need to give comfort here; rather she was drawing it now from this strange young calm, from the curious serenity of this stormy spirit. . . . Was it not true, as this nature in its largeness so spontaneously affirmed, that no one had any concern with consequences? Each must show forth steadily her own best light; nothing mattered but that, and the rest was trash. . . .

Lucy said, a little unsteadily: "I think you take it beautifully. I —"

"Beautifully! — nonsense! There's nothing to take. Not," Miss DeSilver amended, straightening, with an abrupt change of thought, "that I consider the disturbance nothing — or funny either — don't misunderstand me there. I must say I thought some of them gave a pretty sorry exhibition."

"Don't you think that was rather human too, considering the — "

"Considering nothing. If we can't observe the ordinary proprieties of assembly, let's stop and go back to kindergarten. If I'd had any power of discipline, I should n't have let them off with a talking to, not I."

"Oh!"

"Who was it that hissed, do you know?"

There was a second's dead pause, at the end of which Lucy said, flatly and firmly:

"I did — and I'm glad of it."

Miss DeSilver, who had suddenly started pacing about, stopped still, and stared at her. Lucy met the gaze defiantly. And then her late leader did one of those completely natural, yet completely unexpected, things which Lucy found, from her, supremely endearing. Her blankness dissolved in a stream of rippling laughter, very girlish and merry, and throwing both arms about Lucy's neck, she gave her a great hug.

"As your former chairman," said Teresa, really giggling, "I am reprimanding you severely. Do not fail to consider this — and this — and this — as the severest of reprimands. I am utterly ashamed of you, I am at a loss to understand your unladylike conduct, and I love you very much. And you wrote me a sweet letter, too, when all the time you think I'm dreadfully wrong-headed like the others —"

"No — no! I think you're — "

"Come! — We must fly if we're going out!" said Miss De-Silver, suddenly releasing her. "I've plenty to talk about. . . . Oh, hang it, no!" she said in another tone, looking at her watch. "I can't go, Lucy. I'd no idea it was —"

"Oh, *do*, Teresa! Just — "

"I wish I could — it's just not possible, Lucy. . . . I'm off to Cohaxie at eleven, and there's an immense lot to do at the office first — I'd no right to be away this afternoon at all. And then right now . . . well, I've got to try to see grandfather again," said she, "and this is my only time."

Puzzled by that, Lucy asked: "But — Mr. DeSilver's here, isn't he?"

"Oh, yes, he's here — still. The trouble's just that he doesn't want to see me. . . ."

Her tranquillity became a little clouded. Dropping down in a camp-chair as if she were tired, she said with a sort of deliberate lightness:

"It's about come to the breaking-point, as everybody knows! Now he's told the housekeeper that he's going to leave me altogether — move to a hotel — something of the sort. I think he means it, and the thought's not a happy one — it takes all the heart out of quarrelling with him. No more wonderful rows. . . . I'm very much afraid that he'll do something rash — and he knows I'm afraid. . . . Ah, Lucy, he's so old!"

But Lucy, who pretended to no sympathy where Mr. De-

Silver was concerned, said only: "How do you mean that he'll do something rash?"

"Ah, one can never say! . . . I'd hate it like the devil if his life ended with anything ridiculous — any sort of trivial mess. I'm going to make one more effort — now — to avoid at least a final smash. . . . But enough of troubles. Sit down a minute, Lucy, do! I've not seen you in weeks."

Lucy willingly sat. The two young women — not far apart in age, but of how different an experience of life — chatted briefly of things near and far, including "Dark Happiness" and Mr. Steinfeldt. It appeared that the burning question of the meeting had been completely disposed of; as for the sin of intolerance, upon which Mrs. Flanner had been full of pointed reflections, what need to broach that subject here? Beside her, the strange Teresa, notorious "outlaw" from civilization, newly come from a stab in the house of her friends, had begun to speak of a new poet — some one of whom Lucy, who herself loved poetry, had not even heard — was reciting in a stirred voice lines which Lucy was destined to hear and to read often again:

> 'If I should die, think only this of me:
> That there's some corner of a foreign field
> That is forever England. . . .'"

Out of which the singular girl — who did after all betray a certain controlled restlessness, faint sign of the tremendous strain she was undoubtedly under — said suddenly:

"Oh, by the way, Lucy! I've not had a chance before to thank you for that man you brought me — Masury? I've wanted to tell you that he's proved a treasure."

"Oh! — Has he?" said Lucy, whose consciousness for some moments had been turning toward just this topic.

"A pearl without price. I wish I had a staff all just like him — or almost."

"I'm so glad you like him! He's a —"

"I did n't exactly say I liked him, my dear, but that's a detail — and, in fact, I do like his sincerity at least! But his work, which is the point, is admirable. What he's accomplished in these two weeks, under the most trying conditions imaginable, is a marvel, nothing less. It's as if he had given me a new office — absolutely."

"That makes me happy," said Lucy, returning her friend's gaze steadily — "and at the same time, it does n't quite surprise me either. But — I hope you are n't saying that he — makes himself disagreeable in any way? He *can* be —"

Teresa's brief laugh interrupted her.

"Why should n't he? He's more determined than most to get Whitestone away from me, you see — and after all, I did n't engage him for his manners! —"

"Get Whitestone away from you?"

"Of course you know that? You and he are good friends, did n't you say?"

Lucy, staggered by the extent of Dean's intentions, felt ready to sink through the floor. But she said firmly:

"No, I did n't know it. He's very apt to keep his own confidences, I've found. But if you believed that I knew it, you must have thought it strange indeed that I intro — "

"Bless your heart, don't say it — the idea! Why, everybody in town would like to see the company taken away from me, Lucy — why bar him from the fun? Besides, he's been most honorably straightforward about it from the beginning — and besides again, the chance of anybody's turning the trick is so small that it very seldom worries me! . . . No, really!" said Teresa, with what seemed a faintly inquiring inflection, "the only possible point in the matter is why he wanted the place at all — since of course he would n't use it against me?"

On that point Lucy, with her oddly divided loyalties, was

scarcely prepared to offer surmises of her own: the ice seemed
disagreeably thin. Still, the subject retained for her a risky
interest.

"Why do you keep him, Teresa?" she asked suddenly, out of
her real uneasiness. "I mean, knowing that he's hostile to you,
and finding him disagreeable besides —"

"But I've just said, he's an office man in a thousand."

"Aren't there dozens of men in New York who would be just
as good?"

"I doubt if there are two. . . . And I'll tell you, Lucy," said
she, obligingly, like one struck by a new thought of possible interest — "I daresay another reason I've passed over the irregu-
larities in your friend's position is that he's rather believed I
wouldn't! There seems to be a sort of challenge in his bearing,
don't you know — I noticed it the first moment I saw him — as
much as to say that he thinks I'm going to be afraid to have him
around. Perhaps I'm obstinate enough to keep him around just
for that. Anyway, it's not important, as I say: the real struggle
just now is not so much to keep the company as to keep the business — which unfortunately is a subtler difficulty!"

Her listener, who had not forgotten that Dean Masury, at the
first sight of this girl, had also experienced a sense of "challenge,"
felt something deep in her abruptly stir. In the over-close meeting-place, Lucy was a little cold.

She said, rather at random: "You mean — they're trying to
take your trade away?"

Teresa laughed monosyllabically. "That's what *they* mean,
yes. Well, we'll see. . . . I've just had the honor of a visit from
Mr. Porter. Of course, his ultimatum was the same as grandfather's; quite possibly grandfather sent him, who knows? Give
it up, or take the consequences. Or, to quote him more exactly,
he had a fancy to buy some Whitestone stock — name my price.
. . . As a matter of fact, I'd already felt his iron hand, as of

course he knew I knew! — and it certainly must look like pretty easy pickings for him. Naturally lots of people are saying, without being put up to it, that they don't care to deal with a German concern. . . ."

The inflectionless tone betrayed no feeling. Yet Lucy, rather staggered by this new glimpse of the pitfalls besetting her friend's path on every side, felt suddenly like crying out: "Oh, Teresa, it's too much for you to carry alone! This is n't the way for you to wear out your youth! . . ."

She did say, nervously: "But, Teresa — is it possible for you to stand up against Johnny Porter?"

"I think so," said Teresa calmly. "Nothing in me, of course — but my father's power is in my hands. He left me, I'm discovering, besides money, some awfully valuable connections. There are a good many people who must do what I say, regardless of what Mr. Porter says. . . . One does one's best, that's all. And if they should break me — why, of course I'd just get something else at once, and start again."

"You mean — steel? You do like that part of it?"

"I adore it," answered Teresa simply. "The days I'm at Cohaxie are the best days I have at all — or ever have had, I believe. No moral problems there. . . . Oh, the plans I've got for Whitestone, once I can be let alone, just to make steel. . . . Lucy, I must run! 'George, it's half-past six."

The figures of the two women, as they rose, stood small in the perspective of the immense and noble chamber; and Lucy was rather the taller of the two.

"What a dear you are to be grieved by my troubles!" said Teresa suddenly, and put her hands on Lucy's shoulders. "But you must n't, my sweet friend — you must n't. I'm used to fights, and I don't mind criticism the least bit — truly, truly. I do assure you, Lucy, there was n't one thing here this afternoon that even touched me at all. . . . At least — perhaps . . .

"Yes," said the girl, dropping her hands soberly and staring off toward the door. "I do except that gentle good woman who waited there to speak to me — and then would n't. . . . Do you know her, Lucy? — Mrs. Merrill?"

Lucy said, a little painfully: "No, I — know she's an English-woman — and in mourning — but no, I've not met her."

"I scarcely knew her either, till she came to see me the other day — at the office. . . . Came, doing her bit," said Teresa slowly — "in that forbearing and considerate way that is often so much more effective than force don't you think? . . . Just delicately laying before me a few facts about England's shortage of munitions. Her brother's Granville Ashby, it seems, high up in the Admiralty — she knows a great deal. The Northcliffe press is about to make a broadside exposure, and the Government will fall, she thinks. That is — the need for shells is as plain — and as bad — as that."

"And she?" said Lucy. "Has she lost — a soldier?"

"Both her sons," said Teresa; and went on after an instant: "Those stories have got familiar long ago, of course — still, they can never be commonplace, perhaps? . . . These boys, both just out of Harvard, were in England visiting her people last August; they cabled for permission and stayed. Both had had a little military training at school, I believe, and, perhaps by pull, they got into replacement battalions and were over in September. One of them was killed right off, at Mons. The other was badly knocked up at the same time, but was sewed together again and was back in the line in February. The boche got him last month, at Neuve-Chapelle. They do say that the shell shortage at Neuve-Chapelle amounted to a scandal," said Teresa, and fell silent.

Lucy said, now with open distress: "But surely, Teresa — surely she did n't — "

"Imply that I'm responsible for killing her sons?" supplied

the girl quietly — "and other mother's sons to come? Oh, no, she's quite too kind for that. Still, the implications are pretty plain. It's a fact — their artillery can't protect their infantry — and that's all. . . . Strange, how things work out. In wanting to have nothing to do with bloodshed, I incur a direct responsibility for bloodshed."

The president of Whitestone stood looking at the floor, her young face colorless and sad. Lucy's eyes stung under a mist of tears.

"Oh, it's there. I have a responsibility so big, don't you see," said the pacifist, but hardly as if speaking to Lucy, "that by the side of it any little hostility against me personally is simply beneath all notice. . . . Good-bye, Lucy dear! Let's meet again soon."

The older woman's heart seemed to twist within her.

"Teresa, Teresa!" broke from her. "It's too much for you! It is n't fair! — it is n't right! *Could n't* you bring yourself to give it up — till this horrible time's over!"

Teresa, who had already started hurriedly toward the house-door, just stopped and turned a little. Lucy never forgot the look on her face then.

"Why, don't you know they'll all see I'm right some day?. . . I'll never give up."

CHAPTER XIII

THE Whitestone Steel Company was in serious straits. Even the stenographers, even the pallid office-boy Elmer, were aware of that, pleasurably enough. The resignations and the quittings, once a topic of exciting possibilities, had become a stale matter now. Louder and ever livelier news seeped and spread through the rooms. The mills at Cohaxie were going to close down at the end of the week; the office would close a week later; Whitestone had been bought by other interests; Miss De-Silver was going out of the steel business. Everybody in the office knew these things; everybody knew the reasons for them too — reasons transcending either the bad conditions in the steel industry or the special odium under which the company struggled. No, as even the dullest clerk could have told you, high finance was the trouble here — high finance most satisfactorily embodied in the person of Johnny Porter himself.

The visit of the financier had, in fact, created a great stir in the office. As Mr. Porter's large and deceptively kind features were almost as familiar as the President's, his presence had, of course, become known immediately; the young tongues were almost as quick in interpreting it: he had come to tell her that she must re-open the shell-plant at once — or be squeezed out of business. How rumors start — especially in an office where gossip is no longer tolerated — and why they are so often and mysteriously correct, Dean Masury, for one, had no idea. That this report was substantially correct he was certain: for it happened that he, and he alone as he believed, had got a first-hand account of the visit from its only eye-witness.

It came from his favorite informant, Miss O'Neill. By chance, Mr. Porter's call had fallen in or near the lunch-hour. Miss

Janney, who seemed to be always gliding in and about, had gone "for a little bite," as she expressed it; and Miss O'Neill, who was making obvious efforts to "please her," and was slowly learning to dispense with both talcum and gems, had been placed "on the buzzer." Thus it fell out that the little guttersnipe actually received the Olympian caller from the doorman and ushered him in to Miss DeSilver's presence. It was a tremendous moment for her; however, a still greater awaited. Miss DeSilver, wishing to verify or exhibit something, had rung the bell; and Miss O'Neill responded, with her heart thumping in her throat, she said, like it would bust. Having returned with the needed papers (by a miracle the file-room produced them almost instantaneously), she was bidden to wait; as Miss DeSilver either forgot her then, or was indifferent to her presence, she had remained an awed observer of what remained of the encounter.

Reappearing about quarter past one, she had come straight to Masury, her cheeks quite pale, her eyes starry with wonder.

The child's interest was such a real thing that the acting office-manager hardly had the heart to enforce his iron rule, the less so as they were in the privacy of Kappus's old office, which he sometimes used now as his own. Besides, not to put too fine a point on it, he was interested.

"You know — he was tryin' to make her do sump'n," said Miss O'Neill eagerly, floundering for words, "an' she never had no idea of doin' it, and, Mr. Masury, it was just like a fight in the theayter! Gee! Johnny Porter that owns half the world, and goes with kings in Europe and his income per annum is ten million dollars I seen in the paper — against one young lady, that ain't hardly much older than me and that everybody's fightin' and all. And she wasn't afraid of him one bit! And Mr. Masury, they was so *pleasant* — so easy-like, I don't know, I can't put it, but all the time they was just smilin' away at each other, and she was laughin' and kiddin' back at him like a young lady passin' a few cracks with a gentleman at a party. Just as *friendly* — and all the time you could see they'd both kill the other one just as lief as not, rather'n not have their way. Ooo! He was tellin' her like that if she did n't leave him have White-stone or whatever it was, I don't know, he was laughin' and sayin' he was going to ruin her, and she was laughin' back at him and sayin', 'You try, and be damned to you.'. . . Ooo! I never seen two great big fine people scrappin' before and the easy way they done it, and just murder behind what they was sayin' all the time — there was minutes when the goose-bumps run right down my back! And then he laughs and waves his hand and gets up and says 'how's your grandfather, I don't see him much these days,' and tells her a funny story about sump'n him and old Mr. DeSilver done once. And she laughs, and says 'come see me sometime, for I'm goin'a be in the steel busi-ness right here,' she says, 'for far ahead as I can see.' And, Mr. Masury, I was so excited, I coulda cried. . . ."

Inevitably the office-manager, who stood listening in hat and coat, about to go out, recalled the woman's claim, in their last talk, that the channels of business were being closed against her because of her opinions; it was conceded that this episode indi-cated support for her claim. As an editorial writer he had often enough attacked the workings of the so-called "system"; and in fact he felt no welcome at all for the powerful, but for him quite extraneous, support of Mr. Porter. Now that parting fling of hers about "far ahead as I can see," had turned his thoughts in another direction. The end of the girl's narrative found him staring at the wall.

The words, no doubt, were mere fighter's bluff; still they con-nected themselves too readily with other matters in his mind. He no longer questioned now, alas, that the woman's position was strong, any more than he sought to evade the fact that his own position, never really strong, was growing weaker. Nothing but false clues had come as yet from his elaborate advertisements, nothing from the voluminous correspondence upon which he and his friend and lawyer, Bill Brockenbrough, had embarked. . . . The dragnet indeed was drawing up Coits, and representatives of Coits, of every description — all of them believing that money was to be left, each insisting that he or she was the very party desired — but of the lost DeSilver or his agent there came no word. Nearly two weeks now he had been pursuing the elusive quest, and he had to confess that he had not advanced an inch. . . .

"Don't repeat to any one what you have just told me," he said to the thrilled stenographer.

She tossed her head.

"No, *sir* — I would n't! I'm 'most like her assistant secretary, it's confidential. I would n't tell nothing to anybody but you. And she's . . . she's — Ooo!"

The girl stared off into the spaces toward the window, with wide blue eyes that saw nothing, and presently said in a stirred, rapt voice:

"She's like what I seen in a book once — 'all fire and ice.' The Woman That —"

"Go to your lunch," said Mr. Masury.

He was satisfied that Miss O'Neill kept her knowledge to herself; nevertheless detailed accounts of the great captain's call were soon flying about. As usual, the common understanding seemed remarkably sound. At any rate, following this incident, the state of Whitestone began to go visibly from bad to worse. The market for the company product had been feeble; it now seemed on the point of drying up altogether. The approaching "boom," scented by Ellison from afar, seemed freighted with no hope here; to the contrary several considerable contracts, counted on to keep the furnaces going, part-time at least, come what might, were abruptly cancelled. Novel difficulties developed. There was trouble in buying raw materials (the company needed "pig" continuously, it seemed); there was trouble in getting cars for shipments; there was mysterious trouble with the workmen at the mill. Despite the strength of the interests controlling the company — i.e., Miss DeSilver — credit became suddenly "bad." There was a matter of arranging a "little line," a mere routine thing; astonishingly, a vice-president of the bank, who called in person, pursed his lips solemnly and was "very sorry."

It was from Ellison that Masury learned most of these happenings; and Ellison's round face was growing longer and longer. The sales-manager and the office-manager were by now on the best of terms, exchanging opinions with great candor, while the one knew nothing of the other's reserve. As Ellison argued it, he and the new man were in much the same box: each of them had a detail of the company's work to do, and as that detail involved no responsibility for policy or management, each could honorably proceed with his duty without regard to private views. But Ellison's situation had its special complex too. He was "as good as a Canadian": he had spent his boyhood in Alberta, his sister had married a Canadian lumberman, his sister's boy — "Fred his name is, but we call him Pete" — had gone over with a Canadian regiment, the Princess Patricia's Own. On the other hand, Ellison felt a strong loyalty to the "old company" and a quaint devotion, as sentimental as Lucy's or Miss O'Neill's, for the new chief.

The affair with the bank had made the good fellow indignant. It seemed that the banker, Mr. Simonton — after much smooth talk about the troubled times — had not failed to drop the hint in passing that Whitestone seemed scarcely as sound a risk as formerly, owing to the recent loss of large profits, and uncertainties due to the change of management and dismissal of that fine steel man, Mr. Ball.

"How're you going to fight that kind of thing, Masury? How?" he asked angrily, pacing up and down Kappus's little office. "God damn him, what's Johnny Porter got to do with Whitestone! The power some men got in this country, it makes my blood boil just to think about it!"

Masury left him to worry it out for himself. He had no concern with the general difficulties of "my enterprise"; and in fact he had troubles enough of his own. He had not seen Miss De-Silver since the day when he had so narrowly avoided calling her a liar; she seemed to spend half her time, at least, at Cohaxie. The pacific vacancy left him unsatisfied, but he could force an interview when it suited him, and expected to do just that: what else in truth, was he here for? Meantime, he had accepted the responsibilities of his promotion, within the limits he had indicated: he undertook to keep a working force together; he hired and fired. He had replaced with five new employees the eleven who had left the company following the newspaper explosion; by the end of the second week, he had taken in three more to offset still further quittings. The prospect of becoming a regular customer of Haversands, the employment agency, and of starting each Monday morning with new help to break in, was displeasing to the efficient mind; the suggestions of ambushed hostility, which survived in hardly tangible signs, and which tended to operate against his plans no less than against Teresa DeSilver's, were more deeply irritating. Still, he had told the lady that he would not do detective work for her; and so he would n't. What "arrangements" of her own she was making or thought she was making, he could not imagine. The new purchasing agent, Mr. Hocking, had appeared last week, bringing with him his own "assistant," a pimply youth named Stumpf; it was conceivable that Stumpf, who seemed to find very little to do, might be an "investigator," more or less disguised. However, nothing developed there, one way or the other.

The outward routine, at any rate, had begun to run smoothly enough. His constant attention to all and sundry parts of the little machine was producing its logical results, despite extrinsic obstacles. In the matter of discipline, to overcome quickly the previous laxness, he had become a martinet, and an alert one. If a girl foregathered with a friend or two in cloakroom or corridor, if she broke any of the rules which he promulgated and posted from time to time, he was apt to know of it, and trouble was sure to follow. The summary dismissal of two male clerks who were found whiling away the time at the dusky golf-game, and his physical ejection of one of them who undertook to be impudent, had markedly wholesome effects. There came a day when, happening to glance round the general room, the organizer was himself suddenly struck, not without definite satisfaction, with the competence and orderliness of his creation.

And that day, within an hour, something happened, or rather two things happened surprisingly together, which showed that orderliness was the very last thing he had effected: that in fact he was busily building upon the sand, and the developing organization — his organization — was undermined to its foundation.

The incidents fell out of a clear sky. The day was Friday, at the end of his third week. As it chanced, the day had started inauspiciously for Masury with a telephone call, at breakfast-time, from Walter E. Ball. The late president telephoned frequently in this period, demanding news of Masury's progress — an intrusion the more annoying in that there was never any progress to report — but this time he was the bearer of tidings. Ball had just learned, how he did not state, that Miss DeSilver herself was taking steps to call the "protest" meeting, not waiting for the minority petition; moreover, she was going to call it for the earliest date possible — about the middle of next month. The discovery was plainly upsetting to the ousted executive; he had shouted over the wire that if he, Masury, expected to do anything, he had better not let the grass grow under his feet another day. How the grass grew in Indo-China these days, Ball did not mention. Masury, too, felt that the news was ominous. What possible reason, in fact, could the woman have for taking the step which her opponents had reserved to take against her, except that she knew she could control the special meeting, now, and wished to get the matter disposed of and the means estopped? Another meeting could not be petitioned within a year. He remembered that faint betrayal of amusement, when he had told her that Brockenbrough's advertisment was his own, and again he had the disagreeable sensations of one lost in the dark. . . .

He arrived at the office considerably out of humor, though unaware of that fact. By now, perhaps, as Lucy Flanner had vaguely surmised, a certain strain involved in his position and private struggle was beginning to tell on him. Work immediately engulfed him. From the printer presently came a bale of proofs of the new blanks and forms, upon which he had spent no little thought. Having hastily run through the set of sheets, he took the bundle to Ellison, according to agreement; for the sales-manager had shown a lively interest in this phase of the work from the beginning. It was then about ten-thirty, the heart of the morning. Somewhat to his surprise, he found the "peppy" Ellison sitting entirely unoccupied, staring out the window. He rose at the sight of Masury and solemnly shut the door on Miss Alice and the rest.

Masury was in no mood to listen to mushy talk about the chief, whom Ellison, mooning like a gaby, had lately referred to as "that little woman." However, the sales-manager's intentions this time proved different. Out of the floundering talk he began about his "position" and what he called "the dictates of my conscience," the fact emerged that Ellison had made up his mind to resign.

Masury, for once, was taken altogether by surprise. Ellison's vacillations, indeed, had been limpidly clear. He could rebound manfully enough from Ball's broadside attack, or the more sinister manifestations of "pressure"; the matter of his personal position, with a pacifist company, was a more pervasive and recurring difficulty. He was astonishingly well-informed about the progress of events on the Western Front; to this day he maintained an elaborate war-map, with pins. Steeped in the writings of the military experts, he caught dark meanings between the lines of the barrenest communiqués; hanging on a strap in the subway, mornings, he read and read again of the overwhelming force of the German bombardments; and then, arriving at his office, he was — without doubt — reached and affected by that subterranean buzzing which the acting-manager knew to be going on, though, for some reason, it never came to his ears.

That Ellison had had his struggle Masury knew well; however, there had been the best reasons for believing that the good fellow's loyalty, his interest and his native pugnacity, had finally overcome his qualms. . . .

"Seen the papers to-day — the big battle that's bust loose at Ypres?" said the sales-manager unhappily, pacing about. "Read about the poison gas those swine are using, damned stuff that eats the lungs right out of your body? Special dispatch in 'The Republic,' had a line saying that a Canadian division was called in to patch up that line, all punched full of holes — and the Germans driving through hell-for-leather for Dunkirk and Calais. . . . I don't doubt for a minute that as I stand here smoking this cigar in this comfortable office, that boy of mine is right in the middle of *that*. That's my sister's boy I'm speaking of, Fred, but we call him Pete — always have. . . . Well, you can see my angle. I feel as if I ought to be *helping* that boy — and, my God, I feel all the time as if I was fighting against him!"

He let the cigar fall nervelessly from his hand. In a low voice that had positively a tragic ring, he said:

"I've got to go, Masury. Got to go. A man's got to follow the dictates of his conscience."

Masury, standing with an elbow on his colleague's desk, was eyeing him without favor. Sincerely as he wished misfortune to Miss Teresa DeSilver, it was clear now that there were kinds of misfortune he did not wish her, and this, in fine, was one of them. His sense of resistance to the wobbly pronouncement was strong and instant. To see others give the woman "pin-pricks," as she had put it, had never interested him; it was, of course, desirable to keep Ellison for her successor — even though no one could take oath to that eventuation now; and the serious crippling of his organization, just as he had got it to functioning passably, was hardly a prospect to be viewed with patience. Beyond all this, the fellow's indecision came on him as an exasperating affront to consistency and fair reason.

"On Tuesday," he said dryly, "you told me that for you to leave the company while it was being hammered below the belt would be no better than cowardly desertion. This is Friday. I see you've changed your shirt."

Color came into that candid and woe-begone countenance.

"No, I haven't, old man! I hate that more'n I can possibly say — leaving the company and leaving *her* — to fight all this alone. No — it isn't me, it's the situation that's changed. Fact is — well, I guess I've kind of exaggerated the importance of my staying or going."

"How?"

"Well," said Ellison, with rather a wry laugh, "I don't guess I'm as necessary to the chief as I thought I was. Seems she don't like me any too well. I've heard a few things. For all I know, she'd as soon see me go as not."

That took the matter deeper at once. From whom came this "information"?

"I don't know what you've heard, and don't care. You know

as well as I do that you're necessary to the company, and unless your idea is that the president needs a guardian, you know she knows it too."

"Think so? Well, that's what I'd always thought up to . . . Well, I don't know," said Ellison. But he brightened visibly.

Masury tapping out a cigarette against the desk-side, gave him a searching stare.

"What's up? We've talked of this often enough. I thought you'd satisfied yourself that shell-making was n't the steel business — that it was as if the company had never taken up the side-line at all. Suppose you'd been a grocer or a doctor? — would your conscience dictate to you then that you ought to be helping that boy, Fred, Pete, whatever his name is?"

But Ellison's little silver lining had soon clouded over.

"It is n't that. If it stopped there, no," he said hesitantly. "But — I guess it don't. If the company's skirts are n't as clear as I hoped they were — well, you can see I'd have to take a different angle."

So that was it.

"You're saying, then, that you think she's out to help Germany?"

"Well — don't you?"

"No."

The two men measured each other. On the whole, the sales-manager looked as firm in his position as the office-manager.

"I did think that at the start," said Masury firmly. "I now don't believe it's true. However, I've put myself in position to know positively before long."

Instead of noting that, which might have been important, Ellison flared out: "You speak as if it was a crime! As for that, why should n't she, if she sees it that way? This country is n't at war! — "

"No reason at all. But I'm speaking of facts, not . . . Oh, I know, I know!" he said impatiently, as Ellison sought to launch on a defensive harangue. "You don't wish to seem to reflect on the president. That's agreed — you don't wish to. But, Lord, how you're doing it! She made a public statement, solemnly declaring that her only motive was her pacifism. You read that statement — but have decided that she was lying."

Ellison's clear skin again turned a little pink. He floundered unhappily: "No! — lying — no, certainly not. That was true too. But — oh, damn it, Masury, this is *war*. You can't go around telling your plans to everybody. You've *got* to have *some* secrets!"

The office-manager's eye upon him, oddly, perhaps, resembled that of a prosecutor, grilling a witness of doubtful intelligence or veracity. As if in shame at having had to use so feeble an argument, Ellison flung out:

"Well, you know I'd never have reached this position unless I just had to! I may have had my thoughts and all, the same as Tillinghast and the rest of 'em. But you can bet I'd never desert this old company that I love — and her, though I don't know that she minds so much — unless, well, by God, unless I *had to!*"

"I suppose I'm right in understanding that you've just heard something concrete — to the effect that Miss DeSilver has plans for selling material to Germany?"

Ellison nodded, gloomy and a little defiant. "And you know I never would have believed it, if I had n't got it — well, pretty straight."

Well, that was two things that Ellison had got, presumably inside the office. In the first place, the chief did not reciprocate his admiration; in the second, she was working against Fred, or Pete.

"Does n't it strike you as strange that she could have plans like that without you, her sales-manager, knowing anything about them?"

"Not necessarily — she could work direct from the mill. Keeley's an Irishman incidentally — he hates England. Or she might work through another company, for all I know. She's got connections everywhere."

"I see. And deliveries?"

"Oh, hell, the underground through Switzerland and Holland's as wide open as Hudson River."

"No doubt. But you don't get to Switzerland or Holland till the British navy have frisked you pretty well for contraband."

He felt like saying: "You poor gull. You've read spy-stuff till you're seeing things at night."

Ellison perhaps interpreted his regard. He burst out unhappily:

"I don't like to argue this way, and I'm not trying to influence you in any way, old man. Last thing I want. I'm just explaining my position, that's all — different from yours. You're going to leave in a couple of weeks, anyway. But every fellow's got to follow the — "

"You don't influence me a hair's breadth. . . . I gather you don't want to tell me where you got your stuff?"

Ellison's eyes fell.

"I would, of course — if I could. But — I'm not at liberty to. Confidential. In fact I'd have never been told at all, except that the — the party thought I knew already."

Masury laughed.

"Yes, indeed! I've noticed that people who go about repeating dangerous gossip are usually pretty careful to prevent their responsibilities from being pinned on them."

He tossed the bale of proofs down on the desk with a thump.

"As I told you just now, I've taken steps to learn the *facts*. The report will be ready in a few days — if I were you, I'd wait. It's devilish easy these days for people who believe everything they hear to get off on the *wrong foot!*"

Ellison began, uncertainly: "You've taken steps? . . . Well, I — "

"Look over those just as quickly as you can — I'm in a hurry."

He stalked out disgusted and angry.

The office-manager's duties awaited him, but he did not at once return to his duties. In the public hall, outside his precincts, he walked up and down, contending with himself. Often enough he had thought of those two characteristic and foolish sayings of the woman, "The situation is in my hand — I will make my own arrangements"; now he remembered them only with a certain indignation, and no longer with any sort of satisfaction. He was of two minds to go straight to her now and say: "Look here, either make those arrangements of yours immediately, or my work here can't go on." However, he overcame that somewhat inviting impulse.

He walked the hall for five minutes, and decided to do nothing at all. Ellison was not personnel; he, the organizer, had no responsibility for him. Let the cocksure girl deal with her dissolving "situation" for herself. He would put the whole matter from his mind. . . .

By a considerable act of the will, he put the matter from his mind. He had hardly succeeded in doing so before it bobbed up again, in the most definite form imaginable.

In the basket on his desk, he found his elaborate memorandum on the rearrangement of offices, with sketch-maps drawn to scale; submitted yesterday, the papers came back now with the stereotyped "Approved, T. DeS." He telephoned the outfitters, and arranged to have the workmen in on Saturday afternoon and Sunday, outside of office-hours. Pale Elmer laid before him the first collection of outgoing mail, and he took it up, thinking of the carpenters. His interest in the correspondence was purely routine; he inspected it for form only and sent it on for visé and signature. Running hurriedly through the batch, he came upon a series of letters, dictated by the new correspondence-clerk, which were written in blithe disregard of his prescribed "style." Having checked the stenographer's initials by his list, he called into the spaces of the well-filled room:

"Miss Kelsey!"

A tall, tow-headed girl, at a desk down the room, raised her head from her typewriter. He beckoned to her absently, and she rose with no alacrity, and advanced.

The matter was the merest detail. Miss Kelsey was one of the new girls who had come in with Monday morning's awkward squad. While there was little excuse for her carelessness, such things, of course, had to be expected under the upset conditions.

"You initial A.K., Miss Kelsey?"

"Yes."

"You have n't happened to mislay your rules and style-sheet?"

"No. Why? — what's the trouble?"

He glanced at her contentious face, which had turned a brick-red in color, with some surprise.

"The office style calls for an inch-and-a-half margin at the left, one inch bottom, one inch right. You've done these boxed — single-spaced, margins nearly half the page."

Miss Kelsey muttered something that sounded like, "Well, what of it?" Aloud, she said, "I guess I must have forgot, that's all."

"In that case, get out your rules and study them carefully. That helps to refresh the memory. Here, take these. They can't go out like this."

The girl, who had turned to go in the middle of his remarks, turned back, flushed and scowling. Having unwillingly received the condemned letters, she stood a second irresolute, and then snapped out, with curious heat:

"If my work don't suit, I guess I'd better quit to-morrow — that's Saturday."

At these words a number of eyes from neighboring desks became fastened on the small tableau.

"All right," said the manager indifferently. "Now do those letters."

As if urged on by her dramatic sense, now that she knew she was watched, the tow-headed girl flared out:

"I'd decided to quit anyway! I don't want a place like this!"

"Oh, you'd decided to quit anyway," said he eyeing her, and his attention then was entirely captured. "And why don't you want the place, Miss Kelsey?"

"'Cause I don't want to work for a firm that makes its money tryin' to drown innocent American women and children, that's why!"

Had she slapped the manager's face, he would hardly have been more thoroughly aroused. A fine organization, indeed, was this he was building up, rotted through with a hidden poison....

"Oh, that's your reason, is it?" he said in a changed voice, louder. "And why do you think this company is trying to drown innocent women and children?"

"I don't think it. I know. How I know is my business, I guess. And I don't want to work for a woman like her, either. I'm not used to working for women that ain't nice."

"Get your hat and coat, Miss Kelsey. I'll tell the cashier to give you your money."

The girl stood staring at him, angry and confused.

"Come, don't you speak English? You're fired. Ten minutes to be out of the office."

Miss Kelsey, her thin breast heaving, threw the letters he had just returned to her on the floor and stamped on them.

"I said it first!" she shouted. "I'm quitting — because I won't work for a lot of dirty, sneaking Germans!"

"You shut your lying mouth," said a high voice far down the room, and Miss O'Neill rose noisily from her typewriter, her handsome face quite white.

The large room was in commotion. Inquiring faces appeared in the file-room door, others in the doors to the corridor. There was the murmur of voices. Masury, having rapped sharply on his desk, raised a long arm and pointed it at Miss O'Neill; the forefinger, alone moving, indicated a direction.

"You sit down."

The girl sat, but unwillingly; her blue eyes looked afire. In the same moment, the rebel Kelsey, seeming taken aback by the discovery that public opinion was not completely with her, glared around, said, "Shut up yourself," and flounced away toward the cloakroom.

Masury was standing. There was hardly need of his upraised hand. Every eye was fixed upon him; the room had become intensely quiet.

Without pause or premeditation, the temporary office-manager addressed his personnel with incensed words:

"I have just discharged that young woman, Miss Kelsey, for open disloyalty to the Whitestone Steel Company. She repeated, in your hearing, false stories — slanders — about the company. I take this occasion to tell you all that such conduct will not be tolerated. Do not listen to, and do not repeat, these silly and malicious stories. I want to remind you that libel is not a joking matter. It is a criminal offence. If I hear of any one else repeating such stories, that person will be lucky if he or she does n't leave the building on the arm of a policeman. I give you fair warning. . . ."

He paused, involuntarily. His gaze, moving slowly as he talked, rested by chance upon the face of the president's secretary, Miss Janney. In the file-room on some errand, she had come to the door with the others, and now stood listening respectfully, her slant eyes downcast. Miss Janney's air and bearing were, as ever, all that an employee's should be; she was the model secretary; and of course it was only the trick of tint and shape that gave her face, permanently, that mysterious and mocking air.

Looking at that suddenly seen face, Dean Masury might have felt a fleeting awkwardness: the secretary would tell the mistress that he had done, in effect, what he had vowed he would never do. No such thought touched him. In fact, his flashing conception was as different as possible. With incredible swiftness, in a second, in a wink, little fragments from memory had begun to fall into place, forming the outlines of a strange pattern.

But was it conceivable?

"I warn you all who listen to me," said the manager, in a resounding voice — "for the first and last time. *Watch your step.*"

He sat down fascinated by the sensational quality of his thoughts. And then for some moments, while the office settled back into its normal routine, he did nothing but turn and turn again, under eyes that saw nothing, the sheets of the unsigned letters before him.

Thereafter, he became exceedingly busy. He did not stay now to debate whether spy-catching was outside his technique; his temper had swallowed up all those resistances. When Miss Kelsey reappeared for her departure, her eyes rather red, the office-manager escorted her to the cashier, speaking kindly the while; next he went with her into the hall. Returning, he called Miss O'Neill, presumably for dictation. For the sake of quiet or for other reasons, that session was held in the Kappus cubicle; it lasted a long time. Afterwards, Mr. Masury returned to his own desk, where the collected mail had waited all this while. It was the custom for the office-boy Elmer to carry in the letters to Miss Janney, but on this occasion Mr. Masury himself was seen heading toward the secretary's office with the large wire-basket under his arm. He was not seen again in the general room till long after lunch-time.

CHAPTER XIV

THE sound of the buzzer brought the conversation to a standstill. In the model secretary's little office, bright with April sunshine, there was a second of dead silence. Rather unexpectedly, she made no move toward answering her familiar summons. Mr. Masury, who was as cool as if nothing had happened, and did n't even glance toward her, turned, nodded and spoke:

"Answer that."

Miss O'Neill, who was the recipient of the nod, and the reverse of cool, said with a little gasp: "Yes, sir — But I gotta get my book —"

"You won't need a book. However — take that one."

As the girl seized Miss Janney's book almost from under Miss Janney's elbow, the manager continued in his easy and rapid way:

"Take her orders. When she asks why you come, say that I assigned you to do her work. Perhaps it will stop there — for the moment. If she asks why again — don't say anything more, but refer her to me."

The girl nodded up and down, breathing loudly, too full for utterance, and turned feverishly away.

There were the little noises of the opening door, then the little click as it automatically shut again. After that there was silence.

On the other side of the thick door, there was quiet too.

The young president of the company, who had many visitors, was now alone. A moment earlier she had nodded adieu to a committee of women, whom Janney herself had ushered in almost half an hour earlier; now came the period reserved for her executive duties, and already she was deep in them. At her desk by the windows, through which for the brief hour a golden light streamed, Miss DeSilver sat conning a long typewritten sheet full of figures, which might have been a mill report, and which she, evidently, found completely engrossing. Papers surrounded her.

After a space, becoming aware that her call was answered, she looked up briskly, ready to function, no doubt. Then she paused, faintly surprised.

"Well, Florence?" said the voice that Miss O'Neill could never hear without a thrill. "And what brings you here?"

The stenographer, having kept a most respectful distance, was standing rigidly at attention, wide eyes staring out of a face that looked unprecedentedly colorless. She answered in a voice that seemed to tremble a little:

"Mr. Masury he 'signed me to come and do your work, ma'am — Miss DeSilver."

The president's gaze was not unkind.

"He did, did he? And why? Miss Janney out again, I suppose?"

"No'm. She's — in there, Miss DeSilver."

"Well, why did n't she come, then? Teeth again? Busy? What is it?"

"N-no'm — it is n't her teeth, Miss DeSilver. I — and she is n't busy, ma'am."

"Well, great Scott! Can't I have my own secretary when I ring for her?"

Miss O'Neill swallowed, but struggled to hold on to her conception of the secretarial manner.

"Mr. Masury said, if you asked me about it, I was n't to say nothing, but was to refer you to him, Miss DeSilver."

A faint frown appeared on the marble forehead which had revealed to the present observer the larger possibilities of the eyebrow.

"All right — ask Mr. Masury to come in. Let's get the point clear while we're on it."

"Yes, Miss DeSilver."

"Wait one moment."

The girl, halting, stood motionless under that exalted scrutiny, large-eyed, unconscious arms clasping the note-book to her bosom. The pose, the childlike gaze, were not devoid of grace.

"You look much better with the paint and powder off, Florence, and that simple blouse is becoming to you too. Now, why don't you pull back most of the hair off your face, and stop using that wash on it? I think those artificial things just cover up what you really are — a very nice-looking girl."

Miss O'Neill said, with another gulp: "I will, Miss DeSilver — just like you say."

"Good. Send Mr. Masury."

The stenographer went out hurriedly, feeling rather trembly. She was shaken with a fierce happiness. Oh, what a day was this!

In the room adjoining, where all had happened so swiftly and dramatically, she found the scene as she had left it. Mr. Masury sat on the small table, swinging his long legs and nonchalantly smoking a cigarette. He was talking as she entered, and having calmly finished his sentence, barely turned his head.

She said in a voice which she strove to make easy too:

"She wants to see you right away, Mr. Masury."

Mr. Masury nodded, rose, dropped his cigarette on Miss Janney's immaculate floor, and stepped on it. Standing, he eyed Miss Janney herself, who, just a little while before, had sat down abruptly in the springback chair by her typewriter. No stretch of the imagination could suggest, however, that the refined secretary showed signs of breaking up; rather, beyond the temporary disadvantage at which she found herself, she seemed keyed to the last notch of resistance. Sitting there in her familiar place, the figure of a persecuted woman, she looked as hard and cold as ice.

It seemed a further proof of the remarkable creature's confidence that, at this critical juncture, she made no effort to assert herself.

"Sit here," said the manager to Miss O'Neill. "If the buzzer rings, you're to answer it. Don't speak to Miss Janney — don't answer her if she speaks to you. If she attempts to leave — or to do anything you think she should n't do — open that door and come to me at once."

"Yes, sir."

Miss O'Neill flung upon the silent secretary a young look devoid of all mercy. As Mr. Masury went by her toward the door, her attitude changed instantly. Clutching his arm in her passion, hardly troubling to lower her voice — and indeed after the words that had passed a little earlier, a nice courtesy would have seemed superfluous now — she said imploringly:

"Mr. Masury! — *don't let her keep her!*"

"Don't worry, my child." Mr. Masury smiled, but the look on his face made her heart jump a little.

On that the thick door opened once more, and his back went through and vanished. The patent-shutter clicked again.

Dean Masury passed into the executive chamber, where he had not set foot in these two weeks. He found the bare room, though sunny now, almost as cheerless to the eye as before; its occupant, his chosen enemy, in her wonted place, looked as quiet as her room.

This time, however, she was frankly awaiting him; he had hardly come into view when she said with cool briskness, distinctly in the presidential note and without preamble:

"What's the difficulty about Janney?"

The complicated expert, coming forward, did not answer immediately.

Had he had this announcement to make a fortnight earlier, he would have been conscious chiefly of a triumphant hostility. It was otherwise now. Time, indeed, and the bitter flavor of his unsuccess, had but deepened and solidified his fundamental opposition; but this matter was beneath their conflict. Perhaps the strongest feeling in him at this moment, beyond the mere sensations of the crisis, was only his will to carry through now what he had so unexpectedly begun.

In front of her desk, looking down at the expectant pince-nez through which came intimations of impatience at his tardiness in replying, Masury said slowly:

"You see, Miss Janney's no longer in the employ of the company."

"She is what?"

"She's dismissed from the services of the company. I," said he, "have just dismissed her, for cause."

Miss Teresa DeSilver stared up at him like one who put no credence in her ears. At the end of five seconds of complete silence, she emitted an annoyed laugh, as the strong greet the evidences of unbelievable stupidity or effrontery.

"Oh, no, you have n't, Masury," said she positively, flatly, and yet reasonably too. "For one thing, you have n't the authority, you know — you could n't if you wanted to. For another, I would n't let you if you could. But surely if this is some pleasantry? — surely my —"

"No, there's very little pleasantry about it, I'm afraid," he answered with a sort of hard composure, "and the fact is, if you'll pardon me, I have the authority. You'll not have forgotten the special request you made of me, regarding the disaffection —"

"I remember a request, certainly. I also remember withdrawing that request. But what's that —"

"True you withdrew it — on the understanding that you

would deal with the mess yourself. That was two weeks ago. You've failed —"

"Enough! I'm asking permission to see my secretary. You're scarcely trying to suggest that Miss Janney has succumbed to the virus?"

"You understate the case. I'm afraid you must adjust your mind to the thought that Miss Janney is herself the virus."

"I don't think I hear you aright."

"I'm saying that your precious secretary is the origin and source, the deliberate source, of most of the trouble I've been having with the personnel."

After one second's pause to let that thought sink in, he supplied it firmly with a background:

"You remember you felt, when I first brought the matter to your attention, that the disaffection here lacked the spontaneous touch."

Miss DeSilver came slowly to her feet. The movement was unconscious; it was as if a spring hoisted her by an unseen device. Her face had lost a little color. Her gaze upon the informant, the reluctant spy-catcher, was hard; that look could scarcely have been called complimentary; and yet he saw that, incredible though his allegation must have been to her, her mind had not instantly rejected it. At least, though he had so nearly called her a liar in their last encounter, she did not seize the opportunity to retort in kind.

"You appreciate the seriousness of what you are saying?"

"The situation is serious, you see. Otherwise, naturally I should not be here."

"And that under the circumstances it seems to come oddly from you?"

"I really don't care how it seems to come from me. The fact is, the conditions existing in this office make it impossible for me to do my work. You undertook —"

"Where is Miss Janney now?"

He gestured slightly with his head.

"She's insisted on laying her case before you. It's just possible that she's reconsidering now, since it occurred to me to mention the police. While I know nothing of her past, I rather suspect she has encountered the machinery of justice before to-day. ... However, she's safe — I've got her under guard."

At that, the young woman's look, which had passed beyond astonishment, visibly stiffened; the lengths to which the clerk had gone with her secretary staggered her, no doubt. She said coldly, even sternly:

"You are here charging that Miss Janney has spread through the office stories calculated to damage my interests?"

"Yes, I charge that."

"Your evidence?"

"It is cumulative. To lay it before you fully, as I mean to do, involves —"

"The high point of your evidence, then?"

Chafed by the grilling, cold and hard too, he threw out: "Are you aware that it's believed in the office that you are planning to make parts for German submarines — or, as it's popularly put, that Whitestone's business is to help drown innocent women and children?"

"That's one of the least things said about me, I've no doubt. Well?"

"The tale originated in this office, I'm certain — I've never heard a hint of it elsewhere. Half an hour ago Miss Janney herself confided it to me, under interesting circumstances, and with some original touches of her own. However, luckily, the case does n't rest there. The fact is, she admitted to me, almost in so many words, that she wanted to break up the company — though, to be sure, as her position is delicate, she assigns herself the most considerate, and indeed noble, motives."

"What motives?"

"She thinks you'd be so much happier if you were out of it," said Masury dryly.

There was a slight pause.

"I don't follow that."

"She says that your situation here has grown impossible, that the strain of the constant struggle and misjudgment and criticism is wearing on you — breaking down your health, as she put it, I believe. She thinks that the sooner you give up this business, unsuited to a lady, as she said, the better off you'll be — especially," said Masury, in a voice through which a certain pointedness somehow obtruded, "as she thinks that, with the powerful opposition against you, you're sure to be beaten in the end anyway. . . . Accordingly it occurred to her, if I follow the jesuitical reasoning correctly, that to help break up the office, while indeed it might give you pain for the moment —"

"I see," she broke in, crisply. "One of those blessings in disguise, as it were."

There had flitted over the cool, hostile face, confronting him, a look which seemed unmistakably touched with relief. . . . Was it not possible that she recalled a day when Janney had said to her, too, in a perfectly human and trustworthy manner: "If we could only give up this terrible fight!" It was, then, but some extraordinary misunderstanding, now about to be adequately resolved. . . .

"Well, women argue in strange ways at times," said Miss De-Silver, with a distinctly ironical inflection. "Many sincerely believe that the end justifies the means. But we must hear Janney set out her theories for herself."

She picked up a pencil from her desk, threw it down again, and went on in her characteristic way, mistress of herself and the strange crisis too:

"This whole situation is considerably muddled from my point

of view, Masury, I confess. You won't expect me to accept at once all your own conclusions, however natural and honest — and I am sure they are both." She paused, as if somewhat at a loss how to make her meanings politely clear, and went on with some evidences of restraint: "The feminine motives you speak of, this notion that it would be a blessing for me to have to shut up shop — all that seems to indicate a confusion which I don't connect with anything at all in my knowledge of Miss Janney, and which I don't pretend to account for. It's the more puzzling in that she has n't the remotest interest in the issues involved here, or any knowledge of them. It is n't that she does n't sympathize with my views, which I should n't object to at all; the point is that she has no views. . . . However, if the plunge into this atmosphere has been too much for her, and the circumstances have got her badly mixed without my knowledge — why, obviously, she must be straightened out at once. I'll have her in now, and we'll thrash it out in your presence."

"Oh, no, you must n't do anything of the sort," said Dean Masury.

The looks of the two remet. The young woman's hand, already on the buzzer, remained there; but she did not ring. Her voice came tinged with a deeper irony:

"I must n't?"

"Not if you care anything about being just to your other employees who have *not* deceived you — and who are at the mercy of your sense of cöoperation and fair play."

His manner had the quiet certitude which convinces beyond heat; his gaze was firmer than her own. Her desire to compromise, standing by her secretary, while not completely repudiating her suddenly zealous office-manager, was of course natural and human, and had been expected. Still, it was clear to him that there could be no compromise here.

"If you've made up your mind to whitewash her regardless,"

said he steadily, "do say so plainly, for that will save a lot of trouble. On the other hand, if you're interested in getting at the truth, don't give her, unprepared, the immense and unfair advantage that comes to her through the fact that you like and trust her. I tell you, she's a clever and dangerous woman, who's relying on just that knowledge to go on pulling the wool over your eyes and hoodwink you into ignoring what she mistakenly let drop to me."

Miss DeSilver's face betrayed that his positiveness, and perhaps the force of his argument too, were impressing her. However, her distaste, and mere incredulity, were also strong; she answered with a sort of stoniness:

"You hardly ask that I shall condemn my secretary unheard, on your belief of her guilt?"

"No; I ask only that I, having made a charge, shall be allowed an opportunity to substantiate it. I'm asking only that reasonable degree of support from the head of the office which an organizer, officially, has the right to expect. As for thrashing it out on your present information — I think you'd do better to thrash it out with Ellison, or even Miss O'Neill, than with Miss Janney."

"Ellison?"

"I don't consider it confidential. In fact, I imagine he'd prefer to have some one else tell you. Ellison's decided to offer you his resignation this week. He's taking this step, I understand, because of confidential information he's just got about your supposed private plans. If you still have any doubt as to where that 'information' came from, I think Ellison should be invited to tell you for himself."

Miss DeSilver, who stood motionless, had been regarding him with her peculiar grave fixity. Now it was as if, for the first time, a doubt of Janney, inconceivable yet real, slid into her mind. Her look indefinably changed. She made a slight movement

worker. It also convinced me of the need of having a chat with Miss Janney, for myself. So I went in there, an hour ago, with a basket of letters, and let a conversation spring up casually, as it appeared.

"My problem was to make the woman betray herself out of her own mouth. It proved easier than I had ventured to hope."

The measured words fell pithily into the still room. The president, a quiet auditor now, looked at her desk-top, hardly moving. The temporary clerk sat down suddenly on the chair-arm — exactly where he had sat that other day, when she had asked him if his opposition was chiefly personal. . . .

"I'd posted the girl O'Neill outside the door, to be called if needed: as it happened I did n't call her till the case was proved. It's regrettable that I can produce no witness for the conversation that followed, but the presence of anybody else would, of course, have made the thing hopeless. As it was, I had an excellent opening, in the little scene she'd just witnessed. I spoke of it with suitable embarrassment. Growing franker as we chatted, I confessed to her that my position here grew more and more awkward: on the one hand, it was my official duty to weed out disloyalty to the company, on the other, I myself, in my personal capacity, was in opposition to the company policy. She followed me easily. I had rather supposed that my — my views would come as a surprise to her, but her manner convinced me that she had understood them all along — how I don't undertake to say. What surprised her was what she had just heard me say to the personnel. Now, as I prattled along, she suddenly saw, as I'd intended, that I'd presented her with an ideal approach — to me, the acting-manager of the office. It never crossed her mind, you see, that I might already have told you of my views; no, I'd stupidly betrayed a guilty secret, and she had me covered thenceforward. Feeling perfectly secure, then, but looking only concerned and upset, she began to show her hand in the most gratifying manner. As if the words were dragged from her by a tyrannical sense of justice, she told me that my splendid principles did me the greatest honor. I had indicated a tyrannical sense, too, you see, that of duty, impelling me to go instantly to you and tell you what was afoot in the office. It was, of course, the last thing that she wished. Opening bit by bit, like a dark flower, she applauded my intentions as, if anything, carrying magnanimity too far. Under a little pressure, she obligingly produced some remarks you had made about me, behind my back, as she said. That touch was particularly interesting, since Ellison —"

The young president glanced up again, and again he paused. He saw that those masked eyes which had often annoyed him by their studied blankness, were unmistakably disturbed.

"Remarks? — I don't understand. What were the remarks? Perhaps we might check up there."

Dean Masury bowed, not without a distant enjoyment.

"I believe the first thing she cited, chronologically, goes back to the Sunday I called on you, to consider taking this position. She informed me that in the afternoon, when you and she were going over the day's appointment-list and came to my name, you laughed and said to her, 'Janney, did you ever see such an absurd young man in your life?' Then — let's see. She said — that — "

The speaker's voice lost momentum and ceased. Upon the lily cheek of the celebrated Miss DeSilver, beyond mistaking, a faint pink rose and spread. The two adversaries contemplated each other through a moment of silence; and an odd moment it was too.

"I'm extremely sorry," she spoke up in a forthright way, which yet betrayed a distinct confusion, "but — I'm afraid I shall have to support my secretary there. I believe I did make some — hasty — remark of the sort, though naturally it was never meant to be repeated."

The acting-manager sat briefly nonplussed. The unexpected turn was indeed as gauche in its trivial way, as graceless and impossible, as could well have been imagined. And yet, in some way, the girlish color and the unflinching gaze with which she met it came nearer to appealing to him than anything about this woman had ever come before. In the sharing of this human awkwardness, in her young embarrassment which he felt to be quite superfluous, his dislike seemed momentarily to recede.

"It was merely," she added firmly, "one of those unthinking and really jesting speeches which — literally have no significance whatever."

Masury laughed abruptly.

"Really, I beg your pardon. May I say that it was n't, of course, the sentiment that roused my doubt, but only the occasion, perhaps? — the confidence to the secretary? But I won't press further on that line — if you'll just be good enough to ask yourself what Miss Janney's motive could have been in repeating the speech to me?"

Having emphasized that point by a slight pause, he proceeded on his way:

"At any rate, her conversation interested me because I thought it shed some light upon her changing methods. But — possibly I'm mistaken there, and you have spoken disparagingly of Ellison too? He —"

"Of Ellison? Naturally not."

That made him smile a little, too.

"Well, he's picked up the idea somewhere, very recently, that you don't think as much of him as he thought you did, and it's hurt his feelings considerably. I'm certain that's played its part in his decision to leave. Anyway, I soon understood that Miss Janney was spoon-feeding me with bright thoughts which came to this: if I did n't like my situation, why under the sun did n't I do what everybody else was doing — resign? She admitted that she knew of Ellison's intentions, and took the moment to say, like one ready to weep, that it was probably dreadfully weak of her and everything, but she could n't, simply could n't regard the development as an entire calamity. It was then that she elaborated, in a fairly clever way, the disguised blessing theory. She asked me if I did n't remember her saying, only the other day, that she wished you would give it all up. I did remember some such remark of hers, though naturally I had attached no importance to it at the time. Her point was, you understand, that she and I, though from totally different motives, were entertaining precisely the same hopes. Well, I could n't see Miss Janney as exactly qualified to play the rôle of the Almighty, chastening others by adversity, and I thought the time had come to push matters along a little. I told her, solemnly, that I'd undertaken certain responsibilities here, and did n't think it right to let mere personal considerations count; I said it would take something big to absolve me — for example, the positive knowledge that you . . . But you perceive my simple drift. It's impossible to describe how easily the talk proceeded, how inevitably one thing led to another. By this time she was convinced that I was one of the babes in the wood, born to be plucked, and she'd no sooner seen what I needed than she began to shove it out to me — though in a reluctant, distressed sort of manner. By the way, O'Neill had just heard 'confidentially' that Miss Janney herself was going to quit on May 1st: so I conclude that with others she's taken the simple direct tack — dislike of your policy. With me, for some reason, she was much more complex — wholly defensive: why should n't you do thus and such if you wanted to, why was it any better to help one side than the other? — and so on. But about the fact itself, she seemed surprised that I entertained any doubt. I said that a responsible person could n't act on hearsay or gossip; I, for one, must have proof, or duty was duty. She obliged at once — reluctantly. She said she overheard part of a conversation between you and this fellow Byers, or Beierstein, which left no doubt about the matter. I told her I could n't regard an overheard conversation as positive evidence; she might have misunderstood. She then sadly confessed that about ten days ago she wrote a letter to Mr. Byers for you; she could n't understand all of it, she said, the allusions were too cryptic or technical, but the intention of dealing in some way with a certain Great Power was unmistakable. I, of course, asked for a copy of this letter. She said that you had instructed her to make but one copy, and you had taken that and put it away in your private safe. I then asked for her notebook, in which —"

"Stop! Stop!" said his listener, in a loud voice, for her. "I think I've heard enough!"

The flat of the woman's hand fell heavily on the desk-top, and she came to her feet. The movement this time held nothing of the flashing dangerousness which had so interested him on that other day; this seemed merely the visible recoil of energies too long repressed. Yet it was clear that the cultivated composure, the affected turning-off of personality, was shaken through again — and by feelings deeper, perhaps, than pure anger. . . . Did she think now of that over-confident speech of hers about the situation's being in her hand?

Still, he, rising with her, hardly felt that his case was won. He said gravely:

"Just one thing more. . . . Upon my word, as I tell it, it hardly seems credible. You'd be justified in simply declining to believe it — just my word against a woman you've hitherto trusted unreservedly. As the matter's open now, suppose I call in — "

"Nonsense!" said Miss Teresa bluntly. "Of course I believe all you say."

At that, his chest lifted a little; a breath went out from him and instantly he was relaxed. The inner stiffness which had gathered to support his will subsided, now that he had won his way, and he could consider her a little.

With troubled abstraction, unconscious and hard too, she was saying: "Now that my mind turns in this direction — I can see that she's been a little different. . . . Ever since we came down here. . . . Yes. Only . . ."

And then what must have been growing in her mind since the moment conviction began to take hold of her, exploded in speech:

"But — good God! It's *unthinkable!* . . . What possible *motive* could she have? What?"

Hardly regarding that question as addressed to him, Masury stood silent.

The headstrong young woman, eyeing him yet scarcely seeing him, continued rapidly in an engrossed way, a little excited, like one thinking it out aloud:

"Corrupted! — but who could have corrupted her? — And how?. . . Bribery? I'd not believe it if she told me so herself. She's fonder of me than she is of money — that's often been proved. Blackmail! — through her fears somehow? . . . Conceivable, perhaps. Perhaps — I daresay there is some shadow out of the past. But she knew she was safe with me! . . . Her hopes, then? Yes, but of what? . . . Her affections? But I'd swear that Janney hasn't got a lover. I'd have been her confidante there as in everything else. . . . What then?"

Consciousness came abruptly into those intent large eyes, fixed upon her hostile manager.

"I suppose she let fall nothing to you which threw any light on — what's behind this?"

Again Dean Masury hesitated. However, to spare this woman's feelings was no concern of his.

"I can't say," he answered slowly, "that she gave me any

real clue. At the same time — I did suppose that this matter would connect itself — in some way — with what you told me two weeks ago."

"With what that I told you two weeks ago?"

"You remember you not only believed that some one was agitating against you inside the office; you were also certain that some one was passing out information to persons outside. Your inference then — and I must say I think it was correct — was that the same person was doing both these things."

That association of ideas, it was clear, had not as yet occurred to her; that she found the thought interesting was also unmistakable.

"But no," she said, straightforwardly, yet a little confused, it seemed, "no — there's been nothing of that sort, so far as I know, since the disturbance of the first few days. I've — had reason to believe that the steps I took at the time disposed of that — permanently. So — "

Masury, of course, had not forgotten Walter E. Ball, and the information Ball had got, so very recently, about this woman's plans. However, the want of ease he began to feel did not proceed from that.

"I was n't speaking of it that way," he said quietly. "My point was — I'd thought that if you knew to whom she betrayed your confidence — even once — you might know, or guess, what's behind it all."

She had stood staring at him, actually wide-eyed; a moment after he had finished speaking, the gaze terminated in a novel way. The dusky eyes, needlessly decorative for commerce, suddenly closed; behind the pince-nez, the incongruous lashes lay thick on the fair young cheek. The feminine signal of weakness, from this strong and violent girl, was curiously disconcerting. . . . Really, whatever she had done or deserved, it had to be admitted that no one quite deserved this.

He ended, with some effort, in the least combative tone and manner he had ever used toward her:

"I ought to add one further detail, and then I've finished. When Miss Janney realized that she was in serious trouble, and got both frightened and angry, she warned me that in attacking her I was opening up a great deal of trouble for myself. She said she was no friendless girl like Miss Kelsey, that I little knew what powerful protection lay behind her—something of that sort. I—I merely pass on the remark for whatever it may be worth."

The tag was for appearance's sake, to try to keep up the distant surface of formality: he well knew now what worth that remark had for her. Miss DeSilver's eyes, soon opened, had returned directly to him; and it was as if, by a subtler language than the tongue's, a conversation had gone on while he spoke. Some part of her had inquired of him clearly, "You know, then, who this protector and instigator is?"—to which his voiceless self had answered, "Yes, yes, I know—and I don't mind admitting that it's pretty rough work"; and then she had said something else much more complicated, which possibly ran about like this: "It's a little trying to have a family skeleton exposed before a stranger and a hostile one; please remember that this is not of my making, and it does n't affect any differences that may exist between us...."

"Thank you," said Miss DeSilver, in a low voice as he ceased speaking. "That's enough."

She pressed the palm of her left hand to her brow, and turned abruptly away; she stood at the window, looking out, her back to the still, bare room.

Masury was glad that the dialogue, spoken and silent, had ended. This intrusion of feeling, this approach to some sort of sympathy even, while doubtless unescapable under the circumstances, was quite unwelcome. The clear line of his action frankly had no room for this....

Turning, too, he loitered in another part of the room, by the bare council-table. He gazed attentively at a large framed photograph of the many-stacked mills at Cohaxie, hanging on a wall. The enfolding silence seemed to deepen.

There was much that he did not understand about this ugly incident, and did not care to, but that it was the froth of a decidedly ugly mess had been pretty clear from the beginning. As Janney was no casual employee, ripe for the sickle of Walter E. Ball — by the way, he would try to avoid Ball for the future — it was obvious that it had taken a strong lure to seduce her; and his mind had inevitably connected what Lucy had told him of the "old monster," Mr. Josiah DeSilver, with the fragment of the scene he himself had chanced to witness that Sunday, at the beginning: the sinister-looking old gentleman bundled up in the wheel-chair, and the figure of Janney, shapely and smooth, bending solicitously above him. Had n't there been something distinctly "coming on" in Janney's slant eye that day? Well, perhaps. At least for a long time past she had been all but a member of the DeSilver household, and undoubtedly she had come somehow under the sway of the vindictive old man who, if Lucy did not exaggerate, would stick at nothing to hurt his strong-willed and spinster granddaughter. The pleasant conception of discrediting her with her own employees had been his, no doubt, and Janney, willing to please, even to this malodorous extent, but with a rather elementary imagination, had worked out the embroidery for herself. Probably she hoped she could entice the old lecher into a position where she could marry him. Well, possibly he would marry her. Possibly he already had. . . .

How were that odd pair, the Misses O'Neill and Janney, getting on in there, all this time? Did the serpentine Janney — seeking neither to bolt nor to break in on him prematurely — still think that she could bluff it out perhaps? Well, they would see about that. . . . Really, she had taken this in a manly way, you had to say that for her. No heroics or blustering at all. . . . By the way, should n't he admit to Lucy that he had rather overdone the heavy sarcasm as to all that "protection"? Certainly it could n't be denied that those eyelashes, left to themselves, were quite unnecessary in the steel business. . . .

"Mr. Masury."

The manager turned, a little hastily, to find his employer regarding him. She stood at her desk again, and he was at once conscious that her look took some note of him: as if now, when the crisis had been fairly met, though not yet quite settled, she could think of all this, a little, as from his point of view.

The strange woman spoke, and for once this man, the least impressionable of her critics, did not question her perfect sincerity.

"I want to thank you, first," she said, her voice sounding vaguely subdued, "for the trouble you've taken about this — and to express regret for all the trouble the situation has given you earlier. I'm sorry, too, if I made it unnecessarily difficult for you at the beginning of this conversation. That was due to the complete surprise of what you had to say, and — and was not meant to involve any reflection on you."

At that, which he would have wished unspoken, her adversary colored faintly. His impulse was to say, "Don't consider me, I beg — I never consider you, and what I do is not done for you." But that reaffirmation, now, seemed over-crude. Having no apt words with which to greet the "just" speech, he bowed in silence.

"You perhaps remember an old prophecy," she said, with a hardening of her tone, "about a man's enemies being those of his own household. I find that unexpectedly come true for me now. You'll forgive me, I hope, if I don't go into my —"

"No! — please!" he said hastily. "My relation to the incident was purely accidental — it is now quite ended, of course."

She continued to look at him.

"Thank you, I'll not question your position again, at least ...
Well, we'll have her in now —"

"I'll get her."

"There's just one thing," she began slowly, "which I — owe
it to you to say.... I hope you won't feel that a — a public dismissal is necessary? I think I'd rather — just let her resign."

That surprised him. Where was the implacable fighter of
legend, the rough and ruthless Saint Teresa?

"If you do that," he said non-controversially, "you of course
appreciate that you throw away most of the force of the incident. A wholesome example would be helpful at this — this
juncture."

"I know, I know. Still — there may be considerations even
more important than that."

Looking down, fingering the tassel of her fez, the notorious
woman added, almost gently, "Who can say how she has been
tempted? I am not her judge, and I know she has been fond of
me."

"That's for you to decide, of course!" he answered, rather
abruptly. "Besides — the matter's hardly settled yet, I should
say. You may feel very differently after you've heard her
version —"

"Do you think she can deceive me now? Not in a thousand
years! ... But I want you to stay a moment, if you will. I should
like you — to see for yourself."

He nodded, strode to the door, opened it, passed through and,
holding it half-open behind him, said to the secretary within,
who surely needed a protector now if ever:

"Miss DeSilver will see you."

The woman, who was standing, turned toward him a face like
a white flint. The scene in the little room had changed. Miss
Janney appeared to have been surprised in the act of walking
about, whipping herself up a little, maybe, for the coming inter-

view; her excitement was obvious now. Miss O'Neill stood with her back to the door leading into the corridor, as one prepared to defend the pass with her life, if need be. Two brilliant spots flamed in her cheeks. That words had passed between the two, despite his injunction, was only too evident. However, that scarcely mattered now.

Approaching him, as she moved toward the door, the woman threw out in a low voice that sounded a little strangled:

"You wait — till I tell her about you — you *spy!*"

That indeed seemed a case of the pot and the kettle. Letting the door close further, looking into that artful eye, Masury murmured, with a steely smile:

"Why, my good woman, don't you know yet that the game's up? That's what you say in your set, is n't it — when the bulls are hammering at the door?"

The timely thrust, or the hostile sureness, or both, seemed to have their little effect. He saw that her white face had a faintly greeny cast. She passed him with no further speech.

So the model secretary, though a little tardy, came answering her mistress's summons. Miss Janney crossed the familiar threshold as she had done a hundred times before; behind her, this time, walked the office-manager. The door clicked shut upon the vivid, questioning face of Miss O'Neill.

In the austere president's office, there was quiet for a space. Nothing broke the stillness but the light fall of the secretary's feet, advancing. The woman's eyes, having rested at once upon her mistress, had remained there, as if caught and held by the grave gaze they encountered. That still, fixed look between the two women, one waiting motionless, the other slowly advancing, lengthened; it seemed to go on and on.

Masury had halted near the door, prepared, if necessary, to bear testimony in the coming clash. He had expected that Janney would begin at once an outpouring in defence of herself, in attack of him, perhaps; now he saw that, too clever for that, she did n't mean to commit herself till she knew what attitude her mistress meant to take to her. Yet it came as a slight surprise when the woman, having traversed scarcely half the well-trodden path to the desk, came to a halt. Her feet seemed to falter.

He glanced at the president, the old man's granddaughter. Standing behind her desk, gazing above the pile of letters which she had expected Janney to answer for her, she raised an arm in a beckoning gesture, and spoke two stern words:

"Come here."

Thus invited, Miss Janney, whose taut face was taking on a certain pinchiness, set her motor machinery going again, though still in silence. When she had arrived at a point about five feet distant from the desk, she once more came to a pause. It was now seen definitely that her steps had grown uncertain.

Miss DeSilver spoke again; "Come here! . . . Good heavens, woman, I'm not going to bite you!"

The secretary came on her shaky legs to the corner of the desk, which was her customary halting-place, and her young employer then took a step forward to meet her. The moment for explanations had clearly arrived. But that duel of will and wits, which Masury stood alert to bear a hand in, did not begin even then. The two women, both slender and black-clad and pale, stood regarding each other in a moment of silence. And then the wild woman, Saint Teresa, merely took the secretary's hands in both her own, and said in a grave way, gentle and a little sad:

"Poor Janney, you don't know how I hate to see you like this."

And that was all that the awaited grilling came to, literally all. To the observer's astonishment, Janney made a low noise like an animal in pain, horrible to listen to, and fell on her knees. Those clever and unscrupulous hands clutched at the cowl-like robe, that forsworn face mouthed in the shapeless folds. The collapse was startling in its completeness. After that one stifled cry, there was, indeed, no more sound. But the sobbing of the self-contained woman, broken at a stroke, was frightful to witness. Those dry rackings, those long spasmodic heaves and hysterical shudders, seemed bent upon tearing the slim body to pieces. . . .

Then observation ended. The company president, lifting her eyes above the head of her former secretary, looked at her temporary clerk, standing there silent by the door. . . .

He had previously become aware that the mere affectations of this woman, his adversary, no longer oppressed and affronted him as they had once done. Perhaps he had grown used to the mannerisms by familiarity: perhaps the controversial character of their conversations tended, each time, to shake and break through them; perhaps it was true that she unconsciously came to forget them with him, intuitively recognizing that "protection" was not needed here. In their talk two weeks ago, as he thought of it afterwards, she had seemed distinctly less posing to him; through this talk, from the beginning, she had been almost like a natural person; and now this look that she suddenly raised to him seemed striking for nothing so much as its utter candor.

The firm and colorless young face was full of trouble. The misplaced fringed eyes, which could gaze so straight, were dark with feeling. Regarding him, she seemed to shake her head a little; her brow moved just perceptibly with an expression indescribable and faint. Once again from behind the pince-nez — and it was rather as if he could see behind the pince-nez now — she seemed to speak to him, as to one who understood: "Well, but isn't it just like life? . . . You sin, and then you wish you had n't. This is awful, is n't it? — but I've done things too and afterward been sorry. . . ."

That look recalled Dean Masury at once. It seemed mysteriously to change matters further, and he in especial desired no changes. He had seen this interview purely in terms of conflict, and of his will successfully asserted. But what it had yielded him, most importantly, was these moments of appalling intimacy.

He turned instantly on his heel and left the room.

CHAPTER XV

GEORGE DAVIS, as the days passed, grew less and less satisfied with the way things were going. His interest in his friend's "crazy" impulse had, of course, broadened greatly when he found the whole matter first on the front page of his newspaper, and next in the place of honor in his "Literary Digest" — than whom that innately neutral periodical had no more faithful reader. The rub was — and a strange rub it was — that no fresh material flowed in to feed this now nationalized interest; no offerings were made, absolutely none, to keep George's abilities, as confidential adviser in the case, intelligently at work. Dean's silence on the subject of Whitestone grew, in fact, more and more marked; he neither reported any developments nor seemed disposed to discuss the known status; and the Elder was presently convinced that the wild undertaking was not prospering at all.

George had his own reasons for feeling no surprise at that. Very early in the proceedings he had perceived that the private plans of Dean and this fellow Ball were based upon a fallacy. They assumed, because they had to, that a man couldn't disappear; well, the simple fact was that George personally *knew* of a case where a man *had* disappeared. That instance, once it had returned to him from memory, seemed strikingly though gloomily apropos, and George felt in duty bound to relate it to Dean at once: the moment the latter came in one evening from some of those mysterious calls he was always paying, here lately — trying to chase up that fellow in Indo-China was what he was, and a fat chance he had of finding him in his, George's, opinion.

"This fellow I speak of," said he earnestly, walking along with Dean to the bedrooms, "used to be Aunt Sophy's prize Sunday-school scholar down at the old brick church on Bleecker Street, remember? . . . Well, rovin' kind of a fellow he grew up to be, but he always kept his religion, Aunt Sophy said, and always kept up with her too. Used to come to see her, and talk and play the organette every time when he got back from his travels, and write her letters when he was wanderin' around and all — gettin' ready to translate the Bible into dialects, he was. Well, sir, and then this thing hit him and he just vanished, that's all. Aunt Sophy had a postcard saying he was starting off for some place, Madagascar, as I recollect it, to take the Word, and that's the last she ever heard of him, and that was Christmas of 1913. She's about made up her mind that he's been eaten by cannibals," said George. "Anyway, nobody knows what's become of that fellow, for she's asked all around, and nobody's heard a thing. . . ."

The remarkable incident proved beyond contradiction that men could disappear, in especial men who wandered loosely in heathen lands; yet George hardly felt that Dean was much impressed by it, even when he had pointed out its teachings clearly and fully. That, of course, was because Dean was hoping to find somebody in town who could act for that missing fellow, dead or alive — and a fat chance he had there too, in his, George's, opinion.

Later, George had had another thought, even more directly to the pessimistic point.

"You can bet your life on one thing," he said suddenly, one day, laying down his newspaper beside the morning rasher, " and that is your boss won't let this ragged situation stand very long. Either you and Walter E. Ball find that missing stock *pretty* quick, or you can bet she'll take steps to eliminate it altogether!"

This time he saw that Dean's attention was caught at once. He inquired, with a stare, how that could be done. George legally informed him that there were various ways.

"Simplest plan would probably be to sell the company," said he. "She'll incorporate a new company. The DeSilver Steel Company, you might name it. Then she'll call a stockholders' meeting and put through a sale of the Whitestone Company to the DeSilver Company. This missin' fellow don't respond to his chance to take shares in the new company, so she buys his allotment, or her pro rata share of it, and he gets a check in the mails to his legal address. Simple as a change of name, pretty near — and makes her control final and absolute."

Lighting his after-breakfast cigar, and smoking for a time in silence, he demonstrated still further the advantages of talking things over with him:

"Likely she'll use that protest meeting that Ball's plannin' to call, to do just that. She'll grab that meeting and dig herself in for good. . . . Yes, sir, she's a smart woman, with a jaw on her, and she's got smart lawyers, I don't question. Don't want to butt in on your affairs, of course," said George politely, "but if I were you I'd have Ball lay off callin' that meeting till you knew you *had that stock*."

He was certain then that Dean looked a little queer. However, he just threw out in a matter-of-fact way:

"Suppose she ups and calls it herself?"

"Then o' course you'll *know* you're licked!" said George.

To that, surprisingly, Dean only nodded, and picked up his own paper again. No confidences whatever dropped from him. What was the fruit, if any, of those letters he was forever composing at his typewriter there in the corner, he never mentioned, then or later. When approached indirectly — as through the munitions question, upon which George's views began to show a certain modification — he proved unwontedly laconic; when questioned point-blank as to what he was doing or meant to do, he was significantly evasive. Gradually his unresponsiveness seemed to sharpen into a kind of irritability, and there came an evening when his marked touchiness on the subject of Miss De-Silver's alleged pro-Germanism convinced George that something decidedly unfavorable had happened.

The Elder became vaguely troubled. Friendship doubtless made allegiance; principle or no principle, a man was flesh and blood before he was an institution; and it may be that the American People would rather have seen neutrality tampered with just a trifle than Dean dished in a matter upon which he had set his heart, as he had so plainly though unaccountably done in this case. Why all the mystery? George felt a need to talk over the situation with somebody — preferably some woman of the helpful, understanding sort; but alas, Alice Williams was away, visiting her great-aunt in Philadelphia, and besides there were parts of the matter that he was n't at liberty to tell even Alice. And then one day, while he thought in this vein, he happened to run into a friend of Dean's who not only seemed to know all about the matter, but proved in addition almost incredibly easy to talk to; and then he did succeed in unburdening himself just a little.

That incident happened in rather a remarkable manner. It was Sunday, and coming out of church less full than usual of the beauty of holiness, and with a touch of an earthy something in his veins that might have been spring fever, George found himself confronted by a lady who, not content with greeting him in the most cordial way that you could imagine, came to a halt directly before him. No Lothario by habit, George would have preferred to meet the surprising emergency by merely doffing his hat and passing on; but the lady's position, at the critical instant, made this practically impossible; and in another moment, not to put too fine a point on it, escape hardly seemed so imperative a need. In short, the apparition enveloped George with such an atmosphere of friendliness, her opinions about the pleasant month of April proved so sane and safe, everything was so obviously reassuring, that almost before he knew it the Elder was walking down the street at the lady's side, in full view of the general public.

What made the position particularly stirring was that George, though he remembered the face perfectly, could not for the life of him recall who this lady was. By great good luck, however, she said almost in the first step: "And oh, how is Mr. Masury? I have n't seen him for *ages!*" And that offered at least a rough working basis, making the whole situation less precarious at once.

"He's all right, I guess. Workin' pretty hard," said George, and he added with sudden bold cunning: "You and he are great friends, I believe?"

"I like to think so," said she, smiling and stepping gracefully along, "though as a matter of fact, I see very little of him nowadays. But you say his work keeps him very busy?"

"Yes, certainly does. He's at it all the time. . . . You know what he's doing, I suppose? Temporary thing — organizing the office of this Whitestone Steel Company."

"Yes, indeed! In fact, I got him the job," said Lucy, for it was indeed no other.

The Elder was surprised into looking down and around, but seeing that his companion's charming face was turned up toward him, looked hastily away again. Still, it occurred to him that it would be rather nice if Alice Williams could but look over the spaces from the Quaker City and see him now.

"Yes, oh, yes! Certainly! . . . Let's see," said the shrewd fellow, "I believe you're a great friend of Miss DeSilver's, are n't you?"

"But not any more than I am of Dean's," said she, and the words instantly conveyed, as they were possibly intended to, that she was aware of a difference there.

"Well, that's a big thing she's doing, my opinion. Giving up all those big profits, and laying herself open to being criticized

and abused and all, just for principle. That takes a lot of courage, the way I look at it, Miss — that is, it takes — "

"Mrs. Flanner," said the silvery voice.

"Yes, yes, certainly. Know you very well, Mrs. Flanner,"
mumbled George, ready to bite out his tongue for having let the
cat out of the bag. "I was just going to say . . ."

There followed a détour, while George conscientiously set
forth some of his leading thoughts about Americanism. When
he paused, the lady returned to the muttons.

"What rousing arguments you and Dean must have!" she
said gaily. "For I know he thinks that what Miss DeSilver's
doing is too dreadful for words!"

"Well," said George hesitantly. "Yes — I s'pose so. Well,
it's a big question."

"Or perhaps he does n't think it's quite so dreadful as he did a
month ago? As I say, I have n't seen him for *weeks*."

"Well, I don't exactly know, Mrs. Flanner. You know — he
does n't talk much. . . ."

However, having chanced to speculate considerably upon this
very point, George resumed:

"I think he's worried about the whole matter — more or less.
I think he's kind of unsettled, in a way. Well, these are funny
times, if you know what I mean."

"Unsettled? Just how do you mean, Mr. Davis?"

"Well, not that maybe, but — "

The benevolent man, desirous of pleasing this so pleasing
lady, considered more carefully just how he meant:

"Well, far as I know, he thinks Miss DeSilver's just as wrong
in her *views* as he ever did, but — I don't know. . . . All this attack on her — callin' her a paid German agent and all — he's a
great one for fair-play, even with people he don't agree with, and
I kind of think that all that has just sort of turned him the other
way, if you know — "

"Oh, do you *really* think so?"

"Yes, I do," said George, more positively, seeing that he had impressed her. "I just guess it — you know, from little things, the way he does. I kind of imagine he sees her point of view better now and admires her more as a — a person, even though he's dead against her *position* — "

"That *is* good news," said the lady, smiling up at him. "And I only hope it's typical of what's going on everywhere too. . . . But here's my corner — too soon! *So* nice to have met you this way, Mr. Davis! *So* glad you remembered me! . . ."

Lucy smiled, and it was as if a finger had touched her heartstrings. She rejoiced at the news of Dean's improving opinion of Teresa, and as soon as she had got home, she looked at herself in the mirror, took off her things, and laid herself down on the large new lounge. She lay that way, scarcely moving, for a considerable time; in fact, until a knock on the shut door recalled her to place and circumstance. The little servant, entering, found her young mistress standing by the window.

Lucy bathed her eyes in hot water, bathed them in cold, put some powder on her nose, and went out to lunch. She was very merry at table, two women commended her hat, a third could n't take her eyes off it, and a strange man sitting next to her, who had an eagle's beak and a mustache as fierce as a pirate's, but whose name was merely Professor Pitcoe, took an instantaneous fancy to her. This man, having walked home with her, strongly desired to ascend and pursue the acquaintance on the spot, but Lucy mentioning that she had to go out to a tea-party a little later, and in the meantime would be busy, firmly said good-bye. She was "rainwashed," she was at peace, and in the lift she thought with a pensive melancholy, but with no bitterness at all: "I don't suppose I'll see him again now — not till all this is over."

As she unlocked the door of her empty apartment, her telephone began to ring. She answered the summons with a listlessness not characteristic of her: it was Masury. He was calling from his office where, it seemed, he was putting in his Sabbath, and proposed to celebrate an hour off by running up to see her. Though she had meant to go out, Lucy said, without hesitation, that he might. Then, when another second would have been too late — for he sounded very brisk indeed — she bethought her of the obvious counter-prosposal. Could n't he, and would n't he, in short, go with her to the Jedds'? As she had supposed, Dean had forgotten all about that occasion, valued friends of his though the Jedds were; however, the plan seemed to appeal to him at once, and after he had talked a little with somebody named Fogarty there in his office, it was so arranged.

In the subway, Masury became interested in his own thoughts, forgetting the unread "news-section" he had brought along for company. From the "extra" work he was doing to-day for the Whitestone Steel Company, his mind passed readily to that extra service he had done the company three days earlier, the results of which promised to be so far-reaching, and which had been "appreciated" in proportion. Before he had passed Fourteenth Street, thinking of some point or other, he had plucked from his pocket the missive, received yesterday, in which the president of the company had officially conveyed her thanks. Then while the train hurled itself through the darkness with a deafening uproar, and a weeping Polish infant with eczema sprawled over his knee, he examined for a space this strange testimonial which — ignoring the unpleasant aspects of the incident itself — inevitably stirred a sardonic humor:

24th April, 1915

DEAR MR. MASURY:

Allow me to express my thanks for the unusual service you have just done the company, and at the same time to offer you an apology which I hope will not seem unduly belated.

In our conversation some days ago, you considered that I had questioned your official loyalty in respect to the special duties you had undertaken here. At the time I assured you that I entertained no doubts of you in any direction, and I made that statement, as I then believed, without reservations. As I look back now, however, it seems to me that, because of the peculiarities of the situation, I did perhaps feel some uncertainties — however unformulated; and I think you were quite justified in objecting to any such uncertainty, and in resenting it. I beg leave to say that, whatever doubts I may have unconsciously felt, you have most effectually destroyed them; and it only remains for me to express my regret for the injustice I did you in my thought.

I assure you, you have put the company, and me, as its head, under a very real sense of obligation to you. With appreciation, I am

Sincerely yours

TERESA DeSILVER

A handsome letter surely, a feminine one, and he was promoted to "Mr." now. . . .

Nor did it seem to the acting-manager that "the chief" in any wise exaggerated the importance of her office-manager's service. For two days now, indeed, he had been turning over in his mind a conundrum of no little interest to him: Had he, Masury, saved the "enterprise"? That he had saved Ellison, the centre of the city office, snatching the irresolute fellow as a brand from the burning, there was at least no shadow of doubt. Since simple good faith imposed something, he had apprised Ellison of the facts, while Janney yet knelt and sobbed; and Ellison, immensely disturbed and chop-fallen, yet manly withal, had straightway sought an audience with his chief. From that conference the just man emerged looking chastened almost to tears, and it was freely understood that he had rededicated himself with appropriate solemnity to loyalty and old Whitestone. To the manager's eye the general clearing of the air seemed hardly less marked. It did not appear that the executive clemency had helped Janney much; even the tale she had told a friend or two about a dying mother in St. Louis had hardly whited that sepulchre. Perhaps Miss O'Neill had disobeyed his faintly Pickwickian command to silence; perhaps it was only that the truth was mighty and would prevail. In the subdued and wary movements of the personnel yesterday, Masury had seen the unmistakable effects of a lesson and an example.

And if he, Masury, had saved the office, had he saved it for Miss DeSilver's successor, or for Miss DeSilver? Certainly this letter made an ironic commentary upon his basic and secret purpose. . . .

Dismissing from his mind such and similar perplexities, Dean Masury detached his watch-fob from the predacious grasp of the small Pole, dusted himself with his handkerchief for eczema germs, and emerged into the wholesome day.

Ten minutes later, he and Lucy Flanner were walking smartly up the sunny Avenue, in animated and agreeable converse. It made him think a little of that other Sunday, when all the trouble had begun.

Lucy, in greeting him, had thought again that Dean looked overdriven, and even unwell; but she inspected him in vain for symptoms of that spiritual malaise indicated in Mr. George Davis's prognosis. On the contrary, to her surprise, he seemed perfectly composed and almost ostentatiously cheerful. She took occasion to say at once, resuming the brief telephone conversation:

"I'm glad to note that you're in an amiable frame of mind, my friend, for I'm afraid there may be features about this party that won't please you altogether. I —"

"There are features about every party that don't please me altogether — no, nor anybody else," quoth he.

Swinging his stick jauntily, walking as always a little too fast for her, he said: "I'll go further! There are no features about any tea-party that please the discriminating, if it's larger than two. By the way, when and where did you get that hat?"

"I made it yesterday. . . . You don't like it, then?"

"You completely miss the point of my remarks. But if you're saying that the Jedds have some queer friends, and they have, I — "

"I do say pretty much that, and I honor them for it, don't you? — "

"My dear girl, what's honor got to do with tea? For my part, I'm like the old lady: when it's honor I'm honorable, but when I do business — well! No, no, I don't pretend that I like the queer myself, but then a nimble man has n't legs for nothing. All the same I'd have been sorry not to tell Laura good-bye. That woman, more placid than a cow, has something wonderful in her, don't you think, something inexplicable. Totally devoid of charm in the ordinary sense, she's yet rich with personality. When's she going?"

"Sailing Wednesday — "

"How born for a nurse she is! Well, is n't that substantially what she's been to Arnold all these years, till she made him so he did n't need one? . . . Only wounds to the body hardly seem to give her her full opportunity. Well, you're obliged to envy her, starting off into useful action."

He asked abruptly about her work. When she confessed that it hardly moved an inch, he seemed genuinely disturbed. When she declared that she blamed it exclusively on the times, which seemed so sadly out of joint, he demurred. Seeming oddly full of sententious sayings to-day, he declared:

"Art's not concerned with wars and rumors of war. Did n't Goethe go on calmly grinding out stuff by the ream, while his country was being rolled off the map? Would n't Arnold Jedd do the same? No, come to think of it, I don't believe Arnold would. Well, I'm sorry your writing sticks, Lucy — but if it's the smallest consolation to you, you look as young as a May morning, and this is only April too! By the bye, George Davis tells me that he had the pleasure of a little stroll with you this morning?"

"Ah, that's nice!" said Lucy — "for I was afraid it was rather a case of my strolling with him. Anyway we strolled, and we talked of you."

"So I suspected. Good George has me somewhat on his mind these days. He would like to comfort me, even as Rachel comforted her children. Wrong again — but Rachel would have comforted them if it had been possible. So the old 'un told you that I was working too hard, did he, and in general that I took life and my job too seriously?"

"How did you know?"

"Also that I was troubled in my mind, seeming at once chagrined and unsettled, and was undoubtedly beginning to consider and reconsider all my positions?"

"Well, are n't you?"

Dean laughed easily, looking about him in the great-to-be-alive manner. Oddly enough, he seemed to think it unnecessary to make any verbal reply.

With a sort of deliberation, Lucy said: "I'm not the one to wish a friend worry, of course. . . . Still, it's seemed to me that your uncle has a splendid motto in his live-and-let-live that you quoted to me once, and I can't help thinking it would be nice if all his nephews would adopt it too."

"And everybody be as neutral as old George thinks he is, but is n't! An interesting world!"

"You *don't* reconsider, then?"

For answer, Dean shook his head slightly. While Lucy was far indeed from believing everything that men said to her, especially about a woman, the negligence of that gesture was curiously convincing, and, to her, proportionately puzzling.

"The deuce of it is," he said thoughtfully, "I'm not that sort of volcano at all. I honestly can't intermit for a cent."

And then, in the simplest fashion, he addressed that subject which she had supposed him to be studiously avoiding in loquacity.

"But would it boost my standing with you, Lucy dear, which is the main thing, if I said that I now see much that's remarkable, and even quite admirable, in Miss DeSilver? To that I gladly bear testimony — and after all, that is a large reconsideration, isn't it? — exactly like saying that the Kessler stuff had fooled me in the beginning, and upon my word, I believe it did! . . . And would you like it too if I told you that, though I'm her enemy, I'm the most obliging and positively helpful enemy that any lady ever had? For that also is the solemn truth."

"Oh, is it, indeed?" said Lucy.

"If you doubt it," said he, with the faintest edge to his voice, "you've only to ask her for yourself."

Lucy, though she had already derived a totally different impression from Teresa's own testimony, was silent. After all, that was ten days ago.

"In the office," continued Dean pleasantly, "those who admire Miss DeSilver most look upon me as her personal champion and favored lieutenant — it's a fact. And that's come about by my own words and acts alone. . . . It's the magnanimous though reluctant truth — for," said he, "I must admit that my improved opinion of your friend's abilities and — hem — character — it's all in my head, don't you know, and doesn't seem to touch what I feel — which is me, as I suppose. Don't you think, Lucy, that the telling of anecdote is an agreeable manner of whiling away a walk? Well, I propose to tell you a little *histoire* — quite confidentially. It's gossip, I suspect, but maybe not the less interesting on that account. . . ."

As she offered no objections, Dean proceeded to relate, in the satirical style, a somewhat curious incident which had happened at the office the day before, and which boiled down to this: that a friend of his, a British official named Hedley-Black, whose duties brought him sometimes to see Teresa, had respectfully suggested that she lunch with him some day, to discuss their affairs; whereupon Teresa, "flying into a fury," Dean said, had ordered the man out of her office, forbidding him ever to set foot there again under penalty of being bodily thrown out — him, Hedley-Black, D.S.O., son and heir of Viscount Alingstoke, etc. It seemed that Dean had met the man in the hall as he emerged from this rebuff, dreadfully mortified and angry, and the man, Hedley-Black, thinking that the story might get round to his discredit, had taken Dean down to the end of the corridor to make his honorable explanation.

"How's that for man-hating?" laughed Dean, with relish, as they swung along: "Of course I've assumed that the Colonel's calls have been confined to steel rails — at most that he was hoping to argue her out of her pacifistic ways, just as my live-and-let-live uncle may be doing — who can say? . . . Get her to slip him a few old shells maybe. . . . Well, the poor fellow doggedly explained that it was by no means just a business acquaintance, that he had met the lady socially as the saying goes — that in spite of differences in views about certain matters, he had considered that they were by way of being —"

"Oh, Dean, Dean! — how simple you are!" Lucy broke in, genuinely surprised. "Why, it's as plain as a pikestaff that the man's just been stalking Teresa all the time, I don't care what he says — stalking the great heiress who's inaccessible through the ordinary channels, but could be reached by talk of steel — and that yesterday he let the mask drop, as it were! Why, don't you see it's exactly as if he had said, 'Of course you've known what I've been driving at all this time, my dear, behind this' —"

"Oh, come, Lucy!" he interrupted with his rather careful mildress. "Why the sweet romanticism? Is it your girlish view

that whenever a male asks a female to lunch, it's because
he wants to make love to her? — "

Lucy smiled.

"Ah, I'm hardly so optimistic as that. Even you have asked
me to lunch. . . . Why, Dean dear — I thought you understood!
That's precisely the sort of thing Teresa's perpetually on guard
against — exactly what she'd regard as taking an unfair advantage to begin with, and making an insulting slur on her sincerity
to end with! Whew!" said she, as if lifted by her own strong
words, "I'm really surprised she did n't shoot your gallant Colonel, as they say she shot that Frenchman in 1910 — and I for
one never believed the yarn about cleaning the pistol that his
grandfather carried under Napoleon."

Dean laughed at the odd climax; his answer was: "All right,
all right! — I make it a rule never to argue!" And then, unexpected still, he said, "By the way, do you know something that
I *do* feel — that *is* me — very much so?"

"What?" said Lucy.

He had suddenly turned his keen eyes down upon her, and he
spoke with a sort of abruptness, in another voice:

"It's that you're a wonderful trump — to stand up this way
for what you admire, and to care so much about my feeling —
about having me admire it too. I have to differ with you, I can't
help that — but I claim to be no clod, and you must n't
think I could be blind to what's so fine — and beautiful as
that."

Lucy looked away from him up the sunny street. The peach-
iness of her cheek seemed to fade a little.

"Of course I don't deserve it — far from it," said she. "Still
. . . I'm glad to have you say that."

"It's not the half . . ."

But with what words the man meant to continue his im-
promptu tribute did not appear. He ended short; his next remark

proved to be exclamatory: "Hello!" And then he said in a completely altered manner, thoughtful and struck:

"Well, well! There she is now!"

Lucy looked up with a start.

"Oh!... Where?"

Having glanced hastily at her companion, she followed the direction of his fixed stare. They were then approaching Fifty-Seventh Street; and, in the thin stream of Sunday traffic, on the cross-street, her eyes fell upon a small and smart, dark-blue coupé, momentarily halted by the farther curb for the crossing. Through the open window of the vehicle, which Lucy recognized at once, could be seen, true enough, the unique profile of Teresa DeSilver. Her head, which did not move, was slightly bowed: she sat reading a book.

As the two friends drew near, the car, starting slowly, rolled off across the Avenue.

"But what's she going that way for!" exclaimed Lucy.

"Heavens! Can't the poor woman go in any — "

"But she promised to go to the Jedds'!" said Lucy — "as I've been trying to tell you all along."

"To the *Jedds'!*"

Dean's surprise was so genuine that she thought he was going to stop stockstill, staring at her; his look for the second seemed to say: "Well, you *ought* to have told me, when you asked me to go." But he recovered immediately, in the rather disconcerting way he had, and said almost in his previous manner:

"Well, well! Who'd have thought it! The great recluse you were just explaining to me! — the lady who wants them all to keep away —"

"She's going," said Lucy resolutely, "because Laura, who's one of her oldest friends, begged it of her. And I begged it too, for the same reason — to show that she is n't, and can't be put, in Coventry."

"All right, all right — nothing to me naturally! As I re-marked, just now, a nimble man has n't legs for nothing."

Lucy, glancing at him, saw that his eyes, unconsciously, had turned after that rapidly disappearing coupé. The look she sur-prised on his face seemed singularly out of relation to his continu-ously light tone; she was made to think instantly of that day at lunch when he had said, with just this expression: "Make no mistake, one of us is pretty sure to be hurt."

In that moment, for the first time, Lucy was not so sure that Dean was going to be the one.

It was an author's tea; moreover, it was the very same author at whose hospitable apartment Mrs. Flanner and Masury had met, nearly three years before. Only the author did not live in an apartment now, but in a four-story house with an English basement; for he had learned to make "serials" to order, and out of serials to make pictures to order, and had waxed exceed-ing fat. Still, he was not puffed up with pride, calling other men common or unclean, and thanking God that he was not as they were. In truth, Arnold Jedd's popularity had but grown with his prosperity, for he was a lovable soul, and the street before his door was blocked with motor-cars that day.

After the first slight recoil of his antagonism, Masury had been conscious of a certain desire, hardly stronger than curi-osity, to see and observe his employer in these surroundings: out of an office, out of the chiefship, and set against her equals in a normal human background. Possibly, too, in the reactions set up by his "unusual service," part of him even looked forward to seeing signs of the public disapproval of her. However, as the wide grilled door swung backward under an unseen hand, and the din of voices and laughter rushed down and overflowed them, the likelihood of seeing anybody in particular in this mêlée seemed remote.

The friends ascended; there was a jam on the stairs. The whole house was open, it seemed; there was a jam everywhere. From soft-lit drawing-room and dining-room, from library and study, from small nameless rooms here and there, from nooks and halls and stairways, there came the manifold noises of crowded people at a party. There were hurrying waiters and hat-checks and banks of flowers; the dining-room disclosed offerings beyond "tea"; in Arnold Jedd's study, where thoughts turned serial, and serial blossomed film, the bored or the timid might hearten themselves with ancient spirits, and many did. That was a gathering much mixed in its largeness, and accordingly not without interest. You might have recognized there some of your own friends, the very best people, though, to be sure, only those of them who find amusement as "patrons of the arts"; you could also have seen not a few people who, by the very same standard, your own, were among the worst. Catholic souls were Arnold and Laura; like Gallio they cared for none of these things. Among the artists, dabblers with the pen naturally predominated: though, for that matter, the accomplished Arnold was also a composer of no mean ability and he had many friends in that walk too. In the long drawing-room an ever-renewing group formed itself about the robust, plump figure of the golden-voiced tenor. Small dark men with receding chins and black mops for hair clustered about the dining-table and buffets. Bobbed-haired Villagers jostled dames of fashion on the ornamental stairs. A popular Cabinet minister, leaning against a newel-post, revelled in the conversation of a Jewish picture-director, whose teeth were of gold. In the library you might have seen — provided such a sight had the smallest interest for you — half a dozen celebrated novelists whose names were household words everywhere, including Sweden, chatting amiably together. It was to be observed that these fictioneers were a well-tubbed, prosperous and normal-looking group — not a velveteen jacket or a Windsor tie to the lot. Somewhere, apparently, the day had passed when an author, having eked it out for a space on the duke's bounty, barely escaping cap and bells the while, must die alone in an attic, and so on to Potter's Field.

Mrs. Arnold Jedd, in her place by the doors, remained a centre of attention. This remarkable woman, whose characteristic calm was the expression of a nature of extraordinary poise and depth, was departing for indefinite service in a hospital in Furnes, Belgium: having first completed an unusually intensive training-course, and next having made dispositions of her two children and her husband which satisfied even the most critical. "Going over" was rather less common in that month and year than it afterwards became; and though she and Arnold had avoided giving this annual greeting of friends any special significance, it inevitably took on the complexion of a farewell.

Greeting their hostess, beginning a staccato chatter which there was no hope of finishing, the two new arrivals found themselves straightway pushed on by arrivals still newer. Within, they separated; Lucy found other friends to welcome her, and Masury, on his side, was not lacking. Having lived all his life in this city, with many connections both personal and professional, he had a large acquaintance; there were few people, perhaps, even in this odd assortment whom he could not identify. He moved about, exchanging greetings right and left, and — for all his slighting comments to Lucy — rather enjoying being out with his kind after days and nights of close preoccupation. Horace Checkerman, whose presence made a perfect proof of the Jedds' broad affections, flung one of his rough gibes at him in passing; certain other acquaintances politely aired their curiosity as to his activities; but on the whole there was less of that sort of thing to put up with than one might have expected, and everything was pleasant. However, his time was short, since he had promised to meet the foreman, Fogarty, at the office at six-thirty. More than once as he chatted he glanced at his watch; and he had just decided that he was not to witness a certain occurrence, when all at once it occurred.

The news communicated itself in an unusual way. He was standing at the farther end of the drawing-room by the windows, talking most satisfactorily and non-controversially with Margaret Kane, whom he deemed one of the pleasantest of living souls, when — "something happened." He became aware of it in exactly those terms — a mere vague pricking-up of the ears of his consciousness: what's happened? Upon the clattering and crowded room, which was big enough for a ball, there had descended — something — not a silence, indeed, but at least a kind of hush: much as happens when the word begins to go around that So-and-So has consented to play the harp, or oblige with a few remarks. Masury had just become conscious of the slight abeyance of noise and quickening of the collective intelligence, when Mrs. Kane, who was looking past him, said in an interested voice:

"Well, I see she's come for you, Dean, your beautiful employer!"

On that he turned, without haste; and past many people, over moving shoulders and through the bright plumage of hats, he glimpsed the notorious president of Whitestone, whose grateful letter even now simmered in his pocket. Having entered that moment, evidently, she stood where he and Lucy had stood half an hour earlier, talking with an appearance of eagerness to Laura Jedd, who did not mind queer people, or even know that they were queer, and who was seen to be holding both the hands of this latest visitor. Other people stood about the pair — a considerable group.

By the chance of position Masury had a good, though shifting, view of his chief. It had occurred to him to wonder if she would stick to her "protection" for this public appearance, or whether, on the contrary, she would burst into finery, as a method of declaring that she did not know Coventry. He now perceived that she had done neither. She had indeed left off her pince-nez; she had left off the ugly cap and the cowl; she wore a normal hat and a black dress of some material richer than serge. But the changed costume, while an improvement, was still nothing wonderful for beauty; and besides he himself had come by experience to discount the disfigurements, so that now he hardly noticed that they were gone. Nevertheless, frankly staring, he was aware, not without surprise, that this young woman looked decidedly "different" from the flat executive behind the equally flat desk. The change, as it seemed, proceeded from within, in naturalness or animation or ease; or perhaps it was as if, considering personality as a light, she had elected to turn it on again for this hour. Certainly the girl standing there in the press about the door, laughing, talking, gesturing, now gazing at Laura Jedd's face, which had begun to mist a little under many good-byes, now leaning forward with a movement not empty of grace and kissing Laura's cheek — this young creature seemed, not colorless at all, but on the contrary quite vivid with life. . . .

"You do consider her beautiful, I take it?" added Margaret Kane.

"I'm — obliged to confess," said Masury, smiling faintly, "that such a thought of my pacifistic chieftainess had n't as yet occurred to me."

Still, he continued to observe, while his parlor-chat flowed easily on. That arresting of the general attention, which at least never comes to obscurity, also prolonged itself, noticeably. The party seemed, as it were, in momentary suspense. Why not? Now that the heavenly singer had made his bows and departed, it was no doubt true that this woman was the best-known person in the room, in the house; and she possessed the peculiar attraction of her opprobrium. Countless eyes besides his own were

fixed on that darkly dressed young figure by the door, and from
the groups about him on every side came murmurs, significant
and sharp. Still it could not be said that all this notice seemed
purely hostile. Unworthy though it be, there are creatures in-
festing this earth who care nothing about a woman's "views,"
provided they do not have to listen to them. In the stares of
many males upon Teresa DeSilver, there was to be noted a half-
surprised attentiveness — that odd look on the face of a stranger
which is in some sense recognition and greeting too. . . .

Releasing her hostess, Miss Teresa moved forward into the
room. Behind her trailed a handsome but rather ripe-looking
young man, in the brilliant uniform of a French officer of cavalry,
whom Mrs. Jedd apparently had that moment introduced. He
was fingering his rich mustache. If backs were turned at the
lady's approach, or eyes that were once friendly were averted,
one could see nothing of that. On the contrary, Masury saw,
people were speaking to her. . . . She advanced an inch farther,
and was swallowed up.

Her principal adversary felt that it was a little tame. Not
much Coventry here! He decided that it was time for him to
go. . . .

"Oh, damn!" said Margaret Kane suddenly, as their chat
proceeded — "I'm going to go and find her and speak to her.
That's what I'm going to do!"

While the theme of their talk had changed, moments earlier,
she spoke, oddly, as if it had n't. When Masury asked what this
might mean, his friend explained herself, somewhat profoundly:
a moral performance, she declared, a needed avowal that her soul
was her own. Looking at him speculatively out of her fragile-
looking eyes, Mrs. Kane said:

"I hardly know your handsome saint at all, and I hardly sympathize with a single thing I know about her — except her
spunk — and her looks! Furthermore, I'm perfectly aware that

she does n't care a continental whether I speak to her or not. But my fatal tendency, inherited direct from my grandfather Perkins, is to let others decide for me what I'm to do — and think. Now I've decided I won't. Will you come?"

"No, thanks!"

"What, afraid to acknowledge the acquaintance in public?"

Further surprised at all this, and faintly annoyed, he answered carelessly: "It would n't seem to me that that took a dare-devil courage exactly. Why, I thought she was having quite an ovation. . . ."

Mrs. Kane, in the act of turning away, paused and looked at him curiously. "Are you serious, Dean? . . . A little more of the same sort of ovation, and she might as well be a leper. As to the courage end of it — well, ask Lucy Flanner about that sometime?"

She disappeared, and he sought Lucy, though not for the purpose indicated. The search progressed slowly and ran long. In the end he glimpsed her just inside the doors of the dining-room, where the throng and the din seemed especially thick. However, Lucy stood in a corner which, by comparison, was almost sequestered.

It was understood that, in view of his business engagements, he was not to wait for her; there remained only to take his leave. But Lucy, allowing herself to be easily detached from her immediate environment, who looked like screen-idols, shouted up at him at once:

"Have you seen or heard anything of Teresa?"

"Miss DeSilver? Oh, she's been here for some time. Why, did n't you hear the dramatic pause that announces the entrance of a personage?"

Lucy gazed up at him from under the hat that had been so much admired that day. "How could I hear anything here — even silence? Did — did she ask for me?"

"My dear girl! I have n't had the honor of conversing with her."

"Oh! . . . Well, it's an honor I'm hoping to have, at least. Where is she now?"

"Ah, there I can't help you. . . . By the way, Lucy, is it true that you, too, have been persecuted for righteousness' sake?"

"I don't seem to grasp your Biblical metaphor, Dean?"

"Some one just intimated to me that you had felt the frown of public opinion, because of your friendship for my employer."

Lucy, leaning delicately against a china-closet, noted the skepticism in his face with a certain surprise. In truth she had suffered considerably for her tolerance and her love; and she was proud of her honorable scars.

"Just after you deserted me," she said thoughtfully, "I spoke to Mr. Henderson Lamar. I'm very much afraid that I spoke cordially, though I'm aware that cordiality is never the best form. I'm very much afraid that I was beginning to put out my hand. We were very friendly, you see, the last time I saw him; in fact, to conceal nothing, he wished to hold the very hand I was now offering. But that was two weeks ago. This time he merely gave me a hard stare through his glasses, as if I were an unpleasant thought that he could n't quite remember, bowed just too elaborately, employing only the hips, and passed on. I think at least a dozen people saw it."

Dean was looking at her with a thin frown between his straight eyebrows. It seemed to Lucy that, while he wished to resist the implications of her recital, he was yet much annoyed for her.

"Still," he said, on the resistant side, "who could take that worm seriously? Don't you remember what Bob Whiting said? —' You don't like to call Hendy Lamar a piffling ass. Somehow you feel it is n't fair to all the other piffling asses.'"

Lucy smiled. "How long have we been here, Dean? Half an hour? — three quarters? In that time, three different people have backed me against banisters or into palms and said, 'My dear, I feel it my duty to tell you' — "

Her look jumped over his shoulder, her expression changed instantly and wonderfully, and her sentence ended, as she sprang forward: "*Oh, Teresa!* I'm so happy to see you. . . ."

In the same breath, Masury heard behind him, at his very elbow in fact, a voice easily recognizable among all the voices near and far:

"Well, Lucy! I'd been hoping to find you here. . . ."

The two women joined hands, not at all in the manner of a handshake: it was clear that an affection existed here. Coincidently, Miss DeSilver perceived Lucy's companion. Her expression — for she had expression to-day, quite notably so — did not change by a flicker; she went on with flowing ease: "And Mr. Masury — how do you do? . . . You've actually found a nook, Lucy — how clever of you! And what a perfectly sweet hat! . . ."

So there they stood, as charming a little trio as you would find in a day's march: while around them, over this crowded room, too, there fell that faint and significant hush.

And at once — as an instant premonition had warned him that it would — the contretemps went farther still. The two young women had hardly launched upon the beginnings of a conversation, and the man had not chosen the words for his adieux, when their odd group was invaded from the flank — and a member plucked off.

A person whom Masury recognized as Steinfeldt — a gaunt, frock-coated person with an enormous head and solemn, obscure features — had caught sight of Lucy, it seemed, at just the moment when Lucy caught sight of Miss DeSilver; he now descended with a swoop. Mr. Steinfeldt greeted Lucy authoritatively, without reference to her possible wishes, previous preoccupations, etc.; having greeted her, he began instantly to pour out words in a mournful voice, looking neither to the right nor to the left, but merely indicating, by the bend he gave Lucy's hand as he grasped it, that he desired converse apart. And if the invader, in his complete unconsciousness of any situation, thus set up an untoward claim, it had to be said that Lucy, in her complete consciousness, yielded to that claim. Her quick, upturned glance toward her two friends, who were so far from being friends of each other, was anything but insensitive; it just touched Masury, standing silent regarding her; upon Miss DeSilver the fine eyes rested for a second longer with a fleeting and deprecatory expression which seemed to say, among other things, "I know you'll understand!" — and then, with a slight turn of her shoulder, she was heard to say:

"But I thought you said there was no hurry about that?"

All this consummated itself swiftly. The president of Whitestone, with a little nod and smile to Lucy, was already filling in the small hiatus, with the mannered ease of a woman of the world, mistress of every situation.

"I'm glad to see that you sometimes take a little relaxation from the horrid grind of efficiency. Are the Jedds old friends of yours, too, perhaps?"

Her appreciated clerk answered in a manner just as easy:

"Arnold is, yes. Yes, I remember him from the days when he was a reporter, and a pretty bad one, on 'The World.' That must be all of twenty years ago. . . ."

Untroubled, it seemed, by memories of their intimate hour, Miss DeSilver uttered agreeable commonplaces about Laura Jedd; it seemed that she was coming back to talk with Laura in the evening, when the mob had gone. He lauded nursing as a noble work; she proffered the great name of Florence Nightingale. If she talked rather as one who uses words to occupy spaces, Dean Masury brought hardly more attack to the dialogue. Still, deeply unwelcome though the conjuncture was, he would not lift a hand to change it now. Without a glance, he was aware, if she was not, that she, and he in her strange company, were the cynosure of the room. In this watchful hush, under those lorgnettes, he felt as stripped of privacy as one who rides in a carriage with the honor-guest at a parade: only here the honor seemed considerably wanting. But the knowledge only stirred his combative instinct, which was not weak. Lucy, too, and this move of hers, which he took to be a challenge in its way, laid their restraint upon his nimble legs. At least, mere open rudeness to the notorious woman, an easy snub with the majority behind him, had no especial attraction for him. No, she was to understand the finer subtlety, and the deeper reality, of his disapprobation. . . .

But when she, doubtless sensible to the oddity of the position, let fall some easy words about relinquishing Lucy and passing on, he said at once that he, on the contrary, was on the point of doing just that. He was by now aware that his employer had donned for the occasion a considerable "manner" — quite different from the familiar mannerisms, yet perhaps not less protective in its way? On this near view she seemed, and one had to say that she looked, less like the opinionated steelmaster than the handsome young grande dame, gracious and composed. . . . Oh, yes, she was "different"; she could be pleasant and human when it suited her book, she could smile to "get the best" of her detractors: but the proof of her versatility, which seemed somehow like a trick, did nothing, perhaps, to increase his confidence in her. He, for his part, did not "change. . . ."

Impelled to officiality by a sure instinct, he had added: "I was in the act of starting back to the office." And now she regarded him with a frank attention.

"To the office?"

"I'm putting in a devotional Sabbath there, getting ready for an exceptionally efficient opening to-morrow morning."

"Oh! — the repartitioning?"

"Yes, and that involves a good many incidental changes, naturally. Shifting of desks, moving telephones, rewiring for lights and the like. However, I'll get all that cleared up to-night."

"To-night? Well, that's admirable. . . . Your memorandum brought out very clearly the advantages of compactness. It will be a big step forward."

"I expect it to take up a good deal of slack."

"But was it necessary to put in Sunday at it?"

"Oh, absolutely. To try to do it on a workday would have put the office out of business altogether. I've nine men at work there now, which does n't count Miss O'Neill. They're to keep going till everything's ready."

"That's immensely satisfactory from the office point of view. I'm not so sure that it's quite so satisfactory from yours."

"Oh, quite. The only question was the workmen. It cost something to persuade them to give up their rest-day naturally, but I think it will be found worth it. . . ."

Good sentences and well-pronounced surely; yet, try as he would, his voice and manner began to show the faint signs of effort. Was his extra labor but a jest to make the gods laugh, and did this strange chief, with her serene face and pictorial eyes, know it while she praised him? . . .

Talk and noise flowed all about them. Steinfeldt's dully magisterial tones went on and on. Laying his hand lightly against the leaded door of the cabinet, Masury glanced at Lucy's shapely back. His eye went farther and fell upon the figure, or rather the pugnacious head, of Horace Checkerman. It rested there. Some distance down the room, over the gleaming white and silver of the large table, directly above an unshaded candle and set off by a bower of daffodils, the red face of Horace, seemingly unsupported by shoulders, protruded from a swarm of people like a startled turtle's from its shell. The face was staring straight at him; the heavy jaw seemed to have dropped a little; the small pale eyes were popping with surprise, not untouched, as it seemed, with a sort of triumph. Seeing Masury's eyes upon him, the German-hater suddenly shot his thick eyebrows far up on his forehead; he grinned darkly and maliciously; and then his bullet head disappeared instantly, as if jerked backward by an unseen hand.

With a flare of anger Masury thought: "Damn his impudence! I'll talk to Beelzebub if I like! . . ."

But the dialogue was proceeding:

"Still, I can't be said to have bought *your* Sundays exactly. Incidentally I imagine you've spent a good many evenings in the Edsall Building, too, which also wasn't nominated in the bond."

How had she known that?

"Oh, I'm quite used to work at all hours. In fact, I like it, and with a practical job of this sort there's of course a satisfaction in getting prompt results."·

"I'm fortunate in finding myself the beneficiary of such an exemplary attitude on your part!" said this gracious Miss De-Silver.

But it was on another key that she added, after a slight pause: "I hope you had a note from me yesterday in which I tried to express my appreciation — of *all* your valuable service?"

"A note? Oh, yes — yes, indeed. Thank you. . . . I thought it seemed rather — more — than the facts called for."

There was again a pause.

"In fact," said the manager, glancing about the dense room, "I hadn't felt that the circumstances called for any special notice at all. Whatever I may have done has, of course, been done in mere routine fulfilment of what I undertook to do when I accepted the place — and what the mere 'taking of a salary' obligated me to do."

"Ah! Well, I had n't understood before, you see, that you interpreted your obligations so — liberally."

But that made it decidedly worse. His point was precisely that he had not been, and never would be, "liberal," as to her.

"Really? I hoped my position had been fundamentally clear. If I clouded it — as to some aspects of the situation — I'm obliged to regret any misunderstanding that may have arisen. . . . The fact is I've felt all along a personal ambition to make the place as sound and strong as I can."

"Personal?"

"Because that seems to me the essential justification of my being there — in a position otherwise requiring some explanation."

At that, which was sufficiently pointed, her look upon his unobserving face changed, turned serious. It was as if she considered a totally new thought, recognized at once as of some importance.

"I at least require nothing of you that way," she said slowly, with just a touch of the office manner. "Still — I wonder if it would be possible for us to have a little talk some day — I mean, a quite amicable talk — touching the present and the future?"

Struck in his turn, altogether puzzled, the manager looked at her then directly, for almost the first time: a look which began as a glance, but soon went farther. . . . If there had been a time when this woman was indifferent to his hostility, that time, she now confessed, was past. And his consciousness of her, it was clear, was in this moment somehow intensified. No doubt this nearness, this unprotectedness, did make a difference: she released the aura of a more abundant life. He looked at close range into these quite unsuitable eyes, which probably went better goggled, at the shining young face in which indeed could now be seen that singular something — a purity, perhaps? — which Lucy had cited; and it became with him just as it had been on

274

that other day, when he first caught sight of her there in the De-Silver wing, with that sharp thrill of predestined conflict. The noise about them, the multifold scene, dissolved and dropped from his consciousness: there was nothing here but himself and this extraordinary girl, and between them an undying difference.

He said, in rather an abstracted way: "We can make the attempt, of course — whenever you think it worth while."

Saint Teresa looked down and snapped together the fastener of her glove. She looked up and gave a brief laugh, a little ironical, a little self-conscious, it seemed, yet rather pretty in its way.

"Perhaps! . . . Now I think I've made you quite conspicuous enough for one day. . . ."

Her eyes, glancing away, moved round the Jedds' dining-room; he saw that the laughter faded from them, and her face sobered. In another tone she added, with her characteristic directness:

"Really, I've been inconsiderate, I'm afraid. If I've hurt you — drawing you into a business talk, here of all places — forgive me, for I'm sorry."

Not pretending to misunderstand, for at least small insincerities were n't necessary here, the manager answered with a sort of roughness: "Nonsense! It takes more than chatter at a tea-party to hurt me, I assure you."

The girl turned her eyes briefly back to him; he was aware that her gravity, which was real, was somehow lightened by a curious tranquillity.

"But chatter at a tea-party is public opinion — is n't it? It's not a little thing for an editorial writer to get himself distrusted — or is it? . . . I keep forgetting that I'm an Ishmael. Good-bye!"

She smiled — with just the faintest trace of irony, perhaps? — and turned away.

Laying her hand on Lucy's arm, the young woman said in her *mondaine* manner, gracious and becoming: "Lucy — do excuse me! Are you staying much longer, or shall I have a chance to . . ." And Lucy, wheeling then, detached herself from Steinfeldt with a finished ease which betrayed that she could have done it all along if she had had a mind to.

CHAPTER XVI

HORACE CHECKERMAN, who happened to be sitting with his back to the balustrade and therefore facing the broad French windows which gave into the lounge, said suddenly, in a voice lower than his customary bull-bass: "There's Masury now." Gentle Wilfrid Winslow, who sat beside him, called in almost the same moment: "Hi there, Dean! Come out — Jim Weatherbee's here." And Weatherbee, turning in his chair, thrust his grizzled head and lean "poker" face forward into the light that streamed from the room within, and said:

"Speaking of angels, well, I'll be darned!"

Masury, striding across the lounge toward the reading-room, turned at the sound of Winslow's call, halted and exclaimed:

"Jim Weatherbee! Well, where under the *sun.* . . . "

"From going to and fro on the earth," said Weatherbee, rising. "Stop, and let's have a look at you."

So Masury, forsaking his solitary designs upon the papers and magazines, came stepping from the lights into the shadows and joined the little group of his clubmates.

It was Wednesday, three days after the Jedds' tea-party, which was indeed "public opinion" in its way; nor could it be said that Checkerman's sour grin by the daffodils had been forgotten exactly. . . .

The men sat, under an awning rigged that day, on the stone verandah at the rear of the house, a pleasant spot in fair weather. May was near, and the starry night was soft. Having greeted all his friends — the Major a shade more politely than the rest — Masury dropped down in a wicker chair by Weatherbee, whom he had not seen in so many moons. Nobody in fact had seen Weatherbee, for the excellent reason that he had been in Austria

277

since the outbreak of the war — doing what, none might say. A discreet man of fifty-odd, he had had for many years an intermittent and unexplained connection with the State Department, and his frequent journeys to distant parts, ostensibly for the purpose of gathering material for his books and lectures, were believed to be financed from the privy purse. One of the best-informed men in the club, and one of the most respected, he was listened to when he talked, as now. Masury, having a dozen questions to ask about conditions in the Central Empires, began on them straightway.

However, Jim Weatherbee, a gatherer of facts by profession, was doubtless aware that the tongue gathers nothing but practice. In a very few minutes, lounging deep in his cushioned chair, soothed with much tobacco, he said with the friendliest interest:

"But enough of all that for the moment — *I'm* catching up with news of home. What have you been up to all winter, and what's the big idea now with this German steel company?"

Masury, who happened to be lighting a cigarette at the instant, went on lighting it. The bright spurt of the match disclosed a down-turned face which looked as poised and lean as Weatherbee's own.

He had not been in the club for more than two weeks now; and this was precisely the reason. On that first night when he had had to submit to a quiz here, his annoyance had had its secret offsets. His mind had looked forward to a day when these men here would be piping a different tune, on a sweeter key. . . . "Say Dean, old fellow, what's this? Is it honestly true that you've got control of Whitestone?" . . . "Boys, gather round and hear the news. Who do you think it was that made Saint Teresa bite the dust?" — and many such a welcome saying. But the bright fancies had faded with the passing weeks; that very day, as it fell out, what remained of his hopes had received a staggering jolt; and the gradual destruction of the inner supports had left him, beyond his knowledge, in a state of dry exasperation, spreading downward to the springs of his being.

He had already gathered, from Weatherbee's hail and the expression on certain faces, that he and his "case" had been the subject of discussion, some time during the evening; and now, at the easy and point-blank question, he was aware that every eye in the circle turned expectantly upon him. He was taken aback at the wave of resentment that swept through him, at the effort he had to make to suppress the instinctive retort: "Well, what about it? — and what the devil is it to you anyhow?" But that, of course, was absurd.

Extinguishing his match with a careless wave, while his eye briefly touched the dim red face of Horace Checkerman, stiffened now with a certain air of defiance, Masury said with a creditable effect of good-humor:

"This Whitestone steel company, you must mean. The boys have been giving you an earful already, I see. Well, that affair is a little mysterious as yet, Jimmy — but then no one understands better than you that the very noblest missions sometimes wear a fishy look to the uninformed."

"Oh, it's a mission, eh? You're working against the enemy from the inside out? Well — "

"Maybe so, maybe so, Jimmy! But you don't mean to speak of this pacifist company as the enemy? Blest if I follow you there."

"Surely, you 're pro-Ally, my friend!"

"My dear fellow!"

Gentle Wilfrid Winslow said with a laugh: "He's the original one, Jimmy. His next job after this is going to be driving an ambulance for the French."

"Exactly," said Weatherbee, a little mystified. "But this company's known to be pro-German, is n't it? My understanding was that it's being financed direct from the German Embassy."

All the men looked at the employee of Whitestone. His laugh, again, did him credit.

"You *have* been quick in gathering intelligence, Jimmy! — more quick than cautious, I fear. At least what you say is all news to me — and I'm interested! Where'd you get it, if you don't mind telling me?"

Weatherbee, doubtless perceiving that the friendly talk was acquiring an edge, began what promised to be a diplomatic answer. But Horace Checkerman spoke up, not diplomatically at all, but rather like one cocked and primed for just such an opening:

"He got it from me, if it makes any difference. But of course he might have got it anywhere, because it's common knowledge. Oh, hell, Dean! You must know the talk about this outfit you've joined up with just as well as everybody else."

Masury looked again at the Major, tilted back heavily against the stone balustrade, glowering at him. He felt certain then that the company had been regaled, among other items, with a little anecdote from the Jedds' party.

"Oh, the talk. I see — my mistake. I had the idea that we were supposed to be dealing with facts — "

"And we *are* dealing with facts!" retorted Checkerman instantly, in his hectoring way. "You know that, don't you? You don't pretend to deny that it's a German outfit, do you?"

"My dear fellow, it's no question of pretending or denying anything. Keep in mind that I'm not a defendant in a suit, won't you? As to the facts, my own information is that the company is just as German as you are, and not a bit more."

The positive declaration caused a slight stir among the listeners. Checkerman laughed disagreeably.

"There are none so blind as those who will not see, they say. But if — "

"A sound maxim. Only I, as it happens, am most anxious to see — "

"I perceive," interposed James Weatherbee's seasoned voice, "that my query was ill-timed and impertinent. Disregard it, Dean. You don't have to do any explaining to make me know that you're all right — to a decimal."

Checkerman growled: "Nobody's said anything to the con-trary, so far's I'm aware."

On that, there fell a momentary silence: which, however, no one seemed tempted to break with casual chat, or a return to ear-lier topics. No, Masury and Whitestone, it was perfectly clear, made a more interesting topic than Weatherbee and Austria. The faint night air rustled the pages of a newspaper on Frank Hannasyde's knees. Winslow coughed. And then Checkerman, who had been visibly fidgeting in his chair, broke out:

"Still — my God, Dean! It does go against the grain to hear you defending that outfit, that certainly is working in the Ger-man interest, and that every German in the country is taking up for and praising. Damme if I understand it, or if I get you at all! Seems to me it's a time when all friends of liberty and civili-zation ought to be working together and showing their colors where everybody can see them. Seems to me it's enough that England and France and little Belgium are fighting our battle for us, without us making it harder for 'em by defending and helping those that are working dead against 'em!"

Masury tossed his cigarette over the rail. He was determined to settle this question now, once for all, so that he would not be annoyed by it again.

"You raise a number of questions as you go along, Checker-man — let's stick to the one you started out with. As I recall it, I was taxed with working for a German organization, an organ-ization financed by Bernstorff. So far from defending any such procedure, my reply is simply this: If you can prove that there is a dollar of German money in this company, or that it is actu-ated in any way by German sympathies, I'll apologize to you now in the presence of these men, go in the writing-room, write my resignation from the company, and never set foot in the office again."

"Well! — that's fair enough surely!" said Winslow pacifically. "I'd like to say that I for one have never — "

"All depends on what a man chooses to consider proof!" broke in Checkerman's voice, bullying and eager. "Some fellows'll argue there's no such place as Bombay 'cause they've never been there and seen it. Well, I'll give you the *facts* — if you really don't know 'em — and I'll leave it to any *fair-minded* man to draw his own conclusions."

Then, while the eyes of the others gazed about, now looking at the speaker, now staring at the floor or vaguely out into the dusk, dotted with yellow lights near and far, Checkerman rehearsed with great emphasis a story which had, indeed, grown largely since Masury had heard it last. In sum, it was now declared that the present owner of Whitestone, in the formative period of her life, had spent two years in the seats of Kultur, during which time she had swallowed the formulæ complete; that she had then come to be on the friendliest terms with sundry Teutons high in officialdom, and had reached certain understandings with them apropos of "Der Tag"; that after the outbreak of the war, when German agents of every degree began to arrive in the country, it was to her house that they invariably repaired; that the doctorial press agent was known to be in constant communication with her — and so on, and so on.

"And I'll tell you another thing," said Checkerman at the end, dropping his hoarse voice a little lower. "Thing that I got from a confidential source — not permitted to quote just yet but I will be soon. I have it on the best authority that, not satisfied with trying to cut off England's munition supply, the lady's secretly working on plans to deliver arms to Germany through an agency in France! Think of it, fellows — in *France!* ..."

There was a murmur from Hannasyde at this splendid climax, and Wilfrid Winslow exclaimed: "Well, by George! But Horace — do you think that can possibly be true?"

Masury laughed.

"No — not possibly. In fact, on the best evidence obtainable, the whole yarn's a web of untruth from beginning to end."

Checkerman's face, clearly seen in the filtering light, darkened abruptly.

"Easy there! I'm not accustomed to having my word questioned. What's more — "

"Oh, come, don't be absurd. It's not a question of anybody's word, as you know very well. I merely think you are awfully credulous to accept as gospel any old wives' tale that . . ."

A waiter appeared with a tray of drinks, ordered a little earlier. While the lad dispensed his offering, Masury found occasion to regard Checkerman attentively. Some part of him was perfectly conscious that he was being led into an awkward, if not indeed a morally false, position; but he did not seem to care about that in the least. Into his mind returned the woman's own warning — a little mocking, perhaps? — about the risks of getting "distrusted"; the thought did not stay him. He had always despised and resisted this type of "argument," in however good a cause; and for the moment it seemed that there could be nothing about Miss Teresa DeSilver, literally nothing, that he disliked so heartily as he disliked everything about this bigoted pin-head. Something in the look of that coarse flushed face made him think of the fringes of a mob, jostling in the dark about a tree. . . .

When the servant had vanished through the long windows, Masury resumed:

"You've given us your facts, Major. Allow me to offer you mine. The lady spent three months in Germany, instead of two years. To this day she has never seen Bernstorff. She has never

seen Zimmermann. She has never seen Boy-Ed. She has seen
Dernburg exactly once. That was on the eighteenth of January,
at a little after five o'clock in the afternoon, in the foyer of the
Ritz Hotel. On that occasion, Dernburg's sole remark to her
was, "How do you do?" She made no remark to him, merely
acknowledging the introduction with a bow. That's on the
sworn statement of an eye-witness. There's not a cent of foreign
money in the company, it receives no contributions or subsidies
from any source, and there's good evidence for believing that
the lady's personal sympathies, so far as she has any, are anti-
German."

This circumstantial summary, delivered with no emphasis at
all, was followed by a silence, distinctly dramatic in quality. It
was shattered by a snort, and a loud guffaw, from Checkerman.

"Well, well, well! She told you all that herself, I suppose.
Maybe that's what she was telling you —"

"No, Checkerman, she did n't tell me. On the other hand, I
did n't get it from an anonymous acquaintance, who'd just
heard the whole thing from a dark stranger he met on a street-
corner."

Weatherbee, his face shadowed under the shapeless hat he
habitually wore, indoors or out, spoke up a little hurriedly.

"Ah, yes! Well, that's very definite — remarkably so. Perhaps — ah — you'd care to tell us where you did get it, just for
the sake of the record? After all, it seems to be more or less of a
public case —"

"I imagine there's no reason at all why I should n't tell you.
Most of the detail comes from a confidential report by British
Military Intelligence, which got enough interested in the case to
make a special investigation — going back to the lady's birth.
As I was interested, and happened to have a friend in the right
place, I've seen the report. However, I'd already got the essen-
tials of the matter from some one who has known the person

referred to also from birth. That's my uncle, James Parmenter, who's nearly as good a German-hunter as Checkerman here, but who still believes in giving the devil his due. Or, to put it more exactly — in ordinary fair-play."

These remarks, which had an unmistakably authentic ring, produced a mild sensation among the listeners. Frank Hannasyde, the silent, looked under his heavy lids at Checkerman who, for the moment completely disconcerted, sat glaring speechlessly at Masury, his face the color of a beet. Winslow looked at his finger-nails, a flicker of amusement just touching his well-cut mouth. James Weatherbee, as if taken aback by the unexpected "punch" of the statements he had evoked, murmured:

"Ah, yes — very interesting. In fact, very. . . . And so the British authorities acquit this — acquit the company —"

"Explicitly, as I say."

Checkerman emitted a loud noise into the stillness, half oath, half hooting laughter. The noise had a forced note; the laughter, which he kept up for some time, and by glances round invited the others to share, sounded a little hollow.

"Well, all I can say is, I, for one, would like to see that almighty 'report' for myself —"

"Thanks for the compliment, Major —"

"No, no, no! No aspersions — no aspersions. Ha, ha! But I sort of guess I could read between the lines a little and maybe pick up something that don't seem to have quite caught your attention. F'r instance, I'd like to know who made the investigation. That woman's smart — I'll say that for her. She's smart! . . ."

It occurred to Masury then to cite the name of Hedley-Black, whom Checkerman both knew and admired: for it was the gallant Colonel, none other, who had shown him a copy of the confidential report, assuming that he, Masury, would be eager for such information, and himself rising superior to the humiliation he had experienced at the young woman's hands. However, he forbore to involve Hedley-Black; and in fact felt indisposed toward validating himself further. As for that, further validation seemed hardly necessary; it was sufficiently clear, even to Checkerman, that his "facts" stood badly discredited.

He was laughing and blustering along: "Sharp as a tack. But the fact that she could pull the wool over the eyes of some young officer, and hypnotize him into thinking black is white, don't mean that she could do the same with me. No, sir. Fellows have fallen for her siren song before to-day, if all I hear is true — "

"But all you hear is n't true, old fellow, is it?" asked Wilfrid Winslow in the gentlest voice imaginable.

Frank Hannasyde snickered outright. Weatherbee slightly cleared his throat. Furiously biting off the end of a new cigar, Checkerman sought to recapture the offensive.

"Falling for the siren song — that's what's ruined lots of good men, all through history, right down to the present day! Still — by gad! I never would have expected to hear *you* piping up the soft devil-his-due stuff, Dean! I suppose we'll be hearing you say now that the Germans are pretty good fellows after all, and they got a right to have their little fun."

Masury's fingers tightened on his chair-arm. That personal thrust turned the argument for him; he could feel the blood drawing away from his face. He answered with marked quiet:

"That's on a par with the other suppositions you've thrown out here this evening. None of them, in my opinion, does you the smallest credit."

The judicial Weatherbee again interposed, again rather hastily. With his philosophic manner, which seemed fashioned for scattering oil on troubled waters of every variety, he offered some safe general remarks on American neutrality, pacifism, etc. Unluckily, in the course of them, administering a drop here and a drop there, he happened to refer to the old man's granddaughter as an "extraordinary young woman"; and that, as it proved, was opportunity enough for Checkerman. Smarting under the sense of lost prestige, positive that he was defending civilization against the Huns, no matter what so-called "reports" might say, the Major had sat chafing and sulky while old Weatherbee gassed on. Now he punctured the peace-making sentences with a loud, derisive laugh.

"Extraordinary! You said it — ha, ha! Extraordinary just the way the old man is — only a little different. . . ."

Having previously brought the feet of his chair to the floor, Checkerman leaned forward now, chuckling, dropping his voice.

"Guess you know what sort she is, don't you, Jimmy?"

"What sort?"

"Yeah — this noble dove of peace, that it's slanderous for anybody to breathe a word against — I guess you know about her little peculiarities, when she isn't busy helping the Germans?"

"No," said Weatherbee, not without a certain reluctance. "I really know very little about her. I seem to remember some sort of nickname the papers gave her long ago, suggesting a religious atti — "

"Religious! Ha, ha!" chuckled Checkerman, looking round at the others with raised eyebrows. "Well, that's one way of looking at it, of course! Ha, ha! You know, Jimmy, there've been some damned funny religions since this old planet began to spin, and come to think of it, that kind of thing did cut quite a figure in the ancient ceremonies if what I read in the books is right. But you tell me what *you* think. . . ."

He elaborately looked through the windows into the lounge, craning his thick neck to make sure that no eavesdropper was in earshot; he looked around the empty portico, he even looked behind him into the night, as if to say that he was as careful a man as that. Having thus satisfied his sense of the proprieties, he hitched his chair nearer to Weatherbee, summoning the others by a movement of his almost backless head to commingle and listen. They responded in varying degrees of willingness and unwillingness. The heads, tilting together, gave something the semblance of a male quartette.

When Checkerman had whispered for perhaps a minute, Masury set down his glass on the iron-topped table. The movement, while not devoid of definiteness, was as undramatic as possible. Nevertheless, Checkerman, who had scarcely been unaware that the man for whose especial benefit he was speaking had remained aloof from the intimate circle, stopped short at the sound, swinging his head round like one meeting a spoken challenge.

"Don't like this, eh? — don't like to be told what sort of people you're mixed up with, and that you come in here championing and defending? Well, what your friends here can't understand to save —"

"I don't recall having asked you to understand anything, Checkerman. I'm now about to do so, for the first and last time."

At his tone, from which the last veneer of politeness had dropped, the faces of the other three turned instantly toward him. Weatherbee's mask-like countenance was seen to wear a vaguely pained expression. Frank Hannasyde was a little flushed. Winslow, who looked ill at ease, glanced downward, shaking his head slightly: it was as if he had said: "I was afraid this meant trouble, and now here it is."

"But first," said Masury, his unmoving eyes on the equally unmoving eyes of Checkerman, exactly as two hostile animals contemplate each other before the certain pounce — "I'll give you a chance to explain, if you want to, where you picked up all this servant's gossip you've been tattling around here to-night?"

Checkerman's face became mottled in purple and red.

"I advise you to keep your remarks parliamentary when you address me —"

"I don't see the necessity. Tell me, tell these men here in justice to yourself: Do you personally know this woman informant you were just quoting, or do you know anybody who knows her?"

"Who the hell do you think you are, taking this tone with me? You're likely to hear something —"

"Never mind now who I am — that's a point I'll be glad to discuss with you a little later. Come, in justice to yourself: Do you personally know anybody — for instance, a discharged housemaid or a lying paper-hanger — who has ever been inside this room you speak of?"

Weatherbee sought hastily to scatter oil, but the matter had passed beyond his temperate spray. Checkerman brushed him aside furiously.

"No, no! Listen to that damned cheek. . . . I'll have you understand that who and what I know is n't anything I'm accountable to *you* for. I've had enough of your —"

Masury, coming suddenly to his feet, interrupted him.

"And not even accountable to yourself, that's clear. I'll tell you one person you know, Checkerman. You know a man who despises vulgar scandal-mongering and irresponsible character assassination worse than poison. It makes him sick to listen to it; and he's telling you so right now —"

Then the voices of Weatherbee and Winslow were heard, low and insistent. "There, there! . . . Come, don't let's have any quarrelling. . . . We're friends here." But Checkerman, pushing back his chair, was standing now, his bulky figure noticeably rigid, the veins swelling on his thick neck. His right hand, as large as a ham, had automatically clinched, and he said in a slightly thickened voice:

"I warn you. I won't stand for the tone of these remarks —"

"If the tone's all you object to, you're pretty dull, are n't you? I'm telling you in words of one syllable that a person who goes about repeating malicious slanders is no better than those who make them up in the first place."

That, inevitably, brought the crisis. Checkerman, with a muffled bellow, beside himself, plunged forward.

But the thing was, of course, unthinkable. While the others had watched the quickening clash not without a healthy male satisfaction, the thought of an "encounter" in the ordered precincts of the club, where members should dwell together as one family, was actually shocking to them; and they would not have it. They were all on their feet together. Gentle Winslow, who was so wonderfully adept in every use of his body, flung himself upon Checkerman with a movement quicker than lightning; his slender figure received the brunt of that bull-like rush and checked it. Hannasyde and Weatherbee, hardly less prompt, seized and held the militant arms — no easy task, since the Major was at once burly and sincere. While they forcibly restrained him, the three men spoke in hurried murmurs, arguing, soothing, pleading. However, the quiet of the club was already broken by the unmistakable sounds of scuffling; by ill chance, some one bumped against the table and a glass fell, with a crash, to the floor. In the lounge, eyes were turned toward the verandah. Presently the inquiring face of a member appeared at the windows.

It had become an "incident," a sorry thing. Yet how were incidents escapable in days like these? . . . Here, too, purled the backwash of passions, released a great way off. On this secluded balcony, among these remote men clustered in the dark, there moved the ghosts from Flemish fields. Because the chancelleries plotted and the Wilhelmstrasse had dreams of empire, this distant and obscure friendship must break forever. . . .

But the danger of unseemly violence was passing. Gradually, under the beseechings of his friends, and their hard, unyielding hands, Major Checkerman's higher nature was reasserting itself, his demands to be allowed to settle the affair on the spot, here or "outside," subsided; in the end, they let him go. However, when Weatherbee, encouraged, then intimated that Masury, in the interests of good feeling and to demonstrate the "proper club spirit," should withdraw the words which Checkerman found so offensive, Masury proved unwilling to make that contribution toward the peace. He had stood aloof and still during the small commotion; now he shook his head with sober decisiveness.

"Let me point out to you, Weatherbee, and to you, Winslow," he said coldly, "that as a matter of record, I did n't say that Checkerman was deliberately a liar. If the point's of interest to you, or to him, I have not considered that he is. As for what I said, no, I can't modify it any way."

Checkerman, breathing hard, his ruddy face pale, said hoarsely: "This is the end of you, so far as I'm concerned. Have the goodness to remember that I don't desire your further acquaintance."

"That goes double, Checkerman, and I think I expressed the thought first. By the way, if you find yourself on reflection dissatisfied with this conversation, you know where to find me."

He nodded to the others, turned on his heel, went down the stairs, donned hat and coat and left the club. He was thinking: "I'll never set foot in this place again."

The blue dome was shot with stars. In the open spaces a light breeze played, refreshing to his brow, which all at once seemed on fire. The night invited him, as the bachelor apartment did not, and he began to circle the little park, where shrubs and trees each day showed a thicker coat of green. Round and round the square Dean Masury walked, at first going at a mighty pace. But, little by little, the long stride slackened; the over-stimulated thoughts grew quieter, and from mere anger and resentment, his mood sobered into a deep reflectiveness.

He began to think of his own curious situation, in which the inherent paradox had now sharpened to this acuteness. That day had been a memorable one for him. There was no gainsaying now that, outwardly and inwardly, he had got himself into a pretty predicament. . . .

He had set out to best, put down and publicly overthrow this young woman, Teresa DeSilver; and the singular end of his effort was that he had appeared, in effect, as the young woman's champion and defender. . . . Yes, the end. Why mince words on that point? Why delude one's self longer with hopes that receded like a will-o'-the-wisp? . . . Was not even the vindictive Ball frankly giving up now — on the point of closing with a new "proposition" in Pittsburgh? . . .

His mind, forgetting Checkerman, brooded upon that secret quest of his, his indefatigable search for a needle in a haystack. Now it seemed certain that there had never been any needle; even more certain that the stack had been well combed before him. His immense investigation had yielded results which boiled only to this: "I have n't seen or heard of the man in twenty years." As for his advertisements, which she had smiled over, they no longer brought any answer at all. . . . And then to-day, at a table in a shabby Gentlemen's Café, his unadmired colleague, Miss DeSilver's "predecessor," had given the growing intuitions of failure a fatal push. Once again Ball, the old man's catspaw — beyond his constant and disgusting inquiry: *Had the woman got the stock?* — had yielded up news, dark news again — coming this time in the form of a cryptic cablegram from a person named Hornblower, in Saigon. Hornblower had just learned, in brief, that the certain "party" had left Indo-China at the end of March, suddenly, under an assumed name, bound eastward for an unknown port. At the end of March . . . But Ball knew positively, from the private letter, that DeSilver Coit had intended to go up-country in March, to be gone for months. Neither man doubted now that Miss DeSilver had somehow established communications with the runaway who was the master of Whitestone.

And really had the cablegram been needed at all? Did not everything, down to the woman's strange remark to him on Sunday, suggesting an amicable talk about "the present and the future"—had not the evidence from the beginning pointed straight to the conclusion that she had been sure of her control all along?

With a dark discontent, full of the ashy flavors of defeat, Masury had to-day fairly faced the fact that his chance of overthrowing his powerful adversary was not one in a million. And now, on the heels of that, there was added this sardonic postscript to his defeat, that he had publicly appeared as his enemy's champion. For as to the appearances of the position he had just taken, he did not entertain the slightest illusion. Exactly as if he himself sat in the club lounge, he could follow the murmured conversations going on there at this moment. He could hear the piquant story fluttering from lip to lip, seeping and spreading *sotto voce* throughout the club: "Checkerman made some criticisms of Miss Teresa DeSilver, and Masury flared up and called him a liar. They say he's just about turned pro-German — on her account, you understand." . . . Yes, Checkerman's version at least would include that twist; and since it is the vivid story that survives, unhampered with ifs and buts, the malicious retort would be widely believed. . . . He laughed to himself, a little wryly. The laugh faded, and he was suddenly depressed, and sad.

Was it not terrible that the minds of grown people should work like this, and nine out of every ten of them be ridden wholly by their prejudices? What was poor old Checkerman, after all, but the ordinary human animal, brought to just a little coarser focus? ... By their prejudices and their interests, the poor sheep chose their "views"; having chosen, they cast about for facts to justify their choices; where no facts appeared, they spontaneously invented them; and when some one, less prejudiced, showed them that their inventions were not sound or true, their reply was, not to reëxamine their choices, but to fall upon the disturber, violently attacking his motives and his character. ... It did n't matter in the least that he had not "championed" the unpopular young woman and, as it happened, could not conceivably champion her; it did n't matter that what he had broken a lance for was mere fair-play and ordinary decency, and the chill impersonality of truth. It was enough that he had disturbed strong prejudices, which do not reason; and the revenge of those passions would be to whisper it about that he was a "pro-German" — and "Saint" Teresa's lover! ... Oaths and affidavits would not clear his position now. He had got himself "distrusted" indeed. ...

He recalled Lucy's preachings on the beauty of tolerance which she, rare soul, practised as well, and had suffered for; and those sayings, which went back over the whole period of their friendship, came on him now with a more pointed meaning. ...

Pedestrians passed and repassed him as they circumambulated; fat old women, promenading slowly, led on leash tiny muzzled dogs with legs no longer than fingers; boys and girls sat in pairs in the shadowed places of the coping, their democratic backs leaned against the prohibitory grill. From afar came the hoof-clicks of belated truck-horses, and the silver tongues of the great secular chimes, full of a sweet melancholy, called out the hour of ten. And suddenly Dean Masury, steeped in a helpless bitterness as he was, oppressed with the sense of the inextricable moral tangle in which circumstance and his own nature had involved him — suddenly the troubled man confronted the odd thought that he, in this contact with the herd's treatment of the unpopular, but dipped into the shallows of the woman's own boundless unpopularity, and that the trivial misjudgment that annoyed him now was itself but a splinter of the enormous misjudgment that had pursued her from the beginning.

The heat of his feelings about his own experience, as if melting and fusing the fixed core of resistance within him, precipitated the thought abruptly, finished and smooth. With cold dispassionateness, with a reluctant honesty, he recognized the truth in it at sight. . . . If Checkerman, finding his, Masury's, facts disturbing to his prejudices, spontaneously evolved a falsehood to discredit those facts, through discrediting him who spoke them, was n't that very much what the Checkerman sort of public opinion had been doing all along, on a far more damaging scale, to Miss Teresa DeSilver? . . . Yes; to be just, very much that. . . . He himself no longer doubted, at least, that her motive in closing the shell-plant was exactly as she had stated it: she wanted to "shake an insignificant fist in the face of war." That motive was one which aroused in him, as it chanced, an invincible opposition: the girl herself, opinionated and untamed, dangerous in her power, had stirred him with an antagonism unexampled in his experience; nevertheless, on the facts alone it had to be conceded that, according to her lights, she was literally trying to do what she thought was right — something for the common good, with nothing at all to gain for herself. But because her conception of good and right differed from the conception of the majority, they had unlimbered upon her this punitive and appalling artillery. . . .

But no! . . . No. Was that indeed the true reason — at least was it the whole reason — for the bitterness of the attack upon this woman? In fact, could n't some other person, from a very different background, have done what she had done and carried it off with practically no reprisals? . . . Was n't it true, rather, to say that she, in her own nature and her history, had borne within herself the fatal seeds of this "distrust," which had grown up to throw so vast a shade over her doubtless well-meant undertaking?

Instinctively recoiling from "sympathy" in this quarter, Dean Masury found himself unexpectedly on new ground, contemplating a totally new idea. The idea challenged him at once; it came to fascinate him. She had suggested a reasonable discussion about the future: how if he urged her to listen to reason? . . . For a long time he walked, thinking it out.

In the scientifically improved Whitestone office, the stenographer O'Neill had attained a certain position. She no longer brought along "Confessions of a Nun" when summoned to "take"; her reading nowadays seemed to be confined to a very different book, entitled "10,000 Words often Mispronounced." The girl had created a feminine stir in the establishment by appearing one day with her fluffy hair slicked straight back on her scalp. Oddly enough, the severe mode, while seeming to diminish the size of her poll by about one-half, was distinctly becoming to her, imparting a touch of demureness, almost of subtlety, hitherto quite wanting in her ensemble. That symptom, too, was typical in its way. It was known that Miss O'Neill, at the suggestion of the president herself, was attending night school at the Y.W.C.A., four evenings a week; some even suspected that the moon-struck girl entertained the dream of becoming some day, years and years from now, the president's personal secretary. At present, she was actually and proudly the recognized stenographic substitute for Mrs. Reardon, the cheerful, bustling, and rather incompetent lady who was for the time being filling the vacant shoes of Janney.

On the second day following the incident at the club, late in the afternoon when desks were being locked and typewriters sunk for the night, Miss O'Neill appeared at Masury's desk-side and said:

"They's a genaman to see you, sir."

Engaged in watching the movements of closing, which were certainly far more orderly than they had been a month earlier, the temporary manager answered:

"Who made you doorman here?"

"Nobody, Mr. Masury. I just happened to be out there giving a message to Gertrude for Mr. Ellison, and he come in. He came in. I mean this genaman did."

"Who is it?"

"I think," said the girl carefully; "he gave the name of Winslow. The name of *Mister* Winslow."

Her guarded manner seemed to consider the possibility that the gentleman might be using an alias. However, Mr. Masury seemed to understand at once. He said, with the faint irritability which he often betrayed nowadays:

"All right — all right! Show him in. Don't stand round!"

So the kindly Wilfrid came stepping into the general room of the Whitestone office — which was like Miss O'Neill's head in being but half its former size — looking about him a little curiously as he came, and sat down in a Whitestone chair by Masury's desk.

"Hope I'm not interrupting you too much?"

"Not a bit, Wilfrid. We're closing as you see. Cigarette?"

"Thanks. I'm just around the corner—Beaver Building—and as I had something to tell you, I thought I'd risk dropping in."

"A good thought it was. While I think of it, Wilfrid, what about those plans of yours that we talked of last month — that volunteer escadrille with the French?"

"They're moving, by George! — though not so fast, I must say! Any chance of interesting *you?*"

"I don't know," said Masury slowly. "I'm beginning to look ahead a little now."

Winslow's eyes lighted. . . . He, this gentle and fine-strung soul, was to be, on a day to come, one of the first Americans to fly a fighting ship over enemy lines, and not so much later to have another honor, duly remembered in the first gold star on the club's new flag. Masury in after days often thought of him as he sat here now, kindling to his bright and adventurous plan. . . .

But both men had their duties now, and the talk soon swung. Winslow, looking round him again, said: "So this is the celebrated place where you're doing your bit? Pretty tidy-looking shop it is."

"Doing my bit? Well — we'll see."

The younger man laughed apologetically.

"I sort of guess it'll be something like that, but it's none of my confounded business, of course. I rather think you've taught several people *that*. Let me say, Dean — I'm awfully sorry about that affair, and I must add, I don't think with much pride of my part in it either."

"My dear Wilfrid! You had no part in it — except to keep the peace, which is blessed."

"Oh, yes, I did. These things go in two parts, don't you think? — some one to talk, and some one to listen. I can't deny that I made a pretty attentive audience. . . . Anyway," said Winslow, vaguely embarrassed, "I've felt a decided need to tell you as follows, namely — oh, hang it, I think you did just right, and I hope I'd have done the same in your place, and — well, in short there are others who feel as I do."

Masury warmed to him. Still, the conversation made him, too, uncomfortable. And then it suddenly appeared that, by one of those pure yet not infrequent coincidences, Winslow had not come to speak of the "incident" at all, but of a somewhat more important matter.

"Enough of my idle chatter," he said lightly. "I know you're busy — to business it is. Do you remember asking around, a month or so ago, about a fellow named Coit — in fact, DeSilver Coit?"

There was the briefest silence. But Masury did not start, and his face, turned upon the other, betrayed nothing.

"Certainly. I remember very well."

"I've no idea how important it was," said Winslow, in a manner which repudiated the smallest curiosity as to that name, DeSilver, "and of course you may not be interested now. But did n't you want to get hold of the fellow — some business matter or other?"

"Yes, I did, and do. A business matter —"

"Did you know he was in town?"

Masury's heart seemed to miss a beat. So that settled *that*. . . . He had averted his gaze, affecting to straighten his desk.

"Why, I'd learned he was believed to be on his way here — but no. . . . Where is he?"

"I hoped you'd know that! If you don't, my information's no good, I fear. Your friend seems to be an evasive sort of cuss. He even denies that he's him!"

"Oh! . . . You've seen him, then?"

"Not I — I don't know him from Adam. The man that saw him was Mr. Tebault, a friend of my father's. You know who I mean — John E. Tebault?"

Masury, through his intricate researches, knew very well. John E. Tebault, college and fraternity mate of DeSilver Coit's a quarter of a century ago, had been one of the earliest and most promising names on that hopeful list of his.

"And where did Mr. Tebault see him?"

"At Forty-Second Street and Broadway!" said Winslow, with a merry laugh. "And right there's where he disappeared too."

Settling back in his chair, gesturing with his cigarette, the kind-hearted fellow said:

"I assume that this interests you, Dean? It was really funny the way it happened. Mr. Tebault was coming down Forty-Second Street, about three o'clock this afternoon. Approaching the celebrated corner, he saw a great crowd — whole street blocked, traffic at a standstill — must have been five thousand people. A bystander explained: some fellow had just been knocked over by a motor-truck — row of some sort. Well, presently the crowd parted, and the victim came through in the clutches of the police. No, he was n't being arrested for letting himself get run over — the cop was just giving him a start on his way, admonishing him to look where he leapt after this and so on. Well, the pair happened to come out close to where Mr. Tebault was standing, and the crowd was scattering, so he got a good look. Funniest-looking little fellow he ever saw, he claims — about four feet tall, brown as a monkey, bushy black beard like a gnome. Then all at once he noticed something familiar about the way the chap cocked his eye around, and then, he recognized him. Well, he elbowed his way up, sticking out his hand, and said: 'Why, Silvy Coit!' That's what he called him — Silvy. And what do you think then? The fellow just glanced up from dusting his pantaloons, and said as cool as a cucumber, 'What about him?' 'Why don't you know me?' said Mr. Tebault. 'I'm Jacky Tebault, that roomed with you in Henderson's in '91, and you're DeSilver Coit, or I'm a son of a gun.' 'No, there's a mistake. *My* name's Albertson,' said the little man. And with that he just sort of melted from under Mr. Tebault's hand and dissolved round the corner. Vanished!" said Winslow. "Quite unsociable, don't you think? —"

"I should say!" answered Masury, stirring. "And ... Mr. Tebault saw nothing more of him, I suppose?"

"Not a glimmer. The little chap seemed to be making for a

taxi, he thought — and then the crowd just swallowed him up. Walked with kind of a skip like a tomtit, Mr. Tebault said. . . . Well, I was uptown by chance, and met him — Tebault, that is — just a little after the rencontre. He asked me if I knew you. Said he'd had a letter from you some time ago asking about the fellow, but he'd mislaid it. . . ."

There fell again a slight silence, in which Winslow, at any rate, was conscious of no awkwardness. A door at the farther end of the room opened; neither man heard it. Feet moved on the bare floor; in his intense abstraction, Masury was conscious of no sound. Carefully pushing about small objects on his desk, he said with a business-like air:

"Strange behavior certainly! I suppose, of course, he was sure of his man?"

Winslow laughed. "Tebault said there was only one man on earth who looked the least bit like DeSilver Coit, and that was DeSilver Coit. Said he'd swear to him anywhere in this world or the next. Ah — what he couldn't understand — ah — was why the fellow — why he —"

The amiable voice, having oddly begun to falter, trailed off into a pause. In the same moment, Winslow came unexpectedly to his feet; he said in a changed and lowered voice:

"Perhaps you're wanted, Dean? . . . Well! I must toddle along."

Then Masury, following the just perceptible nod of his friend's head, saw, with a start, that his employer, the president of White-stone, had come into the room. With a stir of sharp and complex sensation, he knew that she had come for an "amicable talk. . . ."

The young woman, as his eye fell upon her, was standing. Clearly, she had come some distance into the room before perceiving her manager in his corner, or at least before perceiving that he had a visitor; having made these discoveries, she had halted, in that instant. There she stood in her cowl and glasses, regarding him — the owner of the company: his gifted and resourceful adversary who had been able to draw DeSilver Coit all the way from Indo-China for her purposes.

There was no pause. As the two men rose, almost simultaneously, and the manager's hawk-eye met her own, Miss DeSilver nodded and said with her brisk composure:

"I beg your pardon — don't let me disturb you! I'd like to see you for a few minutes before you go — at any time?"

Masury bowed. "Yes, certainly."

Winslow, who also stood gazing at the unlooked-for apparition, absently smoothing his hat, murmured hastily: "I am just leaving now!"

He spoke nominally to Masury, but the notorious and pacifistic heiress — who was known, however, not to be a German sympathizer — answered the stranger with direct civility:

"Pray don't let me drive you away. I shall be here for an hour or two yet —"

"Thank you, thank you!" said Winslow, with a bow and a smile for the strange-looking lady. "I assure you, my business is quite finished."

So the gentle fellow shook Masury's hand and departed, and the woman, who was so far from gentle, came on into the room and sat down in the chair he had just vacated.

CHAPTER XVII

H E was certain that she had come to say to him, after whatever preliminaries: "You remember, I wanted to have a talk with you — about *the future of the company*. . . ."

The thought hardly interested him; he had passed that point while Winslow talked, if not days earlier. And indeed, whatever the unlooked-for visit meant, as she intended it, he on his part could greet it with a hoot of welcome. . . . What else had he sought here but just such an opportunity? Why, in truth, had he ever come into this office, why had he leapt into this fantastic and endlessly entangling situation, but that he had a need deeper than reason, and now complicated and sharpened, to remind this woman of his unchanging opposition? . . . By his clerkship he had declared that, in the last sense, their encounter was personal, and she should feel it so.

The first sight of her, halted there, in his room, had revealed indeed — had somehow made visual — a subtly changed relationship: it was as if that community of sympathy he had been obliged to share with her, more than once now, had left behind its ineradicable mark. However, to eradicate those marks was the heart of his intention now. . . .

"I hope I'm not disturbing you too much?" she had added, with almost a hesitating air, as she approached.

"Not at all. My chores are done."

"There were several matters I wanted to consult you about. I took this as the — last convenient opportunity this week. . . . Don't let me keep you standing."

Seating herself, the young president let her eyes move briefly over the altered room. With its improved size and shape, with its new fittings and its still newer orderliness, perfectly exemplified in the two rows of shining desks, spruce and cleared for the night, the reorganized "general" room was indeed a tidy-looking shop, just as Winslow had called it. And the visible order here was symbolical, the slight index of a far larger whole. Teresa DeSilver did not need to look farther to be aware how much her temporary expert had done for Whitestone.

He watched her over his desk-top, waiting for her to begin. Like a lost hunter in a savage country, all his faculties had become intensely alert.

"I've wondered how long the special work here would keep you?" she said. "Can you form an idea now?"

"Why, practically, it's finished. There are a few details. My plan was to stay one more week."

He took her by surprise, evidently; she echoed the last words in a tone less dry than his own, and added: "But! — the files?"

He explained that his task there had ended to-day, when the two men from the Filing Bureau had taken over the installation of the system he had finally worked out, and she had approved, a few days earlier. The work of refiling would run on for weeks, months perhaps; that work was clerical, requiring no manager.

"No. No, you're right. . . . There was the study of costs you spoke of some time ago — the desk-hour analysis —"

That was one of the remaining details he had in mind, he said; conditions now seemed settled enough to make the attempt, at least.

"There's also," he finished officially, "a general rechecking of operations as a whole — making minor corrections as they suggest themselves. That seemed worth a few days' time. Finally, so far as I'm aware, no provision has yet been made as to my successor. The sooner the new manager's engaged the better, in my opinion. He should be ready to take hold where I leave off."

She then said abruptly, but with a sort of diffidence that seemed actually feminine in its quality:

" Need there be a new manager?"

"Need there? Oh, decidedly so —"

"Is it necessary for you to leave off? . . . Why should n't I plump it out at once, since that 's principally what I 've come to inquire about?"

"I hardly think I understand you."

He regarded her as over a gulf, from an immeasurable distance. The young chief gave a little laugh, dissociated from mirth.

"I 'm sorry if I surprise you too disagreeably. . . . May I say, I 'm of course alive to the — the peculiarities of my inquiry — to the various complications, which would naturally be uppermost in your mind? And still . . . Would n't it be possible for you to regard the Whitestone Steel Company apart from the — temporary and abnormal aspects of its situation — ? . . . I mean, to view it as just an ordinary business of more or less interesting possibilities — here long before the war, and to be here, I hope, long after the war is over?"

After a brief delay, his voice said without tone: "Well? — if I could?"

"Then I 'd ask if you could consider, further, staying on here — as an officer," said his adversary, straightforwardly, and yet with some sign of effort too. "I 'd like to keep you — if it 's in any way possible to manage it — as secretary of the company."

Her expert's light eyes, which did not move, seemed to have turned into points of metal. Her words dropped off into silence.

He sat dumfounded. . . . Was it possible that she, who "always got the best of everybody," had bethought her to try a tack with him? She was saying, was n't she, that the time for enmity was past; defeated, why could n't he nicely accept defeat and go on rendering her "great services"? "No harm in asking," as practical persons say. . . . Or perhaps, more kindly, she meant a gracious sop to the vanquished — with an excellent salary thrown in to soothe the little pangs of failure?

Yet it was hardly thinkable that her view of their relation should be so sheerly crude as that. Had she then the deeper thought that he, who clearly had not come into the office to look for DeSilver Coit, might have his own reasons for being loath to go? The same reasons, in fine, touching her? . . .

"The position," she was going on firmly, "would be a responsible one, with large authority in the management of the business. You remember pointing out, as soon as you came, that while I had a superintendent for manufacture, the organization provided no such officer for administration? Well, it's that lack precisely that I want the secretaryship to fill. The position, as it would be fixed, would just correspond, on the executive side, with Keeley's at the —"

"You bewilder me," the man's steely voice broke in. "May I ask why you make this offer to me?"

"Why? . . . Oh, that's very simple, I think. I'm ambitious for the company, the post is an important one, and I want to fill it with — "

"I don't make myself clear. Why did you expect that I could possibly consider such a position?"

"Ah, that! But I can't quite say that I did expect it, you see — it's been long since I've expected anything! . . . At most — well, you *have* a position here now, you see, and — frankly I did n't quite know how you might feel about the business for the future, with the extraneous issue regarded as lopped off — your own freedom continuing unconditioned —"

"How could I regard the 'extraneous issue' as lopped off, when it was that issue alone, as you're aware, that has interested me here?"

Her eyes touched him with a transient scrutiny. She answered, now with her usual assurance:

"As I say, that was the point that I wanted light upon. I'm afraid you've answered me fully! — no matter. . . . In any case,

I wanted to lay the offer before you, for the simplest of reasons. It seemed the best practical evidence I could give that your work here, so admirable in every respect, has not passed —"

"Thank you. Yet you scarcely viewed the offer as just an amiable gesture?"

"Well! — one always hopes, of course —"

"You've concluded, perhaps, that I've changed my mind as to the importance of the issues involved here? — "

"Oh, *no!* Not at all! —"

"You have not?"

"Really won't you view the offer, however ill-judged, at least as meant as a tribute in its way?"

"I have a curiosity in learning whether it's a tribute I can properly thank you for."

On that her look settled, still further. She said in a rather stiffer tone:

"I so consider it, certainly. But you're right — it's for you to judge. . . . Then I'll confess I thought it conceivable that, without swerving a hair's breadth from your convictions, you might have felt the presence of other issues here which — yes, which might seem to change a little the complexion of the —"

"In short, that I'd reached the happy conclusion that all this was, after all, just an exercise in freedom? — your freedom, that is, your 'basic rights'?"

"No; only that you might have come to consider that the issue of freedom — no, let's just say the issue of fair-play — was considerably involved."

Her gaze, which had become steady and grave under his tone, seemed now to take on a sudden pointedness. The man sat suddenly motionless, returning it.

"To that thought I do plead guilty. . . . Will you say that I had no justification at all for it?"

"It's impossible for me to imagine any. I told you, when you raised the point —"

"Then set me right again! I ask for it!"

Having thus checked him, the girl paused; her eyes fell and she deliberated; she went on rapidly, through a faint recurring embarrassment: "I've learned, altogether by chance, that you — you've defended me, in a difference of opinion with one of your own friends — a serious difference which — became more or less public. That in any case seemed to me a remarkably generous thing to do, a thing . . . no matter. But how could I help from supposing, when I heard of it, that you'd found *something* in — in my situation to defend?"

In the silence that followed that, Masury seemed to feel himself pale a little. He had, again, a second of mere stupefaction; then the stunned senses cleared with a snap, and as in a vision, all was clear. The figure of his adversary, in her present pose, regarding him with those strange eyes, decorative yet formidable, faded from his sight, and the eye of his mind saw her otherwise.

For this, as it happened, was not the first time that Masury had seen his employer to-day. An hour earlier, showing out the manager of the Filing Bureau, who had come with the two new men, he had had an accidental glimpse of her: standing at the threshold of her door down the public hall, ushering out a visitor of her own. That visitor, as he had also seen, was Mr. James Parmenter, whose duties as adviser seemed to bring him so often to the Edsall Building. The two, caught in their fleeting scene, were apparently in high good humor. Her smile had seemed the bright banner of success. . . .

Of course, Uncle James, a celebrated gossip, would have heard of the incident at the club: without doubt he had made a charming tale of it. Who could say, in fact, what touches and turns the gallant fellow had n't given it, to compliment this girl whom he admired? "Why, it's evident you've won his alle-

giance completely," you could imagine the old courtier saying.
. . . No, really, you could hardly blame her for any degree of
misunderstanding.

He sat fixing her with eyes which had ceased to see, silenced
and checkmated, pressed down with a sense of the strange inopportunity of destiny. How would he clear now his so complicated
integrity? . . .

She dispelled the awkwardness of the pause with dignity, and
yet with a human feeling too:

"I've hesitated to mention the matter, since I was sure you
would object to my knowing anything about it — and certainly
that you did n't wish thanks from me. I especially did n't want
you to think that I confused this in any way with the permanent
difference between us. That, indeed, would be a poor compliment to you. . . . Still, I wanted to speak of it too — to thank
you nevertheless. As I *had* heard of the — the matter, it seemed
impossible to pretend that I had n't. . . . To pretend that you
had n't, again, put me under a peculiar obligation to you —"

"Oh, no! Really! — not in the least!"

His laugh, not sardonic, not unkind, actually touched with a
desperate humor, abruptly cut through the cumulative sentences
which had seemed to be winding him about as with a net of
fine steel.

"I'm really sorry, but I'm afraid there's been a — sort of
misunderstanding. You, of course, don't wish to be placed under any obligation — I assure you there's none in this case. The
truth is — and I know you want the truth — I did n't defend
you at all."

On the lily cheek a faint color rose; again her expression communicated a slight discomposure that seemed womanly in quality, but the grave gaze of his chief did not waver. "Then I'm
afraid I've made the most unwelcome mistake imaginable —"

"Oh, no harm done! — none whatever! Quite natural!" he

said hastily. "It's merely that some one's seemed to have gotten the cart a little before the horse, that's all. As it happened, what I was defending on the occasion you speak of — a mere casual conversation of really no importance — was nothing personal at all — just an abstract principle."

The inclination of her head silently accepted this statement, while her look said that he would scarcely stop there. On the whole, he acquitted her of blame; this little misunderstanding was not of her making. Besides, he would have his innings yet. He faced it out stoically, while his nerves jangled.

"An elementary principle, which of course you'll agree with — don't make arguments without evidence to support them. Fair-play in controversy, perhaps you'd prefer to put it? By all means. When you asked me just now if that was n't involved here, I hardly grasped the — the application. Needless to say, the question of fair-play's involved in every controversy."

"I'm sorry to seem inquisitive, but was I wrong in understanding that I — that my case — was the occasion of the abstract discussion in this instance?"

"Oh, it was — yes, indeed!" said Masury, like one who willingly ceded that straw, if any one cared for it. "I'm just explaining that the occasion, from my standpoint, was purely accidental. The fact is, if you'll pardon the autobiographical note, I'm often irritated into resisting disorderly methods of argument — quite regardless of my position in the controversy otherwise. It's an old habit — efficiency, perhaps? . . . For instance, there was the affair of the recent disaffection here in the office — you happen to know of that case — a good example. At such times, the original controversy is in abeyance for the moment — just a peg to hang a very different argument on — as abstract as the letter x in a problem. . . ."

The brightness of day was passing fast. From the file-room came the muffled voices of the overtime workers, beginning their interminable task. Down the corridor the old negro porter appeared, in brown duck overalls, with mops and buckets. Seeing the president of the company talking over some matter with the office-manager, he shook his head slightly, after gazing a moment, and shuffled away in his enormous work-shoes, as comic as Chaplin's. Twilight came creeping into the tidy room. The reorganized offices were still.

"I think I understand you perfectly," said Miss DeSilver.

Her eyes dropped to the handful of papers in her lap, encased in one of his new-style file-jackets. Her face betrayed nothing. However, he was quite aware that what she understood perfectly was not his difficult distinctions, but his positive repudiation of part or share with her.

"If I've merely offended you," resumed the steelmaster slowly, "by referring to a matter which you feel I had no right to hear of at all, I'm sorry. To offend you, over that, is of course the last thing I could wish. But my motive in asking you to stay, as I say, was quite apart from that. . . . I mustn't let you misunderstand me there. Your work for the Whitestone Steel Company — which I view as a continuing institution, bigger than personalities and detached from them — has made a deep impression on me, its present head. I wanted to offer, in the company's name, some formal mark of its appreciation. If I offered you the secretaryship, it was only because that was the best I had."

The manager bowed, rather stiffly. Yet even then, some part of the loud discord within him did stubborn credit to the grace of that withdrawal.

"I had also another reason for broaching the subject of the future," she went on steadily. "When I asked if you could consider this business here with the abnormal issue lopped off, I put it in that general way to avoid even seeming to try to put pressure on you — or condition you in any way. Now I must tell you, and I wished to tell you this in any case, that that issue *is* lopped off. . . . That remains as it began, my personal responsibility, now and for the future. Otherwise—it has ceased to exist."

The two unyielding gazes seemed to lock. Perhaps the man's imperturbability surprised her a little, then?

"You're saying, I take it, that you've made your control of the company absolute?"

She hesitated, just perceptibly, and said with a slightly altered look: "That I shall do so, when the time comes."

Was it the guarded locution, was it that look, somehow reminding him that she was, beyond amenities, a determined fighter, guarding her own? He was instantly certain that she had not got the Coit stock, that all his thought in that direction had been mistaken, that that lopping off she spoke of was to be otherwise consummated. . . . Convinced now that the missing block could not turn up against her, she had arranged for a technical "readjustment"; that was all. But suppose the missing block did turn up against her? . . . The small door of chance, which he had thought finally closed, suddenly creaked ajar.

But for that instant, at least, the thought of DeSilver Coit was scarcely interesting; his matter went far further. Legal jugglery was permissible, no doubt; but the knowledge that the young woman was up to it, with the pointed reminder of their external "fight," seemed somehow to release him from his curious inner stalemate; and all at once he was free again, with his need grown. . . .

"I thought it right to tell you this," said Teresa De Silver. "You've laid your cards fairly on the table; I want at least to return that in kind. I've gathered that — for no selfish reasons — you've gone to considerable trouble to — to restore the earlier policy and the earlier management of the company. It may be that you're still going to trouble — still just in obedience to your principles, to your —"

"No, I'm afraid you've misunderstood again," said her manager abruptly. "The fact is, what you call my principles have
been almost incidental with me, from the beginning."

That strange speech stopped her at once. She could hardly
see in it more than another and cruder dissociation of himself
from her, this time simply wilful in its character. Her look
changed, perceptibly stiffening; a sudden reserve seemed to
lower over her like a veil. She made a little gesture with her
hand and slightly inclined her head.

"That must be as you prefer, of course."

And then, glancing at the watch on her wrist, the president
pushed back her chair in the same movement, and rose.

"But I see my time is running short . . . I'll want a few words
with you one day next week, to make arrangements —"

"No! — no!" he again interrupted, hastily. "Don't go! —
just yet, please. . . ."

Standing, the girl regarded him through long-lashed eyes
above which the dark and delicate eyebrows had visibly arched.
This face, in its colorless and now rather haughty immobility,
had indeed the power of conveying a mysterious aloofness.

He came slowly to his feet. At his height, he frowned down
at the desk-top with a sort of hard absorption.

"There's something further I'd like to say — apropos of the
offer you made me just now."

"Yes?"

He had touched his nadir; there was no further to fall. And
surely now, by "toil and pain," he had earned every right. In
that offer of the best she had, she, his adversary, had singularly
testified to the confidence she had come to feel in him. The
inopportunity of destiny had, after all, this obverse: that he had
an approach to this difficult "headstrongness" such as few
men, certainly, had ever attained. . . .

"You made me a proposal," he began, in a controlled voice,

"which, as you were aware, seemed to go contrary to certain beliefs — and intentions — of mine, yet carrying offsets, as you believed, which might make it still acceptable. . . . Well, I want to make you a counter-proposal of the same sort. Except that my proposal actually *supports* your fundamental sympathies — and it's on that basis alone that I urge it upon you."

"I will listen willingly," said Teresa De Silver, "to anything you have to suggest."

Dean Masury's head lifted with a sort of jerk, and he flung out:

"Miss DeSilver — why don't you give this up?"

Then for a space, while these two stood confronted, there was heard again the unintelligible murmur from the files, and the vague clatter of the porter in more distant parts.

"I don't understand," said the girl's colorless voice. "Why don't I give up what?"

Words poured from him, the unconquerable adversary, in a stream, rapid and cold:

"Give up this pacifistic demonstration you've tried to make here! Acknowledge and yield to the vital facts that are so much bigger than any theory, yours or mine. In your own time, in your own way, for the sake of your own cause — yield! For surely you must know now that what you've undertaken to do here you, at least — fairly or unfairly — cannot do. In your heart you must have felt now that your meanings, in the essential sense, have already ended in failure. Well! — you speak of obedience to a principle: do you know of a finer obedience than unselfishly to withdraw from a position you can no longer justify? . . ."

All the light had died out of her face while he spoke, and she stood staring at him with eyes full of incredulity and distaste. The clear pallor of her cheek had deepened; she was suddenly quite white.

"Are you serious?"

"*Why!* — could you conceive of a *fool's* jesting —"

"Still less could I conceive your imagining a solution here in shocking self-stultification for me — "

"Stultification! You miss the point altogether! It's vindication that I propose to you — the opportunity —"

"How do you feel free to say that my undertaking has ended in failure?"

"How? Good God!" broke from him. "Does n't the hostility to you everywhere convey any thought *at all* to you? — except that 'it is n't fair' that your little 'rights' should be interfered with? Has n't it once occurred to you, in a month's full experience, that that very unfairness — and it *is* unfair, I say it willingly! — that the extraordinary bitterness of the attacks on you — means that there's something *peculiarly* wrong? That very discussion you just referred to, when you were told that I'd defended you — can't you really see anything in your immense *need* of such defence, except that I've turned my coat —"

"Enough, enough! Your drift is clear," Teresa DeSilver interrupted, peremptorily. "I scarcely have to be told, at this day, that my cause is unpopular, and my —"

"But what do you gain by *making it more unpopular?* . . . Don't you understand that what I'm saying to you is that your advocacy only injures the cause you say you want to help?"

There at last he struck her; not only struck but silenced her. In full flight as she was, obviously near to anger, the sudden thrust checked her instantly. Her whole being seemed mysteriously to subside. She stood gazing at him, wide-eyed and speechless.

"Which do you value most, Miss DeSilver," finished Masury, with unconscious sternness — "your cause, or your privilege of personally asserting your cause? I think the time's come when you will have to choose between them."

Her eyes left his face.

With an experienced gesture, she knocked off her glasses, which fell to the length of the pendent black ribbon. Quite as if she were alone, the bagger of the company pressed the tips of thumb and forefinger against her closed lids, as people do when their eyes are tired. Then with the palm of her hand she pressed her forehead vigorously with an upward stroke or two; that again was the gesture of fatigue, and of those who pray for patience. Next she paced a step or two away from him, in a sort of controlled abstraction, and, turning thoughtfully, came a step or two back. Last of all she stood and looked at her manager again, out of those incredible orbs of hers, beautiful and hard.

"All right," she said with a naturalness which all but startled him. "I'm not only gazing down the crossroads you indicate, but I invite you to point the way. Pray explain to me how I'm injuring the cause I say I want to help."

She had a largeness of spirit, one must give her that. Was not that, in fact, already fully given her in this counter-offensive of his, which no wise man, surely, would have essayed with a small-minded opponent? In her known large reasonableness, he had glimpsed his slippery approach. . . .

"I speak," he began deliberately, yet with quickening breath, "of the unbreakable connection between the cause and — the person who offers the cause. I speak of the merciless — and unfair — judgments of public opinion — to which you alluded the other day — and I say that those judgments can be avoided — in a controversial issue — only through the public confidence *already won*. Do you recall, giving me a sentence from a book one day, to point a moral? Let me give you another from memory, from a pen older than Bury's. . . ."

And in a voice which, through its iron substance, yet somehow disclosed the color of feeling, Masury recited old words that had long possessed to his ear the finality of an epitaph: "*All men*

*are not fit to be champions of righteousness, but many, having rashly
stormed the troops of error, do but leave themselves for trophies with
the enemies of the truth. . . ."*

Between the perfect arched brows, there had appeared a faint
perpendicular line. The straight gaze prolonged itself. So far
from betraying anger at his damning text, the strange girl leaned
casually against the corner of his desk, and said, in an even
voice:

"You interest me. Tell me, how have I become a trophy for
the enemies of the truth?"

Thus specifically, the too celebrated Miss DeSilver authorized, nay asked, her "temporary clerk in the local office" to
point out her faults and her foibles. He was conscious enough of
the cold excitement within him. And yet this too seemed curiously foreordered and inevitable: what else had his quarrel
with her pointed to so straight from the beginning?

He began to speak, and the sentences came crowding:

"I'm a good deal older than you, Miss De Silver, and through
my interests it's happened that I've thought considerably about
this subject in the large. Reform — propaganda — the advertisement of a new idea. . . . I'm convinced that it's a delicate
business, requiring distinct and peculiar qualifications. My observation is that reputation — that is, the general position in the
community of the person who offers the revolutionary idea — is
of the first importance. It does n't do to say, you'll agree, that
the truth's the truth, whether Brown speaks it or Jones.
There's no such thing as the abstract truth, and when it's a
question of a speculative hypothesis, there's necessarily an enormous difference in the weight it carries in the public mind when
it's Brown that sponsors it instead of Jones. And that's the reformer's sole object — to *convince the public mind.* . . . Now, my
experience is that what convinces especially — beyond ability
and character, or deserts — is a reputation for 'soundness,' as

people call it — a record of *regularity*. If the person proposing the new idea is known to be perfectly orthodox in all his other ideas, then the public mind recognizes him as part of the safe established order — he speaks the accepted language of the tribe, and people will listen fairly while he 'demonstrates' his theory. If, on the other hand, he has constantly come forward with new ideas, if he passes quickly from one proposed change in the common establishment to another, the tribe, which did n't erect the establishment without a great deal of difficulty and suffering, becomes first uneasy and then suspicious, and in the end simply vindictive. Their revenge is to label that person an 'agitator' or a 'crank,' to attack his motives and his character and to distrust and oppose him in whatever he recommends.

"That is why I'm justified in saying that, in practice — fair or unfair — the more vulnerable the reformer, the weaker grows his case — and it falls out often that he is cited against it.

"You're a public figure, Miss DeSilver, and your views are necessarily well known to the community. Do you find behind you to-day a large backing of public confidence already won, which alone could bring any hope of success to your moral purpose here? I'm quite familiar with the whole situation, and I don't see any — not any. I'm satisfied that another person, from a different position, could have closed that shell-plant, just as you did, and roused little or no opposition — and won far more support. . . . If you'll think the case over dispassionately from just that standpoint, I'm certain you won't be able to escape the conclusion that at least *one* issue here, seriously complicating and coloring your whole undertaking, has been and will continue to be just — yourself."

His listener leaned against the desk with slightly lowered head, showing him a profile which might have been cut from marble. At some point in his address she had picked up her pince-nez, where it swung; and, producing a small handkerchief from a

recess in the cowl, moving her fingers only, she was carefully
polishing the enormous lenses. Now, with the same curious
stillness, she set the hideous contraption back on the bridge
of her nose, and said in a voice from which all tone was pressed
out:

"I follow your argument, I think. Doesn't the application
seem a little excessive? Viewing myself as a reformer — which,
by the way, I hadn't done — I don't recall having identified
myself with so many public issues as to have forfeited —"

"That's true, no doubt. But in this particular case — naturally — not much would be required that way."

"Naturally? . . . I am puzzled, since I'd understood that it was
in the multiplicity of my new ideas that I had proved my un-
soundness?"

The man, having briefly paused, said with a hard deliberation: "But not all new ideas can be described as public issues,
should you say? I suspect there are idiosyncrasies that are even
farther reaching."

The woman's head lifted; her eyes came up to him with an inquiry whose challenge he did not miss. He gave a laugh, odd
and dry.

"You're hardly unaware that yours is a very special case —
and one illuminated by a great white light these many years?
That must excuse the familiarity of strangers. . . . It's true,
your sex would be a handicap in any case, for a leader of lost
causes. I don't go into that. . . . It's a handicap that many
women have successfully overcome. In their fundamental attitude toward their own prime responsibility, that is, toward
their womanhood, they have been so sound and sane, so poised
and trustworthy, that every one observing them has been
reassured —"

"Has it occurred to you," she interrupted sharply, "that you
make your argument unnecessarily personal —"

"Ridiculous," he said, with a sudden roughness. "If the argument is personal, don't you know very well it's not my making? . . . And don't tell me that, having expressly invited my views, you are n't strong enough to sit and listen to them."

The look that went between them then was a pure revelation of conflict.

"These are fatal times and fatal questions, Miss DeSilver," said Dean Masury. "Beside them, little civilities from me to you hardly matter much, do you think? Be big enough to consider the facts judicially. . . . Is it, or not, true that at just the point where the community is most sensitive, you've managed to give it your hardest jolt — that just where the public mind most insists on orthodoxy in a woman, you've made it known everywhere that you're — fantastically almost unorthodox? Great heavens," said the clerk, in a curious, quiet voice. "What do you suppose the average normal person who makes up the world feels, when he reads an article about 'The Woman Who Hates Love'? Don't you know that to him it's exactly as if he'd read, 'The Woman Who Despises Truth' — 'The Lass Who'—"

"*Stop!*"

"'The Lass Who Loathes God'? Don't you know that if he'd never heard your name before —"

"Stop! . . . I will not listen to you!"

The strange woman had come to her feet with her first sharp command; now, with a swift movement, she seized the man's wrist in a grip unexpectedly strong for so small a hand. The odd manifestation, it was clear, was as unconscious as a reflex: as if the inner power of her resistance to him had compelled a physical expression. Still there she was, Saint Teresa, surprisingly gripping him — looking into his eyes with the curious, unconscious, hard insistence of a strong-willed man prepared for any trouble. The slender fingers tightened on his arm. Then ab-

ruptly, as if becoming aware of herself, she released the domi-
nating grasp, relaxing with some effort. The hand fell at her
side.

In a moment she spoke, and he was aware of her rapid
breathing.

"It's a coincidence that having come to thank you for scrupulous fairness, I should be met with such peculiar unfairness."

The excitement within him mysteriously ebbing, Masury felt
suddenly remote from her, all but indifferent to what she said
now. She wasn't big enough to view her own situation ob-
jectively, that was clear; she could learn nothing in considering
the profound roots of his hostility. She had seen them, at least
— and this was the end.

All at once he was weighted by a sense of irreparable disaster.
A great lassitude possessed him.

With a slight shrug, he murmured distantly: "If fairness toward yourself is still your principal concern!"

"More unfairness! But when one's made responsible for what
any penny-a-liner cares to say, the verdict is easy. I'm —"

"Again you miss the point. Come, do you say that the penny-
a-liner had no justification for —"

"I'll not discuss my 'idiosyncrasies' with you."

"As you like. Nevertheless that has been the chief subject
of my discussion with you from the beginning."

He had the way to her, that was clear. Again a speech of his,
by its strangeness and point, successfully checked her. These
quiet words, charged with the naked truthfulness of one who has
no more to lose, seemed indeed completely to divert her thought.

"May I inquire what that means?"

The man shook his head with a wintry smile. "You wouldn't
understand if I were to tell you."

"You think not? . . . At least I don't forget your saying that
your principles were hardly concerned here. And I've necessa-

rily wondered, before to-day why you, wanted to come here —
drudging in an office to help the cause *you* wanted to injure!"

"There are sentiments that are deeper than principle, Miss
DeSilver."

Her look upon him became curiously intent.

"Then perhaps I was n't so grossly *gauche* after all," flashed
from her, "in thinking you might *want to stay!*"

And though the clerk found it unnecessary to make any reply
to that, something far away inside of him concluded then that
she understood him sufficiently well. At least, she could hardly
fail to think that he had fully recanted that unforgotten speech
of his, about seeing no promise of interest in her. . . . Well, antagonism was interest of a sort; one must concede her that. . . .

The soft twilight had faded while they talked; dusk stole into
the quiet workplace. The man and woman eyed each other in
the deepening dimness, and all at once it was seen that both unyielding faces looked tired, a little spent.

"I thank you for the elderly counsel you 've been kind enough
to give me," said Saint Teresa, in a somewhat stirred voice.
"It was certainly ingenious of you, but the truth is I don't *convert easily a bit.* . . . I don't know how to take my principles on
and off like a hat, and I can't see my way clear to handing over
Whitestone to you and Mr. Ball. I'm an unfit champion of
righteousness — that's conceded. And still I'd a thousand times
rather try to champion what I think's righteous — and fail —
and die . . . than be content as the unfit champion of nothing at
all — than make a shameful surrender under fire —"

"You'd rather be!" he interrupted with a devastating absence of all emphasis. "Still thinking of yourself, I see. What
you're doing to your righteousness does n't matter —"

"No," said she, all at once as quiet as he, "odd as it seems,
I'm not thinking of myself, but of my righteousness. The point's
just that I don't accept your offhand opinions there as equiva-

lent to the word of God. . . . And even if I knew that I were injuring my cause — and I've abundant evidence to the contrary,
by the way — I'd still not dream of giving up — for the excellent reason that that would injure my cause far more. It's
curious if you are n't aware that for me to do what you propose would be to justify every one in concluding that either I
was beaten, or that I knew I was wrong. Well, I'm *not* beaten
and I'm *not* wrong, and I'll not stab my own righteousness by
falsely acting as if I were!"

Dean Masury smiled, and thought of Coit; his lean face
looked dark.

"I listen to you, Miss DeSilver. About how wrong I consider
you, there's nothing more to say. As to whether or not you're
beaten — and I've been drudging here to help *you* — I prefer to
wait and see for myself, *when the time comes.*"

The girl continued to gaze at him for some seconds, with an
expression beyond his fathoming. And then, to his surprise,
without a word, she turned on her high heels and went away.

The man's eyes moved after her. She had a natural dignity of
carriage; even in that robe, she did not lack grace. Receding, she
traversed the breadth of the general room to the door that led to
the secretary's office, where he had sat and trapped Janney, one
memorable day; her hand touched the knob. However, his
withdrawing adversary did not at once open the door, and disappear from view. Her hand, as it were, paused on the knob; she,
the resolute, seemed to suffer a moment of irresolution. And
then the incalculable woman turned on her heels once more and
came slowly back: back over the floor she had just crossed, halfway to her manager's desk, where he stood silent in the vague
dusk, regarding her with his lidless gaze.

"I'm not willing to have your connection with the company —
which has deserved so well in every sense," said she straightforwardly, yet with some constraint too, "end on this note —

just a trivial wrangling of personalities. That does n't seem fitting to me, and in fact, it puts all wrong — what I came in here to say."

A slight change, a faint relaxation, flickered over the man's controlled face. In fact this act, these words from her, through and above his conflicting senses, profoundly disturbed him.

"You're perfectly right in saying," continued the young steelmaster, in measured tones, "that nothing matters beside the reality of the questions involved, and there's the less cause for me to take offence, since I know that nothing you've said or done here has been for yourself at all, but always for something bigger — for an idea. . . . It seems much truer to assure you that I shall keep, rather, a vivid sense of just that — of your pure disinterestedness through all this relationship. Perhaps I understand your course here better than any one else, and I must tell you how impressed I've been all along, by your perfectly single-minded devotion to *your* righteousness — a quality which I can admire without reference to the fact that it's brought you, in this case, so vigorously against me. I — could only regret that we might n't have met on some other issue, where our fundamental purposes could run together — regardless of sentiments — for indeed no one could desire an abler or more valuable ally."

Dean Masury's eyes had fallen from the pale face whose allurement was visible to him now under whatever disguise; and the discomposure within him was spreading and deepening. It was as if this valediction, so far finer than bitter phrases, was utterly disarming him; in a quite new and better sense, this girl was getting the best of him. Frightfully embarrassed, he pushed back the rumpled hair from his forehead, and with an immense effort stammered:

"You — you're very kind I'm sure, to — to say this."

"No, I'm merely unwilling, as head of the company, and therefore embodying its relation to you, to leave you thinking

I could — could entertain a grievance toward you. My chief thought, you must permit me to add," said the president, a little diffident again in her resoluteness, is "really very different.... I'd like, since you wish it, to confine myself to the abstract — even to think of myself as just the letter x in a problem. But that's difficult, since to myself, you see, I'm not abstract at all but necessarily quite personal. . . . To say a word for me, or my case, takes a good deal of courage in these days, as I know very well; from one so deeply opposed to both, it seems to me to take something quite above courage. For that generosity, Mr. Masury, I'd have to be a stock or a stone if I did n't feel under a peculiar debt to you, and that's the way I do feel, transcending every difference. I'm sorry to pain you, and affront your conception of my proper attitude, and everything, but for what you did for me the other night, I thank you — and I thank you and I thank you, and I always will."

The voice of the headstrong and mistaken girl had become a little moved. Her shadowy eyes, fixing in him the dimness, were beautiful and grave. The gaze broke: she had turned away; this time she did not pause. Janney's door presently clicked. She was gone.

Dean Masury sat down in his manager's chair, full of a nameless depression.

CHAPTER XVIII

YET the end of conflict was not yet. Generous words, though one admire them, butter no parsnips. In him she had, in truth, an adversary not easily bested or tired. Within five minutes of the clicking of that door, Masury had begun to think of DeSilver Coit.

His mind came to fasten with extraordinary tenacity upon this slender but astonishing hope.

If she had had the Coit stock, she would not have given that guarded answer; if she did not have the Coit stock, it followed certainly that Coit himself had it, and that his return at this time was for his own reasons and a pure coincidence. From that premise, in turn, sprang a train of interesting reflections. . . . If the unfathomable idiot who controlled the destiny of White-stone was loose in the city, then the control of Whitestone was loose in the city. If the cursed monkey had appeared once at Forty-Second Street and Broadway, then he might appear again at that corner — or at some other corner, or in the middle of some block — at any moment. If the woman were not clever enough to go out and find him — "Pardon me, but are you the mysterious Mr. Raffles of the '*Morning Bugle*'?" — then the way was open to somebody else to go out and find him. The man was here; he was somewhere. . . . Maddening, indeed, it was to think that at this instant or that, as he sat here at his desk in the Whitestone office or in the rooms on Irving Place, the little brown rascal who had what he desired more than anything else on earth, might stroll nonchalantly by the door.

When these considerations had pursued Masury steadily through two nights and days, he found himself resolving to do what he had meant never to do. He would take his secret to

Walter E. Ball. The thought of conspiring with the vindictive predecessor — a man whose scruples were regulated solely by the revised statutes, and his honor kept by the police — remained indeed repellent to him. Still, it was emphatically no moment for squeamishness; rather the case presented a desperate necessity.

For there was, of course, only one thing to do. That was to go and find De Silver Coit — Mr. "Albertson": to employ searchers, ten or a hundred or a thousand searchers, to ransack New York and Brooklyn and Jersey, and go on ransacking till they found him. By luck he had a unique description of the fugitive; by the same luck, the trail behind him would be broadly marked: no stranger who had seen that bearded gnome, skipping like a tomtit, was likely to forget him. All that was required — urgently required, since the time was short —was an alarm and search on the largest possible scale. Such a search passed beyond his personal resources; on the other hand, it had already been made clear that Ball's associates both possessed unlimited resources and were ready to go to any lengths. Certainly it did not seem that "interests" which had been ready to comb the jungles of the Far East should be staggered at the thought of canvassing Broadway.

Yet Masury deliberated. He would stomach Ball, since that was necessary; Ball's mysterious "backers" offered a queasier pill. In his inmost thought he was certain that Ball's backer was none other than Mr. Josiah DeSilver — who, as Ball himself had said once, was bitter against his granddaughter "till it'd curdle your blood to listen to him." Thus to plot with Ball about searchers was actually to plot with that sinister old man. Another step, through the tangled net of circumstance, and one would find one's self working shoulder to shoulder with Miss Janney. The thought fell across his plannings like a fence. . . .

On Sunday, when the problem of what to do had grown acute

— for he meant to act on Monday, without fail — Masury had a chance meeting with Lucy Flanner.

For reasons not far to seek, the rencontre was unwelcome to him: yet so it fell out. He had been lunching — reluctantly — with his sister Millie, Mrs. Haskell, who was an inquisitive woman, and a boring one, he thought; and returning, happening to pass along Thirty-Ninth Street, he fairly ran into Lucy, just emerging from her own doorway with an escort of two high-hatted gentlemen. Avoidance being out of the question, Masury greeted her with unusual marks of pleasure.

One of Lucy's companions was her director Steinfeldt; the other was a ferocious-looking stranger, presented by Lucy as Professor Pitcoe. Pitcoe, as it chanced, welcomed an opportunity for a man-to-man chat with Steinfeldt; laying a hand on the director's arm, he dragged him aside at once. From snatches of conversation presently overheard, Masury gathered that the Professor was explaining, in a few words, what was the matter with the movies.

Thus the two friends, who had conspired on Easter Day, might talk together.

"You were n't by any chance coming to see me, I suppose?" Mrs. Flanner had asked at greeting, in the sprightly vein.

He laughed, and said no such luck for him. He mentioned that he had work to do; also, that she seemed adequately provided.

"To the office — another Sunday?"

No, this was some stuff he had promised to do for "Parson's" a long time ago. Weeks overdue, it was.

"But you'll soon have plenty of time for that? — you've nearly finished with Whitestone, have n't you?"

It would be through with him very soon, he conceded, while wondering how she had known that; Saturday, in fact. And a good job he had made there too, if he did say so.

"But where are you off to with the drove of swains, Lucy?" her mumured, rallying. "You look too beautiful for a mere walk — more parties, I'll be bound?"

Lucy, unfemininely, was not interested in the matter of her appearance. If she could have passed for twenty-five at this moment, she felt forty at least; and as to looks, Dean's, which betrayed to her eyes the unmistakable signs of strain, had given her, at the sight of him, a curious sinking of the heart, exceedingly mature in nature. More pointedly than George Davis, Lucy was aware that she was far outside of this man's confidence. But what was the good of pretending, or beating about the bush? For a month now, she and he had had but one topic.

"We're going to the studio. By the way — I went to see Teresa, this morning after church. She's in a state, too."

Coloring faintly at her slip, but not attempting an impossible correction, she added hastily, with an exasperated laugh: "I declare I wish Whitestone had never been born! It seems meant to bring nothing but trouble to everybody that touches it!"

"Why, a little trouble's very wholesome at times, don't you think?" said Dean, with his annoying air of amiable indifference. "But why in the world should she be 'in a state too'?"

"I'm sorry! . . . But I can't help knowing that you have a will that does n't bend easily, either. It's one thing I like you for — yes, and fear you a little too. . . . Oh, nothing unexpected — just that Mr. DeSilver's broken with her definitely. He left the house yesterday."

"Oh, did he?"

"Cut her off with a curse and no shilling and moved out bag, baggage and retinue, to an apartment in the Plaza. Good riddance, I'd say," said Lucy briskly; "but unluckily Teresa, for reasons that must be in her blood and tissues, feels otherwise. He's too old to live alone, she says; therefore he'll either marry

ridiculously or die at once — and either way, she's the cause.
It's the first time I've ever seen her really upset."

Resisting the admission of any of this into his consciousness,
Masury said with unmoved pleasantness:

"But then, as you say, she's foreseen all this for a long time?"

Lucy laughed oddly.

"Still, why should she tax herself with having broken his
heart? Why should n't the old monster on his side prove, to begin with, that he has one? Is it a crime that Teresa has n't forsworn her identity, forfeited her very soul to his —"

"My dear girl! — why put these posers to me?"

"Why indeed?" said Lucy quietly, but again with a trace of
a rare irritation.

She glanced away from him to Steinfeldt, whose solemn voice,
infinitely bored, began to answer Professor Pitcoe. Her mysterious sense was that of one gazing down upon, nay, caught in,
strange rapids — dark rapids that were hurrying to an unknown
fall. . . . Why? She could hardly have said. Her eyes returned
to Masury's face, and she said suddenly:

"Dean, I've thought a thousand times of that Sunday four
weeks ago, when I, to tease you, suggested your taking the
place with her. . . . Do you know, I've come to see that as one
of those somewhat ironic jests — through which poor helpless
people make themselves the instruments of fate?"

"How so, Lucy?"

But Lucy only shook her head slightly and turned away.
Over her shoulder, she called back with staccato vivacity:

"She said some awfully nice things about you, by the way!
— charming! Come to see me when you're not so busy!"

He went on his way in a deepened abstraction.

Why was it, in this worthy fight, that he thought of defeat as
a purely personal defeat — the case of Willie Connaught over
again, but magnified a hundredfold? Why did the very sound of

the woman's name, even now, when he was not defeated, stir in
him this sense of a personal something, personal and necessary,
forever left unfulfilled?

George Davis had had a nice Sunday. Yielding to the slight
religious anticlimax that followed Easter, and to the subtle in-
vitations of spring, George had named deputies to teach his
Bible class and pass his plate, and had vacated worship for the
day. Sleeping late, sallying forth in informal attire, he called for
Alice Williams at her home on President Street, and together
they had gone to Babylon to "spend the day" with their friends
the Ditmarshes. The Ditmarshes were charmed to see them, the
daffodils were blooming in the beds by the back door, and Alice
Williams, in her new spring dress, which was of blue foulard with
white polka-dots, looked positively pretty. As if George's guardian angel were determined that he should not go wholly secular
for the day, the Babylon rector and his wife came to lunch, and
he and George held the table with a pretty far-reaching talk on
the probable future of interdenominationalism; while afterwards,
as they sat in wraps upon the glassed-in porch, which Ella Dit-
marsh called a loggia, all listened while George alone, in a thirty-
minute talk, expounded the newer aspects of the war. And then
on the journey back, Alice Williams, who had already let out
that she was knitting him a purple sweater for his birthday, invited him to address her Girls' Club at its social next Saturday,
on the issues of the hour: a rather gratifying climax to a very
happy day.

The holiday Sabbath, continuing with half an hour at the
club, ended, by custom, at Miss Sophy Winterbotham's. Here,
as it fell out, the talk proved so unusually informative and fruitful
that George lingered beyond his wont, and it was eleven o'clock
when he climbed again the stairs on Irving Place.

The rooms-mate was seated in his familiar place. He wore an

eye-shade and an old jersey coat patched at the elbows, usually
the signs of literary preoccupation. As he looked round at his
friend's entrance, the light of the lamp fell over his face, and
George's thought changed instantly.

"'Lo," said he casually. "Well! — started working on those
articles, hey?"

Masury, who had in fact taken his manuscript from the
drawer at the sound of George's step, answered as easily: "Yes
— Hendricks has been after me. You're late! . . ."

While the Elder sat, unlacing his tight boots, the two men exchanged the habitual commonplaces of question and answer.
Seven years they had lived together, a model to the neighbors,
and in all that time had never exchanged a sharp word. Had
George had a nice day in the country? Yes, George had had a
fine day. The Ditmarshes' place was looking fine, the country
was looking fine, and he had had a fine talk with Reverend Dr.
Bartemus.

But George, conversing, seemed less expansive than might
have been expected; and in a moment, standing, sock-footed and
eased, he changed the subject altogether.

"Say, Dean . . . I was over at the club before supper. Saw
Lyman White, and we got talking about that Checkerman business. Seems there's a good deal of talk of calling Horace before
the board, for a reprimand."

Continuing to look at the wall in front of him, Masury said:
"Why, what for?"

"Well," said George slowly, "I guess there's some that
would n't be sorry to see Horace come a cropper anyway. Seems
a good many members think he's been getting a little too big for
his breeches here lately. . . . Well, the way the story's gone
round — and Doc White had got it straight from Wilfrid Winslow — the understanding is that he made some pretty nasty
remarks, and when you showed you objected to 'em, he just kept

on, getting worse, till you gave him a hard call-down provin' he did n't know what he was talking about; and then, instead of apologizing like a gentleman, he tried to make a pass at you, right there in the club —"

"Well, what of it?" interrupted Masury with creditable quiet. "There's a difference between war-times and a pink tea, don't you think? These squabbles have got to happen nowadays — and one side's usually as much to blame as the other. I hope you'll stand against any idea of reprimanding Checkerman. It would be ridiculous — and unfair to both of us."

"It'd be a board matter," said George, more authoritatively, for he had been a governor these five years. "We could n't consider either your wishes or Checkerman's, but only the good of the club. Still — well, I don't guess anything'll really come of it."

Rubbing the thin spot in his hair with his thumb-knuckle, the Elder shot his rooms-mate a curious glance, touched with a vague bewilderment.

"Well, anyway," he concluded deliberately, after a pause, "the sentiment speaks for itself, I guess — and this particular squabble's going to have a wholesome effect, my opinion. There's been a lot of loose talk around the club here lately, a lot of unfair, un-American talk. Why, great Scott! — did n't Ed Doolittle, when I said we licked England about her old search-warrants in 1812 and we could do it again *if* necessary, did n't Ed go and tell Roscoe Skipwith that I was no better than a pro-German! Me! And that's a sample of this kind of talk — they can't answer your argument, so they go lyin' around that you're a pro-German. Well, what I hear, certain people will try to be a little *fairer* after this, and some of these loud-mouthed know-it-alls'll think twice before they begin shootin' off their old bazoos. . . . Well, just thought I'd tell you," said George.

"Yes. Much obliged, George — appreciate it. . . . How'd you find Miss Sophy to-night? Rheumatism better?"

"Yes — she's fine," said George, a little set down. . . . "And hear! — well, just as good as you can. That aurophone, the Little Marvel, they call it, is sure a wonder. Oh, that reminds me — kind of a horse on me. . . ."

He was looking at the back of his rooms-mate's head, while with slow fingers he unbuttoned his collar, releasing a large Adam's apple, chafed to a ruby hue. With an odd touch of embarrassment by no means characteristic of him, he continued:

"Remember my telling you about a fellow, an old Sunday school scholar of Aunt Sophy's, that rovin' fellow that nobody had heard of for years — and she thought he must have been eaten by cannibals — and I did too? Well, blamed if that fellow has n't turned up again after all, and was there at the house to-night!"

"Well!" said Masury, polite but with an effort. . . . That *must* have been a pleasant surprise for Miss Sophy!"

"I should say. The old lady was in a real flutter when I got there. Said it was like one returning from the dead," said George mechanically. ". . . Funny. Just shows you never can tell. . . ."

This time the rooms-mate, rocking slightly on the hind-legs of his chair, fingering manuscript vainly conceived as a shield, was slower in offering suitable comment. George, though he had possibly conceived his anecdote as encouraging in its way, hardly noticed the inattention. In truth, the minds of the two men in that moment were closer together than their words revealed. For the deepest part of George was thinking, while he talked: "But what's it all *about*, that's what I'd like to know! . . . I declare, I'd as soon he'd have gone off to Nooyey as ever got mixed up with this blamed steel company." And Masury, sitting with deaf ears and straining patience, was also considering that very same mix-up, upon which kind George's words about the "sentiment" had furnished the last sardonic commentary. . . .

He had set out to take the Whitestone Steel Company away

from Miss Teresa DeSilver; he had succeeded in giving her a model office with which to carry her enterprise to success. He had viewed himself as her predestined and invincible adversary; she had asked him, in gratitude, to remain as her ally and first lieutenant. He had embarked with the resolve to hurt her as badly as he could; now here he was back in port with the assurance that he had done her nothing but good. The final exquisite flavor of the anti-climax was surely this: that his acquaintance henceforward would criticize Teresa DeSilver less, and some at least would always think better of her, because of what he had said and done. . . .

"Well!" he said stirring. . . . "And what had he been up to all this time?"

"Gettin' ready to translate the Bible into native dialects, is what he claims," answered George, without heart. "I don't know. . . . Well! — anyway, that's one time I was wrong."

But it was impossible to leave the matter like that, literally impossible. To do that would be to falsify his whole course, a simple dishonesty. This was a fight supremely worthy, without quarter, beyond personal niceties. He still had his chance: and that chance would be immensely strengthened with the power of Josiah DeSilver behind him.

He would swallow this squeamishness; he would telephone Ball the first thing to-morrow. . . .

"Well, it's late," said George's voice, rather vaguely. "I guess I'll turn in."

The Elder began, with slow movements, to gather up his apparel. At the end of the happy day, he found himself not happy. These were worrying times. George yawned heavily, very tired. And then, something pleasanter came back to him out of the evening, a rare humorous bit that he had been unable to share with anybody at the time; and from his gloom and silence there broke unexpectedly, a little chuckle.

"Say, Dean, you'd have laughed to hear that fellow! *Talk!* — whew! Runs right along for two hours together, and never draws a breath — and the funny way he puts things! Well, he certainly does know a lot about native customs and religions and all, but between you and me, I believe he's got a touch of the sun — though o' course I'd never say it to Aunt Sophy."

All that the rooms-mate produced to that was a clipped, "Really?" Yet George, standing loaded like an old-clothesman, warmed a little under his thought.

"Blamed if I don't. First place, he's such a sight to look at — he don't look right! Black as the ace of spades, and bushy whiskers all over him, and so small he would n't make a mouthful hardly — and a little black eye that never looks at you! And the funny turns he gives! F'r instance, I said to him at supper, 'Mr. Coit, is it your honest opinion that you can ever make a real Christian out of a Papuan?' — and you'd have died to hear him. He — "

The front feet of Masury's chair, descending, struck the floor with a tap. His head turned abruptly, and he stared at George with a sudden piercing intentness which, though gratifying to a raconteur, yet did seem a little sudden. His voice, too, came out quite unlike his own, harsh and thick:

"*Who?* . . . WHO?"

"Who? — Why," said George, thinking that old Dean was certainly queer these days — did n't listen when you talked, that was what it was — "why, this fellow I been tellin' you about, that was at Aunt Sophy's to-night, Mr. Coit. 'Silvy,' she calls him, and I declare he looks as much like silver as I look like a bunch of violets! Well, I said to him, 'Mr. Coit, is it your honest opinion . . .' Why, what the devil's the *matter*, Dean? . . . You look as if you'd seen a *ghost!*"

The rooms-mate had astonished George by rising slowly and rigidly from his chair, with round glaring eyes that seemed to be popping from his head. The chair fell over behind him with a crash, but neither of the men heard it. George often said afterwards that he had n't known that a person *could* turn so white.

About quarter of twelve, Miss Sophy Winterbotham, in her discreet bower on West Ninth Street, was roused from a deep dream of peace by the peremptory ringing of her telephone. Starting up confusedly, thinking with vague forebodings of her brother Eugene, who was low in the hospital with diabetes, Miss Winterbotham clambered in alarm from her tall tester-bed, not even pausing to light the gas in her haste, and in consequence suffering a painful blow of the great-toe against a chair in the dark boudoir — all this to find that the ominous summons came from one of her nephews, George Davis, who had a fancy to learn, in the dead of night, the name of Silvy Coit's hotel! Greatly incensed, the aged churchwoman informed her nephew that she was not a public bureau of miscellaneous information, that she knew nothing whatever about Mr. Coit's affairs, and did not care to, and that she would not fail to think of George if she had to spend the next few days in bed with her lumbago. Paying no attention to her nephew's dismayed apologies, the indignant lady thereupon clicked up the receiver and went to put arnica salve on her foot.

Next morning, refreshed with an excellent sleep, and, contrary to expectations, feeling unusually well, Miss Winterbotham inclined toward a more tolerant view of the night's alarums. George, after all, belonged to the younger generation, which could not be expected to have the manners and the nice decorum of the old; moreover, to do him justice, he was as a rule anything but wanting in considerateness. Remembering dimly that he had made some mention of an urgent matter, the Christian woman had just made up her mind to let her servant call George on the telephone — a concession in itself, since her views about "calling" men at their offices or clubs were well known — when the doorbell rang and George himself was ushered upstairs.

Completely mollified by this evidence of contrition, Miss Winterbotham then conceded that, in point of fact, Silvy Coit had provisionally promised to come to tea with her on the following day, Tuesday, bringing his private pictures of the man-eating idolaters of Papua; graciously adding that George, since he had a business matter to discuss with Silvy, and to Silvy's advantage, might join them on this occasion, if he cared to — provided always that he said nothing to upset Silvy who, with the wild noble life he had led, had become so shy of strangers.

George, it seemed, did care to join them. He thanked his aunt with a sudden gushing warmth which showed that the kind forgiveness was indeed appreciated. On the other hand, he left her almost instantly. Within three minutes of the first mention of the provisional tea-engagement, the honest fellow, in a cigar-store on Sixth Avenue, was calling his rooms-mate at the Whitestone office.

Masury sat dining alone at a bleak basement restaurant on Seventeenth Street. After the strain of these weeks, and above all of these last nerve-racking hours, he was possessed by a great contentment, positive as a benediction, realer than peace out of pain. Scarcely touching the frugal table d'hôte, remote from his surroundings as a man in a trance, he mused on the marvel that had so suddenly befallen him: how the unreal had magically turned real, the dream come true, and the longest arm of coincidence ever seen, thrusting out of time and space, had made him master of Whitestone.

For so it was. Old George had done it. That block of long-dead stock, which had for weeks occupied the centre of his thought, was alive now; and it was his.

It was Wednesday again. For three days — down, in fact, to five o'clock this afternoon — the acute matter had stood at the touch. In the watches of Sunday night, it had seemed probable enough that the bearded idiot, having paid his call on his Sunday school teacher, would hop on the next boat and go back to Indo-China. George's message next morning had been an immense uplift. Yet of course it had settled nothing. In the first place, Silvy, the "shy," might not keep that provisional engagement. In the second place, keeping it, he might not have the stock — he might, after all, already have disposed of it to his cousin Teresa. In the third place, having it, he might eccentrically decline to sell. However, none of these mishaps had befallen, nor any mishaps at all. Indeed he found it astonishing to think with what simplicity this mighty transformation had been effected.

At half-past six o'clock yesterday afternoon, Josiah DeSilver Coit, "wanted" on sundry continents by divers people, stood — true enough — by the old organette in the chaste drawing-room of Miss Sophy Winterbotham. The little rascal had then been standing there for nearly three hours. Not only had he exhibited and reëxhibited his photographs of the misbehaving Papuans; not only had he dispensed native lore, excitedly and without cessation; this time quaint Silvy actually sang a large number of native chants, used for the feasts of the long pig, while George, in the most winning manner, endlessly improvised accompaniments on the organette. It must have been a mad tea-party; one could smile at it now. But then at last, Miss Winterbotham, pursuant to the solemn understanding, had flatly broken in on Silvy to go and get her knitting, and George, exhausted but determined, confronted his memorable opportunity.

"Say, by the way, Mr. Coit," he began, as one struck by a casual thought. "Did n't I hear somewhere that you were one

of the original stockholders in this little DeSilver steel company
— Whitestone? . . ."

Of the long colloquy that followed between the Elder and the
idiot, Masury by now, through much telling and retelling, knew
every phase and turn. The little psalm-singer had proved a
hard trader. George was early convinced that he not only knew
nothing of the present struggle for control of the company, but
had all but forgotten the existence of his stock, having long ago
marked it off in his mind as worthless. At the scent of cash,
however, Silvy at once pricked up his ears, while his whiskered
features assumed a falsely dubious expression. By cautious
steps he admitted that he might have a little of that stock; that,
in fact, he did have a nice block of the stock; that he had, specially reserved for his declining years, an exceedingly choice lot
of it — a block that would give a fellow a tenth interest — make
him a director, if he wanted to be — in one of the most promising steel propositions in the country. George, moving with
equal caution, pointed out that, through the odd chance of having a friend on the inside, he had happened to hear that this perfectly worthless stock, in a company that had been practically
insolvent for years, had lately acquired, through war conditions,
a certain ephemeral and fictitious value; in consequence, provided that Mr. Coit acted instantly, and could find some one to
guide him to the right market, he might at this moment hope for
as high as 30 for his block — 35 even, George conceded. (The
latter was, in fact, the price that Miss DeSilver had paid to one
Cecil Coit for a few shares, in March — the last known sale.)
So far from betraying elation at his windfall, Silvy had let his
bushy face lengthen and shaken his head with great gloom.
When he gravely pointed to Bethlehem as a fair indication of his
reasonable hopes, George, without regard to age or lore, gave a
short horse-laugh and began to strum on the organette. Wild
noble Silvy lighted a hookah and thumbed his ugly pictures.

Since both men powerfully desired action, however, the dickering was of course soon resumed. George admitted with manly frankness — what he knew the rascal had guessed from the start — that by an odd coincidence, he knew of one certain party — not a client of his, of no interest to him, George — who for special reasons of a sentimental character had a whim to buy in on the company; and that he, George, out of regard for Mr. Coit, and in appreciation of his talks and chants, might possibly induce this party to do a little better than even the present abnormal and purely fictitious price — say 37 or 38 — well, 40 then. Reciprocating, Silvy confessed that he harbored a peculiar affection for Miss Winterbotham, who had first taught him the consolations of religion; because of it, he longed to do anything in his power to oblige Miss Winterbotham's nephew, or Miss Winterbotham's nephew's friend. But still — a man did n't rob himself, and toss away property long passionately cherished, without a struggle, etc., etc. In the end the two men agreed at 45, and Aunt Sophy came back with her knitting.

That was Tuesday. To-day, as the upshot of those proceedings, Masury had sold all the marketable securities he possessed for what they would bring. Excepting his clothes, some furniture and ordinary personal possessions, this represented everything he had on earth — the sum of the acquisitions of an, on the whole, industrious lifetime. The yield in cash was just under thirty thousand dollars; his bankers and brokers, not very eagerly, had put up the rest. Thus, shortly after lunch, he had met George by appointment at an oyster bar on Fulton Street and handed over a certified check for forty-five thousand dollars to the order of Josiah DeSilver Coit. A memorable moment! Some hours later, George had met Coit, also by appointment, on the northwest corner of Broadway and Vesey Street, Silvy having positively refused to bring his certificate to George's office, or to any office whatever. There finally, on the windy street corner, while thousands of people streamed and jostled about them, the momentous exchange had taken place — not, it must be confessed, without the frankest precautions on both sides.

So it fell out, that Dean Masury's entire economic situation this evening was summed up — temporarily, indeed, for he had a contract with Ball to fulfil later on — in a debt of fifteen thousand dollars and a frayed yellow paper, lying in a locked dispatch-box in a locked trunk in the spare-room next his bedroom. So too it was that, with eyes still touched with a sort of wonder, he sat now staring at another paper — the private memorandum he had scratched off that first night, in Ball's den — which now, amended, made graphic his staggering triumph:

Distribution of Stock

Miss DeSilver — inherited		2,000 shares	
purchased		2,700	4,700
Blagden Estate	1,500		
Mr. Josiah DeSilver	700		
Mrs. Wilmot	500		
Mr. Lovering	500		
James Parmenter	400		
Mr. Ball	400		
John DeSilver Wilmot	300		4,300
D. Masury			1,000
			10,000

In the bleak restaurant, the last customer but one rose and went out. At a table in the corner, by the pantry door, the three waitresses had seated themselves to their dinner, for the hour was late. The last customer, lost to his environment, sat staring at those magical figures. . . .

In what she had said to him, Miss DeSilver had unquestionably been honest; she simply had not thought it possible that, at the last moment, a miracle would happen. But so it was. He and

George had thrashed it over twenty times. "She can't do a thing without the consent of the stockholders," said the lawyer, "and o' course she can't get consent if the voting majority's against her. As to that," he had added, more than once, for George, despite the loyalty of his heart, had reluctances over the forcible ejection of Miss DeSilver — "as to the alignment of the stock at that meeting o' course I don't undertake to say anything." But on that point, Masury himself undertook to say everything. Most of the shareholders had been associated with Mr. Henry Lovering in his proceedings for an injunction; all of them, beginning with Mr. DeSilver and Mr. Parmenter, were on record as being unalterably opposed to Miss DeSilver's policy. Ball had said again and again: "Not all the money the woman's got would buy her a share from any party on that list." No, there was no loophole there. The minority had marvellously turned itself into the majority, and he controlled the company by six hundred shares. . . .

Now, from thoughts of the meeting when the recapture would be effected — he had decided to confer at once with Mr. Henry Lovering, over the necessary arrangements there — The late diner's mind skipped on to the interesting public aftermaths of the meeting. In a flash, his journalist's fancy saw the front pages of the newspapers as they would be on the day following — May 16th — a Sunday again — six weeks to a day. . . . That the dramatic redemption of the "notorious" company would cause a sensation, there could of course be no doubt. There would be new headlines, of a different kind; and his name, inevitably, would figure in them. In fact, the newspaper stories, however prosaically written — and prosaicalness could not be called the weakness of reporters — would necessarily disclose a sort of personal duel between himself and the supposedly pro-German heiress, in which he, acting secretly and alone, had outgeneralled and overthrown her; performing thereby a service to the Allies, to "civilization," worth a regiment of infantry. . . . Those head-lines — slightly prejudiced, to be sure, not exactly "tolerant," or even fair — would be the most brilliant vindication conceivable of the equivocal position he had been forced to occupy for weeks; by the same token, he perceived, they would fall rather heavily upon his vanquished adversary.

That brought up another point — a little matter of personal procedure. Hitherto, his fancies of the triumphant climax had always included the element of surprise; he had pictured a sudden confrontation at the meeting itself, with the young woman completely demoralized by his startling emergence in control of "my enterprise." Now he saw at once, without any argument, that such crude melodramatics — even if they could be managed, which was doubtful to say the least — would be quite superfluous. . . . No, she had given him fair notice when she thought she had beaten him; he would of course do the same for her. He would go to her and tell her the facts, one day this week. . . .

Masury stirred and called for his check. However, by the time the slip was laid before him, he had relapsed abruptly into thought; and the waitress, after hovering about an instant, and glancing at him expectantly a time or two, went back to her dinner.

In fact, the last customer had been struck by another thought, novel and not devoid of interest. To this moment, no doubt, he had been so preoccupied with his own concerns that his mind, like a full sponge, could not take up fresh considerations. Now, in the release of utter victory, he had begun, without intention, to think of the other side of the picture, of the vanquished; and he had no sooner done this than he was aware, with a distinct surprise, that in the progressive circumstances of their encounter, his conception of the young woman, his adversary, had been singularly modified.

He stared at the tablecloth, coarse and thin with many washings. Presently he lighted a cigarette. . . .

By repute, Miss Teresa DeSilver had long been an example to him; she had stood in his mind as a striking embodiment of everything that was untrustworthy and unlovely in a woman, undesirable and untrue in a human being; he had met her, and the shock of his eyes and ears had confirmed, as it seemed intuitively, the worst that he had imagined of her. That was his beginning. And then — what? By the curious nature of their relation — promoted, he did not doubt, by his rude, sexless, genuine indifference to her — he had come to know this difficult and complex girl as not many men had ever known her; and in that knowledge, purely by what she herself did and said and was, she had gradually broken down his ancient criticism, and in the end pretty well dispersed it. . . . Yes, that was the fair truth; why haggle over it now? Of all the hard adjectives with which he had belabored her a month ago, nothing seemed actually to survive now, except that she was assertive; no, let's say — assured. Teresa DeSilver was certainly assured — and hang it all, she had a right to be.

He had said that she had seized Whitestone to exploit and advertise herself; that charge was as meanly untrue as an argument by Checkerman. It certainly was for nothing selfish that she had thrown herself, open-eyed, against a powerful and savage public opinion, submitting her name to become a plaything and a byword; those who sought publicity chose softer paths. She had been trying to do something, definite and large, for the common good. . . . She was wrong in her theory, of that he was perfectly convinced; but it would not be gainsaid now that her error was a generous one, and certainly put forward with rare courage and indifference to consequences. Was n't it possible that, *sub specie æternitatis*, what a person believed mattered rather less, on the whole, than the manner in which the person showed forth his beliefs? In this girl's reckless disregard of herself, in the strange unfeminine salience of her idealism and the unconscious largeness of her spirit, there was a touch that seemed not far from greatness.

Even that "self-expressiveness," which had once so offended him, seemed different on closer, and calmer, view. It appeared, rather, as the manifestation of a more abundant life. This girl had had more life than any one else he knew. She was nearly ten years younger than he, and had made a great stir in the world. She was full of aspects, and sides, and surprises. He had, of course, never met any women in the least like her. . . .

His mind went back over the course of this encounter; and he fairly met the thought that, in the essence, in the personal, the honors remained with his adversary. He recalled his rash abuse of her, in their first meeting; he remembered the day when he had affronted her honesty and virtually called her a liar, without any warrant whatever; and neither recollection yielded him credit now. He thought of the letter she had written him, ignoring every quarrelsome difference, going straight to the fact of his "great service": and that was an act of grace and magnanimous acknowledgment which he had never been inspired to imitate. . . . He stirred a little in his chair, and some of his pride, some of the pure triumph of victory, seemed to ooze out of him. He thought again of that moving moment in her office when, in the shock of discovery of the baldest treachery, the girl's denunciation of her false friend had been only this: "Poor Janney, you don't know how I hate to see you like this." He thought of that not less moving hour the other day when, again in the face of his hardly pardonable criticism, she — surely the least petty of women — had once more returned firmly to what she thought important — looking at him out of grave eyes which might have been a coquette's but were so much finer, saying: "I thank you, and I thank you and I thank you. . . ."

Oh, yes! — this generous enemy was entitled, at least, to have fair warning. . . .

The bells in the Metropolitan tower began to strike nine. Suddenly, the late diner sprang from his seat, clutching up hat and coat with a haste contrasting quaintly with his previous long-drawn abstraction. Having vaguely frightened the waitress with the gift of a dollar accompanied by a stern stare, he rushed out.

In the club, where he had not set foot since his quarrel with Checkerman, not pausing at the cloakroom, Masury clattered down the steps to the telephone-booths. The switchboard boy, who had known him many years, offered a conversational greeting, but Mr. Masury, this time, took no notice of him. Having rapidly thumbed the pages of the book, he flung out a number, and the glass door of the nearest booth swallowed him up.

In the airless chamber, a voice, a manservant's evidently, spoke suddenly in his ear: "Well?"

The new owner of Whitestone, the new bagger of the company, was aware now that his quiet mood was gone. He felt himself all at once excited — oddly, indeed unaccountably so. Hence he said with great deliberateness:

"I should like to speak to Miss DeSilver."

"I don't know if Miss DeSilver's at home," said the voice conventionally. "Who shall I say?"

"It is Mr. Masury. . . . M-a-s-u-r-y. From Miss DeSilver's office. The matter is urgent."

"I'll see."

There was a considerable silence, of a somewhat tense quality, and then another voice, a woman's, said cheerfully: "Hello?"

He recited his request anew, spelling and all, and the voice returned:

"One minute, please, Mr. Masury."

Another silence, and then Miss DeSilver's voice, familiar and natural: "Yes, Mr. Masury?"

Dean Masury's strong fingers wrapped themselves around the stem of the receiver. He could hear his heart beating. Why?

"I hope I don't disturb you, Miss DeSilver? I wonder if you could see me for a few minutes this evening? There's a matter of some importance I should like to tell you about."

There was the faintest pause, during which the doomed president, two miles away, possibly wondered why the matter, whatever it was, could not keep until to-morrow morning, at the office. Or perhaps — who knows? — her thoughts might have been of a totally different sort.

Her assured voice came back: "Yes — certainly, if you wish. At what time would you come?"

"In quarter of an hour, if that will be convenient?"

"Perfectly. Till then!"

He picked up a taxi on Fourth Avenue and, in twelve minutes by his watch, dismounted in front of the enormous mansion of the woman who hated love, through whose doors, in these days, few visitors entered.

CHAPTER XIX

A MAJESTICAL butler received him with an impassivity faintly touched with disapproval, and deposited his things on a carved cathedral chair, made of ebony and magnificent as a throne. In silence the old servant led him down the stately hall to a lift, and shot him upward two stories. The great house seemed unnaturally still; Masury recalled that the former owner of it had lately taken his retinue and departed.

Above, at the lift-door, a white-haired woman in black dress and apron, inspecting the visitor through steel-rimmed spectacles, greeted him by name; and escorting him forward again, through a dim, thick-rugged corridor, broken with silent passageways, paused and pushed open a door which already stood ajar.

"In here, sir, if you please."

Then the caller, the owner of Whitestone, passing over the threshold, found himself with a sense of suddenness in a charming and spacious chamber, rich with light and color. From a small desk toward the farther end of it, a young woman in a hat rose smiling.

"Mr. Masury?"

"Yes. Good-evening."

"Miss DeSilver's expecting you, Mr. Masury," said the young woman, and her pleasant voice was the voice he had heard on the telephone. "Won't you sit down? She's in her office for the moment — I'll let her know you're here."

She briefly tidied the little desk, which appeared in some disorder, picked up a coat from a chair near the door, nodded brightly and withdrew. Despite the absorbing nature of his business here, Dean Masury, left alone, looked about him, with frank interest.

He thought the room, which was without doubt his chief's private sitting-room, quite captivating in its odd beauty. Its dignity, and a certain graciousness it conveyed, came in part from its fine proportions, which were the architect's. But its charm flowed out from more personal use and original design, from furnishings and possessions and multicolored lights, and from sumptuous stuffs, shimmering or severe, that covered cushions and chairs and draped the many windows. The dominant tones seemed to be purple and a pale gold-brown, a combination bold to hazardousness; whoever had done the place, however, evidently quite alive to the perils of the scheme, had as boldly steadied it with black — a little pure black in the hangings, two large black-and-gold lamp-shades, black-and-purple on the small deep sofas which flanked the fireplace, vague faded grays and purples and golds on the floor. The effect of the whole upon the eye was sensuous and lovely. The room expressed something — what exactly?

A fire of small hickory logs, no bigger than saplings, burned in the fireplace. On one of the black-and-purple sofas, whose imperial hues were considerably softened by time, rested a large padded basket, in which a wire-haired terrier puppy, with a pale lemon spot on his tiny nozzle, slept deeply: one of her famous "Highlands" undoubtedly. The walls were lined high with books; by the long-chair, which was the only feminine thing in the room, stood a large reading-stand, littered with books: he noted there, successively, an anthology of war poetry, the "Oxford Book of Mystical Verse," Bernhardi's "Germany and the Next War," Bucke's "Cosmic Consciousness," and somebody's "High Speed Steel." An interesing admixture! . . .

Within the desk a large photograph stood, slightly awry. Unframed, a little faded and defaced, thrust back carelessly against the side it tilted, half concealed by packets of old letters which the secretary, no doubt, had been interrupted in sorting over.

Falling by chance upon this neglected souvenir, Masury's eye rested there; after a moment, quite unconsciously, he took a step nearer.

The photograph, evidently an enlargement of a snapshot, showed a young girl, some fifteen or sixteen, perhaps, walking up a winding driveway through a park full of splendid old trees. She was in riding-clothes and hatless, with a loose white shirt like a jockey's, white breeches and high shining boots; and the camera had caught her with upraised crop, in the act of greeting some one not shown in the picture, who was possibly the photographer. The picturesque costume, the singular lifelikeness of the pose, the wide scene caught in small compass, would have made the print noticeable enough in any case. What struck the observer especially, however, was the child's face, framed in a mass of dark hair, falling so low on her forehead as to give the effect of a thick bang, under which there looked out enormous dark eyes, larger and more liquid than the Countess Potocka's. More arresting than spectacular effects of shape and color was the subtler quality of expression, which seemed less a matter of feature or pigment than an inward, or moral, contribution to the charming total. The girl was smiling as she recognized that distant friend — smiling, but not very much; and the faintness of the welcome seemed to emphasize something in the face that was altogether unsmiling, an indefinable grave aloofness, dissociated from youth or beauty. By some gift, at least, the young countenance conveyed a singular, proud austerity, mysteriously self-contained, dedicated, and marvellously pure. It was such a look as Artemis of fable might have worn — Artemis the virgin with her face like the morning, and her limbs like marble and her heart pure and cold as a mountain spring.

He thought, unbidden, "*Saint Teresa.*" . . . And then the light sounds of movement came into his consciousness, and wheeling hastily, with a conscious start, he saw that Miss DeSilver had en-

tered the room. She was coming toward him, greeting him with
her faint smile, and for the flying second, by some white magic,
it was as if that faded pasteboard presentment had come to
life. . . .

"You are welcome, Mr. Masury — forgive me for keeping
you waiting, after all. Ellison was with me. Our talk ran
longer than I'd expected. . . ."

"Good-evening. . . . Oh, certainly! — yes!"

His hostess spoke in an easy and not unfriendly way, apparently unaware that her caller had been illicitly looking at her
picture. Her eyes turned at once toward the sofa, and then
her steps.

"Perhaps you've amused yourself making the acquaintance of
my littlest puppy — Hotspur Second, if you please! . . . Ah,
he's fathoms deep, I see."

She bent a little above the padded basket, while he, vaguely
murmuring, struggled against his novel embarrassment: this
curious and profound disturbance set up within him, by the
sudden visualization, in the person of his doomed chief, of the
beautiful and austere child whose pictured face had bewitched
him. . . .

Turning, she continued:

"I must tell you that I was thinking of you, not five minutes
before your message came. Ellison came to tell me that he landed
another contract to-night — a big one that we've been scheming
for for weeks. It's really quite a coup for him, personally — and
so I found myself glad, again, that you had helped him to feel
that he needn't leave Whitestone."

As her manager offered no comment to that — finding it indeed impossible to devise any — she went on quickly, in a considerate tone:

"You understand, of course, I'm thinking now of our people
at the mills. I've been so anxious to avoid a shut-down, if I

could. . . . To throw a thousand men out of work is a serious thing."

"Yes."

Was it her own thought, or again something in his look that made her add gravely? —

"I did that once — and more. I hope never to have to do it again."

A gentle knock sounded at the door and the voice of the secretary said:

"Do you wish anything else, Miss DeSilver?"

"No, thank you, Evelyn. Run away, and sweet dreams."

The thick door shut softly. The stillness around him seemed to emphasize the novel intimacy of this place and hour. The girl's extraordinary eyes, which the lamplight turned into shadowed pools of violet, came back to him.

She wore a black house-dress of some soft material that might have been crêpe de chine; the dark hair was arranged simply, low on the forehead; the face was bare of the pince-nez which commonly both "protected" the eyes and cunningly destroyed the lines of this perfect profile. But all this, he had thought, had long ago been understood and allowed for. Why then this sense of "difference" and discovery — this befuddled sense, like one suddenly disclosed to himself as the credulous victim of a somewhat far-reaching hoax? Was it the "Kessler stuff," now discarded for him, was it his own prejudices, now somehow scattered by overwhelming success ? — why had he needed the key of an old photograph to find pure beauty here, to discern in the face of his enemy, now of all times, this strange and moving beauty, to which the virginal dedication gave the last fatal piquancy? . . .

"But," she ended thoughtfully, "I'm sure it won't come to that now. . . . So, Ellison's visit has left me happy."

Her caller answered, rather curtly:

"No — you won't have to do that now."

Her brief look then seemed to question him. And nothing in these speeches surprised him at all. . . . No, it was probable enough that she, with her ample reasons for misunderstanding, thought he had come to say that he too had decided, after due reflection, that he "need n't leave Whitestone."

She turned suddenly away.

"But your time's valuable, and you did n't come to discuss unemployment. Shall we sit here? . . . The fire seems a little warm, I think. . . ."

She moved toward the front of the room, where the curtained windows made lashes of opulent color. From the reading-stand she picked up a pair of large spectacles, of which she seemed to possess so abundant a supply; these particular lenses were rectangular in shape and had rims of light green celluloid.

"It's quite apropos seeing you to-night, for I'd meant to ask for you to-morrow in any case, to —"

"*Oh, don't!*"

Miss DeSilver, with arms raised toward her small ears, turned her head in some surprise. She found her manager regarding her with a peculiar attentiveness, and was no doubt aware then of the unusual constraint in him.

"What?"

He laughed oddly, in a monosyllable.

"That is — need you put on those things? . . . Why, what's the use?"

For the space of five seconds, perhaps, the young woman remained motionless with upraised arms, exactly where the strange command had overtaken her. Her gift for stillness was striking. Then, curiously, her hands fell at her sides; turning again, in silence, she dropped the ugly thing back on the table.

Moving on a step or two, she said, rather as if she were continuing a speech of which part had already been spoken: "But indeed my eyes are quite bad now. What with reading in bed to all hours and — various things — I've injured them permanently, I fear. Once they were keen as a falcon's."

She dropped down negligently on the end of the chaise-longue, saying: "But to business! Sit down, do."

"Thank you.... Though my errand is soon done."

Different this charming scene from the dramatic and violent confrontation his fancies had so often pictured: where was the pure joy of triumph now? And yet the peak of the man's heavy confusion had already been passed, and his senses, which had seemed briefly liquescent, were hardening again. He had remembered — what he so often forgot altogether — those trainloads of vital shells, and the more distant conflict where quarter was neither asked nor taken. . . .

He sat, not in the easy-chair she had indicated to him, whose spring-cushioned arms invited like an embrace, but in the slender desk-seat whence the secretary had risen. The eyes of his fated employer lifted to him with expectancy — with something else that might have been encouragement, perhaps? He spoke abruptly.

"In fact, the briefer I am the better. I've succeeded in getting the Coit stock, Miss DeSilver — a thousand shares. . . . I wanted you to know it."

The strange girl did not move a muscle. For an instant the two sat staring at each other in a sort of fascinated silence, as if struck dumb together by the sheer wonder of these words of his. In her eyes the light of expectancy died, yielding to mere bewilderment; but that was all. She sat beneath the splendid lamp still as a marble woman, not betraying herself by a flicker, while she took in these tidings of an incalculable disaster.

She spoke suddenly and simply: "How under the sun did you do it?"

"Why! — you've known that I've been looking for the stock — for weeks — "

"But — every one's been looking for it! I've been looking for it for months —"

"Did you know that Coit was in town?"

"*No!* . . . Is he?"

"Yes. Singularly enough. I've no idea why. . . ."

The beautiful startled eyes searched his face. His vague astonishment at her controlled stillness, meeting his determination not at all costs to feel sorry for her, gave his manner an added stiffness. He went on, laboring a little:

"I'd learned of it, first, through some inquiries I'd started — at the beginning. Still — it was luck. In fact, pure luck, all along. . . . He'd been seen and recognized on the street — and then he just vanished. Lost again — hopelessly. . . . And then, by a coincidence, the only person he's been to see at all — so far as I know — happened to be an acquaintance of mine. The whole thing was extraordinary. . . . Well, that located him, you see, and — and the rest followed naturally."

"You've seen him?"

"No — he preferred not to deal with a stranger."

"And — when was the sale made?"

"Just a few hours ago."

Teresa DeSilver's eyes fell. Her rigidity of attention was breaking up. She sat staring at her slim hands locked together in her lap.

The owner of Whitestone regarded her fixedly. To the senses of his spirit, the conversation, the whole scene, retained a strange air of unreality, in which nothing was stranger than his adversary's mastery of herself. . . . Utter rout in the moment when victory was counted as sure, a crashing overthrow, an unforgettable humiliation to come — and there she sat, under the stunning impact of the revelation, composed and still, beaten but not defeated.

What happened then? A clock ticked, the prize puppy snuffled in his sleep, the honk of a remote horn came up from the street somewhere. That was all. Yet in that precise instant, without warning and without reason, doubt slid into the man like a lance, and he was sick with a sudden misgiving. How if it were he, and not she, who had been confident with a fool's certainty?

But no; that was not possible. There was no way there. . . .

She had lifted her eyes; and the look in them, which was the very reverse of explosive, brought him no reassurance.

"If you don't mind my asking, is Mr. Ball associated with you in the — the purchase? . . . Or — any one?"

"No one is associated with me."

"You bought the stock for your own account, then?"

"Yes."

The two gazes, in their utter absorption, were equally unwavering. Now, in the same instant, the man's face turned a little white and the woman's fingers locked themselves more tightly together.

"Have you . . . May I hope then that you would reconsider — on any terms — your decision to leave the company?"

"No, I'm leaving the company on Saturday. . . . Why?"

There was, again, silence through five ticks of the clock. Through his being there began to spread a dizzy and immense excitement. But no, it was n't thinkable. He and George had thrashed it out twenty times . . . .

"It had n't occurred to me," said the girl, with some effort, "after our conversation last week, that you would wish — or find it any advantage — to buy an interest in the company. I'd be tremendously glad if —"

"I think you misunderstand. I have n't bought merely an interest in the company. I've bought, in effect, control of it."

"Ah. . . . I was afraid you might think that . . ."

Then together, curiously, as if moved by a single unseen lever, the two came slowly to their feet. Now in their pose, in their

colorless faces and unwinking regard, their unchangeable difference seemed, again, nakedly disclosed. Here was a memorable
opposition, a lasting and insoluble clash of wills. And still in
the girl's look, at least, there was no hostility; no, these eyes,
pure and unyielding, seemed suddenly full of a genuine com-
passion.

And she spoke first, a little breathless, all but apologetic:

"I know how much your heart has been in this. . . . I — I'm
so sorry."

"You seem to be implying . . . that I have *not* got control
of it?"

She hesitated.

"Do you remember my saying the other day that the — the
matter was settled, that my control —"

"I remember perfectly what you said — which was only that
you expected to settle the matter, when the time came. I have
the best possible reasons for believing that your expectations
were founded on a mistake."

"No. . . . I — in fact, in a matter so important to us both, I
shouldn't have felt justified in saying that — if there'd been
any possibility of a mistake."

"But how do you suppose that you can wash-sell the company — that you can do any sort of legal trick — without an
absolute majority of the stock?"

Her look changed a little at that; her eyes became somehow
less concerned with sympathy; still it was in the same forbearing
way that she announced:

"Ah, but that is what I have, you see —"

"No! . . . You have forty-seven hundred shares."

She shook her head, repeating: "I have a majority of the
stock."

Her caller's face had darkened curiously. His hand closed over
the back of the chair, where he had sat just now reporting his

miracle. Her speeches were indeed unbelievable; she was like one madly using words out of their meaning, she talked rigmarole like a tale told by an idiot; and still he knew, instantly and finally, that she spoke the truth. Once again, wheel within wheel, the incredible had come true: and the lovely saint, whom he had been trying not to feel sorry for, had somehow managed to trick him of his victory.

All his early distrusts of this woman seemed to come back to him in a single shock: and he cleared white and cold as ice within.

"You're stating that you've acquired additional stock, since you got hold of the company in March?"

"Yes. That is the fact."

"But that is impossible. There was no stock for sale."

"Nevertheless, I have bought some."

"Then who sold me out?"

She made no answer.

"I say, from whom did you buy this stock that gives you, as you allege, permanent control? . . . Who sold me out?"

Her face, changing further under the hectoring cross-examination, then unmistakably conveyed a warning, just touched with something as personal as reproach. However, she spoke in a controlled way, a little dry, like one promised to patience:

"It wasn't a question of selling out anybody. Not every one feels so certain that I'm wrong as you do, and I have bought plenty of Whitestone stock before to-day. . . . As to your questions, I must remind you, as you have often reminded me, that we are adversaries — and that when I offered you information the other day, you refused it, saying you preferred to wait and see the outcome for yourself."

If these measured words affirmed her understanding, too, that their difference was irreconcilable and must proceed to its ordered finish, her beaten adversary, holding her with a lidless and sightless gaze, was not interested in her just summary. He did not listen to her, he hardly heard even the sound of her voice as she continued, after a brief hesitation:

"I am sorry — sorrier than I can well express — that there should have been this — this misunderstanding. As you're aware, I've appreciated all along — and admired — the — the disinterestedness of your position and — whole attitude. . . . As for the practical side of it, as for my cousin DeSilver's stock, of course, there are any number of people who would most gladly relieve you of it. You would not care to sell to me, but —"

The sentence stopped there, destined never to be finished. The man, the caller, all whose intense thought had turned inward, suddenly broke through it in a low voice, violently still.

"I know. It was soft old Parmenter."

Then for a space the gracious room was quiet while the adversaries merely stood, confronted and staring. Her face, Saint Teresa's, had become like a mask, yielding nothing; to reply to him, evidently, was not in her mind. Indeed, it seemed that, with the tone and meaning of those words of his, the whole matter had passed beyond speech: what profited question and "explanation" now?

The beaten, for his part, desired nothing that way of his victor. Once the eye of his mind had turned in the unimaginable direction, all the business was plain on the instant. . . . Uncle James. Yes, Uncle James — who had flatly refused information at the outset, and curiously urged tolerance toward the "interesting experiment"; Uncle James, who so obviously liked and admired this woman, forever dropping in to see her on inexplicable "business"; Uncle James, the handsome husband of an ailing woman, who, if rumor did not slander, had had his gallant diversions before to-day — poor soft old Parmenter had weakened and betrayed him. All was plain.

And she . . . Oh, but had he not been right all along to listen to his profound instinct reiterating that she was not to be trusted!

Why, how else could it be? There was no room here for an honest "sale." James Parmenter understood perfectly the moral issue involved in this struggle; he was as staunch against Germany as he himself; he could not conceivably "change." No, this girl, with her deceitfully "austere" countenance, had simply seduced him. Oh, they could veil it with silences and drape it with sophistry: but that was it. She had seduced James Parmenter. She was a calculating saint, she was a false posing Diana, and she had played on an elderly amorousness and whistled an honor away.

The recollection of his sensations, such a little while before, as he stood and looked at the old photograph and thought romantically of Artemis, struck the visitor acutely in his cold straining fury. He found his thought exquisitely ironic. The room's stillness was shattered with a burst of licentious laughter.

"Oh, that's rich! . . . I think it's the juiciest thing . . . I ever heard in my life."

He leaned against the sofa-end, in an abandon of ferocious mirth. Overwhelmed, he ha-haed without restraint, barbarously; his body racked with his insane and unbearable revulsion.

The little puppy Hotspur, jerked from sleep by these astounding noises, leaped to all fours with a fierce yowlp. A word from his mistress silenced him. She herself, having instinctively backed a little away, stood regarding her clerk, her adversary, from under those perfect brows which the mass of dark hair, like a thick bang, almost met. Her gaze for the moment showed less of resentment, or anger, than of a strange, grave distress. The look, perhaps, was not calculated to subdue the man's terrible derision. . . . No, truly: that virginal gravity, which she would take off at her need, was the final perfect touch in this historic jest, this staggering and deathless quip. . . .

"Really, you must p-pardon me. Pardon me. . . . Pardon me."

He straightened abruptly, wiping with his forefinger eyes that had dwindled to bright points of steel, and strove to share with her his poignant pleasure.

"But I'm sure you see — in your own original way — how absolutely perfect it is . . . I'd been a little puzzled about you, you see — and now I understand you — just a little suddenly. I —"

"Do you think you are quite yourself, Mr. Masury?"

The voice, breaking her pained silence, came suddenly sharp. As from a distance, Masury was conscious that her face, never conspicuous for color, had lost all that it had. Her body, too, had become still with a peculiar rigidity, reminding him, again, of that other day when he had made her successfully angry. Oh, yes, this was her punishment, this was the way of his perfect farewell: a full discussion this time of her little idiosyncrasies— with no sweet "forgiveness" afterward.

"Why, that's it, Miss DeSilver — I'm just beginning to be, as I say. I promise you shall hear me explain myself clearly, before I'm done. It's only that this — this *bon mot* came on me so abruptly. . . . Do you know, I honestly think it's too good to keep? I must spread it — it's a duty. You and the old squire — 'Saint' Teresa and Uncle James. . . . God!" said Dean Masury, with sudden savagery — "*what a headline!*"

The president of Whitestone took two quick steps toward him, and then halted — halted dead, like one colliding with an unseen barrier. Perhaps that obstacle was but the pure interposition of her will. He saw that her face had gone from white to chalk. Her breath came rapidly, like a runner who has come too fast. Her voice threw out unevenly, with an odd huskiness:

"I'm trying to make allowances — for the strain you've been under . . . the shock of disappointment — but there's a limit. I think you'd better go."

He laughed in his dark rage, furious with contempt.

"Yes, indeed! — and let you go free with the price of your —

amiability! . . . Oh, come, that's it, is n't it? You don't even pretend to think that poor old Parmenter would have let you have that stock if you'd been a *man*, do you? No, no," he said hoarsely, "even you draw the line at that sickening insincerity. You could insult Hedley-Black like a pickpocket for asking you to lunch — Hedley-Black did n't have any stock. But you did n't insult gallant old Parmenter! — no, you could lunch with him, and have him calling on you five times a week — and smile up at him — Oh, I saw you that day in the hall! — *He* had your price. . . ."

The puppy Hotspur, who had been watching the proceedings with great alertness, went abruptly into a fit of treble barking. His effort passed unnoticed. The attention of the man and woman were all for each other. Their engrossment had assumed a peculiar fixity. Now a faint spasm slightly distorted the girl's pure face. Her enormous eyes regarded him with a mortal significance.

She said through shut teeth in a voice hardly articulate:

"Go quickly. . . . We shall both be sorry."

The man's chest gave a fierce heave.

"You will be — yes. I'm going to make you very sorry before I go. Do you want me to tell you something for your good? In all the green earth, there's nothing I despise so much as a woman who trades on her beauty for gain, and gives nothing in return — but calculated smiles. And that's you! You with your posing pretensions and your false 'complex' — you with your sham saintliness and your bogus 'ideal,' you've cold-bloodedly sold just enough of your . . ."

He ended; it was his turn to leave a sentence forever unfinished. Trouble, incredible trouble, impending ever nearer for some moments, broke then quicker than a thunderbolt. With a stifled cry, guttural with pain and anger, the girl flung herself upon him.

Yes, Saint Teresa DeSilver, whose life had left her no stranger to violence, goaded past any desire for control by these insufferable insults, hurled herself bodily upon him, her adversary. The retort was executed, it had to be confessed, with marked skill and effectiveness. It was quite as if the amazing creature had been divided into two distinct parts, her body and her will: and her will had picked up her body, as an angry man picks up a stone, and cast it with all strength at its target.

By its extraordinary swiftness, the movement found Masury unprepared. The impact of the young body, which had known how to give itself such astonishing velocity, was greater than his unbraced legs could withstand. A smart thrust from her fist settled the matter. He went down with a bang.

All the man's raging discontent vanished, merged into a startled and incredulous content, and he heard himself laughing as he fell.

The girl's headlong attack — which perhaps took her somewhat unprepared too — in a sense overreached itself. Resistance collapsed, but momentum continued: she fell with him. The descending figures struck the frail desk-chair with a force for which its makers had not calculated it. There was the sound of splintering wood.

The puppy Hotspur bounded to the floor and began to race about the room, barking terribly. Nobody noticed; and none came to answer his call. The walls of the great empty house were thick, alas, and the little pipe was unready.

The man and woman, whose difference over a steel company and other matters had come to the ultimate expression, had become intensely busy. She had managed to fall clear of him, but he, easily guessing her design, would not let her rise. He was no burglar, or devoted Frenchman, to stand and take cold lead. She was astonishingly strong and reckless and quick, and even more astonishingly efficient. In a wink, wildly struggling, she had wrenched loose the broken chair-leg and struck him a thwack across the forehead. Instantly following that slight advantage, she pulled herself freer and struck again, harder. This time the cornered weapon took him just above the eye — a rather nasty rap. Ignoring other features of their common predicament, Masury set himself to disarming her.

After perhaps a minute of activity, unexpectedly furious, he had his way: though he rather thought that he broke one of the small fingers in the process.

He had, as it were, a flying glimpse of her face, like that of a beautiful wild animal, just above him; in the serene light of lamps and hearth, her eyes glowed down upon him, under co-quette's lashes, with a lethal ruthlessness. She madly fought to free herself. Dean Masury laughed. Quicker than light, he shifted her two wrists, and with his open hand struck her a soft box on the ear.

"Let that teach you not to cheat, false saint. . . ."

At once, the puppy Hotspur, darting and snarling, bit him on the cheek, and Teresa DeSilver, with convulsed force, tore her wrists from the single hand which held them.

Then action speeded, and little events followed each other in rapid succession.

The girl was on her feet in a bound. She was springing away toward the farther end of the room. All her movements had an extraordinary beauty and grace. She was light-footed as a doe. That she was animated by a deadly purposefulness was also evi-dent, and it was this fact, at the moment, that most interested the man, her adversary. Unluckily, though he was up half a sec-ond behind her, she had already cleared him. His first headlong lunge caught only the loose part of her dress, about the shoulder; the soft stuff tore in his hand. His second thrust proved even less fortunate — becoming indeed a distinct reverse. For his gifted chief, turning sidewise, actually succeeded in clutching his arm;

whereon, stopping short, adroit as a professional wrestler, she blocked his feet with uncanny precision, simultaneously giving his arm a powerful jerk. He was thrown heavily to the floor.

He was on his feet again directly, but the little gain was all she needed. From a table-drawer she had plucked, not a pistol, luckily enough, but a knife: a jack-knife of the sort that hunters use, heavy and very long when opened — and it was open. As Masury stumbled up, necessarily somewhat shaken by his fall, he saw the mænad standing almost above him, poised, with upraised arms; he heard her gasp something husky that sounded like: "Take back that lie. . . ." As he sprang, she struck; in the awkwardness of his position he could not quite evade the blow. The murderous point took him in the hard flesh where the underarm joins the body and glanced toward the breast. He felt a thrill of pain, and a start of warm blood.

The two closed and clenched, both breathing hard.

He now understood that the matter went past a joke, and in the same moment was aware of his fixed handicap, his inescapable male inhibition. The knife, clearly, was not the girl's weapon; her gyrations left her fatally exposed; one sidestep now, and he could — how easily — knock her over the sofa and into peace. Something deterred him from doing that, or anything like it; and she was steadily benefiting through his restriction. The puppy Hotspur, understanding thoroughly now the nature of the proceedings, continually snapped about his legs, and the puppy's mistress, actually contriving to break nearly free, struck at him again, as one beside herself. However, in far firmer position now, he "gave her the arm" this time, with perfect success. Her descending wrist met his forearm, rising: it was as if she had struck it, full-force, upon an iron railing. The knife bounced from her hand.

It fell, by ill-luck, behind him. They pounced for it together. The woman was the quicker, and got it.

He closed with her again, both struggling desperately, each to the settled purpose. She sought to extricate herself from his merciless grasp, and stab; his need was to fasten up this force unleashed upon him — for that had to come first, it seemed — and then to wrench away the knife.

His plan, which seemed both sensible and simple, proved curiously difficult to execute. Holding this young body at all was rather like restraining a hydraulic ram. She had unexpected means of attack, in which her feet played their considerable part: and her wrists, which he had easily secured, but had n't yet managed to pinion together, were darting everywhere with clever feints which made the nearness of the knife a constant menace. He was faintly troubled, too, by growing pain and numbness in his shoulder, where the knife-wound seemed to be flowing freely.

The blade was perpetually just missing him; now, by a tricky jab, the young devil fairly laid open his cheek. About the same moment, in the midst of their noiseless commotion, he suddenly heard her voice again, panting, unnaturally deep:

"Take back that lie — on your knees. Or . . . one of us — does n't leave this room alive."

If she had really set out to seduce old Parmenter, would she have found the taunt so utterly unforgivable? . . . Through some part of Dean Masury's busy consciousness, the thought just shimmered — was it then or later? It scarcely interested him; doing exact justice in this quarter was no more a matter of solicitude for him, and he would find epithets not less stinging when their talk was resumed. Other matters engrossed him now, and as he at last forced those dangerous arms resistlessly upward and backward, he answered laughing, with gasping breath and an ugly trickle down his cheek:

"Take it back? . . . I have n't begun with you yet."

The girl's reply was to produce another surprise from her unwomanly bag of tricks. Without the slightest warning, her head, on which the dark hair was tumbling loose, dashed violently into his face, faintly stunning him: simultaneously she used that dextrous foot-block again, this time behind him, and as he gave backward, unsteadied, she jerked down her pinioned arms with a cogent thrust.

Once again, astonishing to relate, Dean Masury was thrown to the floor.

He fell backward heavily, with a sufficiently audible thud. Still, the faint squawk or gurgle which came with the sounds of falling, and which then passed quite unremarked, could hardly have emanated from him, or from her. However, all that was a detail. . . .

As no effort of the woman's could loosen the man's hard grip, she necessarily went with him in his descent. Having fallen, they partly broke, and scrambling up together came instantly to a clench again.

Then for a long time, for what seemed to him an interminable time, the conflict resumed itself as before. She could never quite succeed in reaching him with the knife, he could not succeed in getting it away from her.

Now, after his third incredible fall, and in the endless struggle that followed it, Dean Masury's view of this strange dénouement underwent a still further change. With surprise, and the beginnings of concern, he recognized that this frenzied athlete, who used her body like a bludgeon, as if she had nothing to do with it, was a match for him. He was half a foot taller than she, many pounds heavier and certainly far stronger; but it was clear now that these advantages were completely offset — by her superior quickness, by her repertory of tricks, resembling those of an accomplished bargeman, and finally and above all, by her sex. Without doubt he could still manage, dropping all tactics, to batter her into unconsciousness with his fists: but he did not want to do that. Well, what then?

For a long time there was no sound but the noises of hacking breath and the soft pad of feet, as the two moved up and down in their hopeless and final deadlock. The man's case did not improve. She must have cut an artery with that damned knife; otherwise how account for the fact, more and more evident, that his strength was mysteriously ebbing? His wind had gone all to pieces; his throat was as if choked with hot ashes. Blood from his cheek ran into his mouth, blood from his temple half blinded him. A little more of this defensive temporizing, one misstep, one more trick, and she would have the cursed blade between his ribs. Indeed, it began to look as if that grim alternative she had indicated just now was not far from the reality.

Odd thoughts, these, here in this serene and gracious room, embracing a girl whose beauty but assumed in dishevelment a more gorgeous splendor. Truly it had not been for nothing that he had felt for her, from the beginning, a mortal antagonism. . . .

Still, the choice she left him was not yet between their two lives, but between his chivalry and his life. He held her slim wrists at the level of his breast, with the blade turned, as he had done a dozen times before; now his extremity demanded that he declare his choice: and it was odd how quickly his situation was improved. With a sudden jerk, he snapped the two wrists together backward and downward, in a pitiless compulsion. He had a vague sense of something cracking. The girl gave a strangled moan, and involuntarily came to her knees.

Then in a second he had twisted the knife from her weakened grip, and dropped it, open, in his coat-pocket. In the same instant, she wrested herself free from his single hand, and rising, struck him feebly in the face.

He took her again, but on a changed basis. With a surprising uprush of relief, he knew that his crisis was past.

Now, in the anti-climax, the results of their terrific pace, too long continued, became very evident. Abruptly, together, the adversaries were both far spent. The hard-pressed bodies trembled from overstrain, the tired legs tottered; there came seconds when there was no movement, when the man and woman seemed merely to lean on each other, one form helplessly supporting the other. Of the two, it was the girl now who seemed suddenly the worse off. It might have been mere reaction from strain, it might have been the loss of the knife, it might be that he had actually broken her wrists: but all at once it was as if something within her had been destroyed. Her manœuvres visibly ran themselves out, her struggles grew feebler.

She was a sight to behold. Her long hair, fully loosened, streamed downward like a dark veil. Her dress to the waist was long ago torn to ribbons, disclosing bare her splendid arms and shoulders; whiter than milk when first revealed, they were now splotched with red and blue where his hands had fallen. Blood oozed gently from her temple, where she had taken a chance scratch. Her face, dead-white, was faintly spotted and smudged with blood, where it had rubbed against the man's coat. Her breath came in dry sobs, painful to listen to. . . . Miss Teresa DeSilver, the permanent president of Whitestone.

With scarcely an effort Masury did what he had vainly tried to do through long minutes: he pinned the girl's arms securely behind her. The move, with his firm embrace, reduced her at last to impotence: it was as if she so recognized and acknowledged it. The fringed eyes closed, the body drooped against him; her head, with the magnificent mane, hung weakly on his shoulder.

Another trick, perhaps?

Well, and what to do now?

Tie her up? Certainly. There was no trusting her otherwise. . . . Tie her to the chaise-longue with strips of that pretty black-and-gold spread. Gag her? — probably. . . . Then resume the little talk she had so unwisely interrupted. . . . About how she

370

had got round sentimental old Parmenter, and cheated him of his victory. . . .

His blood slid down his body, his head swam in surging circles. Lights smarted his hot eyeballs, and his saliva dried up in his mouth. . . . Yes, but was that enough? That would merely be going on with what he had meant to do anyway. It would n't be punishing her for these new tricks, for this vicious foot-fighting and jiu-jitsu, for the nasty cut she had given him with a rusty jack-knife. . . . It was letting her off too cheap.

What happened? . . . As if warned by an instinct of his hostile thinking, the woman, roused from her brief repose, moved her head a little, and suddenly looked up at him. . . . Her eyes, one could not fail to see, were quite unconquered. . . . These glorious orbs, so near his own, regarded him with the same ruthless defiance, the same implacable fixity, with which she had first sprung on him.

She began to struggle again, and unexpectedly her voice gasped out, broken and small, yet curiously menacing:

"Liar and coward. . . . Let me go."

She kicked him, prisoned as she was, rather painfully; and at once he had his flash of inspiration, transcending reason and surpassing speech. Her face, wildly beautiful, was very near; splotched and smeared, glaring and deadly, it yet mysteriously retained that vaguely "sainted" look, that strange virginal purity, which she could forswear for a price, to turn a dishonorable triumph. And that look came now as an invitation, supremely fitted to his need. With an ugly laugh, Masury sank his head, and set his lips upon the lips of the false Saint Teresa.

For a second, gone as he was, he felt a thrill of ferocious satisfaction. He could feel the ravished mouth quivering under the infamy of his kiss. And then, in a wink, in a trice, all changed. Unable to extricate herself from the shameful embrace, Teresa was yet not resourceless. Her head jerked ever so little, her

mouth opened convulsively and she bit him through the lip. . . .
Clear through. Her teeth clicked and ground together.

Well, that was fair enough. One does n't outrage even a sham
saint for nothing, of course. . . . The trouble was that the young
hell-cat would not let fair enough alone. Galvanized with a sudden spasmodic strength, she was drawing her head backward;
now she began to tug with her neck, this way and that, as a puppy
yanks at a string. In her madness she was tearing his lip
away. . . . Very nice. . . . Marking for life the man who had . . .

He said, indistinctly: "Let go."

With her marvellous suppleness, she pulled farther back.
Blood ran down his throat, strangling him.

He released her pinioned hands, flung his arm behind her
neck and crushed her face to his. That stopped the violent jerk-
ing, indeed, but it did nothing else. Her hands freed, she began
at once to strike at him feebly.

He mumbled again with a gurgle, just articulate: "Drop that.
Do you hear?"

She did not drop it. He felt her fingers at his coat-pocket. She
was after the knife again.

He put his hand on her throat, white as a swan's, and found
the wind-pipe. His fingers closed over it.

Her difficult breathing ceased. After a moment, she stopped
struggling altogether.

The two adversaries, the two baggers of Whitestone, stood motionless, locked in their strange embrace. Now and then, the
woman's bosom heaved paroxysmically: that was all.

The clock ticked on in the still lamplight, the gentle flames
leaped in the fireplace, a log crumbled and softly fell. The small
sounds of the street became startlingly audible. By the way,
where was the puppy? . . . The girl's rigid body gradually relaxed. Her lids, which had closed, slowly opened. The eyes,
faintly glazed, an inch from his own, were beginning to start from

their sockets. Her face, which had first gone from white to gray, and then become vaguely shadowed, began to turn dark. He could just see her cheek, downward; bluer and bluer it grew, and on the curious darkness odd spots appeared. Still the teeth remained gripped through his lip, as if set in lockjaw.

He thought, "This won't do," and immediately another thought, more practical, came to him, as from a great way off. He released the throat, and turning his hand upon the insensible jaw, squeezed at the locked hinges, with thumb and middle finger on either side. To his dull surprise, the mouth fell limply open at once, and he extricated with his fingers his half-dissevered lip.

With her, the first instinct had set strongly to work. Her throat released, she had given a weak gasp and shudder; and instantly her stifled lungs began to fight, fitfully, to catch again the trick of sucking in the revivifying air. She made queer noises, little moans and sobs. . . . Was she conscious? He slacked his hold to test her, and she seemed to waver; he moved a little farther, and her head drooped on her breast.

He picked up the limp body in his arms, and, staggering five steps to the sofa, laid his enemy gently down.

Thereon he leaned against the sofa-back — briefly hung there, in a state near to collapse, like a bundle of clothes on a peg. His overpowering exhaustion attracted his own attention; it was rather as if he had no insides; the marrow was gone from his bones. He couldn't understand it, and then he remembered the cursed knife-wound again, and knew that that was it. He must really have lost a great deal of blood. . . . He would have to try to do something about that. Pretty soon. Stop it some how. . . .

He was staring vaguely down at the black-and-purple sofa. . . . Strange. Strange sight. Teresa DeSilver. . . . Yes, that was the wilful president of Whitestone, the arrogant heiress — who ex-

pected to have her way with everybody . . . lying there with her
clothes torn to strips, unconscious, moaning and gasping, dark
hair falling wildly over her bare and blood-stained breast. . . .
His work. Who would have thought it possible? . . . Now, remembered sentences, somehow characteristic and never forgotten,
went dancing across his cloudy mind. . . . Extraordinary, hell.
You've never made a success of anything in your life. No assumption about it; I've given you the evidence. Nothing to do with
my management of the company. . . . It does n't seem fitting
that your connection should end this way. I know how much
your heart has been in this. No one could wish a better ally, and
I thank you and thank you, and always will. . . . Yes, and there
she lay, where he had dropped her — and still not beaten. . . .
What a woman! Beautiful and untamable like a leopard, and
like a leopard, like a woman, she would n't fight fair. . . .

Yes, but still — beautiful and untamable. He had always
liked them so. What a woman!

That breathing was pretty bad. Rumbling and rattling, very
irregular. . . . Perhaps there was risk of choking in unconsciousness? He had better try to bring her to. . . . Yes, and when he
had brought her to?

The man's eye, moving round the room, fell at once upon water. . . . No mistake. There it was — on the small table near
the door, where she had gone running for the knife — a tray,
carafe, glasses. At the sight, there came into the visitor's eyes
a gleam that was not Samaritan. His parched and disfigured
mouth lusted.

He went, with slightly reeling steps, toward the distant table,
as a lost traveller in the desert descends upon the sudden oasis.
Greedily he poured and drank, and the icy water ran down his
throat sweeter than nectar and milk and honey.

Behind the table hung an ornamental mirror and the drinker, the
formal caller, suddenly caught a glimpse of himself. For some sec-

onds, he thought, with remote wonderment, that he was looking at a stranger. Never had he beheld so repulsive a countenance.

His straggled hair was matted with perspiration, his collar was a filthy rag spattered with crimson, his face, or what remained of it, was an odd greenish smear of blood and sweat. Over the right eye there was a knob as large as a hen's egg; the left eye, where she had punched him once, was nearly closed; both cheeks were ragged with scratches, from the knife-point, and from the puppy. Even more arresting was this hideous wound on his lip, already swollen to three times its natural size. But, as for that, there were swellings, queer puffs and lumps, everywhere: the whole countenance was comically out of drawing, like a fantastic caricature.

Dean Masury smiled at that strange and revolting reflection. The reflection smiled back revoltingly. The greetings were halted, diverted by a vague sense of motion, back in the room. . . . In a corner of the mirror he could see the reflected sofa, where the bagger of Whitestone lay; she had turned over, in her difficult stupor. Now he saw that she was making uncertain movements with her hands, like a frightened sleeper in a dream of falling. . . . Or did these movements, jerky and feeble, suggest rather an imperative need to lift herself? Was it possible that he had broken something in her throat — that this was a hemorrhage? . . .

Masury seized the water-bottle by the neck, and turned back, rather hastily.

He had thought, many times, that his hostility to this woman was founded on the intuitive faculty; now it was as if the instinct for enmity had been transferred to her. He had scarcely turned his face toward her when her eyes unexpectedly fluttered open: quite as if something that was deeper than consciousness, subtler than pain and more important than death, had sounded within her an ineluctable alarm. Her darkened eyes fell upon him, ad-

vancing, and life sprang into them instantly. From her throat
came a noise, a cry; and struggling frantically, she pulled herself to a sitting position. Another struggle, and the incredible
girl was standing: standing crouched there by the fireside, sway-
ing and holding to the sofa-end, glaring at him an immortal
unforgiveness.

He always thought that he said then: "*Water! — I'm bringing
you water!*"... But there was room for doubt, for his brain was
fogged, and all happened quickly. He had but a flying glimpse
of that disordered face, at once terrible and terrified; he just
thought, almost humorously, that perhaps he should have tied
her up, all the same; and then he was aware that the astounding
Teresa was in motion again, and understood clearly that the end
of these things was not yet.

The water-bottle dropped to the floor with a clang, the caller
started forward with a weak bound. Through his consciousness
shot the fretful thought: "*Great God! ... Have I got it all to do
over again!*"

His concern in that respect proved to be superfluous. The
responsibilities of punishment had passed out of his hand. Halfway on his headlong rush, which he had started just too late, he
encountered the welcome the mad girl had so hurriedly contrived
for him. He met it as a crash; it took him as a singing and a roar.
The serene and lovely room, having tilted fancifully, exploded in
a sheet of flame and went out. All was dark.

CHAPTER XX

OUT of the blackness crept the knowledge of light, and the light was like an ache; into the void came thrusting the edges of consciousness, and consciousness was a woe, diffuse and inescapable. The rumbles of obscure distress, the vague intuitions of adversity, the faint far rumors of an unthinkable calamity, all the troubling hints and shadowy uneasinesses were swimming together, resistlessly concentrating. They took substance, sharply, as a physical pain: a mighty pain in the head. The pressure of the pain grew overpowering, and the man's eyes fluttered open.

They rested upon a sofa, done in black and purple, which flanked a fireplace. All about, as it seemed, was dusk and stillness; but on the hearth a fire, new-replenished, crackled brightly. For a hazy space, through half-opened lids, the man gazed at that unforgotten upholstery, faintly frowning. Then his eyes closed again.

He remembered. One look proved enough to take him, at a leap, over twilight processes often tortuous and long: *Where am I? What has happened?* By its intensity, perhaps, his recent experience easily projected itself across the dark gap, and his mind, though conditioned by a head that seemed ready to split from his shoulders, yielded up at once the tale of his immeasurable catastrophe.

He had lost Whitestone; he had lost the fight; he was beaten everywhere. And the causes of his utter overthrow were one. . . . Yes — a thing that he had sensed clearly from the beginning, and then been somehow lulled into forgetting. She was a person who could not be trusted. . . . He had fairly won the company, and it was his; and then she had used means not open to a woman of honor, and had stolen it; and now it was hers. . . . The fight was the same. He had been going to tell her what she was, as fitting punishment for her dishonesty; it was she who had turned it into a rough-and-tumble, and he had beaten her well — handicapped at every turn as he was by the wish not to hurt her too much. . . . Yes, she had lain right there on that sofa, pretending to be dying, choking to death, and he had felt sorry for her because she was a woman; he was sorry he had punished her so hard. And then, when he had come hurrying up, bringing her water, off guard entirely, she had come alive at once and . . . what? . . . Shot him? It did n't matter. Something characteristically shifty. . . . Something dishonorable. . . .

She was a person who could n't be trusted. He'd not make the mistake . . . forgetting that again. Seduced. . . . Oh, lovely nun's face . . . Chaste Artemis on a mountain. . . .

He was slipping down again into the borderlands of consciousness, where there was neither waking nor sleeping; he caught himself sharply, just in time. . . . Oh, no! No, you did n't. He was not to be trapped that way. The thing now was to get away — to sever quickly this quite hateful connection. That meant keeping all one's wits about one — all one's will. . . . Let 's see now. How badly was he off?

A kind of canniness possessed the man, befogged as he was: it had occurred to him at once that he might be watched. Lying with closed eyes, just stirring, he made a faint sketch of lifting his head. . . . All right there; shaky though his hold on himself seemed to be, the faculty of levitation was not gone. He tried moving his arms and legs a little, feebly, under the covers. Good again. Nothing broken evidently, and he could coördinate as well as another. As for these capital pangs, as if something large and blunt were pressing upon the brain, that was bad, certainly, but just as certainly it could n't be serious; otherwise, note well, his consciousness would not be clear, and steadily growing clearer. All right; his chief enemy then would be this exhaustion, making heven tese slight efforts arduous; a really overwhelming fatigue. . . . Yet, already, it seemed, strength was growing in him to meet his need.

The beaten man was continuing his tentative explorations, and, little by little, he made interesting discoveries. It was the chaise-longue he was lying on, from the end of which she had risen when the trouble began; it had been moved a little nearer the fire, though not so near as one could have wished. The great room had been darkened like a sick-room; his nostrils detected the faint odors of drugs. He was lying with head and shoulders propped high with pillows — a professional touch surely; he wore a loose woollen robe; under the robe, from the waist up, his body was bare. The wound under his shoulder was expertly bandaged; swathes of bandage ran round and round his breast. His lip, by the stiff feel of it, was bandaged.

Dean Masury lay still, vaguely frowning. When and how had all that happened? Those bands and compresses, these props to draw the blood from his head, were a doctor's work. But was it possible? . . . What might not have taken place, then, during his interlude?

The man's eyes, opening suddenly, searched for the remembered clock. . . . On the mantel — there. . . . He could just make out the small face of it in the dusky light. Twenty minutes past nine. Good.

But no. . . . That could n't be right. Not possibly. It was quarter past nine when he had looked at it last — and that was before she had come into the room, even. The clock was slow. It had stopped. Or . . . it was quarter to four.

He closed his eyes for a moment, as one does to clear the vision, opened them, blinked them a time or two, and looked again. . . . No — no mistake. Inconceivable, but true. It was quarter to four. Then he had lain here six hours. . . . Or was it still worse than that? He was lost to time — how if it were the next night, or the next?

Startled into strength, oppressed with sundry misgivings, the sick man abruptly raised himself from his pillows. The scene danced before his eyes, giddiness overcame him, and he fell back. But his mind and will were now thoroughly aroused: he must get away. He had taken it too suddenly then, that was all; a little rest and try again. Easy did it. . . . He must shrive himself speedily of this hideous hospitality. He must get away.

He opened his eyes, steadied for a decisive move, and was aware that a woman stood beside him. The knowledge presented itself in the form of a black skirt, brushing his covers. Frustrated, he let his lids lift further; and the shadowy pale face of Teresa DeSilver was bending above him.

So the eyes of adversaries must meet again, in circumstances fantastically novel. And at once, as he encountered the gaze of his victor, Masury was aware of a curious sense of distance here: as if all that had happened to-night — no, last night — had happened last year, or the year before. Or, no; this distance seemed to be less temporal than moral, though it was temporal too. He contemplated this false and beautiful face, now somewhat drawn, with a mere remote speculativeness, coldly inquiring; and it was rather as if she, by what she had done and was, had somehow removed herself from the range of his interest: she had finally outlawed herself, like a too cowardly enemy. . . . Strange. Their counter was long ago finished.

The look of his conqueror, on the contrary, came down upon him wafting a great, a shining, relief. She seemed even to attempt a smile, ghostly, yet quite in the cheering nurse vein. With a solicitude born of tardy compunctions and, no doubt, of some wholesome fears too, she said in a low "encouraging" voice, grating to jangled nerves:

"How do you feel now?"

Her caller's eyes fell indifferently. Having cleared his throat experimentally, he said in a voice of some strength, though with utterance marred by his wounded lip:

"Where are my clothes?"

"Yes, yes. They're right here," the voice answered above him, soothingly. "Whenever you want them. . . ."

The black skirt vanished.

Cleared of its normal litter and covered with a white cloth, the reading-table stood near the head of the couch, bearing a hospital array: bottles and bowls, rubber gloves, thermometers, cotton, scissors, unguents, spoons, everything. Thence now came the slight sounds of movement: the clink of glass presently, and then the lively gurgle of water pouring from a bottle. Now his captor materialized again, this time as a small hand extending a tall tumbler toward his lips. From the tumbler came the emanation of a heady liquor, powerfully inviting him. He did not stir.

"Drink this, please."

"No, thanks."

He was aware that she had slipped her arm under his supporting pillows, ready to lift for his convenience. Now the tall beaker pressed nearer; the cool glass, holding warmth and life, touched his patched lip. The low voice grew urgent.

"Do! — please! You have n't had any stimulant at all. I was afraid to give it to you. Now it's what you need most — it will make you feel so much better. . . ."

Did n't she suppose that he knew that? In this moment, he thought that he would have given whatever else he prized most upon earth to feel that life-giving stuff thrilling away inside him. But one must draw the line somewhere.

"No, thanks."

The odd ministering angel pleaded: "But indeed — it's absolutely necessary. You must have something — to go on with —

to live on. I'm afraid you lost a great deal. . . . Your pulse went down very low. I — it's not safe."

He shook his head, scowling with exasperation and pain. Her arm gently withdrew itself. The glass receded. She passed from his vision.

At once the man in his canniness, dedicated still further to his single purpose, lifted his head from the pillows, pushed back the piles of blankets and swung his heavy feet to the floor.

Executed at one swift stroke, the coup was almost entirely successful. The room rocked briefly; he was dizzy and a little light-headed, his feebleness was more than ever troubling: but that was all. The pains and aches were unaffected; lying or standing, that would be the same; and now, the floor actually under his feet, he felt a confidence that he would manage somehow. He would get away. . . .

The scene had straightened, and his eyes came to rest upon the young woman, his victor, and his nurse. She had made an exclamation, as she became aware that her patient was revolting from her ministrations; now, standing motionless by the hospital table, she regarded him fixedly, with some air of alarm, out of those grave virginal eyes of hers. He observed that her assiduous hands held an electrical warming-pad; well, he had circumvented her there, at least. . . . Abandoning the idea of coming straight to his feet — for it seemed unnecessary to risk that, under this scrutiny — he now took some note of her, rather in the manner of a coldly curious stranger. Outwardly — superficially — she appeared much as before: no one would have believed that this decidedly intriguing-looking creature had lately participated in a fight to the death. She wore a soft black dress that might have been a duplicate of the one he had torn off her; and her hair, which he had last seen falling like a dark cascade over her bare shoulders was arranged again in that simple, yet striking style, like a bang. . . . Very becoming it was, too. Very effective above this large-eyed

382

white face, which cut out of the dimness, above the single shaded candle, with the startling clarity of a tragic mask. . . . Blacks and whites. A stunning poster. . . . Still, it could n't be said that all was with her a; it had been then, that she had got off scot-free with her shady plunder. Oh, no. The strain of the thing — these hours of practical anxiety, if not the aftermath of the drubbing he had given her — had told on her, that was clear. She looked considerably caved in.

But no doubt she had had comforters, sharing with her the night-long vigil?

From the side of the feminine chair, sitting, to say truth, a little bowed, supported by crooked arms on unsteady knees, the man said suddenly, in his blurred voice:

"Pardon my curiosity — but who's been here?"

The owner of Whitestone gave a little start, stirring from her trance-like stillness, and answered hastily:

"Nobody at all — nobody but me."

She laid the pad in a purple-and-gold armchair beside her — where she had sat earlier, perhaps, inspecting him? — and came back a step.

"Everything's been — been perfectly quiet. It's all right," said the encouraging voice. "Now don't you think you'd better — "

"In that case, who put these bandages on me?"

"I did — I'm afraid it is n't done very well? Do you — do they seem comfortable?"

When the patient failed to answer that query, she came another step forward, and bending, with a murmur of apology, unexpectedly took and lifted his hand. He felt her cold fingers drop along his pulse. Not roughly, indeed with the chilliest impersonality, he removed his wrist from that solicitous grasp.

"You're saying that it was you who lifted me — and carried me — and put me over here?"

"Yes, I — it was. I assure you no one else even knows that you are here — or of anything's having happened. . . ."

Her low voice seemed to strain a little, yet it was controlled, not wanting in sureness. She went on hurriedly:

"You'll understand. . . . Of course I wanted to have help and advice — to call a doctor. It was hard to tell how bad the injury might be. I was very much afraid of doing the wrong thing. But I felt sure you would n't wish me to call in any one. . . . I had to do the best I could."

All of which was true or it was n't true, just as you looked at it. He, for his part, would not have believed her on Bible oath. He felt decidedly ill. He said:

"I'd like my clothes now, if you please."

The obstructing, the fatiguing, black skirt did not move.

"Yes, yes — whenever you say," came the voice, humoring again, soothing. "But — do you think you'd better go quite yet? Why not rest just a little longer? Rest and sleep. You'll feel — "

"No, thank you."

"Just to avoid any — any possible risk? I don't believe it's wise for you to start just yet — especially — without any stimulant, even. . . ."

And then, as the patient merely sat there in his guarded position, looking no doubt a little odd, the low voice, nearing as she bent, pressed into entreaty.

"Rest till morning at least, I — I beg it of you. You'll not be bothered by me — I'll go at once. There's an old servant upstairs — my grandfather's body-servant for many years. Let me send him to you. He is dependable — altogether discreet. I —"

Dean Masury raised his weighty lids again and looked at her. He looked with remote distaste at the haggard and lovely face of the bagger of the company, and he was conscious now of a puzzle here, vague and annoying.

"It strikes me that this concern is a little belated," he said clearly, though with a peculiarly elaborate enunciation. "I can understand that you may have been a little upset when you thought you might have a homicide case on your hands. But now, as you plainly observe, you have n't. Pray dismiss these superfluous anxieties from your mind —"

"Can't you imagine," came from her abruptly, just above her breath, " that I've felt something besides — fear? And I have felt fear. . . ."

"It's not a matter I'm interested in imagining about. By the way, what was it you threw at me?"

A little quiver passed over the girl's face. But the fixed gaze, whose power of steadiness had often struck him in days past, did not falter; and the thought then just flitted through his mind that some part of her, at least, would be well content that she had so punished him for his infamous kiss.

"It was . . . I . . . It was the fire-shovel."

"Oh, the fire-shovel!" Masury repeated dryly. "But you knew I was coming to help you — did n't you?"

His conqueror drew her tongue once across her lips, which were a little pinched and without color. She answered, with obvious effort:

"No. I did n't know that. I did n't seem to know what was happening. I thought you were — coming after me. . . . It was a long time before I took in . . ."

"It does n't matter in the least. Now, as I've several times suggested, I'd like to go."

Miss DeSilver then said, in a voice that self-control had strained thin and flat:

"If you would try to remember the state I was in . . . if you would try to allow — and forgive."

He looked at her, frowning under his bandages, puzzled further, unsettled afresh. Who had produced that "state" she spoke of, if not he? How then this cheap "feeling sorry" for him? Was her memory for deadly insult so light that it couldn't survive a little blood-letting? ... His head, his whole being throbbed dizzily; he desired to end this bedside chat. He glared up at her, his swollen lip twisting into an ugly smile.

"Suppose we wait for all that till I've withdrawn the remarks that — as I recall it — brought on the little trouble? ... Then the continuance of this conversation will be indefinitely postponed — which is what I especially desire."

Under his gaze, the long-lashed eyes closed briefly. The face seemed to give in a little, as at a physical impact. She turned away, saying:

"I'll get your things."

Light clicked into the gorgeous tall lamp behind him; the nurse's table, bearing that beckoning drink, rolled closer; the pad, wired and hot, dropped gently beside him. The voice said:

"Will you move nearer the fire?"

"No, thanks."

The black skirt receded; the woman disappeared. Almost instantly, as it seemed, she was back again, his folded clothes over her arm. Having pushed the easy-chair to his side, she draped the garments, one by one, over the back of it, convenient to his reach.

That done, the skirt still hovered.

"I'm afraid dressing is going to be — an undertaking," the voice said. "Won't you let me send some one to you?"

"No, thank you."

"All right. ... I hope you'll find everything here that you need. There's a bathroom down the passage, beyond that door."

She receded again. Halfway down the faint-lit spaces, she hesitated, turned back and said:

"I'll be just outside, if you should want anything. If you'll call — or knock on the floor —"

He made no answer.

The door closed on her.

So he had his welcome privacy, won at last. Having frankly reclined for a moment among the cushions, he rallied for the great experiment of rising. . . . With some aid from the chair, that affair passed off in quite a gratifying way. Boldly abandoning the crutch, the caller stood free, with no support but his legs; now he took a few tentative steps about, just to see if he could, and he could. . . . Good. Feeble though his pins admittedly were, they could yet be relied on for reasonable locomotion. He would soon be off.

Seated again, Masury threw off the blanket bathrobe, and set himself, with what speed and skill he could muster, to dress. To say truth, he could muster little of either. Out of his covers, he was suddenly very cold; his teeth chattered a little, and his fingers were without life. The breath of the electric-pad, which he forbore to touch, mocked him with its feeble warmth. At the outset, too, he struck an obstacle, in the inability to lift his left arm, for the swathes about him, above his shoulder. It proved impossible to put on his undershirt, and giving up the attempt at once, he balled up that garment and stuffed it in the pocket of his coat. For the rest, chiefly by the force of his purpose, perhaps, the enterprise proceeded with fair steadiness.

He was well along with it before he noticed that these clothes of his — like the restored room and woman — had received attention during his noncomposity. Undoubtedly they had come off him blood-marked and wet; they were clean now and agreeably warm. Shirt and undershirt had been washed and ironed, evidently; coat and vest, by an unmistakable aroma, had been scoured with alcohol — benzine maybe. She had n't been idle, it would seem. . . . The thought of this attentiveness — liberties taken upon his helplessness — was vaguely disagreeable; but it very soon slipped from his mind.

His collar and tie, doubtless ruined beyond repair, were missing from the outfit; in their stead he was offered quite a choice of haberdashery, belonging to somebody else. Leaving these where she had laid them, he searched for and found his handkerchief — also relaundered — and clumsily knotted it about his neck, bandanna-wise. Then, picking up a handglass from the supply table, he inspected himself, with reference to his coming appearance on the public highway.

Though the collarlessness was a debasing touch, he considered that, on the whole, he did very well. Moreover, his overcoat collar, turned up, would conceal that principal weakness, just as his hat, pulled down, would nearly conceal the head-bandage. The cover on the bitten lip was tidy — just a cotton pad held by a trim adhesive strip. His judgment was that his physiognomy, in its contour, looked notably less humorous than when he had seen it last. But he felt a gleam of cold amusement when he observed that she had neatly parted his hair.

The visitor rose, suddenly and a little scramblingly, ready to go. To quit the house on the instant, to sever the connection without another sight of her, would have precisely met his view of things. That, however, was scarcely to be hoped for: she had admitted in so many words that she would be prowling in the hall outside. Besides, if it came to that, there was an official word to say; and now was the time to say it, avoiding communications hereafter.

He took a few steps down the dim gracious chamber, in practice, and felt master of himself. He took another step, toward the fire, and without warning his legs rocked under him, the floor rose, and he listed sharply against the sofa-end, and clung there, dizzily. . . . Well! . . . Well, here was the old stand. . . . Just where he had stood, laughing his mind out at the deathless quip — and again a little later, hanging just like this — all in, but beginning to be sorry that he had choked her to death — ha! An expe-

rienced sofa-end, you might say. . . . Yes, and here cute little Hotspur had come bounding down, barking loyally — and where was
Hotspur now? Killed somehow, he'd be bound. . . . His mistake
— should never have trusted her. . . . Sprawling round the storied
landmark, the man plumped down heavily on the cushions.
Scanty cold beads bedewed his forehead, and he was very sick.

The vertigo receded, the spell passed, but the sudden reverse
left him no little disquieted. Very nice to part forever, and then
pitch over in the hall or on the stairs, to stay here God knew how
long — in the midst of this terrible solicitude. . . . Enduring this
trivial and cheeky "sympathy" — on account of that shovel, as
if that were all. . . . He would master this weakness if he died
of it to-morrow. His eyes closed.

They opened again smartly at the sound of a low but insistent
knocking. He made no response to that due notice; and then the
door opened, and first the dark head of his hostess came through
the opening, and then she herself came through, moving on
noiseless feet. She looked about as she advanced, and at first
did n't see him. He, in his corner, noted that the thoughtful creature had brought this time his overcoat, hat and stick; and
through his slightly disordered fancy wandered the conceit:
Here's your hat; what's your hurry? Still, he was glad to see that
stick; overcoat too, for that matter. . . . Then her inquiring eyes
fell suddenly upon her caller, sitting there stiffly on the dark sofa,
dressed in his washed clothes, in his bandages and kerchief; and
at the unexpectedness of that sight, or perhaps at the look of his
face, her visible anxiety betrayed itself in a little jump, curiously
like fright.

Her look, like a drink — though a feeble one, be it said —
seemed to put some fire into Masury's thinned blood. He came,
almost jauntily, to his feet. And from his trousers pocket he
plucked his key-ring, with the most business-like precision.

His conqueror, having placed her burden on a chair, as if to say that she had not surrendered him quite yet, came forward into the space between the sofa-ends. She spoke, with some uncertainty:

"You seem to have managed wonderfully well. . . . You do think that you feel — all right?"

Masury answered, rather oddly: "Thank you, I feel perfectly content."

Having found what he sought, he methodically detached it and laid it on the mantel.

"There's the key to my desk. There are papers there," he said, with his careful enunciation, only mumbling a little — "that will be of some interest and help to the manager. In the top drawer on the left, there are a few of my personal belongings. . . ."

A faint sound had escaped the woman's lips — of surprise or protest. He eyed her, rather forbiddingly perhaps, and resumed:

"Including my watch, which I inadvertently left there this afternoon . . . the other afternoon. . . . Be good enough to tell Harger to send them to me. He has my address. You'll also find — "

Then she spoke up, suddenly, breaking in on his meticulous remarks in a voice which, though steady, seemed hardly like her own.

"I'm to understand then — that you won't be in the office again?"

"Really!" said he, with less of sarcasm than mere dull patience. "Had you thought it probable that I would be in the office again?"

Her voice, having lost its soothing quality, now seemed to harden a little. It said, directly:

"Then if I'm not to see you after this — I want the chance to explain about that stock now."

"Explain about what stock?"

"The shares I bought from Mr. Parmenter. I . . . I can't be expected to rest satisfied — like this."

In the still dimness, they eyed each other fully. The light from the flickering fire, and from the single lamp, rising out of the twilight like a splendid flower on its tall stalk, just touched her; and he was now aware that strain, like dishevelment, somehow but enhanced the austere loveliness of this flesh. These show-girl's eyes, regarding him, far sunken and blackly circled, held a look mysteriously celestial. . . . Yes. The tricky hellion had, indeed, an unearthly beauty.

He was frowning at her like one trying to grasp a recondite and inopportune allusion: more talk was, in truth, of all things, what he least desired. Under his implacable look she went on as implacably with her "explanation," — possibly hoping, in addition to everything else that she had, to hear him say that, after all, she had been "right"?

"I'd not trouble you about it to-night — perhaps not at all," said her hurried voice, not without difficulty, "if it were just a case of being fair to me. . . . But what you think does such an injustice to him — and I've thought perhaps it makes it all worse for you, too — more — bitter than it need be. . . . He's said from the beginning, months and months ago, that he'd sell me his stock if I needed it — simply withdrawing from any responsibility in the — the matter. He's been interested in my idea — philosophically — all along; he believed in it, halfway — he thought, at least, it was worth a fair trial. And then you see — neither of us supposed that his shares were even specially important, one way or the other. I'd never dreamed that this dead stock — "

"Really! — if you please!" her late manager interrupted, his voice and manner now harsh with effort. "Won't you spare me this? I've tried to make it plain that I want nothing now, but permission to *go!*"

"I know! — I know! Indeed I had n't meant to detain you
... But you say I'm to have no other opportunity — and I
thought that — even now — you'd want to hear *the truth!*"

He answered deliberately: "I have n't the smallest interest in
anything you say you did or did n't do, or in anything you say
you'll do or won't do for the future. As I've already told you
once, I'm perfectly satisfied with things as they are!"

That silenced her. The enormous eyes, whose fixed gaze had
taken on a somewhat tragical character, convicted him then of
open injustice, great and irreparable. But the wholesome power
of anger, for which he had first admired her, which would have
been so welcome to him now, restoring to him his fighter's dignity, seemed to have forsaken her altogether. Her lips formed
the words, "All right"; and she turned away.

In stubbornness, in the bravado of the defeated, perhaps, the
man resumed:

"The manager will also find in the desk my notes and figures
for a study of costs — ready for the memorandum. All other
matters ... in the special file marked 'Manager.'. . . One more
thing. I've drawn no salary during my stay in the office. You
may tell Mathewson to send a check for the amount. . . . Tell him
to send it direct to ... to the Commission for Relief in Belgium. I think that's all."

She nodded, to show that she followed his remarks, and held up
his overcoat for him to put on. He took it from her hands, and
proceeded for himself. The simple operation proved unexpectedly tedious. That was this damned weakness: though at the
same time, for that matter, his head seemed about to explode
from his neck. By ill luck, exactly as he had finished the trick,
and was reaching for his stick, ready, his legs treacherously
folded away under him and he sat down.

At the unfortunate betrayal, the woman, actually, began it all
over again. . . . Rest a little longer ... call some one ... stimu-

lant. . . . The murmur of her voice, at first remote, grew sharp, recalling him. . . . God, was there ever any one so set upon having her way? But then, it chanced that he had preferences that way himself. He grasped his stick and rose.

"The conversation repeats itself," he interrupted clearly. "High time to conclude it."

On that, having turned his coat-collar about his neckerchief, the caller picked up his hat, and inclining his head a little, started with rather a stately tread for the door. But the woman, impervious to all rebuffs, went with him still; her voice, sounding distinctly alarmed, was peppering all about him. Somehow, all that was a challenge to him; it strengthened him.

"There's a car at the door to take you home. One more request. Let me go with you — just to see you safe. I beg it as a kindness —"

"Why should I show you kindness, pray?"

"You'll take the car?"

"Certainly not."

"It's madness for you to go alone. Suppose you fainted — fell in the street. . . . Grant me this at least. I'll promise not to speak — not to annoy you in any way. Just let me go with you! Let me —"

"Look here! What's the matter with you?"

At the door, in a corner of the spacious room, whose serene areas now lost themselves in lovely shadows, the adversaries stood briefly eye to eye once more: he, odd and sinister with his wounds and his ashy skin, she with her sainted face shockingly pinched; he leaning heavily upon his cane, she frankly steadying herself with a hand against the wall. Both spoke with a sort of breathlessness.

"I thought you plumed yourself on being a fighter," said the man, desperate with fatigue and pain. "I confess I can't imagine why. Perhaps if you remind yourself — again — how this trouble started, you might be able to muster — a little becoming pride — and spare me —"

"There'll be time enough to think of my pride afterwards," said she in a small voice, hurriedly. "Now I think of nothing but that I can't bear to see you go — like this —"

"You must try —"

"No! Don't leave me to remember — after what's happened — that you could be just cruel now!"

The words, the odd appeal, heartened the man wonderfully. Cruel! . . . Well, at least he was curing her of her cursed sympathy: this was the way.

"Cruel? — oh, no," he said, almost smoothly. "I'm just not interested in morning-after remorse, that's all. Pathological — childish, it seems to me. . . . Really, if you break up so easily as all this, wouldn't it have been well to remember that, before you started your tactics? . . . First smiles for the squire — then a fire-shovel for the Samaritan. Let me pass, please."

A little convulsion twisted the mask-like face. But it seemed that her anger could not rise now even to that insult. She did not move. . . . Where was the relentless and invincible Saint Teresa of legend? He was looking, surely, into the eyes of a badly frightened girl.

She answered, with a spreading agitation:

"Never mind now what I've done. I don't ask for forgiveness again. Now I am begging your pity, your —"

"I've none for you —"

"Not when you've reduced me to this?" broke from her, uncontrollably. "Not for to-night only . . . but to-morrow and to-morrow and to-morrow. . . ."

The man shot her a look at that: and an odd one it was. By a score of evidences clustering thick about him, he was one who had taken a beating, and a bad one. Yet the look he rested now upon his adversary unmistakably laid the claim of a victor; and his disfigured mouth bent into a smile, dark and slow.

That look, or that smile, settled her. The wilful Teresa moved suddenly from his path. In the shadowed corner, she laid her arm against the wall. Her dark and beautiful head fell into it.

He gazed at her for a second or two, darkly smiling, and not knowing it; and then his voice broke the stillness, suddenly rather soft with a sort of contemptuous kindness:

"Oh, don't worry any more about me! I assure you, I'm not hurt easily."

Thereon, the caller passed through the door and out into the wide silent corridor; passed into the magnificent well of the stairs, went downward through the great still house.

Under the impulsion of his immense resolve, mightily buoyed from within now, he walked for this moment with a springy firmness. From somewhere out of the dusky reaches beneath him, a dim sweet gong began to sound: it was five o'clock. On a landing, he passed an oriel window, and he was aware of the whitening dawn. Above him he heard the sounds of faint movement; of light feet, perhaps; but he did not mind that now. He was free. In a flash, he had mysteriously understood that his catastrophe of the night was only material, was only practical. She had the steel company; she had beaten him bodily in a physical encounter; but she at least would always know, that in the subtle and essential sense, the victory had not been hers.

CHAPTER XXI

WELL, that was a time of controversy: a time of strained nerves, deepening concerns, and of differences of opinion sharpening steadily into feuds which time would hardly resolve. From street to street and coast to coast, rifts opened and widened. Warm human preferences and prejudices, the tastes, cultures and traditions of folk, bade fair to prove stronger than the pallid ideal of "neutrality," heavily coarsened with advantage as it was. Now the homogeneity of the hundred million had proved a delusion and a snare; here was a "nation" heterogeneous to alarm, and under their standards the tribes were gathering. In pleasant drawing-rooms gentle women said, of those once dear to them, "We never see them now"; in the clubs there were good men who saw familiar faces averted as they approached; in the highways, hot speeches led to blows. The country was neutral, the country was at peace, the country had neither foe nor quarrel; but the blood of the countrymen was ominously rising.

In those days, the views of George Davis, the American People, were imperceptibly shifting. Why, exactly? When did a logical turning-point come, and this stout mind first open to the searching doubt? George himself could hardly have said. In his club, where he hobnobbed exclusively with responsible family-men, his position as to the secret chancelleries and their trade-grabbing machinations had been clearly laid down for months. The trouble was, really, that the situation changed: things kept happening which he, George. personally did n't like, no, and had never for one moment pretended to. From the "restricted zone" announcement in February to the drowning of an American citizen in April, from the proofs of sly "propaganda" on American soil to the criminal blowing-up of American munition-plants, from the Zeppelin raids to the chlorine gas — things kept happening which a just man was obliged to take some note of. More annoying than any of these, perhaps, was the tone persistently adopted by the spokesmen of a certain power, a peremptory bullying attitude which seemed strangely out of place as applied to free America. The Germans themselves were a fine people, and their national character was fine; what was objectionable was simply these particular fellows' *tone*. However, Masury, to whom he had offered this distinction, had answered briefly: "But these fellows *are* Germans, fine Germans, and what you call their tone *is* their national character." More and more as the days passed, George wondered if that saying might not contain a truth.

And then, just when he was growing conscious of strange wobblings within him, and was struggling against his unneutral irritations, there befell that sad thing, that heart-cracking and fateful thing, which many had vaguely apprehended for months, and yet which to nearly every one had remained all but inconceivable. Through a chance meeting with a young acquaintance of his, who was a cable-clerk in a great banking-house, George heard the wild news about eleven-thirty o'clock, that May morning: thus, as he often pointed out afterwards, he was undoubtedly one of the first persons in America to know the fact. True, he did not believe it then; but almost at once he heard it again, and then again and again; by telegraph and ticker and word of mouth, the rumor was spreading through the city and the country, rapidly gaining in circumstantiality; then extras blossomed blackly on the streets, and thick crowds gathered before the bulletin-boards. Long before nightfall every one knew that the horror was true; and men looked startled into each other's faces with eyes which said: *Is it war?*

George Davis took the news very hard. Here was a climax indeed of that most reprehensible "tone." Devouring column after column of tragic print, he felt himself possessed by an im-

potent rage, unbecoming to his philosophy. He looked for a
ringing word from a high place, and none came. As the voice of
an obviously unwarlike Uncle Sam to the avowed desperado of
nations, the pale rhetoric of that hour fell ashily into George's
expectancy. Haunted by day and by night with the thought of
those down-turned faces in the vasty deep, rocking aimlessly
with the lapping of the waves, drowned women and children,
wilfully drowned Americans, George became aware that his cool
judiciality was cracking off him. Was it so certain that just *keeping out of trouble* — when you came right down to it — *was* the
prime duty of a great people in troubled times? . . .

"It looks to me," he declared one night, with the slow gravity
of one who counts his words, "that either we've got to stop
right here and now and show these fellows where they get off —
or else the time's goin' to come when we'll have to fight 'em *by
ourselves.* . . . And that's my deliberate opinion."

Mr. Lyman White, who was the recipient of this pronouncement, seemed disinclined to contest it. Yet, as if himself sensitive to its revolutionary character, George, having risen heavily,
continued with a sort of bewilderment:

"Why, you would n't have believed it possible! A fellow
blows up an Austrian prince — at *Serajevo* — and now here it is
reachin' way over here and doin' this to us. You knew two
people personally that went down on that boat, and I knew
three. You just would n't have believed it! . . . Well, I'm tired.
Guess I'll go home now. . . ."

"What's this I hear about Masury's going over?" asked Mr.
White.

"Don't know yet, nothing's decided," said George non-com-
mittally, and tramped away down the steps.

Entering the dark diggings on Irving Place, where for some
days now he and Mrs. Roorback had been keeping bachelor hall
uncompanied, the Elder felt old and sad and sore at heart.

Walking about, snapping on the lights, he was oppressed with a sense of lonesomeness. He grunted and sighed to himself. . . . Bad times. One worry after another. And all due to this rotten war, which so plainly ought to have been just a European mess — but which, instead, had now reached right over into these rooms here. . . . Yes, sir, when you stopped to think of it, if that Servian fellow, that *Slav*, had n't thrown that bomb, Dean would probably be sitting right there at this minute, writing away on his articles or something, and there never would have been any of this trouble and mystery and Lord knew what-all. You just would n't . . .

A sharp ring at the telephone, breaking in upon his sombre reflections, actually caused the Elder to jump a little, his sense of solitude was so pervasive. But he unhooked the receiver absent-mindedly enough, his thoughts already returning to their channels.

A pretty voice which sounded somehow familiar said in his ear: "Is Mr. Masury there?"

"No — Mr. Masury's out of the city just now."

"Oh! . . . And can you tell me when he's expected back?"

"I'm expecting him very shortly now — probably to-morrow. Who is it, please?"

"It's Mrs. Flanner? Am I speaking to Mr. Davis?"

"Yes — how-de-do, Mrs. Flanner?" said George, flustered, but rather pleased. "Thought I sort o' recognized your voice —"

"So sorry if I disturb you, Mr. Davis! I tried to get Mr. Masury at his office, you see, this morning, and they told me he'd left there the middle of last week! That was rather a surprise —!"

"Yes. Yes, o' course," said George, laboring a little, for who was more surprised by it all than he? "Well, he'd really finished his work there some time ago. You know it was only a temporary job —"

"I know! — of course!" answered the understanding voice, with its high, "social" inflection. "And I suppose he went off then — for a little rest, perhaps? I know he's been working dreadfully hard —"

"Yes — yes, exactly. He did need a rest," said George, and he was wondering now, with a mounting perplexity, how much, if anything, this lady might know. "And then he had one or two little matters to attend to, you know — in connection with his plans and so on — "

"Oh! . . . I see! Thank you so much, Mr. Davis! Would you be good enough to tell him I called, then, and say — there's a small matter I'd like his advice about?"

"I certainly will. You understand," he added, suddenly, whether from caution or a sort of curiosity — "his time here *may* be a little short. I don't know definitely about that yet — but I guess you know what he's expecting to do, and all."

"Why, no," said Mrs. Flanner, in a more thoughtful tone, it seemed -- "I'm afraid I don't. I don't seem to remember his mentioning —"

"Well, just what he's been talkin' about — off and on, here lately," said George, more and more surprised by the proofs of ignorance. "He's about decided to go over and join that ambulance outfit — you know — at Nooyey? That's really what he's fixin' up on this trip."

After an appreciable pause, he prompted, uneasily:
"Hello?"

"Yes, I'm right here!" the voice came back with sudden brightness. "I was just trying to think — but no! I shall have to scold him, I see, for keeping so many interesting things from me! And when will he go, do you think?"

"I think his idea was to go just as soon as he could make the arrangements," George confessed, sadly.

The lady thanked him again, reminded him delicately of her

message, apologized for detaining him and said good-*bye*, with a smart, rising accent. Hanging up, frowning into the spaces of the empty sitting-room, George thought:

"By gad, I don't believe she knows anything about *anything!* And she's her friend too. . . . Well, I declare. . . ."

The telephone began to ring again, loudly; it kept on ringing, annoying him. The conviction that this was a meaningless ring-off was not shaken, but he answered at last, sharply, to get rid of it. To his surprise, the voice of a lady, again, inquired:

"Is this Stuyvesant 9824?"

"Yes," said George.

"May I speak to Mr. Masury, please?"

"Mr. Masury's out of the city."

"Out of the city!" repeated this voice, calmer and more business-like than the other, but like it, betraying surprise. "When will he return?"

"To-morrow or next day, I expect. Who is calling, please?"

"Thank you. I'll call again," said the voice, rather hastily. George heard a click on his tympanum, and was again alone.

The sense of mystery had somehow deepened about him. The solitude was more than ever lonesome. Moving gloomily toward his bedroom, the Elder felt, again, a great need to talk everything over with some sympathetic and trusted soul. It was, unluckily, a need that there was no hope of gratifying. Not only was Alice Williams away again — visiting college friends in Massillon, Ohio, this time — but this was something that just could n't be mentioned to anybody. Mrs. Flanner here did n't even know that it had happened, that was plain, though it was she who had got Dean into Whitestone, to begin with; he, George, if it came to that, knew very little more, though Dean had had the opportunity to tell him everything if he had wanted to. . . . No, it would have to stay a puzzle as far as he was concerned — just a painful but unmentionable puzzle.

Yet this talk with Dean's friend, unsettling somehow, seemed to rake up the whole matter afresh: now he could n't seem to get it out of his mind. Doing about, making his preparations for a dreary hour with the "Literary Digest," George's thoughts turned back for the hundredth time to that strange day and night — to the strangest experience, maybe, that he had ever had in his life.

He was thinking of last Wednesday — just a week ago to-night. That afternoon he had landed the Coit stock, for which Dean had been scheming for weeks, and to buy which he had that day mortgaged everything he owned. At six, they had met by appointment, here at the rooms, and talked for over an hour; Dean had certainly been in fine spirits then, laughing a great deal over "wild noble Silvy," and showing in a dozen ways that he had n't a care in the world. Then, about seven, he, George, had rushed away to dinner with the Whites, feeling exceedingly satisfied with everything; and, getting back about 10.30, tired but happy, had gone at once to bed and to sleep.

The next thing he had known, there he was sitting bolt upright in bed, staring about him into the dark. He had a roaring in his head, doubtless explained by the violent breaking of his slumbers; beyond this, his fuddled brain-cells retained the memory of a loud noise, as of something breaking or falling, very near. He thought of burglars. Now the rooms, just vaguely lightening to a new day, were stiller than a tomb. Lifting himself noiselessly from bed, tiptoeing through the spare-room to the arched doorway of the sitting-room, he had stood listening behind the portières, scarcely breathing, intensely alert. Nothing stirred the unnatural stillness. After a minute, he had walked into the room, and switched light into the nearest lamp.

He looked about him, and saw nothing. His glance had rested on the clock on the mantel. It was twenty minutes past five.

Rather late for burglars — what then? His eyes had moved further, and he all but jumped out of his skin.

Just over the threshold of the little entrance hall, Dean was lying, face downward. He had fallen on his hat. His head, bared, was wrapped with bandages.

Bounding forward, George had tumbled down and gently rolled his rooms-mate over; the face, a curious gray in color, came into the lamplight and George moaned aloud. Dean was inert as a dead man; his breathing was feeble, his skin was cold. George put his hand inside the shirt to feel the heart, and was shocked to find more bandages there.

What terrible thing had happened to send Dean home like this — Dean, whom he had last seen so triumphant and gay? An accident? No! — for whoever had bandaged him then would not have turned him out alone like this. Footpads? — a frightful beating up? To this moment George had almost no idea.

But it had been clear, at least, that the matter was serious — serious perhaps to the last extremity. Sick with fear, the Elder had lifted his friend in his arms, taken him to his room, hurriedly undressed him and laid him out — piling blankets on him because of his bloodless skin, and damning himself madly because he could n't remember more of that First Aid book he had so faithfully studied, years ago. Next, leaping down into the subterranean regions, he had roused Mrs. Roorback with knocks and shouts — an accident! — come at once! — and then, ramming himself into trousers and overcoat, while she sat on guard, he had bolted out into the dawn to fetch the doctor.

The doctor was McLachlan, on Stuyvesant Square, who had counselled George upon his aches and pains these many years; but McLachlan was old now, far past seventy; the milk of kindness ran thin and a little sour in his veins, and he stuffed up his telephone at night. Not to be denied, George did not remove his finger from the new electric bell, while he kicked without ceasing on the fine walnut door. In the end, the ancient bonesetter, querulous and swearing, took his head in from the window, dressed and came to Irving Place.

At the sight of the patient the old man's profound pessimism had seemed to lift a little. He removed all the bandages, asking neither questions nor help, and proceeded, in silence, to look the possibilities over. To George's surprise, the deep jagged gash under the arm, still oozing blood, the ugly wound on the swollen and blackened lip, had seemed to interest him scarcely at all. But he had examined with the greatest attention the slight but curious-looking purple welt, just breaking the skin, beyond the right temple where the hair began to grow; here — and finally over the whole head — he had felt round interminably with his omniscient fingers. In the end, abruptly, he had announced that there was no fracture, and probably no brain complication at all. The chances were, old Mac had said, with anger and considerable disappointment, too, it seemed, that the young fool would be walking round before the day was over.

"Where'd he get all this?" he then barked shrilly. "Who's he been brawling with? Who put the clumsy cloths on him, and did n't have sense to see 't was stimulant he needed?"

George said he did n't know, and sat down suddenly. McLachlan had prodded him up at once. Had he no eyes to see either that the young fool would be wanting liquor now? Then, just when his best bottle had been opened — the old man having fortified himself at once with a mighty libation — Dean, without notice or preliminaries, had opened his eyes.

He had blinked them a little in the strong light, from McLachlan to him, George, and back again; and in that moment, it had certainly seemed that he was trying to remember something, and that having remembered, he was not dissatisfied. You could n't be sure, of course; still, that had been the way it looked. He had then said, quite naturally and clearly, through that queer looking mouth:

"H'lo, George. . . . Howdo, doctor?"

Old Mac had then given him the whiskey. He drank greedily; and almost at once that deadly grayness began to leave his face. Then, after some characteristic badinage, McLachlan had asked: "Well, sonny, how'd you get this way?" Dean had obviously deliberated over that; that was as certain as anything could be; but in the end he had said quite pleasantly, in his feeble voice:

"I had a difference of opinion with a friend."

And there, really, the matter still rested. He and the doctor had had some further conversation, but it came to nothing. McLachlan had asked:

"Anything the law's entitled to know about?"

"The law? Why, the idea, doctor," Dean had said. "Just a little talk — one thing led to another. You know how it is."

"And I suppose I ought to see the other fellow, eh? All damned fools, you young lads — all hot blood and no sense to ye. You can thank your stars and the thick pate God gave ye that I don't have to make ye a silver plate to your skull. How d' ye feel?"

"Pretty sleepy," Dean had answered, just as if nothing had happened at all.

"Well, you'd best have gone to sleep after your dinner last night. Then you would n't be rousting an old man from his bed at crack o' dawn to help ye out of your deeficoolty. Well, you'll stay awake for a bit now, with what I'm going to do to you."

"What say to another drink, then?"

"Not so fast, sonny. When I'm through with you, maybe. Now hold yourself still while I clean up this pretty lip you've gone and got yourself. . . . H'm! Teethmarks, I daresay, and odd it is, but I don't trouble meself to ask questions. . . . Eh, yes, it brings its own punishment. You'll have it there to remind you, next time you feel your dander going up, that quarrellin' and fightin' and cussin' and damnin' don't pay."

"He's marked me, then?" Dean had asked, with a flicker of drowsy interest.

McLachlan, peering into his little black bag for knife or needle, answered with unmistakable satisfaction:

"Yes, sonny — to the longest day you live."

Dean had said nothing more. Long before the doctor had gone, when it was broad day, he was fast asleep again. He slept like a log till ten o'clock that night, got up, pottered about the rooms in pajamas and dressing-gown, ate an enormous meal — and chatted freely of everything but his trouble. In the course of this interval, he had mentioned casually, and not as if it were of any importance, that he had decided to leave the White-stone Steel Company at once, and to go to France as soon as he could make a suitable connection. Then, at the end, he had said just one thing, in a kind of apologetic way: "Of course, you're entitled to an explanation of the affair last night, George. I'm awfully sorry I can't give you one — just yet. It was a fight and I provoked it, and I'm glad of it, and that's all I can say for the moment." On that, he had gone back to bed and to sleep again. Next afternoon when George got back from his office, rather early — it was the afternoon when that wild news from Kinsale Head was flying around town — Dean was gone. He had left behind a note saying that he was going to take a few days' holiday at his brother's place in Darien, Connecticut, and would then go on to make some inquiries at the ambulance headquarters in Boston. . . . Now, here a week had passed since that night, and the whole business remained as dark as it was in the first minute. No, it was darker really — yes, darker — for the points he had picked up for himself, that Dean didn't even know he knew about, had actually deepened the mystery. They finally reduced the thing to impossibility, as you might say: a solution was simply not conceivable.

When Dean had mentioned a difference of opinion with a friend, George had thought at once of Horace Checkerman. For all his bluster, Checkerman was known to be an ugly customer when aroused; and it had seemed reasonable enough to think that the two men had met somewhere and, renewing their quarrel, had proceeded to fight it out to a finish. But George had hardly set up this plausible hypothesis before something happened to upset it. Balling up the discarded bandages after McLachlan had gone, he had happened to notice among them several long strips of old linen or table-damask, of a very fine quality; turning these over curiously, he had come, with profound bewilderment, upon an embroidered monogram: *DeS*. ... Then, hours afterward, as he sat at his late breakfast, Mrs. Roorback had given him the surprising news that, soon after eight o'clock, a lady had come to the door to "inquire" after Mr. Masury. The landlady's description of the inquirer was vague but romantic: she wore a heavy black veil, and she was beautiful.

Thus George had known positively — even before Dean's announcement that he had quit the company — that the mystery was somehow connected with the fight over Whitestone: but that, of course, only tangled the knot further. You could imagine that Dean might have gone to see the woman that night, to arrange his victory, and even that she, a known fighter, had gotten angry over her defeat; but when it came to those terrible wounds — no, the mind balked there. Nor could you imagine any connection that way with the other trail — the Checkerman one. You could n't imagine, for instance, that Checkerman, having beaten and stabbed Dean into insensibility, had delivered his form at the DeSilver mansion, saying: "Here's the fellow that took up for you, and look what's happened to him." No, even Checkerman would balk at that. . . . And besides, either way or any way, how was it that Dean had come home alone, in that state, at five o'clock in the morning? . . .

The Elder — who had been conscientiously touching the floor with his finger-tips while he pursued these reflections — cast off the single garment in which he was clad and reached for his pajamas. He sighed aloud. Trouble, trouble — and all because of that *Slav*, at a place nobody ever heard of before. . . . What would it be like when Dean was gone for good? This Nooyey business was only a starter for him, that was clear; he had that flying thing in his mind, there was no doubt of that; once he had spoken with interest of the Foreign Legion. Why, it might be years before he was back. . . . If it came to that . . .

In the act of thrusting his leg into his pajamas, George, who had become rather jumpy here lately, all at once started violently. The silence had been broken by the grating of a key in the lock; now unmistakably the door of the rooms came bursting open. Then, while he stood motionless, hardly able to credit his ears, a cheerful voice rang toward him through the stillness.

"Hi, there, old 'un! Where are you?"

"*Dean!* . . . You son of a gun. . . ."

And he sprang for the passageway, clutching up his trousers as he leapt.

In the cheerful sitting-room, the rooms-mates remet with unwonted warmth. Seven years they had shared these diggings in amity; now, through one reason or another, it seemed rather as if they had been parted for eventful months, instead of days. There was a rapid crackle of question and answer. Dean, it appeared, had got through his business a day earlier than he had thought possible; therefore he had not lingered — and glad he was to be at home again too! . . .

George hardly needed his assurance that he felt like a fighting-cock, hardly needed to draw him under the lamp for minute and paternal inspection. The doctor's patch was gone from his lip, and the wound, as George had seen in the first glance, had already turned into a healthy red seam, not beautiful certainly, but still nothing for children to run from in the street. Otherwise, his face showed no traces of the late unpleasantness; his color and general appearance, indeed, were better than they had been for weeks. His spirits seemed excellent.

"I'm top-hole — how could I help it?" he said serenely, turning to pitch hat and overcoat into a chair. "Sleeping fourteen hours out of the twenty-four, and out of doors the other ten — never had a better holiday in my life. I don't know that *you* look so fit, old cockalorum. . . ."

That was fine, could n't be better. But the moment greetings were over and they began to talk, there was trouble again — of course. Dean was going to Nooyey — right away. That was settled, once and for all; he had signed up the papers in Boston, this morning. From the void within him at the casual announcement, George was aware that he must have kept some hope — without exactly knowing it — that he would n't go, after all. . . . Still, it could not honestly be said that the Nooyey idea seemed quite so crazy and quixotic as it had six weeks ago. No, there had even been moments this last week . . .

"Well! When 're you going?"

"Sooner than I'd expected," said Masury, reaching for pipe and pouch in his opened suitcase. "That is, if I can make my arrangements — passport especially. I've got to do some telephoning about that now — but I rather think I'll have to go to Washington to-morrow — or to-night, perhaps."

"*Why!*" said George, astonished. "What's all the rush? — when did you think of getting off?"

Turning then with a sort of affectionate defiance, not untouched with embarrassment, Masury plumped it out:

"I'm expecting to sail on Saturday."

George's mouth fell open.

"*Saturday!* Why, you can't!... Why, this is *Wednesday night!*"

Masury, stuffing his pipe, said that he believed he could still make it. However, it remained to be seen about the passport: You could n't pick them up at a window like postage stamps just now.

He explained, rather apologetically:

"You see, it just happened that they're sending over a contingent that day — twenty or so, college boys mostly. It'll be a general convenience if I go with them — so that we can all be handled and broken in together. It seems they're short of men, too. Besides, when you come down to it, there's nothing to wait for — and I confess this Lusitania business has made me tired of sitting around — talking."

The Elder leaned against the table, in his pajama-trousers, looking at the floor. He felt so nonplussed, so desperately at sea, that for a moment he hardly trusted himself to speak. His voice, when it did come, was devoid of all inflection.

"What about that meeting, Dean?"

"What meeting, old fellow?"

"That special meeting of the Whitestone stockholders.... *That's* Saturday."

"Oh, yes," said Dean. "Well, that's all off, George. My plans there did n't work out, you see — far from it."

He was sauntering about, smoking his pipe. To his friend's wonder-glutted eye, he had a curious air of detachment from his surroundings. A pile of letters lay waiting for him on his table; he had seen them, but had n't even troubled to turn over the envelopes. A telegram lay beside the letters. He did not pick it up.

"I ought to have spoken of that before I went off," he was

going on, with a sort of offhand amiability — "but it's very simple. I learned, by a chance, that the other side had managed to rope in some stock, after all — enough to ensure control. I was dished completely — so I naturally lost interest in the meeting. . . . By the way, I must do something about that stock we bought — I'd like to talk with you about that before I go. . . ."

George's sense was that nothing could ever surprise him now. For once in his life, he felt actually a little nervous.

"This comes unexpectedly to me," he said, dully and politely. "I am sorry your — your plans did n't work out."

Caught by that tone, perhaps, Masury turned; and then abruptly, he came up to his friend, put his hands on those broad shoulders and gave him an affectionate shake — a rare testimonial from one somewhat grained in reserve.

"Forgive me, George, for all this silly mystery — and don't worry your old heart about what does n't matter in the least any more! The whole thing's as empty for me now, and as uninteresting, I swear, as a last year's bird's-nest. . . . Some day, I'd like to tell you about it, and have you judge. Now, because you've helped me so much, I just want to tell you, on my word of honor, that I have n't a worry — or a regret. . . . And, George — *I have n't been licked.*"

"Well, that's what I wanted to *know*," spoke up the Elder, rather gruffly; and he turned away, clearing his throat.

His next remark came with perfect matter-of-factness, quite markedly hearty:

"Well, you have n't got much time — you'd better tackle those things. That telegram's been here since last night, Mrs. R. says. You'll find a good many phone calls there too. And, say, Mrs. Flanner called you up just now. She said . . ."

Lucy was that rare thing under the sun, an intuitive woman. She had called up the bachelor apartment, finally, in a state of

genuine anxiety. Why? She knew, as George Davis had surmised, literally nothing: she had scarcely clue or hint: how then
was she certain, deeper than reason, that something pretty serious
had happened, involving her two friends and herself no less?

The thing was unexplainable, no doubt, after the way of genius;
still there had been stages in the process after all. The first
tangible intimations of trouble had come to her two days earlier,
when, making a somewhat diffident move toward seeing Teresa,
she had encountered a puzzling obstacle. It was Lucy's disadvantage, all too clearly recognized, that these two closest friends
of hers should each occupy a position superior to her own —
Teresa because she was a personage, Dean Masury because he
was a man — so that she found herself anything but free of
their company. Nevertheless, feeling a genuine longing to see
Teresa, in the shadow of the public calamity, she had conquered
a considerable hesitation and telephoned to the DeSilver house,
early Monday evening, meaning to propose to "run up" for a
few minutes. However, a servant's non-committal voice informed her that Miss DeSilver was unwell, and had retired for
the night.

As Teresa possessed celebrated health, there was perhaps some
reason why Lucy, pervasively sad as she already was, should
have found this news a little disquieting. There existed, indeed,
a perfectly rational explanation for it, in the very causes, most
distressing ones, which had finally prompted her to telephone.
Not only had the woman who was reputed to be Teresa's dearest
friend in the world — Mrs. Herbert Burney, of Philadelphia —
gone down in the ill-fated ship, and her two little sons with her;
but, beyond the common misfortune, it was as if Teresa herself,
in her notorious pacifism, had almost been sunk under a fresh
wave of obloquy. Just what was Miss DeSilver's connection
with the dark triumph of the underseas, no one, to be sure, had
succeeded in making clear; more easily, one would say, it could

be argued that if others had done what Miss DeSilver had done, that is, refused to ship arms, the tragedy would never have happened at all. None the less, a dozen people had already said to Lucy, in one way or another: "I hope your friend is satisfied now." And to look at their intolerant faces, cruel with the passions and the fears of war, you might have supposed that Teresa, with her own hand, had sprung the horrible torpedoes from their tubes.

Yet Lucy remained more subtly and irrationally disturbed. Next afternoon, the process went further. Stopping at the DeSilver door about six, anxiously hoping to find Teresa at home — that is, back from her office — she was told by a grave footman that Miss DeSilver, though better to-day, was still confined to her room with a severe cold. As Teresa never had colds, the report was plainly fictitious; and Lucy was then certain that this inaccessibility was not due to the public catastrophe at all. The more she thought of it, the more she was convinced that Teresa, with her wonderful strength, would have made a point of going steadily on her way. What had happened? She became at once full of a vague foreboding, in which, curiously enough, thoughts of Masury came to figure more and more constantly. Next morning, overcoming reluctances again, she called Dean at the Whitestone office. All the gathering omens of an unguessed disaster seemed somehow confirmed when she learned that Masury had left Whitestone days earlier. Here, again, there was a rational basis for any degree of surprise, since both he and Teresa had told her definitely that he was going to stay through the week: but the growing anxiety that she felt was altogether without such basis. Certainly there could be no rational accounting for the fact that she had instantly connected Masury's sudden change of plans with Teresa's unprecedented indisposition.

The knowledge that Dean had been out of Whitestone a week, without even apprising her of the fact, was a severe blow to

Lucy's pride; she saw that she could make no further move in that quarter. All day, her uneasiness pressed in upon her, and when evening came her spirit wilted, and she had no pride. At dinner-time, she called his rooms; there was no answer. She continued to call at intervals through the evening. On the seventh attempt, which was to be the last, his friend, the good and kind Mr. Davis, had unexpectedly answered. Thus she had learned, finally, that whatever else was or was not true, something sufficiently bad had happened. Dean was going away to France. He was going off to the war.

Alone in her pretty living-room — which pictures had given her for her happiness — Lucy called a bright good-bye to Mr. Davis, replaced the receiver, and dropped her face into her hands.

Her weakness was for the moment only. She was devoid of self-pity; and she was not ignorant of the uses of adversity. One must keep one's lamp trimmed: nothing mattered but that. Ten minutes after her telephone talk, she was seated at her typewriter. Through the rest of the evening, and through all the next day, she went busily ahead with her routine.

On Friday, her message bore its rather late fruit. Before nine, as she took her coffee in bed, Masury telephoned. It appeared that he had got back Wednesday night, but then had had to go right off again, to Washington, where he had spent yesterday; and now he was most anxious to see her, to-day. His voice sounded wonderfully natural and reassuring, wonderfully dear too. But when he told her that he was sailing to-morrow, Lucy knew that God sometimes forgets the brave.

"It broke suddenly, you see," he explained cheerfully, and yet conscientiously too — "I'd no idea of anything immediate till day before yesterday! . . . What a rush! I was hard at it here till three o'clock this morning, trying to get things in some sort of shape, and then was up again at six. . . . "

Listening, Lucy had an odd sense of unreality: this considerate voice seemed all at once like the voice of a stranger, some pleasant passer met last week or the week before, and not perhaps to be remet hereafter. But she was steady enough now. Tomorrow or next Saturday or the next, what difference did it make? . . . With understanding and gentleness, she was speaking the commonplaces natural to the moment and the news: that he was lucky to be having a share in it, and that she, for her part, since last Friday, had never wished so much to be a man. . . .

"What time does the boat sail?"

"Ten o'clock, worse luck. I wish it had been three, at least — small favors! Now the immediate point is, when may I see you?"

"Any time that you can manage to find, Dean dear, of course. . . . I wish so much that I could help, with your packing or something."

"Now, my general idea," he resumed interestedly, "would be to come up — say about four? It seems to me I have n't seen you for months! Or let's say, to be on the safe side, between four and five — or maybe just a little later. No — that's getting pretty vague from your standpoint! . . . I'll tell you, Lucy — how's this? Let me call up again about lunch-time, when these crowded hours will have straightened out a little — and then I can make it regular, on the dot?"

"Perfect! — I'll be right here. But Dean! — seriously, you must n't have it on your mind — as one more thing you've got to do! You've —"

He interrupted expostulating: Did she dream he would go away without telling her good-bye?

But she, turning from her desk, felt that they had said good-bye already.

The day that followed proved a memorable one for Lucy. As if the omens were not already sufficient, it proved, by ill chance, to be one of those curious blank days, dropping sometimes into even the busiest life, when nothing at all seems to happen. The mysterious withdrawal of the accustomed trivial detail is, of itself, less than nothing; but hearts that are lonely are thus reminded of that loneliness. Through Lucy's long day, nothing seemed to happen. She, who normally got a fair amount of mail, to-day, all day, got not so much as postcard or circular; Steinfeldt, who for weeks had telephoned her every morning, whether or not he had anything to say, to-day did not call; a picture-queen, his favorite, who was to come at eleven to discuss a new script, did not come; Eva Masters, who was expected to lunch, called up very early, even before Dean, to say that she had a headache and could n't come. Nobody came. If the telephone rang, it was the wrong number; if the doorbell rang, it was for the people next door; if she called any one, nobody answered. Nothing happened. The groceryman failed to come for his order, the butcher-boy forgot to deliver the chops, and just before noon the little maid servant Hilda suddenly sickened and went home. All was negative, all a void.

The day had seemed long up to lunch-time; after lunch, which the celebrated scenario-writer prepared for herself and sparely ate from the kitchen-table, it ran on and on. At half-past two — which almost any one would consider "about lunch-time," to say the least of it — Lucy abandoned all pretense of doing anything. She merely sat, listening to the clock tick: and knew no peace. About four, she thought suddenly: "It's rather lucky I'm not a drinking woman. If I were, I'd certainly start in now and light myself all up like a cathedral." She looked out of the window, and saw white clouds floating tranquilly: but she was strained with much waiting. At quarter of five, without warning, she gave a little scream, hardly stifled — sitting there all by herself. That really frightened her, and then with all her will, she sought for control, and for some harmony within. She closed her eyes and struggled to relax; she yielded and tried to practice new-thought, if that was it; she laid her being out, her soul if she could, to

receive the refreshing visit of a consciousness transcending her
own. . . . She was helped, but not relieved, and knew that her
self was strong.

Then she thought, more practically: "If I stay here any longer
with this childish nobody-loves-me feeling, I'll need pads on the
wall by night. I'll go out now and walk till my legs won't hold
me."

At that moment the telephone-bell jangled, and she leapt to
her feet muffling a cry, both hands pressed hard to her heart.
The nameless summons sounded again and again before she
could nerve herself to approach the instrument.

Having done that at last, she got what was, perhaps, the most
complete surprise of these somewhat surprising days. The voice
that came back to her was Teresa DeSilver's.

"Lucy?"

"Yes, Teresa."

"May I see you for a few minutes? — now?"

To have something happening was at once a help, it seemed:
the spirit could rally to the known. Lucy was colder than snow
within; her heart was beating loud and fast; but the strange
strength that buoys all women in emotional crises was flowing to her now, in her need. She answered in quite a natural
way:

"Oh, yes! — you can't imagine how much I've wanted to see
you. . . . Where are you, Teresa?"

"At the office now — I'm starting uptown this minute," said
Teresa's steady voice, sounding, however, vaguely changed.
"Lucy — shall I find you alone?"

Alone? Oh, yes, Lucy would be alone. In all the world who
was so alone as she?

"I hope it's convenient for you?" continued her celebrated
friend then. "Thank you! — I'll be there directly. . . ."

A little time passed, during which nothing happened, while

she, with character, freshened her appearance. Then the door-bell rang, and the servantless hostess, answering, ushered in her adored and stormy heroine. In the dark little hall, moved together by a common impulse, the two women embraced and kissed. And Lucy thought: "Suppose Dean should come now? . . ."

They came into the sitting-room and sat down among the cushions by the windows. The light of the bright day fell full upon Teresa; and the look of her face, quite shocking in its ema-ciation, was to Lucy like a hand laid upon her heartstrings. She remembered that curious sense she had had one day of being caught in dark rapids, hastening resistlessly downward. One look at this face told her, finally, that the rapids had come to their unknown fall.

She found, at once, that she had nothing to say, literally noth-ing; all was closed to her. But Teresa, the strong, proceeded straight to the point.

"What a sweet place you have, Lucy," she had said rapidly, glancing round as they sat down. "I feel mortified that my first visit to it should have such a practical — and selfish character. For I come frankly as a beggar to-day — to ask your help in my personal concerns. . . . Possibly you know what the matter is?"

The two women seemed to search each other's still faces.

"No — I really know nothing, Teresa," said Lucy gently, "but you've only to tell me. . . ."

"I am anxious to see Mr. Masury," said Teresa, with her fine straightforwardness. "As you know, of course, he left the com-pany a week ago, and . . . I've not been able to get in touch with him since. Unfortunately, the matter's grown more and more urgent. . . ."

Lucy's look did not change. In the surprising implications of that announcement she felt no surprise. Of course she had under-stood as much as that.

"You must know how it would please me, Teresa, to think that I could help you — about anything."

Teresa gave her hand a firm squeeze.

"The situation is both difficult and acute, Lucy — I must n't leave you in any doubt there. In brief. . . . Not quite by my own fault," said the rapid voice, at once stirred and subdued, it seemed, "I find myself in a — a false position, as to Whitestone. To-morrow, as it happens, there's to be a most important meeting of our stockholders — a decisive meeting, in fact. To correct my position, it is essential that I see Mr. Masury, who happens to be primarily concerned — before the meeting."

Lucy said, with what might be called some bravery, perhaps: "Well, seeing Dean Masury is n't the most difficult thing in the world, Teresa. I'm sure that can be managed — even now. Only, as you probably know, his time, too, is very short."

"His? . . . No. . . . Before the meeting? —"

Lucy shook her head.

"That, of course. But he's leaving the country, you see. . . . He's volunteered for the ambulance service that the Americans are organizing in Paris —"

"To go when?"

"He's sailing at ten to-morrow."

Teresa, unconsciously, came to her feet. The movement, being without purpose, betrayed unmistakably a nervousness till then perfectly concealed. Yet Lucy, rising with her, felt no surprise. She saw that her friend's face, already sufficiently white, had gone a little whiter; one of her hands rose unconsciously to her breast, whose rise and fall had suddenly become noticeable. Otherwise Teresa was immobile; and the huge sunken eyes, staring at her, looking curiously ethereal above her hollowed cheeks, did not waver.

She exclaimed in a peculiar low voice, which sounded a little startled:

"That *is* a coincidence. . . . Almost funny. . . . Why, I've only to let him sail then — and I'd keep my own. . . ."

To her listener, that saying was dark. She gazed at the stricken and heavenly countenance, and heard no sound but the loud beating of her heart.

Teresa, stirring suddenly, brushed the back of her hand across her forehead.

"I think my guardian angel brought me to you, Lucy. I hadn't an idea. . . . Will you call him up, Lucy? He's certain to be in. . . . Right now?"

But Lucy, after all, had a point of view. It scarcely occurred to her now to say, "I'm expecting him to come here some time this afternoon," for on the whole she did not expect that now. Still, she hesitated.

"I'll do whatever you want, of course — but isn't the direct way the best with him? I — it isn't necessary for me to understand the circumstances — but surely he will listen if you speak to him yourself?"

Teresa's laugh, extremely short and odd, took her quite aback.

"But you don't suppose I'd be troubling you, if I hadn't tried all that!"

Lucy took her hand in both her own.

"You know that he's been away — for a week — ?"

"It isn't that," said Teresa steadily. "He thinks I've been unfair, about — some differences we had — and he's determined not to see me."

Pain came into her candid gaze; her eyes fell. But she raised them again at once, and began to speak in a low voice, hurried but controlled.

"Listen, Lucy, and learn the favor I ask. On Tuesday evening, when my position grew clear, I sent Mr. Masury a telegram and then a letter, asking him to communicate with me at once about a matter of great importance. Getting no answer, I started

telephoning — and learned at last that he was out of town.
This morning I began telephoning again. A woman answered;
Mr. Masury was in — who was calling? She came back in a
moment and said that Mr. Masury was engaged: would I leave
a message? I left a message, in some detail, asking him to call
me immediately. He never called. Early this afternoon when
at last I had a moment alone — for we've had a terrible day
in the office — I called again. That time, I'm almost sure, he
answered the telephone himself. But when I spoke, and my
voice could be recognized, there was a click — and silence. . . .
Now," said Teresa, glancing at her watch and at once back at
Lucy, "I've left the business to go hang, if it likes, for the fact is
I can't rest till I see him — and the time grows short."

As the rôle which she was cast to play began to emerge more
clearly, Lucy grew at once paler and more firm.

"That does seem a little difficult. . . . Now tell me just what it
is you'd like me to do. Is it — to intercede for you — to ask
him — ?"

"I'd like you," said Teresa firmly, "to call him up and make
an appointment right away — *for yourself*. . . . And then take
me along. . . . I — can see no other way."

There was stillness through several ticks of the clock. But
Teresa could have no idea how hard a thing was this she had
asked.

"I adore you, Teresa," said Lucy, whitely. "But — would
that be quite fair, do you think?"

"Fair?"

The young steelmaster flung back the word on the edge of an
abrupt laugh which, small though it was, seemed steeped with
the recklessness for which her line was celebrated.

"I'm afraid I'm a bad judge of etiquette to-day! Necessity
knows no law — you may have heard! . . . *Fair!* Who under
God's wide skies has bothered about being fair to me? You,

421

Lucy — not many more. . . . But I concede something to our common scruples — oh, I still have limits! My chicanery came only to this, that I should be waiting outside the door in the car, while you, going in, begged for me — that I be not turned from the door! Is that too much?"

"For me? — you darling. . . . Why, no. But —"

"But you hesitate? Why? When there's time, I'll make out my case for you, if you like, but now — My sweet Lucy, can't you manage to trust me a little — at least to know that I'd not take a dishonest advantage of you? At least to know that I'd not dream of asking this of you unless it was altogether in his interest — and not my own! Fair!" the girl repeated, with her rather desperate little laugh. "Oh, yes! — I think it will be found, in the end, that I've been fair to him!"

"Oh. . . . It is in his interest, then? You see — as I know nothing of the matter, and as you say he does n't want to —"

"He does n't want to see me — no. . . . Yet I promise you, Lucy," said Teresa, suddenly solemn, and more than a little let down — "that he'll always be glad that he did."

After a moment, she added, still lower: "I'm taking him everything that he's wanted. . . . And perhaps just a little more."

The voice of the headstrong and notorious girl seemed, on these words, to break, just perceptibly. In that instant, singularly, Lucy felt herself the stronger of the two.

"I trust you more than any one else in the world, Teresa," she said steadily. "And now I'm sure — that everything's going to be all right."

She touched her fingers to her cheek, and fingers and cheek were as if carved from ice. She laid her hand upon her heart; after the flutterings of suspense, it seemed all at once to have stopped beating altogether. She walked to her desk.

In a natural voice, only a little hardened, she spoke into the transmitter what surely it had not seemed possible for her to say to-day:

"Stuyvesant 9824."

There came an answer; the voice of a strange man; the stranger said, "One moment, please," and receded, and the moment ran long. Standing with the hard rim of the mouthpiece pressed against her cheek, she glanced around, having bethought her to smile reassuringly; but Teresa, who stood like a classic statue by the cold hearth, and just as still, had turned her back. And then, abruptly, Dean's voice came springing toward her over the wire, warm, contrite, more personal than a clasp of the hand.

"*Hello, Lucy!* . . . I *am* outdone with myself! You've hardly been out of my thoughts a minute all day — but . . ."

He was full of apologies. A dozen times at least he had actually started to the telephone to call her, but always something — or two things or five things — had sprung between, physically blocking him off. Such a day had never been before, on land or sea. . . .

She was trying to interrupt his amiable regrets. Who, she asked, could understand everything, if not she? At last, she could speak.

"I've not called to chide you, Dean! — the idea! — but on the contrary to say that I've decided to simplify your duty for you! I find I'm obliged to go out, starting right now — and where do you think I'm going while I'm out? Be prepared — I'm coming down to call on you!"

"Now, Lucy," he protested affectionately. "That does sound like a rebuke, and I assure you one not deserved in the spirit at least. I was just getting things clear enough to propose a quiet evening hour, which after all —"

"No, but why on earth not?" Lucy broke in, hastily shutting her ears. "You're terrifically busy — I've nothing under the sun to do! Why shouldn't I save your time by coming to you?

Besides — I'd prefer it that way! I — I'd like to pay you a little good-bye attention!"

"A nicer one I could n't imagine. I need n't say that I'd feel honored to see you among my poor sticks. But —"

"That's settled, then! . . . There's the place and the girl — now the time! As all times are equally impossible for you, why would n't this — right now — be just as bad as any? I'm relentless, you see! —"

"Any time that you'd come would be a good one for me, Lucy —"

"You're gallant to-day — practising for France, no doubt! In quarter of an hour then! And, oh, yes! — be quite alone! I've something important to say, you see, and — a little surprise for you."

On that, she put down the receiver quickly, and turned away. Her sparkle died.

"That happened luckily, did n't it?" she said, in a colorless voice. "And it settles everything. Trust me — you'll be talking to him very soon now."

Teresa, who had turned, stood looking at her mutely. Perhaps that brief conversation, of which she had heard half, told her something that had not been known before? Or possibly the thought in her mind, more selfishly, was only that "talking to him" and settling everything were not quite the same? . . . Her great grave eyes, which should have shone relief or gratitude now, one would say, were darkly sorrowful — and something else. . . . Was it imaginable that Teresa too was frightened over seeing Dean?

"I'll get my things," said Lucy.

She moved toward the door, and the wilful young steelmaster, stirring, came forward a step, abruptly, and gathered her into her arms. Or perhaps gather was not quite the word; rather, Teresa clung to her, while the proud head, dropping suddenly, buried itself in the older woman's breast. Lucy felt harder and colder than a stone: in that moment nothing, perhaps, could have moved her. Yet it surprised her, remotely, to feel that Teresa was trembling.

CHAPTER XXII

IN the bachelor apartment on Irving Place, Masury, turning from the telephone, called: "Oh, Mrs. Roorback!" And when the sad-faced woman of the house, dropping one or another of the dozen things she was doing for him in the wild disorder of getting off, thrust her lean head between the curtains, he resumed, with unnecessary loudness:

"Very sorry to interrupt, but do you think you could make us some tea at once? I've just learned that I'm going to have a visitor."

Mrs. Roorback, looking exceedingly depressed by this announcement, as if to say that she, for her part, could not imagine how the whole thing would work out and positively would not answer for the consequences, answered: "Of course a body has but the two hands, Mr. Masury, but if that's what you *wish*. . . . For how many?"

"Oh, just two — just two! And perhaps a little thin buttered toast, Mrs. Roorback, and some of that excellent marmalade of yours. That will be fine!"

Returning to the bedrooms, he perceived that his stentorian hint had not passed unnoted. Hendricks, of "Parson's," and Wilfrid Winslow, who had been sitting on his bed and spilling ashes everywhere, had already risen and put on their hats. They were arch for a moment, and then suddenly a little serious and more than a little wistful, and then they went away.

All day he had seemed to be moving steadily in just this atmosphere: Good-bye — good-bye, good-bye! . . . One hardly liked it.

In the sitting-room again, glancing about, he stood for a second rather staggered by the prevalent chaos. Setting Mrs. Roorback to brewing tea was now seen to have this disadvantage, that he

could n't ask her two hands to come and tidy up for him simultaneously; the thing looked hopeless. To an elderly Polack, who
was nailing up boxes by the hearthside with resounding buffets,
he said hastily: "Take all that stuff to the back somewhere and
finish it there — *noiselessly!*" Through the door into the hall,
he shouted down to George Davis — who, having abandoned the
practice of law till further notice, was at this moment in the
cellar trunk-room on some friendly quest — "Ho, George! Come
help pick up this room, for heaven's sake! Lady coming to see
me!" Next, handing a coin to a small messenger who sat in a tall
chair against the wall, tiny feet swinging far off the floor, he said:
"Can't get it ready for you now, old man — come back about
seven." . . . Then old George came, perspiring and dusty, and ˙
they went at it in earnest.

Lady visitors give a great deal of trouble, if they did but
know it.

The rooms-mates talked little as they plied their task. What
was in George's mind he did not mention; but Masury, as he thus
made ready for Lucy, was thinking of her definitely enough.
In truth, she had been much in his consciousness that day; nor
was it through negligence that thought had not flowered in
word or act. For hours, in the morning, he had been out on a
score of unavoidable errands; and after that, and before, as the
news of his impending departure spread about, people had been
coming to see him, on business or in friendship, steadily throughout the day; or else — like his sister Millie — they had called him
up and detained him indefinitely, with the sublime unscrupulous-
ness of the telephone. It was one day, truly, when the shabby
excuse of "no time" had been literal truth. Now, touched by
this new evidence of Lucy's staunch and understanding friendship, he was casting about for a suitable keepsake for her, he was
thinking that he would keep her for a real visit, though he did n't
get to bed to-night. Plenty of leisure on the boat. . . .

"Half-past five! Great Scott — I must *wash!*" he threw out suddenly. . . . "What you can't tidy, George, just shove out of sight."

He vanished toward the bedrooms; none too soon either. Just as he returned, notably spruced, Mrs. Roorback's face came popping through the other door, looking as if the worst had happened now. She broke the news without hope:

"Lady to see you. Mrs. Flanner."

George, who was loyally dusting about with a flannel shirt, jumped.

"Gosh! *Wait!* Lemme get out, Mrs. Roorback. Just lemme. . . ."

"Grab that towel!" said Masury.

Then, making a hasty survey of the scene, as the Elder scuttled away, he resumed:

"All right — ask her to come up. . . . And oh, Mrs. Roorback! — I'm not at home now if anybody comes."

He set a chair in place, straightened books on the table, and then as he turned, advancing to open the door for his visitor, it opened ahead of him under Mrs. R.'s hand, and she came quickly in.

"*Well!*" he said gaily — "I call this pretty nice! . . . Welcome to the *garçonniere*. . . ."

Lucy had halted just over the threshold, closing the door behind her. She was richly dressed, slender and graceful like a flower, and the sight of her girlish blonde beauty here, under the somewhat disturbed circumstances, was unexpectedly a little moving to him. Yet something in her look and pose, in the complete absence of that reliable vivacity she had exhibited on the telephone just now, vaguely communicated to him, even as he spoke, that something was amiss here, beyond meeting and parting.

She had flinched visibly as her eyes fell on his disfigured lip, his first wound in the war; greeting she neither gave nor took. Abruptly, and with some signs of nervousness, she broke through his amiable nothings with the most unexpected, the most unwelcome, words his fancy could have devised.

"Dean! — Teresa DeSilver is here with me. She wants to see you: I can't stay. . . ."

While she paused, to gather breath perhaps, her host emitted one word, in a changed voice:

"*Here?*"

"Waiting in the car outside. She has something to explain to you — something terribly important — for you both. I — I've come only to bring her — and to beg you to see her. . . . You will — won't you?"

Her hand, which the man had retained, was dropped while she spoke. All the friendliness, all consideration even, faded out of Dean's face, and his eyes, turning sharp like a hawk's and hard like steel, seemed to bore right through her. "So this is the little good-bye attention you spoke of!" that pitiless gaze seemed to say. "And I had trusted you. . . ." And, in fact, it came to that — precisely. Wondering just now if the "surprise" she had promised could conceivably cover something disagreeable, his mind had instantly rejected any such notion, as impossible and unworthy. . . . He said, with cold politeness:

"Of course I know your intentions are the kindest, Lucy, but I'm obliged to regret that you've allowed yourself to be made use of in this way. What you ask is —"

She would not let him finish. Seeing that she must fight for what she had pledged herself, she had steadied at once; she had her weapons, too.

"You don't understand me, Dean! — I've only to look at you to see that. You think I've come to plead for Teresa — to ask you to be kind, or generous or forgiving, about — whatever may be wrong between you! I've not! I — "

"Need we have an argument, Lucy? I assure you, such an interview could have no possible result, except to give her — perhaps — a certain amount of pain —"

"What's her pain to you? You've already given her plenty, by the look of her! . . . That's her risk, as I say. Must I remind you, Dean, that I was your friend before I was Teresa's. Believe, then, that I'd not ask this unless I *knew* that I was serving your interest —"

"No, you don't know that, Lucy! You only mean that she told you you were. . . . You ask the impossible —"

"Tell me frankly — is it that you're a little afraid to see her, Dean? That's it, is n't it?"

"Well, Lucy!"

He drew back a step then, eyeing her formidably, while beneath his sense of human injury and indignation his inward disturbance mounted. . . . How convince these feminine prepossessions that his finished encounter had ceased even to be part of his active consciousness now — a thing slept off, like a fever or a dream, leaving only a secure memory behind? — that what was asked now was that he should help *her* to feel satisfied — "like this," as she had put it that night, trying even then to "explain." . . .

"Then what's impossible?" Lucy was pressing on, as if feeling that she had struck him somehow. "If it is n't that your position — whatever it is — is awfully shaky — then what? To say that you won't give five minutes to what means so much to another human being — to a point of honor, which can mean more than life — to shut your door on a woman in trouble — no, you're not so hard-hearted as that. But if you are — don't wound me with your hardness too. This is good-bye. . . . Am I to remember that your last act was to refuse me this simple — "

"*Dear* Lucy!" said Masury with a kind of despairing patience.

"You can know nothing of the circumstances! I tell you, if you understood —"

"But it's you, Dean, who don't understand what's more important than circumstances. . . ."

Her voice, by its extreme quietude, pierced through his exasperated protest; the changing look of her face somehow checked him. The fine eyes, regarding him, had turned liquid with tears.

"Can't you imagine that I'd never have spoiled my last minutes with you — as you make me feel that I have done hopelessly . . . if I hadn't been certain that you'd be glad that I did, afterwards — as long as you live?"

In the middle of the affecting speech, which had begun steadily, her voice first trembled, and then broke to pieces. Masury always thought that if it had not been for that, just that, he would have refused her finally. As it was, her unwonted emotion threw his will momentarily on the balance; and Lucy, it seemed, understood that, and found it enough. Her long look left him; under his disconcerted but still angry stare, she turned; the exit opened. . . .

"Lucy, Lucy!" broke from him. "You don't know what you're doing. . . ."

But Lucy was gone. The door shut softly; he could hear her light feet on the stairs. . . . And then, alone in his tidied sitting-room, the man, the deceived host, who liked being "managed" as little as most men, perhaps, flung his arms apart and upward in a gesture at once beaten and menacing, and said aloud:

"By God! . . . We'll see about this!"

He moved straight to the windows.

Behind the old lace-curtains, motionless, he stood and stared down into the familiar street — stared fixedly at the smart coupé standing there at his curb, waiting — having its way. . . . From the vestibule, Lucy emerged, hurrying on her high heels across the sidewalk, while the chauffeur, saluting, swung open the car-door. From the coupé a woman descended, veiled, hardly so tall as Lucy and not nearly so well-dressed; the two stood an instant on the sidewalk, exchanging a few words. Then Lucy vanished suddenly into the car, and the veiled woman started forward toward his door.

By chance, her glance, lifting as she advanced, flitted over the front of the house: for the fleeting second it was as if the man behind the curtains had looked, once more, straight into the eyes of his adversary. . . .

Just now, while he resisted Lucy, Masury had discovered, not without disagreeable surprise, that there was a difference between this old affair and a last year's bird's-nest after all: he had somewhat overestimated his inward security. The first sight of the woman herself, stepping out toward him, had made it unmistakably clear that the elemental passions she had roused in him one night, all that barrierless and terrific intimacy, had left within him, indeed, as well as without, their ineradicable marks. Now her upturned face, just glimpsed downward, mysteriously released within him a flood of associations, quite unexpected in their poignancy; and without warning he was swept through with a wave of bitter sensations not easily to be reconciled with the perfect satisfaction he had for days avowed to himself.

Then Masury knew that Lucy, though she understood nothing, had been right in this, at least. The supporting sense of a personal ascendancy in which he had found his secret fulfilment rested, in good truth, upon a shaky foundation. Unless he looked well to himself, his gifted adversary, who had robbed him of everything else, might yet manage to wrest that too from him.

Here she was where she had willed to be: face to face with him, alone with him, primed and resourceful for her post-mortem "explanation." Once again she had had her way with him, once again by a tricky device. And this time, it seemed, she was at her ease in her success. At his inhospitable door, in response to his brisk, chill, "Oh, yes! — come in!" — she had murmured, "Thank you so much!" — almost like the assured executive behind the flat desk; and now as he returned from the door, she, having halted in the middle of his room, by the table, stood regarding him with a directness she had by no means been able to manage, that early morning when they had parted. He was, of course, perfectly aware that her gaze, lowering as if magnetized as he came forward, rested upon his mouth, upon her mark there; he saw that her ornamental eyes, having widened, became fixed; the continuing stare, out of a face as white as paper, took on a fascinated quality. As she did not at once speak, you might have supposed that to inspect and pass upon her work was precisely what she had come for. No doubt she was not ill-pleased?

Yet in truth the man, with his pressing need to reaffirm himself, scarcely waited for her to speak. Facing her with hands clasped behind him, upright and tall, smiling a little, darkly, he said, smooth as a stone:

"I'd fancied that my failure to answer your very kind communications might have been regarded as in itself an answer? As my time unfortunately is much occupied to-day, perhaps you won't mind explaining at once the object of the — interview?"

The veiled eyes had lifted with a slight start, as he began to speak: they were Diana's eyes, beautiful and steady. To his surprise, as he ended, the woman too smiled a little — not a threatening smile like his, but quite a natural one, freighted with a sort of reassurance.

"Yes, I think you're entitled to that, at least! Indeed, I'm sorry to have taken advantage of you in this way — I've been rather terrified with the thought of how much you'd dislike it. . . ."

The speech, the manner, dispelled at a stroke any mere masculine dread of another false "scene." Though something undefinable in her look lent support to her extravagant rhetoric, and though her "saintly" face, as he saw at once, was wasted as with a disease, her composure was unmistakable and perfect. No, certainly, he had not now to deal with a broken girl, begging his mercy: this was Miss Teresa DeSilver.

"Yet I could n't put down the sense," she continued without pause, under the naked hardness of his gaze, "that I should and must tell you, myself, that I've sold back that stock to Mr. Parmenter. . . . I've sold it back — and that made a new situation which was n't at all met by your just not answering."

Her voice came a little blurred through the muffling veil; as she spoke, she was hastily pushing up the thick net with her gloved forefingers: she let it rest on the bridge of her classic nose. If there was silence at all, her host made no move to take advantage of it. He was standing, indeed, staring lidlessly, like a man turned to stone. . . . He had fairly notified this woman, and fully believed, that nothing she could say or do would ever interest him again; now, with a word or two she had not merely captured his interest: she had all but stunned it, it seemed. In this last day or two, when she had been pursuing him, he had thought, with small curiosity, of several things she might want to say, to help her to "feel satisfied"; she chanced to have mentioned the one thing that one's imaginings of a determined and unscrupulous fighter could never have included. Giving up. . . . And still, though his tongue was impotent by the mere shock of surprise, the essence of him — which would doubt first the fact and then the motive — stood scarcely even touched. . . .

"You 'll naturally ask," she was rapidly continuing, "why I did n't just state the facts to you in a letter, and spare you a conversation. I want to make that perfectly clear, if I may. . . . First, I had to consider that you might not read a letter from me. Second, you might read, but not believe what I said — or not fully understand, perhaps. Third, you might both read and believe, but somehow overlook the fact that — arrangements must, and could, still be made. . . . I offer those, in a brief way, as my excuse for inflicting on you what must have been otherwise a — perfectly gratuitous intrusion."

The business-like Miss DeSilver considered fractionally, marshalling her points. Again the man, her victim and her victor, failed to embrace the opportunity to reassert his direction of the interview. His was the loud silence of one who has, literally, nothing to say. Nevertheless, his mind, rebounding from its first stupefaction, when all the tangible foundations of his position had seemed to rock sickeningly under him, had already become intensely busy. "Now let's see," it immediately demanded — "*where's the catch here? . . .*"

But the woman clearly recognized that the responsibility for talk lay with her, who had asked for it. Now a faint anxiety became manifest in the intentness of her thinned nun's face.

"I speak of arrangements. You know, Mr. Masury, the special meeting's to-morrow, and the stock you bought has never been presented for transfer — it still stands in the name of De-Silver Coit. It was that especially that made the matter seem urgent. I've been so anxious to know — I hope you won't mind telling me now — *have you still got it?*"

Stirring then, as the difficult process of adjustment began to settle within him, the man spoke for the first time since his hostile redeclaration. His voice, unchanged, yielded nothing.

"I have the stock — certainly. Why did you suppose that I would give myself the bother of transferring it?"

"Ah! — I'm glad!" said his late employer, and even he could not fail to see that her look lightened instantly. . . . "Well! — you understand that transfer is worth bothering about now! — and luckily as there's no closing of the books, there's still time. Now if you'll —"

"On the contrary, I understand nothing."

"Oh!" said she. . . . "I go too fast, trying not to keep you. But that makes me glad that I didn't depend upon a letter. . . ."

She stood there by his table, which he had just straightened for Lucy, quite composed, easy even, mannered; in look and bearing she somehow reminded him of the *mondaine* Miss DeSilver, whom he had seen at the Jedds' tea-party. To look at her, to listen to her, you would not have thought it possible that this girl, who was not even tall, had thrown him three times in a rough-and-tumble fight, and then knocked him to kingdom come with a shovel. . . . Yet if her words had meant what they seemed to mean, this proud composure would have been indeed incredible.

"You see — when I cancelled my transaction with Mr. Parmenter, it put everything back — back to just where you thought it was last week. That is, you, with your thousand shares — registered, and voting — are in position to control the meeting to-morrow, and — in effect to —"

"Am I? As you correctly point out, I entertained that fancy once before. This time I'll need *proof!* Proof that you can't still —"

"You don't find, then, that the fact that I've sold back the shares I already had is proof enough —"

"As to that, I've no evidence that you have sold them back —"

"Oh!"

"And if you have — pray what's it a proof of? I hope my gallant uncle, believing in your ideas 'philosophically' as you say he does, isn't too much of a coward to go to the meeting now and vote his shares for you?"

"Well, that point at least won't come up," said Miss DeSilver quietly, "for Mr. Parmenter hasn't got them either now. . . . But I thought it probable that you would wish some evidence — yes, and perhaps natural too."

Her face had seemed to give in a little under his severe thrusts, but that was all: the power of anger, which had given worth and dignity to their conflict, was no more in her, it seemed. Yet she remained, strangely, the mistress of herself. From the little bag at her side she took a paper and unfolded it; moving a step nearer, she was holding up the sheet for him to see. As in the old photograph, her eyes, her still face, seemed mysteriously withdrawn.

"Won't you look at this, please? I had it drawn off for you to-day."

His eyes dropped, with a curious unwillingness. He had spoken of proof: perhaps proof here was not quite what he wanted now? ... He looked at an official attestation of ownership of stock in the Whitestone Steel Company, prepared by a firm of accountants, duly certified. Herein, the accountants declared upon oath that Teresa DeSilver's holdings — at the head of the list — were 4700 shares at noon this day, just as he had always had it on that private memorandum of his: which, by chance, he had torn up a few hours ago. Accordingly — unless there were still a catch somewhere — these other lots here must foot up 5300 shares against her. ...

"You will note," her controlled, rapid voice was saying, "that the Blagden Estate now owns 1900 voting shares, instead of 1500 as formerly, and that Mr. Parmenter no longer appears as a shareholder at all. It was to the Estate that he sold his shares, on Wednesday — by agreement with me. ... As for the others — well, I think you'll concede," said she, without inflection, "that there's nobody there I could come round — no matter how much I might wish to. ..."

While she spoke, her host, unconsciously, had put out a hand and taken that startling paper from her. So, no doubt, a line was crossed and he fairly acknowledged that he would receive information from her. But indeed that information was already lodged in him, finally. He no longer doubted now that the unbelievable had happened once more, the wheel within a wheel had revolved again, and he, beyond the bounds of possibility, and on the eve of departing for an indefinite absence, ruled the future of the Whitestone Steel Company. Yet the cold excitement that began to diffuse itself within him did not seem to spring from that fact, alas, astounding though it was, hardly seemed connected at all with this bloodless triumph and the ghost of a victory that came too late. No, the man's instant and curious sense was that positions nearer to him than war and peace, convictions closer to him than hands and feet and fundamentally necessary to his integrity, were being resistlessly taken from him. . . .

"Your stock, of course, stands there to Coit. . . . And oh! I forgot to say, I have here, by way of additional proof, Mr. Parmenter's receipt for the certificate for four hundred shares, which I turned over to him, and a certified copy —

"Oh, never mind that! I don't question — the *transaction's* having taken place!"

He spoke in an abrupt voice, rather harsh, and tossing the sheet on the table, looked up: within him a far-reaching disquiet, through which his mind, skeptical and cool, darted stubbornly about. On his visitor's face, he surprised the end of a curious look which, flitting away, turned as he saw it into a smile. All the same, she laid her new evidence down on the table too; her eyes dropped to her watch.

"That's that, then — four minutes! Two minutes more and I — can release you. About arrangements again. The meeting — perhaps you know? — is called for eleven o'clock. I've wondered — shall you be present?"

"No."

After a second's pause, she said, rather hesitatingly:

"I did n't know till just now about your — your going away. It seems hard — that it had to happen this way. I even hoped

438

that, in view of your interest in the — the matter, it might still be possible —"

"It's too late to speak of my interests now."

"Yes — that's true. . . . I'm sorry. It gives you no time at all to make your plans as to — as to the reorganization. . . . Still — at least it's not too late for you to claim what belongs to you — I wanted to be sure that you understood that. If you'll send your representative to the office with the papers, before eleven to-morrow, I'll — you may of course depend upon everything's being put in order. . . ."

Still his fixed gaze, searching her face, ceded her nothing.

"I assume, then," she continued, as if committed to reminding him of everything, "that you'll have your proxy at the meeting — with definite instructions as to what you want done?"

The inquiry went unanswered.

"I'm naturally curious," said Masury, in a deliberate voice, "to know just what has prompted you to do all this?"

The light of the May afternoon was drawing out of the bachelors' sitting-room. The old adversaries stood, again, face to face. The girl's veiled eyes, meeting his unbelieving ones, did not lower. But her face, whose unnatural pallor had caught his notice at the first sight of her, seemed then to grow a little paler.

"Give up that stock, you mean? Well — you must know there could be only one reason. I couldn't feel right to keep it. . . . Be sure, I tried to!"

"And why? Understand me — I can't consider that your motives have any practical bearing in — in the matter. I'll take what's mine in any case. But — as I ventured to suggest the other evening that you weren't 'right' to have the stock, and as you then objected somewhat vi— "

"Yes! — I know! . . . Still, one can learn a good deal in a week, don't you think?"

"Well? — if you're here in the spirit of fair reparation? . . ."

"What I've been saying then does n't impress you as sufficiently in that spirit?"

"It's precisely what I'm not clear about. . . . Do you wish to say frankly that what I said to you that night was — in its point — just and true?"

"No, I don't wish to say that. Of course — it was n't."

In a voice a little moved, yet full of a young dignity, she added:

"Indeed I don't mind your speaking so — if you think it's necessary. But — from your standpoint, I mean — what's the good now, what's the good? I think I've thought about you every minute since last Wednesday, and you can't imagine how upset I've been. . . . So you don't make me any sorrier, for indeed I could n't be."

Her look, regarding him, had somehow deepened and shadowed; and suddenly, by some trick of memory Dean Masury was made to think of that day in her office, when she had stared at him over the head of weeping Janney with eyes dark with trouble, like this, which seemed to say: "You do things, and then you wish you had n't. It's terrible — but are n't we all like that? . . ." And then the fringed eyes glanced off, and turning, she moved away, a little further into the room: leaving her opponent curiously silenced behind her. Inexplicably, his case grew worse. . . .

"But of course you're entitled to know what's happened," she said quite naturally, receding — "to change my position so completely, and I — I want to tell you, if you're interested. In fact, that was one of the reasons why I particularly wished to see you. Only I — I don't want to keep you too long."

She paused by his desk, looked at it, rested her finger-tips on it and then leaned against it, turning toward him again.

"Still, I can be brief. There is really little to tell. . . . No, if an act's to be judged at all by what one means when one does it —

no, though I'm ready to blame myself everywhere, I can find none there."

She looked at the floor; the man, standing, looked at her, his unconscious fingers curling and uncurling the corner of that other explosive "evidence" of hers. He could easily have spoken then, as for instance to offer to spare her this explanation; he was silent. The room was still. From the street, where Lucy waited, there floated up suddenly the meaningless shouts of a wandering huckster; nearer, from the regions below, came the muffled sounds of blows as the tireless Polack hammered his boxes; and the proud Teresa DeSilver, who "never explained," leaning against his worn and homely desk, spoke in a low voice her intimate apologia.

"In these last months, when for the first time I've been associated more or less closely with Mr. Parmenter, he's been consistently my most kind and fatherly adviser. I've thought more than once — lately — that he was rather like my uncle too. Our relation has been so pleasant and natural that if I'd ever thought of being 'on my guard,' as they say, I feel even now — yes, I still feel that I should have to be a little ashamed of myself. Life, that suspicious way, would hardly be worth living, I think. . . . Well, then, I bought the stock from him, not even attaching much importance to the trade, for I'd been certain all along that I could manage without it. And then . . . You remember you asked me if I honestly believed that he would have sold to me if I'd been a man. As I've tried to say, it would never have crossed my mind to think of it that way, and if it had, I'd have answered yes, right off. But after you'd raised the question — and everything was so serious — I couldn't seem to get it out of my thoughts. My mind kept going back over the whole acquaintance, everything I could remember, inch by inch, trying to reëxamine it from the — new point of view. Then one night, I thought all at once of — a little thing that had happened at the office one day — if one could call it a happening. I remember, it was the day he told me that you — that you'd had a quarrel with a friend, involving me — I mean indirectly — and the day before I bought the stock from him. . . . Just the tiniest thing — that of course I had n't noticed at the time, and could never have dragged up again at all, if I had n't kept going back, over and over. . . . Well, the doubt was so small — in a way, it seemed quite horrid to acknowledge it as a doubt at all — that I tried to put it out of mind, as just something morbid — fastening on me because I was upset — following me like a bogy in a nightmare. I could n't succeed. One does n't care for a dishonest title, naturally, and the thought that I had taken the company away from you by unfair means, however innocently, began to spread over everything like a cloud — poisoning everything. Oh, I struggled most seriously, I assure you. . . . And perhaps," the voice interjected, deliberately — "you'd contend that I should n't lean too much on that word 'innocently,' even? After all, I was n't a child, and by no means inexperienced — no doubt I should know how to protect what's important to me? . . . Perhaps — I don't know. This was a small doubt, certainly. . . . At any rate, it grew clear that I'd have no peace till I'd laid the ghost, one way or the other, so I sent for Mr. Parmenter, nominally about our legal matters. That was on Tuesday afternoon — I had n't been able to do it before. . . . You see, I felt perfectly sure that if I just looked at him again, once, in the light of this odd new thought, I'd know at once — whatever there might be to know. Well, he came — and I did. . . ."

A faint agitation had begun to communicate itself in the speaker's voice; pausing now for the first time in her rapid monologue, she looked away toward the windows. She stood perfectly immobile and white. . . . Artemis in marble, indifferently dressed for the city. . . . In a moment, she spoke with increased firmness:

"In fact, to make it clear that I have n't acted merely out of half-morbid suspicions — which indeed I'd never have done about so important an issue — I must say that it went beyond — just looking at him. . . . It happened that I — I'd been a little ill, and when he came in and saw me, he was disturbed — unduly so, I had to feel — unnecessarily sympathetic. What actually 'happened,' again, was very little. I'll not try to put it into words — at another time it's quite possible that I might n't have noticed that, either. As it was, I knew at once that that rather deep-cutting question you'd asked me was answered — finally. . . . Oh, I ought to say that back in February, when Mr. Parmenter first intimated that he might arrange to sell me his stock if I needed it, I was a little surprised — Mr. Lovering and the Blagdens were so terribly against me! — but after that, everything was so natural, and his interest in what I was trying to do was so genuine, that I forgot my doubts if I'd ever had any Well, then — now I knew, past the possibility of any doubt No — if I'd been a man he would not have sold me his stock –· he'd never have got interested in my experiment to begin with. . . . So there I was, after all, in a quite indefensible position — and of a sort, as it happened, which I particularly resented. Well, there were two steps to take to —"

"All right! — never mind! I understand the case!" the man here interrupted, with a curious abruptness, rather like one who has listened to the limit of his endurance. . . . "I understand. I — except . . ."

Stirring hastily from the sleep-like stillness which had for the second time overtaken him, he moved a step, rather vaguely, toward her.

"His position — I must say seems . . . Had he understood all along — that the fact of the sale would come out at the meeting?"

The girl's veiled eyes, having turned back, regarded him

herself. One would almost say that something in her had actually been broken then — in the fight, or in the strain of the long watch by him, afterwards: broken, yet somehow to leave her stronger than before. *There'll be time enough to think of my pride afterwards.* . . . It was like changing the values of the counters at the very end of the game. Where was the lawless egoist whose wilfulness had challenged him to this conflict, and in the subjection of whom he had found, in fancy, his inward fulfilment? . . .

His eyes returned to her from space; he moved another step, and halting again, said brusquely:

"I'd like to know — is there any uncertainty in your mind as to what's going to take place at the meeting to-morrow?"

The retiring president of the company, who had stood gazing at him steadily through the brief silence, shook her head at once.

"Oh, no! Oh, don't — *don't* imagine that I had pictured you as relenting — changing your mind! . . . That would be quite horrible. . . ."

"Shall you *go* to the meeting?"

She answered briefly that she would not only go to the meeting, she would preside at it; there would be information she should give to the stockholders, it seemed. She added then, with some evidences of effort:

"By the way, I've naturally wondered. . . . As you are going away — no doubt Mr. Ball will be made president again?"

Involuntarily, the man made a faint grimace.

"I don't know. . . . I can't say. . . . Well? — and what are you going to *do*, then?"

"Do?"

"After the — the reorganization? What are your — your business plans?"

They regarded each other, and the girl's composure was the

more marked as the man's poise began visibly to desert him. She answered quietly:

"I'm going to buy another steel company, and start again."

There was another silence. Her eyes fell. She smoothed the wrist of her glove; she glanced again at her watch.

"First," she said, "I'll make the break clean. In a day or two, as soon as the new administration is in charge, I'll sell my Whitestone stock — to Mr. Lovering — or my grandfather, perhaps. Then . . . I've been looking around for several days, you see, and I already have my eye on something — another company. It's pretty big for me to swing alone, but I don't mind that. I know now that making steel's what I want to do, and I'm not afraid to put all my eggs in one basket. . . . But I'm detaining you, speaking of my —"

"Perhaps, then," broke from him abruptly — "you won't in the long run mind losing Whitestone so — so much?"

"Ah! . . . Well!"

Had he still wished to know that he had punished this woman thoroughly, he would have had that knowledge safe forever now. Her veiled eyes, under his gaze, became like dark pools of pain. She covered them hastily with her long lashes, like a show-girl's. Her lower lip pinched in a little, queerly. Her hand just moved, in a gesture of renunciation inexpressible.

"I must go now," said Miss DeSilver.

She moved, to pass him. But her host, who had been so unwilling to receive her a little earlier, seemed now no more ready to let her go; his feet did not stir from her path. His mind's eye, in a flash, again saw black headlines, when he would be far out at sea: paragraphs dark with taunts which he, at least, knew this girl would not deserve; columns and columns of abusive print which would contain no hint of this courageous abdication. . . . Suddenly, above all else, he was obsessed with a sense of strange unreality, like one who, half-waking, beholds a phantasm. Was this, indeed, Saint Teresa who spoke these considerate and impossible words, was this the Whitestone Steel Company she incredibly relinquished to him?

"One thing occurs to me," the new owner was saying hurriedly, yet laboring a little too. "I . . . you are still the largest stockholder in the company — the largest by far. It was your father's company before you. Therefore you have a legitimate claim — such as any one would recognize. You — you have rights. Well! — how would you feel about staying, then — I — supposing something could be — worked out?"

"Staying?"

"Yes! — why not? As an officer, of course, for you — your abilities would entitle you to that. . . . Vice-president, perhaps — something — with of course authority in the operation of the company — large authority . . . ?"

Her look had changed remarkably while he made that difficult speech; her eyes, her whole face, indeed, became wonderfully sweet: you would not have thought it possible that she could look like that. And still, in a singular way, her fundamental expression, which was at once proud and more than a little sad, seemed scarcely touched by that dazzling display; and he knew, while he still floundered, that there would be no easy way out for him that way either.

It was his turn, perhaps, to discover, that the price of peace cut deeper than a little "feeling sorry" . . . ?

"Thanks a lot for that," she said, with a sort of eagerness. "I can't well tell you how I appreciate it — how much it means. It just — takes all the sting out — for good. Thank you. . . . But — you'll understand. . . . I've of course expected that the first step of the new management would be to reopen the shell-plant? And —"

"That is understood — necessarily. But — why, did n't you ask *me* to stay, when you thought the matter was settled against *me?* Why can't you regard the — the war issue as simply lopped off?"

"But you could n't regard it that way, don't you remember?" she answered gently. "And, besides — is n't this really quite different? For you to stay would have been — at worst — altogether negative; for me, it would be — publicly forswearing — and actually helping what I believe to be wrong."

"I'd thought it possible," he retorted, in his last ditch, desperately — "yes, and reasonable — that in view of the crime at sea, which will probably bring this country —"

"No — no!" she interrupted hastily, flinching a little. . . . "No — I — I've often wished that I could change my beliefs — when things have happened to make me unhappy. But I can't. I'm afraid I must be put down as an irredeemable pacifist. . . . Oh! — does it seem inconsistent for me to say that to you — insincere?"

Hardly knowing what he said, the man echoed: "Insincere — what?"

"I mean my calling myself a pacifist — and then . . . the other night? You see — I've never pretended to be a turn-the-other-cheeker in — in personal relations, or anything like that. I've always believed in individuals fighting in their individual quarrels, each to protect what each thinks necessary and right. If wars could be fought just between the individuals concerned, if they could be fought by the old men who want and make them —"

"Oh, I understand all that! I have n't thought you inconsistent! I . . . But . . ."

"I'm glad. I've wondered. Now I — "

"But you're wrong in your beliefs! You argue it all wrong!" the man broke in again, his stubborn voice sounding vaguely unnatural. "We're going to open up that plant at once!"

She answered with her curious serenity:

"You must do as you think right, of course. Well, then, we agree to disagree. . . ."

So, at the end, as at the beginning, the two were confronted: their wills met across an immortal difference. Nothing was changed. And yet, by a paradox, everything was changed. What booted it now that this man should declare his unchangeableness? In the hidden places of his being he knew that everything was changed. She, the woman, from her finer position, was not even interested in that flicker of his hectoring will. She was speaking again: speaking soft words that fell like hands upon this old wound of his, torn wide open now, and this time not to be cheaply healed.

"And since I had to lose, let me say that I'm awfully glad I could lose to you — because I think you've deserved so much! . . . Oh, yes! I meant to ask! Do you remember that silly speech I made in the first talk we had — about your never succeeding at anything? . . . I've wondered if you would n't think it a suitable apology if I told you that those words have come to beat through my consciousness — all the time — like an ironic refrain. For of course I think it's pretty clear that you've made a most fearful success with me."

Her beauty lighted suddenly as with a lamp. The wasted nun's face, fine to haggardness, shone upon him with a brilliant tenderness. And then she went past him steadily toward the door.

The last, at least, was according to her conqueror's wish. Let her go, let her go quickly, lest a worse thing befall. . . . *Look here,* something deep and powerful in him was saying insistently, *this is a pretty big thing you've done, yes, and you've done it in a big way too.* . . . But do you think that he, for his part, would give his whole course and attitude the lie like that, right at the end — letting her get the best of him in a postscript, as it were? Not he. . . . He moved behind her in a crucifying dumbness: through which, nevertheless, stirred a helpless male rage because she had robbed him now of his dearest belonging, his fighter's pride.

Good God! Could n't the girl remember what he had done to her that night? . . .

She had paused — unluckily — by the door; she was pulling down her thick veil, making ready for the street. Her eyes, glancing over his shoulder, went around the room, took in the visible scene of her memorable happening. They came back to him: to the owner of Whitestone, the conqueror of her "experiment," halting before her, silent in his victory, his long hawked face looking perfectly stony, and yet, it must be said, very pale too. All at once then, the girl's eyes upon him, immense and dusky, became vaguely startled; her whole face, shrouded and unearthly — Diana's ghost — seemed charged with a wide wonder. . . . Her fingers pushed the veil a little further, and all was dark.

"Thank you for coming to tell me this," said his involuntary voice then, hardly recognizable, clipped and hoarse like a growl: "It was kind — it was generous of you."

She shook her head a little, smiling absently, faintly disclaiming, as if to say that it hardly mattered to contradict that now. And beneath him then, Dean Masury's legs began to tremble. . . .

"Well, then!" she said, with a reminiscence of her office manner, brisk and sure. . . . "Good-bye — and 'the best of luck!' It's not for me to ask you not to be reckless, over there — especially as that's your nature, I'm afraid! — and, still I say it — don't be . . ."

He had leaned a hand against the door-jamb, steadying himself. . . . Was it her look, was it that voice of his, harshly escaped from his will, was it his words, mocking and humiliating in their hideous inadequacy? In these seconds, the man's stubborn education had gone suddenly further. . . . He had staked everything on the instinctive sense that by yielding her nothing, he would still carry the banner of the essential supremacy. Madness and folly! She bore that trophy, as they stood here: from the moment she had come into this room, and by that act, she had taken his victory from him. . . . He had never challenged this woman for a few shares of stock; he had n't fought her for views of war and peace: those were the chance symbols of their far subtler and more moral conflict. Which of them was the sounder and stronger being? — he had meant all this to say — which could come on the other at the pinch with the harder impact and the truer aim? . . . And now she, merely by being herself, had answered his silent challenge, past mistaking. She could pluck from defeat the fine honors of victory, because she was greater than he; she was beating him here in an epilogue because she was forever his superior. . . . Well, even that could be endured — now. To meet one's betters sometimes was the risk that made a fight worth while . . . no, larger — it was the hope that made life dear. . . . But the luck of it all, on his purely secret side — the stupefying and damnable luck. . . . Hoaxed again, and finding it out a little late, — exactly like that night when he had made interesting discoveries through a chance view of a photograph. Only this self-deception was ten times bigger than that, and was irreparable. And funny too. . . . Oh, God, it was funny, that now, at this inconceivable moment, staring dumbly down at the shrouded face of his enemy, he should so suddenly have divined an inner beauty here, matching with yet far transcending the classic loveliness of the flesh — pure beauty of thought and act disclosed, where he had once seen only pose and ugliness, depth on depth of new and tender beauty, welling up from an unplumbed spring. . . .

"Don't be reckless," the slim veiled girl was saying, the most reckless person that he, for one, had ever encountered "— for, after all — life *is* a trust, don't you think? . . . And oh, yes — I wanted to say. Now that it's all over, won't you shake hands? — and some day, when this is far in the past, forgive me — for making you so much trouble?"

Her victor thrust out blindly a large hard hand — the very hand, by chance, that had so nearly choked her to death one night. Grasping it, regarding him with the fixed open gaze of one who looks forward to no remeeting, Teresa DeSilver spoke again, suddenly and clearly:

"That's going to leave a scar, is n't it? I'm so frightfully sorry. . . . Do you know, you 'll think it a silly thing to say, but I'm quite sure I've the mark of it on my heart?"

And then, no doubt at some look on the man's hopeless face, she added quickly, in an eager way:

"Oh, don't mind my saying that! Why, what harm does it do now? . . . I was so childish that night! — it seemed then like pulling out the pin that held my life together. But not now! — no, I'm glad to know that I can be like this. . . . *Bonne chance!*"

She smiled, remotely; and then her look was gone from him: her hand was upon the knob. Her business here was done; she had perfectly given him everything, and now she was stepping away, through the opening door. But she stopped again, after all: not by her will this time, and not, it may be, quite by another's. She stopped, for a hand fell upon her shoulder; she stopped, for she was spun roughly round. Now she felt her veiled face taken between hard hands, forcibly turned upward; and so upon her virgin lips, other lips, lips not virginal at all and scarred for life for just such a thing as this, crushed terribly down.

What was in the man's tortured mind then? Nothing very clear or fine, I suspect; nothing even creditable, perhaps. Was the tardy act conceived as the candid avowal of his defeat, which meant of love? Far from it. Had he even dimly divined, by some flicker of his deepest instinct, that he, like her, must submit himself to find in surrender his more excellent triumph? That is conceivable, of course. Or it may have been only that this stubborn male consciousness, having deliberately rejected all nobler expression, and retaining an excited memory of another hour and

453

scene, had desperately clutched at the last means to assert himself somehow above her.

But what mattered his intentions now? Only a moment ago, his voice, too long repressed, had risen and cast aside the unyielding will: it was so now with his manhood. The affair proceeded upon its ordered way.

The girl's head had moved a little, under that unprefaced attack, much as in that other moment; her lips seemed disposed to escape; her hands came upward. Had this man in his hardihood, then, provoked again a mortal retaliation? No; all was changed now, all was changed. Her movement was slight; her eyes, which had closed after the fashion of women, did not open; her lashes lay like a curtain on her cheek. Teresa's movement was gentle this time: yet it broke this man, her adversary, forever.

She had put aside her veil — for him.

His hard arms went round her, folding her close.

No, what he in his pride had thought or meant or fancied hardly mattered now. All was changed. These pure lips, softer and sweeter than a flower, yet with the magic to set his blood afire, disclosed to him finally his unconquerable need. And she was his. . . . It was not for her, in her magnificent life, to make a passive giving. Now he heard the hammering of her heart, answering his own; he felt the brave young body, the springs of whose everlasting law he had somehow touched, thrilling to his own. And he understood then suddenly and simply, though God knew how, the essential unity of this so rich and various being. . . . In her thousand activities and her invincible convictions, in the heedless splendor of her rage, defending to the death what was dear to her, in the selfless bravery of her reparation and the tenderness and the passion of her surrender: what were they all but the steadfast faces of a soul which had a perfect faith in the validity of its own meanings and a flawless courage in declaring them? . . . And she was his. He had come up into the mountain